P9-DWW-413

THE EVIL DEEDS WE DO

OTHER FIVE STAR TITLES BY ROBERT S. LEVINSON

THE EVIL DEEDS
WE DO

ROBERT S. LEVINSON

FIVE STAR
A part of Gale, Cengage Learning

GALE
CENGAGE Learning·

Farmington Hills, Mich • San Francisco • New York • Waterville, Maine
Meriden, Conn • Mason, Ohio • Chicago

GALE
CENGAGE Learning®

LIBRARY OF CONGRESS CATALOGING-IN-PUBLICATION DATA

Levinson, Robert S.
    The evil deeds we do / Robert S. Levinson. — First edition.
        pages ; cm
    ISBN 978-1-4328-2967-4 (hardcover) — ISBN 1-4328-2967-X (hardcover) — ISBN 978-1-4328-2976-6 (ebook) — ISBN 1-4328-2976-9 (ebook)
    1. Sound recording industry—Fiction. I. Title.
    PS3562.E9218E89 2015
    813'.54—dc23   2014031310

First Edition. First Printing: January 2015
Find us on Facebook– https://www.facebook.com/FiveStarCengage
Visit our website– http://www.gale.cengage.com/fivestar/
Contact Five Star™ Publishing at FiveStar@cengage.com

Printed in the United States of America
1 2 3 4 5 6 7 19 18 17 16 15

Of Course for
SANDRA
and for JANINE and ERIN

CHAPTER 1

Him.

Harry Roman.

Harry Roman back to haunt her.

Standing on the uppermost tier of the Star Bright Performers Workshop, his back against the wall, his hands buried inside his suit jacket pockets, his right shoulder hanging about four or five inches lower than the left.

Except for her, Roman had no business being here.

Like most Equity-waiver theaters around L.A., the Star Bright wasn't much more than a hole in the wall, fashioned out of a failed mom-and-pop butcher shop on Hyperion in Silverlake, its ninety-nine castoff movie house seats arranged on stadium-style risers facing a concrete floor, barebones props and a painted backdrop designed to hide a walk-in meat freezer now used for storage.

The entrances and exits by her cast were made through the toilet, which Lainie Davies Gardner felt suited her perfectly the first day she walked into the Star Bright hoping to land a teaching gig, desperate for any kind of teaching job that paid, because that's where Roman had helped put her life: the crapper.

Roman must have slipped inside through the production door after the house went to black on the curtain line, or she'd have spotted him before the actors came out for their bows, house lights up, and she could answer smiles from the sparse crowd of relatives, friends, other Star Bright students, a couple minor league talent agents, and two old-line casting directors who had come as a personal favor to Thelma Street, the workshop's owner.

The room echoed with insincere applause, but Lainie knew tonight's show was lousy.

Lousy, lousy, lousy.

Lainie as lousy as her actors after stepping in an hour before curtain for Joy Collins, who had added life to the old saying *Break a leg* while crossing over to the Star Bright from the rut-infested parking lot.

There'd been no time for rehearsal. Lainie had to work from the book most of the show, but she was making no excuses for herself. She was the pro in the cast, granted, not much of a pro anymore, but more than the others. Enough of a pro that she should have done better than them. Better than lousy.

Harry Roman was not applauding.

He was the one unsmiling face in the audience, giving her the gimlet-eyed *Gonna get you* granite stare that still, two-and-a-half years later, gave Lainie nights of fitful sleep. Sometimes, a nightmare shock that caused her to spring out of bed, soaking in sweat, gasping for air, throwing punches at the relentless demons hiding in the clammy darkness who meant to destroy her before they disappeared, taking Sara with them; Sara, her precious fifteen year old, losing a battle with her own raging demons since the night she saw her daddy shot, felt his blood paint her face and clothing, and watched him die.

Lainie studied the ex-cop turned assistant district attorney as he drew closer.

Roman looked every one of his mid-forties years, like he'd gone more than a few rough and tumble rounds and then some with Mother Time. His unruly black hair was turning salt and pepper, but still full of the wayward locks that defied a comb and brush and whatever motor oil he used to give it a shine as bright as his size twelves. His broad, hard-edged chin was growing a chin on a battered face her late husband Roy's lawyers said dated back to the poundings Roman routinely took as a high school football star.

He was a running back who never slowed down or stopped running on his way to being named to the All-City team three times, Player of the Year his senior semester. A nose busted in four places. A jaw broken twice and never reset properly, like the sagging right shoulder he got after becoming a street cop and moving onto the fast track to detective status.

He'd put on eight or ten pounds that hardly showed on his six-foot frame, inside a neatly pressed blue pinstripe that told her practiced eye Roman was still shopping off the clothing racks at Sam's Club. The button-down had struggled through one washing too many, and the skinny tie had long ago gone the same way as eight-tracks and cassettes.

Lainie had never seen Harry Roman smile; as if he thought showing his teeth would be a sign of weakness.

He wasn't smiling now, stepping a respectful distance up to her after the obnoxious agent who'd been monopolizing her finally cruised off. He angled his weight onto one leg, locked his hands behind his back, aimed the good shoulder at her, and began sucking her into his eyes like he was analyzing a painting at the county museum.

She waited him out, not anxious to have the first word, knowing it would be, as it always was whenever they'd faced off before Roy's death—

Nasty.

Something to make the night lousier than it already was.

Harry Roman let his stare go a bit longer, then with no trace of humor said, "Long time no see, Mrs. Gardner. What? Two, two-and-a-half years?"

"Not long enough."

He faked a smile. "Had anybody else murdered since you put out the contract on Mr. Gardner?"

The accusation stunned Lainie.

She locked her knees before they could give out entirely.

Waited for her breath to level out.

Said in a voice not as firm as she wanted it to be, "That your idea of a joke, Roman?"

"That you're still flapping around free as a bird, that's my idea of a joke."

"You're saying I killed my husband?"

Roman tilted his head, squinted and squeezed his eyebrows, pursed his lips and pretended to search the ceiling for an answer. He started a slow nod before looking at her squarely. "Had it done for you is what putting out a contract means, so *yes,* you're definitely the responsible party, Mrs. Gardner."

"In front of our daughter? In front of Sara? I would do a thing like that?"

Roman shrugged, made a throwaway gesture. "I could name mothers who've done a whole lot worse by their children."

"You're sick," Lainie said, choking on her words. Her shiver turned into an earthquake. She struggled against launching her fists, dancing balls of anger, at his smug, arrogant face. "To even think I'd do anything like that, to my husband, in front of my child. It makes you one sick son of a bitch, Roman."

"You're not the first one to come to that conclusion."

"You were wrong then, to indict me with Roy, and you're wrong now."

"Not me. A grand jury named you your husband's co-conspirator on twenty-four of the thirty-seven counts of unlawful business activities inspired by his ties to organized crime."

"Allegations and never proven, because there never was any proof to be found, only you grandstanding for the press, waving around your accusations like circus balloons."

His expression rejected the charge. "The proof was there, if we had gotten that far. Roy Gardner's murder put an end to the indictments, but no chance in Hades you'll have it easy this time around, getting away with his murder."

"When are you going to stop persecuting me, Roman? Ever?"

"Confession is good for the soul, Mrs. Gardner. You think about it after you get home tonight. I'll give you my card. All my numbers are there. Call anytime, day or night. We'll work something out."

Lainie unclenched her fists, wrapped herself in her arms and surveyed the theater. The last of the stragglers had gone. She and Roman were alone. "First, you prove it, prove something, prove anything," she said, her husky voice as threatening as a rattlesnake's hiss. "You can't, or you never would have dropped the indictments. You can't, or you'd be putting handcuffs on me now, instead of playing the sick mind games my husband, Roy, someone I loved more than life itself, always said you were capable of playing."

Roman turned from her attacking gaze. "You are quite the actress, Mrs. Gardner. I don't mean in the play tonight, which I got here too late to see. Now's when I mean. I don't know why you ever gave up a career in acting for the record business. You hadn't, I could be standing here right now talking to a great big movie star."

Lainie took his measure. "And I'd still be talking to a pile of shit."

Home was an easy twenty-minute drive on surface streets from the Star Bright, on South Hoover in the low-rent district behind City College, the bottom half of a double-decker stand-alone duplex from the thirties in desperate need of a paint job, its narrow front lawn a weed-infested garbage dump for booze bottles in paper bags and crushed beer cans; a pee stop for every stray mutt wandering the neighborhood.

Lainie stepped inside calling, "Sara?"

No answer.

No Sara.

No note.

Sara had promised her, sworn she would stay home, finish her homework, and now this.

Not the first time.

Lainie threw her eyes and hands to the sky.

She changed into her nightgown and robe.

She snapped on the TV and fell onto the couch with this week's *Billboard*, the Bible of an industry that turned its back on her two years ago rather than risk fallout and contamination from the criminal indictment brought against her. She flipped through the pages indifferently, looking for familiar names, half-studying the hit charts that barely made sense to her anymore; settling in for another long night of worrying about her absent daughter's safety.

After a while, as she had on so many other nights, Lainie caught herself crying, blaming herself for not being able to give Sara a better childhood than she'd had, vowing to find a way to do better for Sara, before finally crashing under the weight of a memory that had cost her more than her husband—her daughter as well, two-and-a-half years ago, the trial scheduled to begin in Division Four the day after Sara's thirteenth birthday.

The lawyers insisted there was no time for sentiment or celebrations; there was still prep work to be done that would take them well into the night. They backed off the way six-hundred dollar an hour lawyers do only after Roy slammed his fist down on the conference desk and told them it was pointless to argue. He and Lainie were taking Sara out for the birthday dinner they'd promised her, and that was that. His daughter was more important to him, to his wife, than even a "Not Guilty" verdict.

He gave Lainie the kind of look that could last an eternity. "That so, Lainie?"

She squeezed his hand and nodded agreement. "More than life itself," she said.

Sara got to pick the restaurant. She chose her favorite, Sal's Little Sicily, which featured a menu thick with recipes Sal's mama had brought with her from the old country. It was located on a quiet business street about a mile from the Gardners' sprawling ranch-style home in Encino, in Hacienda Estates, a walled, guarded valley haven for the wealthy and famous north of where the 101 intersects with the 405.

Sal, a small man with a salt-and-pepper mustache too big for his egg-shaped face, greeted them warmly, added an extra hug for Sara, and personally escorted the family to Booth Three in the main dining room, the booth usually reserved for celebrities who enjoyed having everybody's eyes on them while they feasted on one of Mama Luciana's specialties.

"Tonight, cousin, you're the biggest star here," Sal told Sara. He released her from his grip after planting a second smooch on her nose and steering her by her shoulders to the booth.

Sara slid along the cracked and faded brown leather to the middle seat. Roy slipped in alongside her with his back to the entrance, and Lainie settled at the aisle position across from Roy. They acknowledged waves and nods of notice from some of the regulars in an unusually large and bustling crowd for a Monday night.

The bar noise, undecipherable chatter and bursts of response to the football game on TV, drowned out Frank Sinatra and Dean Martin on the dining room speakers. Francis Albert and

Dino, as Sal always identified them, were his idols long before the night Lainie brought them in for some of Mama Luciana's *manicotti alla Siciliana*.

It was before the troubles began. Lainie was still in her glory years as president of Blue Pacific Records, a power broker, the highest-ranking woman in the music industry, whose face had graced the covers of *Time, Newsweek* and *Rolling Stone* all in the same week, a first for the business.

Sara had her usual, the *spaghetti alla salsiccia* and a double order of hot garlic toast. Roy and Lainie went for the fried calamari, sharing their orders of cannelloni and linguini with clams and an imported chablis that Sal recommended, allowing Sara to have half a glass because it was a special occasion.

For dessert, Sara ordered the tri-flavored spumoni—unaware of the rich chocolate cake about to be served with fourteen blazing candles, the fourteenth for good luck—and excused herself to spend a few minutes with a school chum who was dining out with her parents in a booth across the way.

Roy hand-signaled it was a good time to pull out Sara's birthday gift, an 18-carat Perretti heart-shaped pendant on an 18-inch chain. She had admired it more than once in the days when Lainie and Roy could afford shopping at Tiffany's and the other Beverly Hills goldmines along Rodeo Drive. To buy it for Sara now, after the IRS had tied up every asset in claims, Lainie had pawned the black-and-white pearl necklace she'd managed to hide from the Feds when they came calling with search warrants. Roy tried talking her out of it, but he'd run out of legitimate sources for loans, and covering the vig demanded by sources you'd never want to meet in a dark alley was impossible, he told her, breaking into horse tears.

Lainie reached into her handbag but after a moment came up empty-handed and did a slap-off gesture against her forehead. "I didn't get a chance to sneak the box out of the glove compartment," she said, and eased onto her feet. "Be back in a minute, darling. If Sara asks, just say I'm in the ladies."

"She'll know better."

"Of course she'll know better. Doesn't she always?"

"Just like her mother?"

"Not best, just always," Lainie said, giving Roy's shoulder a gentle squeeze as she passed by.

Outside, past the dome-shaped burgundy canopy protecting the restaurant entrance, she turned her face against a light breeze and headed through the parking lot. The lot had been full, so Roy parked across the street, about half a block up, where the area turned residential and slim palm trees began forming regimental fashion on the parkway lawns.

Nearing the sidewalk, she bumped shoulders with a man nine or ten inches taller than her own five-seven, half his face buried inside the turned-up collar of his camel hair coat, the rest of him covered in a traveling shadow as the quarter moon glided into a bank of gray clouds. He grunted and hurried on, slouched over like a fullback racing for the end zone. Lainie reached the car, a ten-year-old Toyota Camry one of Roy's friends from the Masons—one of the few friends who hadn't abandoned him— had sold him for nine hundred dollars, on credit, a personal loan with no interest or due date.

She fumbled for several moments in the semi-darkness getting the key into the lock.

Heard what sounded like a car backfiring as she was pulling Sara's gift from the glove box.

Then a second backfire.

She recognized it was more than backfire when she was halfway back to the restaurant. Dozens of customers were racing out of Sal's, their voices tinged with fright as they got into their cars and roared away. She tried to make sense of what they were saying, but it was only a jumble of noise.

The tumult grew louder the closer she got, cries and screams pouring out the entrance.

She heard the words *dead* and *killed*.

Murdered.

Shot.

And a scream louder than any other noise.

At once, she knew in her heart—pounding like a jackhammer—that it was her precious Sara screaming, and—

Sara's scream, loud to the sky, barely a break for a breath before it moved an octave higher.

Higher again.

And again.

Sara's screaming absorbing every other sound attacking Lainie's head.

Terrified for her daughter, Lainie fought through the bottleneck of customers elbowing, pushing and shoving their way out of the restaurant.

She pushed past the last of them into the main dining room, where some customers were still sitting, frozen over their gnocchi and chicken parmigiana, shocked beyond panic, staring as if in a hypnotic trance at Sara and Roy.

She let out her own scream, a burst of horror, when she saw Sara back in the booth, her face and clothing bloodied, covered with bits of brain and bone, shaking the lifeless body of her daddy, what remained of his face drowning in linguini with clams, his left arm dangling, fingers wrapped tightly around an empty wine glass.

It was Lainie's turn to scream.

She got to the booth and somehow managed to pull Sara loose from her daddy, then wrapped her arms around her in a way that sheltered Sara from the sight of Roy. She tried to comfort Sara with meaningless words.

"It's okay, baby. Everything is okay, baby. Mommy's here.

Mommy's here, my sweetheart."

Sara moved past hysteria to gigantic heaves of sobbing, her tears making rivers through the blood and gunk on her face, the blood and gunk transferred onto her mother, who hugged her child closer and harder, adding her own tears to the mix as police sirens grew louder outside Sal's Little Sicily.

CHAPTER 2

The freeways were begging for business. Roman made the drive from the Star Bright Theater home to La Canada in less than half an hour after swinging onto the 134 east from the I-5. He used the time to analyze the hatred he'd seen billowing from Lainie Gardner's astonishing eyes, emerald green randomly flecked with gold, heavily lidded, almost too large for the delicate features of her face.

Hers was not the prettiest face he'd ever seen, but not the ugliest one either. Hers was a face just beginning to show age wrinkles, especially around the eyes and the corners of her tight, sensitive lips. Its maturity was contradicted by qualities Lainie somehow radiated, as the typical all-american girl, girl-next-door, kid sister, bring-her-home-to-mother girl everyone wound up adoring, and no one would believe capable of jaywalking, much less participating in a series of white-collar crimes systematically carried out over a period of years that had the net effect of costing the county and the taxpayers countless millions of dollars.

He had never been entirely sure himself, but the evidence weighed against her.

That was good enough for Roman.

He was confident of getting both Gardners convicted, but the case collapsed when Roy Gardner was blown away on the eve of trial, making Lainie a widow.

Dropping the indictment against Lainie was the only stain on

Roman's otherwise perfect scorecard in the D.A.'s office. He ranked it up there with the last-second field goal he had missed by inches his junior year at South High. It cost the team a win in the big homecoming game, and so what if nobody blamed him and he went on to make the All-City first team again?

He blamed him. That was enough.

Harry Roman was not a good or gracious loser.

He'd promised himself, the D.A., the section, everyone—the media and the public—to make good in the matter of the People versus Lainie Davies Gardner.

He'd given them a rain check on that result.

He'd allowed himself the patience to wait for the sun to come shining again.

With the passage of time, one year feeding into another, he could admit to himself how increasingly remote that possibility was becoming—until the phone call that had branded her an accomplice to murder and put him back on the hunt.

Harry's home was a three-bedroom steal, a foreclosure he fell into on a tip from a contact in the County Recorder's Office when he was still a cop. It was more house than he needed in a wealthy neighborhood outside his league, but the investment was too good to pass up.

What clinched his decision was a backyard that took up most of the almost half acre, a rambling dichondra lawn that didn't need much care and ran up to a fenced-off hillside buried under ice plant, except for trail paths made over time by vagabond deer.

The backyard was perfect for the six mutts currently crowding him in his one-bedroom rental in Echo Park, three over the legal limit, but Harry loved dogs too much to ever pass up strays he found wandering loose and lonely. The total was currently up to eleven, twelve dogs until last month, when he could no longer put off having his dear, sweet bulldog, Drummond, put down. Age had finally pulled past the old boy. To subject him to another round of hip surgery would have been a self-indulgent act of cruelty. Thinking about it now, Harry felt his eyes go glossy visualizing Drummond's last look at him as the dog was led off by the vet. Drummond seemed to be telling him, *It's okay, mate. It's what I want, too.*

Harry stepped through the door connecting the garage to the kitchen. May Whitty and Joe, the leaders of the pack, gave him their usual jump and sniff greeting and growled demands for the Harry's Come Back Home snacks they knew to expect. The other members of the pack had taken up their usual positions and were salivating by the time he dipped into their jar for the requisite number of doggie chews.

May Whitty was a Great Dane named for the old English actress who vanished in Alfred Hitchcock's *The Lady Vanishes.* Joe was a cocker spaniel named in honor of Joe Cocker, one of Harry's favorite rockers, ever since hearing his bluesy version of the Beatles' "With a Little Help from My Friends." Joe Cocker's version of "You are So Beautiful" always moved Harry to tears, although to this day he had no idea why.

Hell, of course he did, but denial was easier.

The department shrink came close to psyching it out during the many sessions they spent together after that messy business with the Moon Pie murders put Internal Affairs on his butt and him on paid leave for a month, until he fed them a mountain of bull that took him off their radar. Harry had become an exceptional liar after he realized that making the lie a fundamental part of his work would pay dividends in the long run, if he expected to succeed.

He always expected to succeed.

Failure wasn't a word in his vocabulary.

Whenever he thought about "You are So Beautiful," more

often than Harry would ever confess to anybody, he tried convincing himself that the song and Joe's rendition brought him solace from all the damn ugliness his work exposed him to on a daily basis, first as a cop and now with the D.A.

He had gone LAPD blue thinking it would be his contribution to a society ritualistically mugged by an army of cockroaches who seemed to think the Constitution and the Bill of Rights were written on toilet paper. Stamping out those bugs became his mission, his life. It got Harry department attention in a hurry. It also got him a nickname, "Hurricane Harry," because "Dirty Harry" was taken.

Between top scores on promotion exams, a record number of busts that would have won him the MVP award every year if the department gave one, and enough medals and citations to decorate a wall in the third bedroom, Harry fast-tracked up the chain from shuffling traffic at a downtown intersection to a patrol car in South Central, then the Heights, then to Detective Two before he bailed out.

His anger had heated up seeing too many slam-dunk convictions waltz out the courtroom door because of sloppy work by indifferent prosecuting attorneys or the out-and-out incompetent lazies who saw plea bargaining as their fast track to the golf course.

His anger became an inferno every time some stone-cold badass paused on the way out to smack his face with a laugh, give him the finger and whisper *Better luck next time*.

He decided better luck would come as a lawyer.

Over a dozen years, Harry fit correspondence courses and night-school classes into his life, emerging finally with a *Juris Doctor*. He passed the state bar first crack and had the right credentials, credits and recommendations to get hired by the district attorney.

Harry worked his rise there faster than he'd made Detective

Two and soon was running the D.A.'s White Collar Crimes. If he had any complaint along the way, or now, it was not being able to put away the bad guys fast enough, more than earning his media reputation as a man on a Mission Possible.

Harry Roman, the one-man justice wave in a sea of slimy white-collar corruption.

But, then—

There were the Gardners.

The ones who got away.

The only ones who got away from him.

He'd never erased the memory of that morning, staring into the TV news cameras from the steps of the County Courthouse Building, saying:

"Roy Gardner's murder makes it difficult to proceed, for reasons the district attorney's office cannot expand upon, but"— his soggy voice stopped dramatically, dropped into a wintry whisper—"Mrs. Gardner is as guilty as her husband ever was, guilty as sin itself. I'm personally committed to gathering the evidence required to get her back in front of a jury and facing righteous justice, no matter how long it takes me."

No matter how long . . .

Harry finished taking care of the pooches and treated himself to a bottle of Dos Equis, the lager he got addicted to during his tour of the Heights, taking heavy sucks from the long neck on his way to the bedroom. He filed his jacket and slacks in the closet he kept as neat and orderly as the rest of his life, parked his Glock in its place in the dresser—a top drawer, slot to the right of the Magnum—and dumped everything else in the laundry hamper.

He hopped into the shower, lingering under the warm, heavy spray while replaying his confrontation with Lainie. He wanted the scenario, all the facts, straight in his mind before he connected with Thom Newberry, the man who'd put him back on the case, promising that this time she would not walk away from an indictment, promising, *"Definitely not this time, Harry, my good man."*

"Why do those words sound familiar, Newberry?"

"The glue wasn't strong enough the last time. This time it's strong enough."

"And the murder?"

"Support for the charge that was lacking the last time. This time, you will have her absolutely dead to rights, which should thrill you down to your cajones, *you have the balls to follow through."*

"You bring the evidence, I'll bring the cajones.*"*

"Forewarned is fore-skinned. Just remember to keep me and my people out of it."

"Like an elephant. You come through, I come through. My word's still good as gold."

"What's gold selling for nowadays, old boy?"

"A lot less than my word's worth."

Harry threw on his robe and sank onto the sofa in front of the TV with a fresh bottle of Dos Equis. May Whitty, Joe and a few other pooches settled by his feet. He'd set the recorder for tonight's Lakers–Heat game before heading off for the Star Bright. The Laker lead was dwindling in the fourth quarter, and he was growling over the fourth misfire in a row by Kobe Bryant when the private line rang.

He checked the time.

On the button, as usual.

No greeting.

Right down to business, also as usual.

"How'd it go, old boy?"

Harry told him.

"No surprise there. Deny, deny, deny. You would do the same thing she did under the circumstances. So would I."

"Even after she almost ripped my face off, I came close to

feeling sorry for her."

"The daughter thing, I bet."

"The daughter thing. But the more I got thinking about the murder, Lainie Gardner didn't come across as the kind of cold-hearted bitch who would lead her husband to slaughter. Not in front of her daughter. Not on her daughter's birthday. My feeling is—"

"You're a lawyer, old boy, remember? You work on facts, not feelings. The fact is she's guilty. I'll be supplying you with all the evidence you need to make your case, solid evidence, not hearsay, not . . . a *feeling*. Get your record back up to one hundred percent again. Get you the kind of press that wins elections, you know what I mean, Harry?"

"I've never claimed I want to be D.A. It's what others say, Newberry, not me."

"Well, you may want to consider saying it after you finish with Lainie, my good man. A great reward for a job well done after years of commitment to a cause."

"When do I get this evidence you say you have?"

"Soon."

"I'd like it sooner than that."

"Sooner than that. Feel better?"

"And what's your reward going to be for getting this on track for me? You still haven't said."

"Down the road, old boy. First things first."

"It's the governor thing, isn't it?"

"The governor thing? I don't know what you're talking about, Harry."

"I can read rumors, too. Those trial balloons floating up there around the time you first punched in my phone number? I'm thinking it's the governor thing."

"What I think, Harry? I think you should save your thinking for the giant splash you're going to make when you put Lainie

Davies Gardner away for keeps."

Thom Newberry added a gargantuan laugh and clicked off, once more leaving Harry to puzzle over what the whole story was here.

Possibly the real story.

Harry's gut telling him there was more to this on Newberry's mind than pinning Lainie Gardner to a murder rap.

Newberry worked without an official title at City Hall, but everybody called him "The Mayor's Man." He had master-minded Lawton Welles's come-from-behind victory in Welles's first bid for the mayor's office and was credited with the strategy that brought Welles an astounding twenty-three percent margin of victory in his race for reelection. The City Hall rumor mill, the media, lately had him developing a strategy to propel Welles into the governor's mansion, so—

That?

Was that it?

Was that where Lainie Gardner figured?

It made no sense, not yet anyway.

Harry fell asleep on the sofa with the question still on his mind.

CHAPTER 3

The next morning, settled behind his desk in City Hall, his arms resting in his lap, legs stretched and crossed at the ankles, waiting for his eleven o'clock appointment to arrive, Thom Newberry replayed his conversation with Harry Roman, to satisfy himself that Roman knew all he had to know for now, would stay the course, play the game the way he'd played football back in high school—to win.

Lainie Davies, whatever else this game was about, that's who it was meant to hurt.

And it would, he told himself with a confidence born of commitment.

Newberry shot the cuff of his custom-made silk shirt. Checked his watch again. Going on twenty minutes since Lainie was due. So typical of the Lainie he once knew better than anybody, showing him her independence, her arrogance, by setting her own terms, even after he'd warned her, "This isn't about me or us, Lainie. It's about you."

"That would be novel, a first for us," Lainie had said into the phone. "Even after all these years."

Newberry didn't have to see Lainie's face to know.

He'd heard it in her laughter.

The arrogance that always set Lainie above and apart from him and the others from the first minute they hooked up—

How long ago?

His thoughts drifted backward.

Thirty, no, more like twenty-five years ago.
Somewhere in between.

Give him another minute and he'd be able to pin it down to the exact day, the date that used to bite into him like a rabid memory whenever he thought about Lainie Davies and seeing her for the first time, in the alley behind the Troubadour, up about a dozen yards from the stage door, where the groupies congregated, like the door was a place on all those out-of-date maps to the homes of the rich and famous being sold on street corners in West Hollywood and Beverly Hills.

Thom was at the Troub trying out for amateur night, sure of his God-given talent even before he bummed the highway to L.A. from Tulsa, the precious Les Paul that had cost him two years' worth of flipping burgers six days a week strapped to his back. The guitar case was full of songs he had written on scrap paper, napkins and cash register receipts, even backs of envelopes Abe Lincoln–style.

He didn't doubt for a second that he was the equal of every player ever to come down the pike, his songs up there with the best ever turned out by Dylan or Springsteen. With one or two exceptions, even the immortal Lennon, who completed his Holy Trinity of rock-and-roll. Only those puss-suckers running the tryouts turned out to be as deaf as Beethoven.

So, there he was outside in the alley, shoring up his ego, at the same time wondering how long before he would need to trade in his Les Paul for some bucks to support a snow habit he had picked up somewhere along the way in L.A.—a little crank, if he could score it, but none of that pharmaceutical shit for him—when he became aware of her, Lainie.

She was trying to con a roadie into helping her get inside, past the stage door, maybe even borrow a guitar for her, so she could get up on stage for a crack at amateur night. Thom sized her up real good, showed her he liked what he saw, and said,

"You need somewhere to flop, I bet. I got the place, me and some friends, you want to get off the street."

The roadie said, "Hey, my man, you see the lady and me how we're talking here?" His voice, so sugar sweet with her a minute ago, now irritated at the interruption.

Thom said, "I see how you're starting to make moves on her. She's just a kid. Fuck off."

"You ready to try and make me, lame dick?" The roadie had half a head and fifty pounds on him, shoulders like a bull, pecs challenging his sweat-stained Sticky Tongue t-shirt.

Thom didn't flinch. He pulled a switchblade from the hip pocket of his jeans, dug one sneaker into the ground, took a long one-legged step back and began slicing into the air like some fugitive from the Three Musketeers.

The roadie thought about it. "Plenty more like that where she comes from," he said. He dismissed the scene with a contemptuous laugh and a gesture, moved cautiously around Thom, who was poking holes in the air and talking French to the world.

Thom waited until the roadie passed back into the Troub before he closed the switch and stashed it. Looking like he had just won a war. "So, you need someplace to land?"

Lainie said, "You talk French, huh?"

"Not really, but it sounds good enough to fake out the heavy thinkers, like that dude. Plan on learning it one day not so far off. Spanish. Probably Spanish first. Lot of Spics here, more'n the French, so that's good business."

"I got enough trouble with English. What kind of flop?"

"Safe. Me and some kids like you who need caring for."

The kids were vagrants who hung together one step ahead of the cops and do-gooders who roamed the streets with missing persons reports, photos and posters they received from parents all around the country who, chances are, never did any mommy and daddy pretending before their children disappeared. After that, only to boo hoo—boo hoo for the TV cameras, like they really gave a damn.

Thom's own parents were disasters from the get-go, Holy Rollers who never failed to pummel into him the belief that the busted rubber that helped produce Thom Newberry was God's punishment for some unspecified sin. They were always dragging him to some crackpot church and making him dig into the glory cage for a snake, never recognizing he only had to reach out and touch them to feel the biggest snakes in his life. Why he didn't mind when the pack, kids alone and desperate on rough, dangerous turf, made him their leader on some silent vote. At first, he thought it was because he was the oldest among them, but he soon recognized what he would go on to prove:

He, Thom Newberry, was a natural born leader.

The realization gave him a natural high, stronger and cheaper than any he ever got from free-basing or the finest grade pure Colombian or Hawaiian. In time, he came to understand that the real leaders are not the front men. The real leaders are their top guns, the trusted lieutenants who are wisest of all to the real ways of power.

Power, not to be confused with *glory.*

He got off on that.

On power.

POWER.

Years later, Thom Newberry was the power behind the throne.

The reason Lawton Welles could even remotely consider running for governor.

Thom Newberry, the Geppetto to Lawton Welles's Pinocchio.

The man who would get Lawton Welles elected, same as twice before, only this time to the governor's mansion in Sacramento.

Thom Newberry along for the rise.

Who and how Thom Newberry was meant to be.

THOM NEWBERRY: THE POWER BEHIND THE THRONE.

He'd begun teaching himself how to control people, move them to his way of thinking while treating his tight little band of street misfits better than any of them had ever been treated before. He figured out schemes for getting them fed and clothed and kept them moving from one abandoned building to another one step ahead of the authorities. He even worked the male perv trade on Santa Monica whenever it was necessary to score food money-bucks for his brat pack.

He became their authority figure.

That day behind the Troubadour, when he finished explaining about the flop, Lainie seemed to study him like his face was a religion before asking a question he could see she'd already answered in her mind.

"What's it make you? Like some daddy?" she said.

"More like a big brother. You know, like in *Big Brother is watching you?*"

"Sure, okay, lead the way. I'll try it out for tonight."

Lead the way.

Thom liked that.

She understood already.

The flop was an abandoned, boarded-up two-story building about a mile away, on Santa Monica Boulevard near La Cienega, posted "Keep Out" signs warning it was unsafe because of earthquake damage. Thom's gang got in and out by pushing aside loose boards on a window off the alley. They staked out space over both floors, keeping their skimpy gear packed in case they had to split fast.

Thom led Lainie to the upstairs room he had all to himself and told her to make herself comfortable. He eased the door closed and, when he was sure they had what passed for privacy, offered her a toot.

Lainie made like a crossing guard halting the traffic.

"My drug of choice is sex," she said.

She didn't seem the type.

He figured she was putting him on, and he told her so.

She answered him with the look of an angel waiting to happen, then closed in on him, lavishing her thanks for rescuing her and taking her in; stroking his ego.

She said, "I was squirreled inside the Troubadour when you hit the stage and started to do your thing, dude. In the balcony before I got discovered, and they dumped my skinny butt back outside, where you pulled me from that roadie creep on the make. Up there on stage, you were awesome, Thom, the one song of yours I got to hear. That's a song can take you someplace, you don't quit and keep on trying."

Her praise caught him by surprise. All he could think to answer was, "You the expert on music?"

"Enough to know." Her confidence defied rebuttal.

He hadn't bawled in years, not even for the worst of the belt buckle whuppings from his pa, but he almost did now, hearing her laud his talent, paint for him the same kind of future he'd once painted for himself, crossing herself and insisting time and again, "I mean it all, Thom. Every single blessed word."

All he could think to say was, "I don't know anything about you yet. Tell."

She made a show of deciding, then:

"Valley brat," she said. "Only child. Orphaned by eleven, my mom and dad killed in a freeway thing—drunk driver going the wrong way, doing ninety—me, almost killed with them. Lot of hospital time, lots of nightmares. I wake up screaming ever and you'll know why. Got bumped from one foster home to the next, me the reason half the time.

"The other half, lousy people only in it for the bucks or because they like beating up on kids. Got molested the first time by a daddy who taught Sunday school and already had plowed through his own natural three daughters. His PTA witchy-woman was one of those who liked to watch . . . Sprung myself loose to the streets early last year and ever since been meeting a higher class of lowlife, exceptions like you seem being rare. How's that? Enough for now, Thom? Can give you more, you like."

"How do you know I'm an exception?"

"I heard your song and heard your heart in it, like I'm hearing your heart now. You're a good person and what I can use in my life, Thom. A good person."

"You're sounding pretty wise for fifteen years."

"Where I've been, you can double that, okay? It's too late to make me back into a little girl. I got made into a woman, and it's worked out. Gives me a head start on taking over the world."

"That what you want, to take over the world?"

"A piece of it. An actress, maybe. Get up there, they know how to live. A singer, maybe. I do some of that. Rock and roll, baby. Nowhere good as you, though. That one song? It'll take you someplace, Thom, if you don't quit on yourself."

Later that night, her nightmare noises woke him. A minute later she was scrambling under his blanket, begging, "You mind? Need someone to hold me, Thom. Need someone to truly love me."

Your eleven o'clock is here, Thom.

His secretary's voice on the intercom fired him from his memory.

Newberry sucked air and shook his head clear, snatched up the phone, and told her, "Coffee, Mrs. Gardner and sit her out there for ten, then send her on in, Winnie."

★ ★ ★ ★ ★

Lainie had a quick nod for him heading to the conversation area, a hand protecting the plastic coffee cup from spilling while her eyes swept the office.

She settled in the giant cream-colored leather armchair he usually took, made a show of caution in putting the cup down on the table and straightened out the stacks of magazines before easing back, hands clutching the armrests like a nervous airline passenger preparing for takeoff. Her body language told Thom she was not as confident about the meeting as her face wanted him to believe.

"You're looking absolutely wonderful," Thom said, smiling, trying to sound warm as he came around his desk. He plopped himself in a corner of the couch across from Lainie, where he would have a clear view of her. He had planned on having her sit across the desk in the visitors' chair, squinting against a bright morning sunlight streaming in from the window, blinds all the way up, drapes pulled, the old disarming tactic she obviously knew.

Lainie said, "I know. I haven't aged a bit, etcetera, etcetera. Have your eyes checked, Thom, first chance. You don't look so bad yourself." Spoken like she meant it. A few moments of awkward silence before she asked, "The picture there on the bookcase. The boy?"

"My son?"

"Reminds me of you that age."

"Three years younger than I was when we met."

"I know. Math still comes easy to me. He have a name?"

"Jerry."

"You *didn't*." Her eyes rolling. "Thom and Jerry?" Hands still gripping the armrest, but not yet ready to let this be his meeting. A shrug. "Always were your favorite cartoons."

"Tweety Bird. He's actually Allen Clifford Newberry. I named

33

him for Lance."

Nodding. "Lance Clifford. How well I remember good old Lance Clifford, world famous singing star, movie star, hero, hunk and man-about-boys. I'll bet it was one tough childbirth for good old Lance. You go to Lamaze classes with good old Lance? It's still the thing to do, very in. Didn't you once tell me how good old Lance, he liked it very in?"

Lainie was playing him. He let it pass. "After Carla delivered, Lance came to the hospital to have a first look. Slapped me on the back—"

"Ass high, right?"

"Lance slapped me on the back and decided, 'Your child is no more than a little mouse. A Jerry to go with my Thom.' How he got the nickname."

"Good old Lance. Same as he originally got a Thom to go with his hairy dick." Betraying no emotion. "Carla, she went along with the idea, of course."

He'd had enough.

"Not why I invited you over, Lainie. If we're going to talk about anyone's child, it's going to be yours. It's going to be Sara."

That got her attention. If looks could kill . . .

"What's that supposed to mean, Thom?"

"In time," he said, aiming a palm at her. "First things first."

CHAPTER 4

Lainie looked for a lie among the deeply imbedded age wrinkles and laugh lines on Thom Newberry's richly tanned face that bespoke years of lazy days lounging poolside or roaming golf courses under the Southern California sun.

Not there.

Either that or Thom had become a better liar over the years.

Probably that.

Practice makes perfect, and he already had the makings of a master liar in him the day they met.

Not that she knew it or was even thinking that way when he moved on her in the alley behind the Troubadour, her hardly noticing him at first, consumed by trying to con that roadie into helping her get back inside, past the stage door, maybe even borrow a guitar for her so she could hit the stage for a crack at amateur night.

Thom had sized her up real good, let her see he liked what he saw and guessed, *You need someplace to flop, I bet.*

At the flop, she'd told him her story and didn't resist when the old nightmares drove her into his arms. He was kind and gentle with her, said words she'd never heard before that brought her more joy. She denied him nothing, submitting to his every suggestion. She came to think of it as her first time ever, always with a smile, until later, when what Thom Newberry gave her and her life was nothing to smile about.

35

The morning after, when Thom told her he wanted her to be his girl—

Magical.

Before that morning, nobody had ever wanted her to be anything.

He said, "I think you and I make a pretty damn fine team. A *great* team, I think." Stretching the word *great*.

"Whatever you say," she answered, meaning it.

For months afterward, Lainie gave him a lot of lip a lot of times over some of the things he wanted her to do, but she never once went back on her word, not even when she knew it was wrong what he wanted her to do, so awfully wrong—

How much in love with him she was.

Too much in love with him.

How she wound up doing the prison gig.

Being too much in love with Thom Newberry.

Doing hard time.

Because of Thom and for Thom, her big brother, her big daddy, whose biggest lie of all was telling her how much he loved her.

Lainie needing to believe him, because nobody had ever wanted her for anything before Thom, because they were a team, the two of them, always there for each other, because that's what teammates were supposed to do.

Some kids in the pack thought it was all about Thom's good looks, what kept her leashed to his side, that shaggy blond hair running wild around a face you'd expect to find on the statue of a Greek god, eyes blue enough to put the ocean to shame.

Never.

Thom Newberry was gorgeous, but what Lainie dug was the goodness inside him.

Thom could have been the hunchback of Notre Dame and it would not, could not, have mattered.

He saw something in her, too. Wanted her to be his girl. Wanted them to be a team.

That's why she loved him.

Enough to keep loving him all through the worst of her jail time, stopping only when—

"You want to know what that is, Lainie, what it is that comes first?"

Thom Newberry's voice retrieved her from their past as easily as it had first sent her there this morning, when his call woke her up. Lainie recognized it was him at once. He was sounding older but still smooth as satin, smooth as *Satan,* the sweetness hiding whatever he wanted from her.

Thom had to want something.

He always wanted something.

She'd learned that the hard way, but what now, on the phone to someone whose life he once came close to destroying?

Now, parked on the couch, giving her his keyboard smile like the old Newberry mojo might somehow work again on her, conceited bastard that he was, he toyed with his coffee cup as well as with her, waiting for an answer to his question.

Lainie leaned forward in the armchair and, hardly trying to mask her contempt for him, said, "First Sara. What's Sara have to do with anything?"

"I needed to get your attention, my good girl."

"In case you didn't notice, I'm a woman, Thom, and not your good anything . . . Talk."

He said nothing.

"On the phone, you also brought up Sara," Lainie said, speaking softer; trying to appear cool. Inside, her heart was racing, and her stomach was verging on spasm. "That time also to get my attention?"

Newberry sipped at his coffee and returned the cup to the table. Bent over and retied a shoelace. Lainie knew the game he was playing. He was showing her who was in charge. How he would speak when he was good and ready to speak.

She thought about leaving, but the way he'd brought up Sara's name. Not just to get her attention. There was menace in the way he'd answered her with Sara's name. She could not leave and let it keep hanging over her like a question mark.

She composed herself. Filled her lungs, let the air breeze out through her mouth. Gave him a slight nod she knew he'd remember, the one from a lifetime ago that always meant she'd do whatever it was he'd just asked of her.

For love.

For him.

For them.

For the team.

The son of a bitch.

He turned his head away from her for a minute, like he was using his stare to straighten one of the framed citations on the wall across the room, and said, "That's my good girl." Lainie swallowed her pride in a false smile and waited him out. "When I said this wasn't about me but about you, you gave me grief and started to hang up," he said.

"I did, yes."

"Hearing 'Sara' kept you on the line."

"Yes."

"And got you up here to my office."

"Yes."

"Late."

"Sara's not well this morning. I needed to spend more time with her."

"Sorry to hear that." Looking not the least bit sorry. "I meant it when I said there was a crisis in your life and Sara's that compelled me to pick up the phone, hoping that you could let bygones be bygones and meet with me."

"You did, yes."

Newberry let the smile slide off his face. He replaced it with the kind of paternal look a doctor puts on just before he springs the bad news. "The D.A.'s office is about to come after you again, Lainie. They're taking the grand jury more evidence than they had last time, linking you like a sausage to your husband and *every* count Roy was facing before he was killed. All thirty-seven counts this time. Not just the twenty-four you were originally charged with. They're going to be sending you away for a long time, leaving Sara motherless. Taken from you and placed in a foster home. A good one, if Sara's fortunate. The reason I called and asked you to meet with me: I wanted you prepared for the inevitable. I felt I owed you at least that much; make up a little for all that bad business that went down between us."

Newberry was being too solicitous.

Lainie shook her head. "The D.A. didn't have a strong case against me then and he won't have one this time. Innocent is innocent, but I thank you for the consideration. So, if that's it . . . ?"

She got up as if she were planning to leave, knowing he wouldn't let her.

Thom Newberry wouldn't know charity if it arrived dressed in a Salvation Army uniform and beating a big brass drum. The leopard had something on his mind that had nothing to do with preparing her for anything but the real reason he wanted her here.

"No, not *it* . . . More, and more serious," he said.

He motioned for Lainie to sit again. Kept the meter running over several sips of coffee while he watched her shift back into the armchair. Studied her as she crossed her legs, gripped her arms over her chest.

"Murder One," Newberry announced, like it was the sad title

to a sadder story.

Even before he got the words out, Lainie had flashed on Harry Roman at the Star Bright Theater, their conversation, Roman laying the same accusation on her head, her laughing it off, as she did now with Newberry.

She said, "Whatever your game, you're trying to scare me into what, saying something I shouldn't?"

"No game, Lainie."

"You know who Harrison Roman is?" She went for her coffee. It was cold. She settled the cup back on the table.

"Harry Roman, of course. The D.A. on the case. He swore to get you back in a court, and now it's looking like he will."

"Roman came at me with the same line. This a tag team? You think I might have changed so much that I'd start quaking at a threat and—then what? I'll say this for Harry Roman: He didn't try to jazz up the jolt by mentioning Sara. I read Roman fast, but what's your spin? I can't see you picking up the phone for anyone, about anything, without there being something in it for you."

Lainie watched Newberry struggle with his composure before glancing away, studying a horsefly loose in his office while it caught a rest on the gold picture window draperies behind the desk. He shifted interest to his manicured nails and said, as casually as he gave them a blow and a buff on the jacket of a black and white herringbone three-piece that must have set him back at least a couple grand, "Roman has your shooter."

"My *shooter*?" She turned as he looked up, hoping he wouldn't catch her astonishment. Roman had said nothing to her about any shooter. She forced down some cold coffee to buy thinking time. Definitely a game going on here with him, but what kind of game? *"My shooter?"*

"Roman didn't tell you?"

She let Newberry lock onto her eyes.

Shook her head vigorously.

"The mechanic who blew away your husband is ready to tell a jury how she got the contract straight from you?"

"She?"

"A her. Says she knew you up close and personal from the years the two of you spent palling around together at the Animal Farm."

The Animal Farm was the name the inmates had for the U.S. Federal Women's Detention Center in San Diego, where Lainie had done her hard time after they caught her coming through the Tijuana border with a left rear tire packed full of pure Colombian.

Newberry said, "Ruby Crandall. Her name bring back any memories?"

"No."

" 'Chips' is what she said people called her, because she always went around the Animal Farm looking like she had two chips on her shoulder."

"Yeah, Chips. I remember Chips. She wasn't a friend of mine or anyone's at the Farm. A lying schizo bitch is what she was."

"She says she did the shoot for you half price, as a favor, because she owed you a big one for something nice you did for her inside the joint."

Lainie swept aside the allegation. "Keeping out of her face was as nice as anybody ever wanted to get with Chips, me included. Somebody's putting her up to something at my expense, same as this crap about the new indictments . . . You?"

Newberry put on a pained expression and moved a palm to his chest, like he was about to pledge allegiance. "If it were me, I'd have had no reason to call you and invite you over to warn you. The grand jury. The indictment. It would happen, and that would be that."

"My concern is for Sara," Lainie said, meaning it, but

41

otherwise playing along.

Putting on a distressed face to go with the act.

Pampering him into slipping on his lies.

He said, "Would be the same for me with my kid, with Jerry, I ever found myself in your predicament."

"Thom, you think you could help me somehow? Parent to parent, and forget about the past?"

"Like I said the first time—bygones be bygones?"

"Bygones be bygones."

"I can help, yes." So much arrogance in his voice. She wanted to shoot him down, but this wasn't the time. "I can see to it that the D.A. withdraws the matter from the grand jury. Get you off the hook now and probably forever?"

"This insanity about the Murder One?"

Blinding Lainie with his teeth. "Also made to go away."

"Chips and what that crazy lying bitch said—"

"Gone, Lainie. Gone, gone, gone. Over and out. Nothing you'll ever have to worry about again. History, and you can go on rebuilding your life, for you and for Sara."

Newberry settled back like some pope, waiting for her to kiss his ring.

Kiss his ass, more like it.

Lainie drew on the acting trick she had mastered studying with Tracy Roberts, before she made the shift full time into the record business, Tracy invoking the names of her masters, Adler and Chekhov, demonstrating how the memory of some past event could sponsor a genuine emotion that put the actor in the moment for real.

Almost at once, Lainie had her eyes moist enough for tears to stain her cheeks. More tears as she struggled to tell Newberry *Thank you.* Even the words cried for her. She gave him another minute to wallow in his supremacy, then, "Level with me now, Thom. There has to be something I can do for you in return.

There is, isn't there?"

Newberry looked up at the ceiling as if the answer were there, adjourned with his coffee to the desk. He played with a stack of papers waiting for her to join him. Lainie padded over and settled in one of the visitor seats. The blinding sun splashed her face when she looked up at him, making it impossible to examine his expression while he said, "Everything comes with a price, my little girl."

"Name it," she said.

CHAPTER 5

"You know who Lawton Welles is, of course?"

"Your boss, the mayor."

"The mayor," Thom said, thinking better than to set her straight on her use of the word "boss." Let her come to understand by herself how much influence he had in the administration. "You've heard the rumors that he might enter the race for governor?"

Lainie turned her head to avert the glare blasting through the picture window and smiled. "To miss them you'd have to be on another planet. Your handiwork?"

Thom ignored the question. "How about Sequit?" She met the name with silence and a look he knew from people stumped by a *Jeopardy!* question. "Gan Eden. Does that name mean anything to you?"

"No."

He watched her wriggle a little. Good. He was letting her see that his being the smartest person in the room had as much to do with knowledge as attitude. He still had both over her. Get that reestablished in a hurry, he thought, so she'd pay him full attention when he moved on to the important stuff.

"Paradise Sands?"

"Something familiar about that one, but—" She hesitated, revealing to Thom she didn't want to give a wrong answer. "Okay, tell me. I surrender."

"It's the latest name of four thousand undeveloped acres over by Topanga. Malibu. That area. Once called Sequit, then Gan Eden, which translates as the Garden of Eden, and now—"

"Yes, Paradise Sands. In the news a lot about a year ago, why the name sounded familiar. So what?"

"The city owns it all, from the shoreline, across Pacific Coast Highway, and up and over the hillside, way over to where the land flats out for about another mile." He moved onto his feet; stood sentry duty behind the desk, ramrod straight, hands clasped behind his back while throwing more facts and statistics at her. When he paused to see if she was taking it in, Lainie said, "Why should I care about any of this?"

"Let me finish and you'll know."

She raised her arms in surrender.

"The city did nothing with Paradise Sands except to protect the beachfront and keep it accessible to the public, the rest a sanctuary for squatters and foliage between earthquakes and fires, while the area grew in value at a rate equal to other coastline property, especially nearby Malibu and the Colony.

"Fifteen months ago, a corporation came to the city and proposed developing the land as a residential, business and entertainment complex, one part Wilshire Corridor, one part Universal City, one part Disneyland. They offered a reasonable price for a hundred-year lease, like a lease-hold in Hawaii, and to cut the city in for a small percentage of the revenues from their various enterprises. On the surface, it looked like a good deal for L.A. Found money at a time when the city's budget was stretched to the limit. The City Council went for it big time, a unanimous vote over protests from local residents, but the County Board of Supervisors had serious reservations, and so did Mayor Welles. He vetoed the Council's bill and promised to reject the plan no matter how or how many times it was adjusted. The mayor was hailed as a hero. The corporation licked its wounds and moved on to other things, or so it seemed—

until a few weeks ago."

Thom paused.

He recognized Lainie's mind working overtime to digest the information, especially the parts he'd left out. She'd always been good at that. Figuring his silence as an invitation to speak, she said, "Your boss—"

"The mayor."

"The mayor was politically motivated. Thinking about running for governor, if you can believe the trial balloons. He decided he had more to gain with his veto—the goodwill of the fat cat voters out Malibu way. Stronger backing from the Board of Supervisors that would translate statewide when the time came. The idea that he wasn't a pawn of big business, but a champion of the people. What a political animal your boss"— she corrected herself—"the mayor must be."

"Mayor Welles respects and listens to good advice."

"That's why he has you," Lainie said, playing up to him and so transparent about it.

"Thank you," he said, as if he didn't know.

"You said 'until a few weeks ago.' What happened?"

"I was invited to visit with someone, and couldn't afford to say 'no.' " He hesitated before hitting her with the name: "Leonard Volkman." Lainie looked at him like she'd been punched in the kidneys. She chased the room with wild eyes while her complexion turned the color of chalk. "The corporation calling itself Rainbows Unlimited was another front for Volkman International, your benefactor at Blue Pacific Records, Lainie, the gentleman who was responsible for your rise and demise in the music business. The same Leonard Volkman who was your late husband Roy's onetime business associate, who bought himself immunity by providing the D.A. with paperwork and a deposition that led to Roy's indictment. And yours."

"You don't have to explain what I already know. A lying

46

snake. Probably what attracted him to Paradise Sands, the former Gan Eden, the Garden of Eden, in the first place. None of what happened would have except for that sack of puke. Roy would still be alive and—What's the rest of it, Thom? Lenny out from under his rock again, feeding you more lies about me, about—?"

"Volkman is dealing in the truth this time."

"Don't tell me you believe he held back three years ago. Has something new that'd make a grand jury dance again on that old indictment or to get me up on a murder charge? Having my husband murdered? While my own daughter watched? Dear sweet Jesus, you think that, that I'm that kind of a monster? You do, Thom, you're a bigger fool than you ever were before."

He let her rattle for a few more moments before telling her, "Not those truths, Lainie. The truths I'm talking about have to do with Mayor Lawton Welles."

That shut her up.

"Volkman called me to say he had come into possession of certain information about the mayor that, if it got out, would end his bid for the governorship before it began, end any future he might have in politics and probably start with a referendum on a recall. We met, and I saw and heard enough to realize Volkman wasn't pulling a bluff. He told me how it could all disappear, go away—"

"If Welles changed his position on the Paradise Sands proposal and made the deal happen for Rainbows Unlimited."

"Exactly, and as a bonus he'd pump in enough soft money to help the mayor buy his way into the governor's mansion."

"You went along."

"I did, but the mayor wouldn't. He's ready to throw his career away—go back to teaching fifth grade, the idiot—and with it my future. I've invested too many years in him, too much time, to let that happen."

"You really think you can stop someone like Leonard Volkman when he puts his mind to something and gets this far out front?"

"Yes. I've done it in the past with other Leonard Volkmans."

"There are no other Leonard Volkmans. He's the best of the worst. The rest rank as amateurs compared to Lenny. And why am I supposed to care? Because Lenny's doing to you what you're trying to do with me?"

"Absolutely."

"Blackmail."

"I prefer calling it *friendly persuasion.* I want you to worm your way back into Volkman International, back into his good graces. I don't care how. You do that, get yourself positioned to get your hands on what I need to get out of Volkman International, and I promise you that you'll never again, *never,* have to worry about anything, *anything,* that'll threaten you or take you away from Sara. Not a grand jury. Not Ruby Crandall."

"You *'promise,'* like that promise you'd never cum in my mouth?"

"Bygones be bygones. Just give me your damn answer."

"What do you need out of there? You haven't said."

"First things first. First, find a way to get back inside Volkman International. I'll tell you what I need when the time is right. Volkman gave me six weeks to deliver the mayor's support, so I'm giving you four weeks. A month. Yes or no?"

She looked to him like she couldn't make up her mind.

"I'm counting to ten, Lainie."

"If for some reason I flop? You going to save me from Lenny?"

"You won't flop. You're too good for that."

"I used to be," Lainie said.

"You listen to me, you will be again, my little girl . . . One . . . two . . ."

CHAPTER 6

Harry Roman worked over the punching bag hanging from the ceiling in a corner of his office for about fifteen minutes, *ratatatat-ratatatat-ratatatat,* after Thom Newberry phoned him to announce he was backing off the Gardner business. He built up a sweat storm punching his way through his frustration, wishing it were Newberry's face, not the bag, turning his knuckles a meat red raw. He'd been too angry to hold off assaulting the bag until he could get the gloves on.

"Just following instructions, my good man. In this case I'm the messenger boy for Mayor Welles," Newberry had said, sounding unusually contrite.

"Why?"

"No explanation, only that we had to hold off."

"For how long?"

"The mayor didn't say. I got the idea it might be for a month or six weeks. Can you live with that?"

"Do I have a choice?"

"No."

Politics, Harry told himself.

What it's all about.

Ratatatat. Ratatatat Ratatatat.

All about goddamn politics.

Bullshit.

For them maybe, not for him.

Ratatatat. Ratatatat Ratatatat.

Harry skipped the freeway. He took Sunset Boulevard west to the Santa Monica cut-in and maneuvered south onto Hoover, slowing when he closed in on Lainie Gardner's apartment. He cruised past the duplex, made a driveway turnaround and backed into a curbside space about a half block away that gave him a clear view of the place. Her porch light was on, although there was still plenty of late afternoon light. A flyer hung from the doorknob. A throwaway newspaper was on the porch. There was no illumination behind the ratty, half-drawn shades on the windows facing the street.

He hunkered down behind the wheel and waited, like the old cop days on stakeout, not sure what he was waiting for or why he was waiting at all; nodded off after about half an hour, catching winks until startled awake by knuckles rapping on the passenger window.

The round face smiling back at him belonged to a Pacific Rimmer in his teens, hunched over and pantomiming for him to roll down the window. Two other teenage Rimmers hung back on the sidewalk, like trouble waiting to happen.

"Cherry Mustang you got, man? A replica?"

"The genuine article," Harry said. "A '64. Original red paint job. Original engine under the hood."

"You get it looking so cherry yourself, man?"

"Spit and polish, but under the hood?" Harry shook his head. "What I know stops where I turn the key. Cost me a few over the years, but it was worth it. Always the car of my dreams."

"What say to taking me and my boys here for a spin?"

"I don't think so, man."

"Around a couple of blocks? I'm not talking any major cruise, you know?"

"Maybe another time."

"Why, you're doing fucking business dreaming behind the wheel, so you can't take time now?" His singsong voice going ugly. Turning to his boys: "Dude's selfish. He says he can't give us a cruise."

"Selfish," they agreed, like a Greek chorus.

Harry let a hand slip off his lap to scratch an imaginary back itch; actually to make a habit-check for the Glock parked under his jacket. His other hand dipped between the driver's door and the seat, where he kept a fifteen-inch length of thick iron pipe with a duct tape handle for fast, easy snatching.

He said, "Let's keep it friendly, okay?"

"Man wants us to keep it friendly, he says."

"Way to go," one of his buddies called over, making an okay circle with his thumb and forefinger.

"Way," the other one agreed, duplicating the circle.

The leader, his smile back in place, withdrew a can of spray paint from inside his bomber jacket.

He yanked off the lid, gave the can a good shaking, and said, "Tag, you're it, dude."

He began spraying a design in grape purple on the hood of the Mustang.

It resembled the gang tag Harry had noticed on the waist-high stucco wall of a house across the street.

Harry watched, commanding himself not to go crazy with these punks. Never one for anyone's orders, even his own, he climbed out of the car and strolled around to the sidewalk, keeping the pipe inconspicuous at his side.

The leader, too dumb to read him as Harry approached within two feet, said, "Price of rudeness, dude."

"And here's your change," Harry said. He brought the pipe up and around too fast for the leader to react with anything more than bug eyes and a squeak. The pipe made a solid connection with the upper arm of his spray hand.

Harry heard the crack of bone as the leader dropped the can, gasped, fell to his knees and face forward onto the sidewalk, the crack this time his nose. His boys were momentarily frozen. They took a few steps backward while reaching inside their bomber jackets. One came out with a set of knuckles, the other one with a Saturday night special.

Harry already had his Glock on them.

He gave them his old crazy cop stare and said in the gutter whisper that always proved more convincing than a shout, "You'll be dead before your next blinks unless you unload, you prick bastard fag asshole fucks."

They got the message; dropped the knucks and the gun.

Harry said, "You, move over and get the spray can for me."

The one he'd indicated, who was shaking so hard Harry could hear his jaw playing a melody on his teeth, did as he was told and backed away. "We were only prowling for some kicks, dude," the other one said. "Don't go and do anything stupid, okay?"

"Thank you for sharing," Harry said, shaking the spray can. He striped the kid on the ground head to toe in purple, then stepped close enough to his playmates to decorate them, getting to their faces faster than they got there with their hands. They yowled when the purple spray spit on their eyes. One upchucked on himself after taking a fat mouthful of the paint.

Satisfied, Harry tossed the can and said, "Now, pick up your fearless leader, move your sorry asses out of here, and next time get your kicks somewhere else." A few moments later he called after them, "Have a nice night."

He was turning to inspect the damage to the Mustang's hood when he noticed the young girl standing by the entrance walk to Lainie Gardner's home. She cracked a smile and applauded as she approached him. He didn't have to flash on the surveillance photos in the Gardner jacket to know who she was. Sara. At fifteen, the spitting image of her mama.

"Slick, the way you put them away," Sara said. "They're absolutely nothing but trouble around here, the whole bunch, whenever they charge up here from down around Korea Town." She moved the knapsack from her shoulder to a sidewalk spot next to the clogs that added three inches to her height and put her almost at eye level with Harry.

She was tall and willowy like her mother, with the same astonishing saucer eyes, more blue than emerald, dominating her red-pebbled teenage face. Her midnight black tresses were streaked with rainbow colors and fell straight down her back, well past her shoulder blades, over a J-Lo t-shirt tucked inside a worn-out pair of faded blue denims. Her speech was less studied than Lainie's, almost too adult for her age, with a rasp that hinted at heavy charges of alcohol and cigarettes and—

He started to check her eyes again.

Sara caught the move, turned her head before he could verify any telltale signs, and said, "You the big bad blue?"

"What makes you ask?"

"The way you used the shooter, like you knew what you were doing. Either the big bad blue or some badass dude. I would've used the shooter. Wish you had. Blow their heads off . . . You don't have any smokes you could spare, do you?"

"I don't smoke. Neither should you."

"Now I read you. A Boy Scout. I see the commercials same as you, Boy Scout. We all gotta die sometime. I suppose you don't drink, either."

A slurring in her speech he hadn't heard before.

Lainie's kid, definitely one of the walking wounded.

Harry said, "I drink, but—"

"I know, I know. I shouldn't. Heard it all before. So, how do you feel about screwing?" She turned her face back to him, her

53

eyes exploding with boldness, daring Harry to answer the question. She pushed out her pelvis and did a few grinds.

All Harry could do was stare at her, wondering if she was serious or only trying to rattle his cage. And succeeding. He couldn't be certain. He had encountered his share of child prosties when he was working the streets. The surprise was getting pitched by the teenage daughter of a woman who had talked like her child was her whole life and breath, who had gone through this herself and should-have-could-have-would-have spotted the signs coming and done everything in her power to keep it from happening.

He tinkered with the thought of flagging Child Welfare as he moved on her and cuffed her wrist with his hand. "Where's your mother?"

The question surprised Sara. She wrestled free, threw her hands at him and sent her eyes to the sky. "What are you, a snitch as well as a badass cop?" Something behind Harry caught her attention. "Jesus!"

Harry turned and saw it was another Pacific Rimmer, not one of the three who had tried playing with him.

Standing by the streetlamp at the corner.

Aiming a gun at them.

"First her, then you," the Pacific Rimmer called out. "For treating my gang-bangers with no respect."

Harry shoved Sara out of the way and in the same motion grabbed his Glock and jumped into a shooter's stance, giving the Pacific Rimmer second thoughts.

The Pacific Rimmer raised the gun barrel to the clouds.

Gave him the finger.

Turned and fled.

Sara was down on the ground. Harry parked the Glock back inside his belt and helped her to her feet. He was asking if she was all right, brushing off her shoulders, when Lainie got out of a junk heap that had just parked.

Sara also had spotted her.

"Mother Shitstorm Time," she said. She grabbed her knapsack and ran toward her house.

Barely a minute later she was inside, and Lainie was confronting Harry.

"What were you doing with my daughter?" she said, her temper barely under control.

It was nothing Harry wanted to get into with her. "Having a nice chat."

"Just happened to be in the neighborhood?"

"Small world, isn't it, Mrs. Gardner."

"Spying on me, Roman?"

"Yes, as a matter of fact."

"What did Sara tell you?"

"She said I should have blown the heads off the gang-bangers she watched make a big mistake by coming on to me." Lainie didn't have to know the rest. "I would've thought a killing was the last thing in the world Sara would ever want to see again, wouldn't you?"

The taunt didn't get the reaction Harry expected.

Lainie seemed to step out of her hostility. "Can you use a coffee?"

"At minimum, but thanks, no. Not a good idea."

"Come on. There's something I want to throw at you."

"Besides a grenade?"

"In addition."

"Maybe some other time."

"When?"

"Some other time."

"I don't like you, either, Roman, but we have to talk."

"About?"

"Coffee?"

"I know all I ever need to know about coffee. Something else?"

"Chips."

"As in *'fish and . . .'* ? For that you'd want a nice lager to wash it all down."

"You truly are some piece of work . . . Chips, as in Ruby Crandall."

Harry had no idea who Ruby Crandall was or why Lainie was taking him there, but he played along. "What about Ruby Crandall?"

"Don't patronize me like I'm some fool," she said. "Thom Newberry let me in on it, the lies you're buying from Ruby Crandall for the murder charge you think you have going against me."

Newberry? What was Newberry doing talking to her?

Harry gave it another beat, then chalk-marked the space between them with a finger, all the while struck again with how elegantly pretty she was—not beautiful or just show biz flashy—Audrey Hepburn pretty, easier to picture in the arms of Cary Grant than behind bars doing life for murder.

Lainie avoided his eyes, like she was reading his mind. "Chips was a lying scuzz before and she's a lying scuzz now. You pin your hopes on getting me convicted on her word, and you're the King of Dumb."

"Ask you a question?"

"Coffee?" She lifted her head, put her hands on her narrow waist, elbows out, and waited, like she was defying a firing squad.

"Trying to kick the caffeine habit, thanks, Mrs. Gardner."

"The King of Dumber than Dumb," Lainie said, and stalked off.

Back home, still grumbling about the desecration of his classic Mustang, toting up the small fortune it was bound to cost to get the tagging erased without damaging the original paint, he went through the usual rituals, adding an extra walk around the neighborhood for the newest addition to the family menagerie, Michael J., a fox terrier he saw wandering the streets hungry and without a license a few days ago, looking like he'd gotten the worst of a fight. May Whitty took to Michael J. instantly, Joe after some sniffing and growling to let Michael J. know who was boss.

He was halfway into his second bottle of Dos Equis when the phone rang.

Jimmy Steiger returning the call he'd put in to him from the freeway.

He and Jimmy had grown up together on the force. Jimmy had stayed with it and was now a detective lieutenant. Harry muted the TV, went through the usual pleasantries and traded some gossip before telling Jimmy, "Need a favor."

"You listening to my amazement explode like an H-bomb? Of course you need a favor. Whenever else is it I hear from you, Hurricane?"

"Is that a yes?"

"Only if what you need from me is illegal, immoral or fattening."

"I need you to run a fast check through the systems for me, Jimmy. Local, but especially the feds."

"Not just as easy for you to do from your place? You're the white collar hotshot of the D.A.'s office, after all."

"I want to keep it out of channels for now."

"Away from prying eyes, you mean?"

"The eyes have it."

"I'm all ears. You want to share the name?"

"Ruby Crandall."

Jimmy Steiger spelled back both names in C-for-Charlie.

"Probably a day or so, we're backlogged on the bad guys, but I'm on it. Give me your e-mail address again."

CHAPTER 7

The Starbucks near Miranda Morgan's place in Burbank, up from the Disney and NBC lots, was packed with show biz types despite the early morning hour, sipping at tall lattés while bent over laptops or working through the trades. When Miranda finally arrived, Lainie was into her second cup of whatever the eager fuzz-faced actor-type behind the counter poured when she ordered "Anything stronger than strong."

"Pure caffeine's coming right up, ma'am," he'd said, like Lainie might be someone worth auditioning for. He was too chipper for this early in the day, not what she needed to go with the killer migraine Harry Roman's appearance and, especially, Sara's smart-ass attitude had brought on last night.

Sara ended their battle of words her usual way, by locking herself inside the bedroom, obliging Lainie to endure a lumpy night on the sofa bed, wondering what it was that always let her let her little brat get away with murder. She knew the answer, of course, but chose to pretend it didn't exist.

Thanks be to God Sara still didn't know the answer.

If Sara did, if any of those psychologists had managed to pry one out of her, she would be a basket case by now; more of one than she already was; or—

Lainie passed on the *"or."*

She always passed on the *"or."*

The *"or"* was unacceptable to her.

Now and forever.

Any mother would feel the same way.

Miranda made the kind of grand entrance that suggested she was a regular here, smiled and waved greetings all over as she streaked to the table for two Lainie had scored at the back of the cramped room. She plopped her tote bag on the empty chair, pushed her shades up onto her orange buzz cut, rattled her hands to go with her apology for being late and promptly excused herself.

"Gotta pee," Miranda said in not quite a stage whisper that had turned several heads and elicited an, *"Is nothing sacred anymore?"* from the bearish man brooding over his laptop at the window table, not bothering to look up as he reached for his tall coffee.

Miranda returned after a few minutes with relief and a fresh coat of paint showing on her overly made-up face. Once settled, she pointed and wondered, "That cup mine?"

"Figured to save you line time," Lainie said. "It's today's special brew."

Miranda took a cautious sip, gave a salute of approval. "Fine. Thanks." A larger swallow. "Definitely what the doctor ordered. Meant to be early or on time the latest, but I couldn't get rid of him any faster, you follow?"

"I notice that everyone here seems to know you."

"Not really," Miranda said.

"Only that she may have a problem with her bladder is what we know now," the bearish man called over, his fingers going non-stop on the keyboard.

"Him, yeah," Miranda said, rolling her eyes. "He used to be a big television writer until he turned forty and then couldn't get anyone on the phone or past a reception desk. So, now he's only big—and getting bigger. He asked me out on a date once, you imagine? Like I'm fresh off the bus and don't know where writers rate in the pecker order in this town? Right behind the circus guy who sweeps up after the elephants. I'm right, aren't I, Paul?"

The bearish man looked over briefly to say, "What goes around comes around."

"He says that a lot," Miranda said, quietly, and took a fresh gulp, tamped lightly at her chubby lips with a napkin. "I do my arrival gag here, other places I hang out to be noticed, you know? Never know when a casting director, some producer, might go for my look."

Her look was somewhere between wild and untamed, cool and contemporary, something for the men and nothing threatening to the ladies. Lainie spotted it the first night Miranda joined her class at Star Bright, but it was Miranda's voice that captured her attention.

Miranda used it in her audition scene, demonstrating a richness, fullness and range in obscure cuts from Sondheim's *Merrily We Roll Along* and *Company* that segued into a stopper moment from Jerry Herman's *Mack and Mabel.*

She was so pitch perfect, she could have lost the piano player she'd brought along and done the bit *a capella.*

Her acting also was first rate, better than ninety percent of the other students, better than other actors in her age range, early-to-mid-twenties, who had caught the brass ring on the movie and TV series merry-go-rounds, but—

Miranda's voice was the reason Lainie had proposed they meet for coffee.

Lainie needed the voice more than she needed Miranda if she was going to score with Lenny Volkman and get inside his organization, not that Miranda's looks wouldn't be an asset if she got that far with Lenny.

Not *"if,"* Lainie reminded herself.

Definitely not *"if"* this time.

"If," absolutely positively not an option.

She eased onto the subject, like the old days when she was romancing some act that also might be on the want list at MCA, Warner Bros., EMI or Polygram.

"You definitely have a look," Lainie said. "And plenty of talent to go with it, as a singer as well as an actress."

"I think so too; thank you," Miranda said, like she was already Barbra Streisand. "Why I wanted Star Bright. The one studio in town offering your kind of class, Lainie, that combination of acting and singing. My real future may be on the Broadway stage, you follow?"

"I follow, or we wouldn't be here now . . . You still doing that day gig at Starshine?"

Starshine, on Ventura in Studio City, was the town's hottest recording complex, with ultra-state-of-the-art gear and a deserved international rep for helping to create Frank Sinatras out of Frankensteins.

"Girl's gotta eat. Either like that or it'd be Hooters for me, some other Tits 'R' Us place."

"The tips would be better at a Hooters."

"Yeah, but I'm off my feet working the reception desk at Starshine. Funny, isn't it? Star Bright. Starshine. You figure I've hooked my wagons to a star, Lainie?"

"You're the star they're hooked to, Miranda."

"Yeah. Gee whiz. What I meant to say . . . Besides, the tips from a Hooters wouldn't begin to cover what kind of cost I'd be racking up cutting my demos at Starshine. It's freebie time for me there, that's the trade-off. There's always an engineer around who's glad to take my smile in trade for his magic fingers on the board—which reminds me . . ."

Miranda pulled a cassette and a CD from her tote bag and offered them to Lainie.

"You didn't say what format so I brought both just in case. Same six demos. I got others, but these are the best, everyone tells me. Like 'All I Ask of You.' Eat your heart out, Miss Sarah Brightman. The best of the best, though, are my originals. Wait until you hear them and—" She paused, gave Lainie a questioning look. "You still haven't told me what this is all about. You said you'd tell me after I got here? So, I'm here."

Lainie let her eat a few more moments of anxiety before she leaned forward and said quietly, like a sister sharing a secret, "Miranda, I've decided to jump back into the record biz. I want you to be the first act on my new label. I want to make you a star. I needed your demos to work with, to let some important people hear for themselves that you are a star, like I've known since your Star Bright audition and ever since."

"No joke?"

"No joke." She raised her right hand to take an oath.

Miranda covered her mouth with her hand.

Lainie watched a million thoughts race across her eyes before they settled for moist bewilderment, then wonderment.

Miranda used the table to lift herself up.

She threw out her arms and shouted: "Watch out, world, here I come!"

The writer at the window table, Paul, groaned and said, "For God's sake, anywhere in the world but here."

The moment Miranda raced off, Lainie got on the phone to the headquarters office of Volkman International in Marina del Rey.

She went through a succession of secretaries until she reached one who sounded like she was guarding the Gaza Strip.

Lainie identified herself again; again was put on hold.

This time, instead of being transferred to another secretary, the power wait paid off with Lenny himself.

"What is it, Lainie?"

"Lenny, I have to see you. It's important."

"It would have to be," Leonard Volkman said.

At precisely three o'clock, Lainie was ushered into Volkman's penthouse suite, which occupied half the top floor of the twenty-two story Volkman International building at Volkman Plaza in the Marina. The suite was comfortably but simply furnished, like you'd expect from a billionaire operating on a millionaire's budget. Lenny had never been one to be too showy, only showy enough to impress any Rothschilds who might drop by to shoot the breeze over a brandy or two; maybe invest in some new scheme Lenny had cooked up to turn a small fortune into an even larger fortune; satisfaction always and most definitely guaranteed.

Lenny didn't call them *schemes,* of course.

They were *programs, plans, projects, promotions.*

Lenny had this thing for words beginning with "p."

To him it was the perfect letter.

The concept of its shape worthy of Picasso, several of whose portraits from various of his periods were sprinkled ostentatiously around the walls, interrupted here and there by a pointillist work by Pissarro or a large-scale Piranesi etching depicting some architectural wonder.

Lainie laughed at her mental picture of Miranda being introduced to Lenny and saying, "Excuse me, I gotta pee."

He'd get off on that, Lenny would.

Take to Miranda at once, with a capital pee.

Lainie wandered across to a display table in the center of the room. On it sat a three-dimensional model of what the miniature easel card identified as *A Paradise Sands for the New Millennium. Presented by Rainbows Unlimited.* The mini was astonishing in its detail, down to the holographic representation of the ocean. The ocean moved when she moved, setting off an audio track;

waves pushing toward the shore; white foam nipping at beach-front estates of radical, revolutionary design.

"Really something, huh?" Lenny's voice, as soothing as bath oil, rolled out from behind her. "I was finishing up a *schvitz.*"

He had entered through an inner door, naked except for the bath towel he was clutching around his ample midsection, leaving wet prints on the parquet flooring that lit up under the recessed fluorescent lighting as he approached. He wasn't wearing his hair and, as always, that made him look twenty years younger than his age, now sixty-three. Even with the added pounds, he was remarkably fit. Wide shoulders on a commanding six-foot frame that tapered to shapely legs Lenny used to say earned better reviews than his acting when he was doing Shakespeare at Harvard. A face so open and sincere-looking, he could close most deals without introducing the grandfatherly smile that also hid a million sins.

"The damnedest thing you have ever seen, admit it," Lenny said. "I never cease to be amazed by what modern technology can accomplish in this day and age. Just look at the details on the hill above PCH, those birds on the trees, some squirrels." He used his clutch hand to point them out. His towel slipped to his ankles, leaving the rest of him exposed but indifferent about his nakedness, a familiar experience for both of them. "Fully animated at the press of a button. Overall, as spectacular as a float in the Rose Parade on New Year's day."

He headed for the window wall overlooking the Pacific, hands locking behind his back, showing off to the world while telling her, "Selling you like you're some investor pigeon, don't know why."

"Habit."

"Habit. Like a pitcher. You have to keep working the fast ball, the corkscrew, the slider, or you lose them. You know what got me interested in Paradise Sands in the first place?"

"The 'p' as in 'Paradise'."

"Yes, what caught my attention. Also, perfect for my crew to go after and score. We have a lot riding on the Paradise Sands project, but so what? Right, Lainesky? So what? So what is it made you pick up a phone and call me when I told you long ago not to bother until and unless I said to bother?" His tone was sweetly dangerous. He was not a man used to being disobeyed.

"I'm drowning in poverty up to here, Lenny. I want to get back into the record business."

"How's Sara?"

"She's been better. So have I. Turn around and face me, Lenny."

"Why? You miss seeing my *schvantz* after three years?" He turned and rolled his arms over. "Here. They come bigger, but they don't come better." She shook her head. "I was making a joke."

"I know."

"The least you could've done was pretend to laugh. At the joke, not my *schvantz*."

"Hah, hah. I want you to bankroll the new company for me, Lenny."

"We could have done this over the phone . . . Forget it."

"You can own the company, then. I'll take my old six figures and a small piece on the back end."

"My *schvantz* and your ass." Trying to make her see she had nowhere to go with him. Showing her how right she'd been to loathe and despise him long before he saved his own skin by blowing the whistle on Roy and her.

"I need this, Lenny."

"Like I once needed you?"

"You never needed me. Used me, yes. The way you use all your women."

"Some I actually like. Unfortunately, they're never the ones I marry. You I would have married. Best sale I never made."

"And getting even with me ever since."

"Not your fault you were married at the time."

"So were you."

His laughter as he moved to his desk, settling in with his feet parked on one corner, could have brought down the Phantom of the Opera's chandelier.

"That wasn't a marriage, Lainesky. That was God giving me a preview of the hell I can look forward to. Do you know what she eventually took me for?"

"A fool."

"That was the ribbon clerk who took up with her, taking Pauline's word for it I would never notice." Volkman bit the tip off the cigar he pulled from the humidor on his desk and lit it. "Don't fret about the smoke. A built-in system sucks it right out of the air. It's a standard feature in all our residential and commercial projects nowadays . . . Pauline got me good. My Gulfstream. My place in Aspen. The chateau in the south of France. My favorite Picasso. She hated Picasso, so that was definitely strictly for spite . . . A monthly check in six figures that goes on forever, on top of all the furs and jewelry and the closets full of crap that kept Rodeo Drive rolling out the red carpet and blowing bugles whenever they saw Pauline coming . . . Not bad doing for someone who only seven-and-a-half years before was washing hair in Patricia's beauty parlor and working part-time as a bagger at Gelson's to make ends meet."

"Patricia. That was wife number two."

"Patsy. Should've known better than to trade her in on a newer model. Should've listened to the advice of friends. Can't say I wasn't warned. Patsy only wanted what was hers when she left me. I made sure to do right by her like I did right by my dear Paulette, right up until the day she died. There was a woman for you."

Volkman looked at her as if daring her to disagree.

Lainie let it rest a moment. "Don't you think it's time to do right by me, Lenny?"

"Not the first time I've heard that from a woman."

"You owe me, Lenny."

Volkman untangled himself, inched forward, elbows on the desk, fingers laced under his prominent nose. His gaze took on a harder edge that bordered on malevolence.

"I did right by you already."

"Cutting me adrift with my daughter? Cutting me out of money that rightfully should have come to me and would have kept our life tolerable? Putting distance and an iron curtain between me and the company, making it plain I'd better not come around, or else? You can't really believe that was doing right by me."

"To do otherwise with you would have been bad for business all the way around."

"Your testimony, your lies. They could have sent Roy and me to prison."

"My truths also would have done that."

"You threw Roy away, threw me in for good measure, to save your lousy skin."

"Not just me. Also my partners. I have the voice, but they have the votes. And the muscle. If they knew I let you come up here today, there could be hell to pay."

"So why did you?"

"On the phone, you made it sound so damned necessary. Also, I was curious, to have a look . . . You're looking good, Lainesky, but you've looked better." He got up. Scratched his crotch. "Now, it's time for you to go, Lainesky."

"We're not finished."

"We are. You park in the lot? Give Petra the ticket on the way out. She's the one with the big bazooms and the Russky accent. We validate."

Volkman pounded out the cigar that had been gathering ash on the lip of a crystal ashtray and headed for the door he had entered through.

"I go from here straight downtown to the district attorney's office," Lainie said, grabbing for something to keep Lenny here. He stopped and rocked in place for a few moments before he turned and looked at her like a disappointed father. "Talk to them like you once talked to them. Talk about things I learned from Roy about how you made all the leveraged buyouts work, the Cayman Islands tax shelters—"

"You shouldn't be talking this way to me, Lainesky."

"The insurance scams involving all those yachts you and your syndicates kept buying and never had long enough to use before they accidentally sank."

"Enough!" Looking like he would have smacked her had he been close enough; might still come at her. "Knowing silence is golden could be a reason you're still here long after Roy got himself a date with the maggots. You telling me you have a different outlook now? I'll have to share the news with my partners. How they'd be inclined to react, I wouldn't wish on my worst enemy. Or you. Certainly not your kid."

Lainie was prepared for the threat. She kept her calm. "Don't go Brando on me, Lenny. Listen to what I brought." Lainie dipped into her bag for the portable CD player and held it out for him to see. It was loaded with Miranda Morgan's demo. "If you don't agree what you hear is my first-class ticket back into the record business, I'm out of here, no hard feelings and as silent as ever. There'll be someone around somewhere willing to take the shot with me."

"And if I like what I hear?"

"You talk to your partners and make it work again."

"My investors would own the company?"

"A hundred percent, if that's the way you want it. I already said I'll settle for my old six figures and a small piece on the back end, say fifteen percent."

"High five figures. Eight percent on the back. A bump to ten depending on how you score on the charts."

"I'll bring home a Top Five single first time out of the box. Twelve percent."

"Six percent flat. Take it or leave it."

"Listen to the demo, then we'll talk some more."

"It's great. We're done talking."

"I want you to hear it."

"I've heard enough. I'm already thinking—How do you feel about Perfect Records for the name of my new company?"

"Perfect," Lainie said.

She left Lenny pleased with herself, thinking, *So far, so good, Lainie.*

Thom Newberry had given her a month to get back inside Volkman International and position herself to get whatever he needed to protect the mayor's gubernatorial hopes and, she had no doubt, to protect his own career.

Step One was out of the way, but it was going to be tough from here on out, even by her most optimistic reckoning, although it wouldn't be the first time she had been called upon to pull off one of these do-or-die miracles.

It would have helped if Thom had told her what he needed from Volkman. It would have eliminated the half dozen or more steps she'd have to take working blind, but at least it was back in the business she loved and had hated to leave, would never have left except for the fact she'd come to love Roy Gardner more, and Roy was dead set against having a working wife.

She could hear him now, explaining, "I'm old school, Chicken

Little. Where I grew up, the man's the breadwinner. The woman stays home and bakes. You don't believe me, you go ask my mother."

That's how he put it after he proposed. Roy was never shy about taking the lead on any subject, never so close-minded he wouldn't listen to contrary opinion, but somehow he always managed to win out.

Lainie smiled at the memory, how she'd given him a stiff argument, thought she had him backing off and on the defensive when she said, "May I remind you your mother passed away six years ago?"

Roy delivered a look that seemed to thank her for the reminder, knighted her shoulder with some love pats and said, "Then I guess you'll just have to take my word for it, won't you, Chicken Little?"

Chicken Little, his pet name for her, struck after the first few times he watched her in action, revving up all the sales and promotion troops at Blue Pacific Records, setting deadlines, pushing them, then pushing them more, threatening and cajoling, whatever it took to get a new release airplay and on the charts. Convincing them the sky was falling and, if they didn't come through, it would crash down on their heads.

She told Roy, "Chicken Little actually believed the sky was falling. I have to will myself to believe it, act it to life. Then and only then can I make my people believe."

"And quite the actress you are," Roy said, meaning it as a compliment. "I don't know why you ever gave it up for your crazy record business."

"The record business is sanity next to the movies and television," she said.

It wasn't the entire answer, only as much as he had to know.

She had found herself loving him enough to share all of it, but hedged on the off-chance she was wrong and this was not

going to last a lifetime, that he'd disappoint her the way Thom
Newberry had disappointed her and ultimately leave her with
secrets she no longer wanted him to have.

How could she be completely honest with him when it was
impossible to be completely honest with herself?

A question then, a question still.

A conundrum she'd given up bothering about when she was
still a kid running wild on the streets, where lies came to work
better than the truth, came faster and easier to her than the
truth. Sometimes, her coming to believe her lies so strongly that
they became the truth.

It was her lying that saved her physically and emotionally
while doing her stretch at the Animal Farm in San Diego, where
time played out like in one of those women-in-prison movies,
like a waltz in slow motion.

Lainie kept to herself in the joint, skirted trouble and tangles
with bull dyke guards and prisoners angling for her body. She
used the time to take correspondence courses that got her a
high school diploma and two years' worth of college credits
before her release on parole almost three years later. She spent
a day at the zoo, devoured a lot of junk food and afterward
caught an Amtrak to Los Angeles, where she made her first
priority finding Thom Newberry.

The good news: She found him.

The bad news: She found him.

And found out why the man responsible for her adding
another layer of dirt to her life and landing in the Animal Farm
had never once written, called or come to visit.

CHAPTER 8

Thom was living in a Colonial style mansion on the flats south of Sunset in Holmbly Hills, around the bend from the pink palace someone once told her belonged to the old actress Jayne Mansfield, then to Zsa Zsa Gabor, and not so far from Hugh Hefner's Playboy mansion and the castle on the hill built by Aaron Spelling, the producer.

Lainie's thumb got her a hitch there, but she couldn't get past the imperious voice on the talk box at the front gate until the gate rolled open for a gardener's truck about fifteen minutes later.

She slipped inside and headed up the long asphalt drive sucking in the lavish grounds, the terraced lawns broken by a nonchalant pattern of flower gardens, mostly sweet-smelling roses in a rainbow of colors, and exotic statuary devoted mostly to naked men in classical Greek poses. A couple of the statues looked a lot like Thom, particularly the one holding his white marble cock like a flashlight.

A butler in full rig and a hairpiece that would not fool Stevie Wonder was stationed expectantly on the front porch, brow tense with anxiety and throwing eye darts at her like she was something the garbage man forgot.

"I've called our armed patrol," he said. "The response time is less than five minutes, so I urge you to leave the same way you came."

"All I want to know, is Thom Newberry here and could I see him?"

"Who lives here is none of your business, young woman." He checked his watch. "We have strict laws about trespassers, and you could be on your way to jail, you don't go quickly."

"Been there, done that," Lainie said. "A statue over on the left, the one of the guy loving his giant salami? It looks a lot like him. Like Thom. What's the story on that?"

He threw her a look that smacked of pity. "We have our video cameras running around the clock, so don't try vandalism on your way back down. Now shoo. Go. Fair warning."

"It's all right, Jasper." Thom's voice, deeper, richer, but definitely Thom, came at them from the driveway side of the portico.

"A trespasser, Mr. Newberry. I have the security patrol alerted and—"

"I heard. I know her. Go on back in and turn them off. I'll take care of this."

The butler frowned and retreated inside the mansion. "Come on down, Lainie," Thom said, engineering a happy face. "We'll go for a little welcome home spin."

He aimed his key ring at the two matching blue Porsche convertibles parked in front of the garage doors.

The doors clicked open on the Porsche with its roof off.

He opened the passenger door for her and tried for contact.

Lainie dodged his reach and angled down onto the posh leather bucket seat.

Thom said, "It's not that I didn't want to. I couldn't, Lainie. Don't judge me until you've heard the whole story." He flashed the old smile full of sweetness and seduction that once meant so much, and now meant—

Lainie didn't know what it meant.

Thom had a lot of explaining to do before she might be ready to let him touch her, as much as she felt those warm body currents challenging her, telling her she wanted to feel him again.

He turned up the stereo player on a "Best of Stax" CD and tooled the sharp curves west on Sunset to the Palisades. He tried inching his hand onto her thigh once or twice, not so much insisting as testing. When she lifted it away and eased it over onto the gear box, he kicked up the speed by ten miles per hour and pretended nothing had happened.

Lainie squinted against the golden sun descending slowly into a red and orange skyline, savoring the wind whipping onto her face and through her hair, kicking harder at her the closer they got to the ocean, but most of all savoring the freedom of the ride.

They settled at a quiet back booth in a deli on Swathmore in the Village, Thom working over what he swore was the best corned beef sandwich in the city when he wasn't firing answer upon answer at her to her one-word question, "Why?"

Lainie picked at her hamburger and fries listening to him deflecting blame from himself to Lance Clifford. She'd reacted with surprise when Thom first dropped the movie star's name, but within minutes Lance Clifford was the third person in the booth.

"Let me get this straight, Thom. You're telling me the reason you could not and did not ever contact me in all that time I was in the Animal Farm was because of him, Lance Clifford?"

"Exactly," Thom said, his head working as fast as his jaws as he took in another king-sized bite of sandwich. "I was always asking him if he'd mind, and he was always saying, yes, he'd mind. Anytime I brought up your name, thought how nice it'd be for me, maybe even with Lance along, to drive down to San Diego and see how you were, maybe bring you a basket of goodies, his green-eyed monster grew the size of his dick. Finally, I just quit, knowing one day we'd find ourselves together again."

Thom bared his smile, and she saw flecks of corned beef lodged between his teeth. He reached over for her hand, but she was faster getting it away and onto her lap, almost tipping over her can of Bud.

There was something boyishly innocent about how he looked at her, especially when he choked up saying, "I won't tell you how many nights I couldn't get to sleep worrying if you were okay or dreamed about the day when we would finally be together again, Lainie. Prayed for that day. For this day."

"Stop it, Thom. You're starting to sound like one of Lance Clifford's movies. What I still don't understand is why he would feel any hostility toward me, him being gay and all, you say, and you making out like you were one of them, too."

"He was insanely jealous of you. I'll tell you why. I didn't fool him for a single minute. Lance knew it was an act with me, but he stayed okay with it because our sex thing together has been good—great—from the night he scored me on the boulevard. And that I definitely blame on you."

"I'm to blame because you had me mule shit into the country for you, because the feds were less likely to stop me than you. You disappear from my life from that minute on, from the minute they clamped cuffs on my wrists, packed me off to trial and shipped me off to do hard time at the Animal Farm. And it's my fault. Now I get it. Thanks. What is not Lance Clifford's fault is my fault. What comes next? You expecting an apology from me?"

"Your fault because I would not have been on that damn boulevard peddling myself to passing cars like a slab of prime stud on the hoof if I still had you around."

"I apologize for getting caught."

"Apology accepted," Thom said, and—as if they'd both seen the inanity of the exchange in the same moment—they exploded with laughter.

Lainie let him take her hand in both of his. It was warm. Comforting. His smile looked real, making her wonder if she were giving in to a need for Thom that had never entirely gone away and sometimes, fool that she was, sustained her during her periodic moments of deepest depression at the Animal Farm.

Sure, she was smarter now, but—

Wiser?

That was still a question when Thom threw a twenty on the table and said, "Let's go. I have a better place in mind."

He got up to leave and headed out without looking back.

Lainie thought about it.

There was still a lot of talking to do, still a lot she needed to understand.

She headed after him.

"It was you, wasn't it, the statue?"

"I'm not telling."

"I can see it was you. Well, okay . . . Not now, but five minutes ago."

Playing with Thom on top of the wet sheets at the Great Sea Lion Inn across from Santa Monica Civic Auditorium, where he asked for a room with a great view of the ocean, peeling off the price from a fat roll of twenties and signed them in as "Mr. and Mrs. John Dough," as if the desk clerk might give a damn. Their lovemaking had been intense, silent and consuming for both of them, Thom seeming as desperate for her as she was for him.

"Give me another five minutes and you can check again," he said, making finger-patterns on her body.

Lainie folded herself inside his arms. "Spend the time telling me about you and Lance."

"Lance is a nice man, a good man. He's been good to me and for me, Lainie."

"Including in bed?"

Thom ran his wet lips down her cheek and drained her neck like a toothless vampire. He rolled into a sitting position with his legs overhanging the mattress, his back to her. "Okay, my little girl, here is where it's at," he said, telling his story like he was talking to the sliding glass door to the sun-drenched patio. "Lance Clifford picked me up for my bod, but caught on pretty fast that I also had a mind."

Lance had liked that, Thom explained. Lance was tired of what he called the noodle-heads he invariably wound up with when he went trolling along the streets of West Hollywood. He liked that Thom shared a lot of his own interests and, of course, that Thom was a fan who'd grown up seeing almost all his movies, especially the few that had trouble climbing as high as zilch at the box office.

When Thom confessed about his life on the street, Lance almost fell to tears. He said, "I want you to come be with me. A physical examination tomorrow. If you're clean, test negative and if you promise me no more drugs, you'll be my young man."

Thom's brain wasn't so fried he didn't know to seize the opportunity. Quitting cold turkey was a struggle, but he kept telling himself the prize was worth the reward and got past the worst of it with Lance holding his hand, telling him he was a brave lad and what a future they'd be able to share together.

Thom said, "From the beginning I had to swear it would only be Lance and me, Lainie. I went for me and have felt lousy rotten over you ever since, but Lance also shut out everyone else who had ever been in his life. You knew who to look for, you would see them in the sculpture court. Nobody ever got away from Lance without posing for Jean-Paul Lachaille." He pulled a pillow to him, hugged it against his chest. "I mean,

78

Lance even married me. A ceremony in the back nine for fifty or sixty of his dearest friends that set him back six figures. Lance doesn't hide me. He takes me everywhere. Only when we're out in public I'm Lance's adopted son, that's how he introduces me. Don't think for a second that doesn't get me the respect I never had before."

Lainie said, "And a Porsche."

"A first anniversary gift, one for each of us."

"His and his."

"And hers. Lance likes to dress up . . . He pushed me back into college. UCLA. I'm a poli-sci major, a minor in business. I'm going for my master's now, and maybe I'll stick around for a doctorate. I think I'm steering towards politics. Lance likes that a lot. Knows a lot of the right people in the right places, already has me meeting some of them. Big names. Important names. I've been to the White House twice. Like that."

"He uses you, you use him. Also like that?"

"He loves me."

"And you love him."

A heavy sigh and an awkward silence before Thom eased back so he could see her face and quietly tell her, "I love you, Lainie."

She wanted to believe him.

"And what do you propose doing about it?" she said.

Lainie stayed at the Great Sea Lion Inn over the three days it took Thom to find a furnished rental for her, a few blocks east of UCLA's Sorority Row and an easy stroll to the campus. It was an older building, two stories set back from the street, only twelve well-kept units, filled with college students doubling and tripling up in order to cover the high rent.

He'd wanted an apartment where she would not look out of place.

Or him, whenever he came over, which was as often as he could concoct an excuse that would work well on Lance Clifford, which was often.

Some of his visits were long, others for hardly an hour. He stayed overnight whenever Lance was on a location shoot or off somewhere promoting one of the low-budget cable movies that eventually become bread-and-butter for leading men slipping past their box-office prime and descending into character parts.

Lainie thought her role as a kept woman spicy.

It also was a turn-on for Thom, a fact evident the instant he turned the key in the lock and swung inside cooing her name, armed with candy or flowers or some other evidence of affection.

When the new semester rolled around at UCLA, he worked whatever magic was needed to get her accepted as a junior, assuring her, "You had the credits. I had the contacts. *Voila!* We are still one great team, my good little girl. Don't you ever doubt it."

They had their share of arguments, usually when Lainie was feeling especially unloved and would wonder if the day would ever come when he broke the news about her to Lance and they could be free to announce themselves to the world. She had fallen that much in love with Thom, although it was not a word she ever used with him—*love*—something always driving her away from it; something he'd say, a stray thought clumsily expressed or a look that raced across his face and didn't fit with his words.

"You don't bite the hand that feeds you as long as you need the handout" was his routine answer about Lance. He used it so often she took to finishing the sentence for him in the same intensely pompous tone, sometimes even starting it for Thom.

Their biggest rift came late in her junior year, after he had treated her to an extravagant dinner at Presto!, a local hideaway always filled with couples anxious to avoid discovery, who would glance furtively toward the entrance whenever the heavy oak door creaked open.

They were back at her place polishing off a bottle of Cristal he'd stored in an ice chest in the trunk of the Porsche, when he asked the question that momentarily stunned her to silence. "I don't believe what I'm hearing," she said. "Are you really asking me to spread my legs for some guy who did you a big favor?"

"Because I need a bigger favor from him. My future and our future. It's like the cost of doing business. Not like it's something you haven't done before, so no big deal. Come on. Is it?" Thom clasped his hands as if getting ready to pray and looked at her like a little boy begging mommy for a cookie.

Lainie's first instinct was to throw the champagne in his face. She acted on her second instinct instead and brought down the champagne bottle on the side of his head, like she was christening a battleship. Thom sank to the floor. "We're still a team?" she said. "You go fuck him then, then go fuck yourself as a favor to me."

It should have ended then and there between them, but she wasn't ready to let go of him, uncertain if it was because he had brainwashed her into believing he was her lifeline or if it was a curse she had wished upon herself.

After a month, he forgave her for the mild concussion he'd suffered, and they were back together as if there never had been a falling out.

At least, Thom didn't expect her to apologize.

She didn't, but neither did he.

Her senior year, Lainie finally met Lance Clifford.

It was nothing Thom had anything to do with, except for trying to stop it from happening.

For the fun of it, on an impulse, she was taking some electives in theater arts: a class in basic acting technique, another in voice and vocal calisthenics. The classes were diversions in an academic load heavy on business management and economics.

On a dare from her drama professor, Thelma Street, the B-movie star Lainie remembered best as Roxy Darvish, a conniving doctor-lawyer on the TV soap *Bedrooms and Board Rooms,* she signed up for the annual UCLA Stage Arts Awards competition. "Your work in class tells me you are talented enough to take it all," Thelma told her. "If you don't trust yourself, take my word for it. Unless, of course, you are afraid of losing."

Thelma knew better, but she also knew how to get a rise out of her.

Lainie made it to the finals with a scene from *A Streetcar Named Desire.*

She and her acting partner placed third. Thelma assured her afterward it was because of him that they didn't finish higher. "Your Stanley froze out there," she said. "Right off, his ripped t-shirt was showing more emotion than him."

Their trophy was presented by Tracy Roberts, one of the L.A. acting gurus. Like all the top finishers, they were now eligible for an acting scholarship at her studio. The second place finishers were given their trophy and promised walk-ons in his next movie by Walter Matthau. The winners were scheduled to receive their trophy and prize, bit parts in the same movie, from Jack Lemmon, but Lemmon was bedridden with the flu and substituting for him, a surprise until it was announced, was Lance Clifford. He swept onto the Schoenberg Hall stage with outstretched arms, like a matador who'd been awarded all four hooves, both ears, the tail and a night with Ava Gardner, shedding finger-kisses in answer to the outpouring of enthusiastic applause from the audience.

Lainie hadn't known Clifford was there until that moment.

It explained why Thom had made a furtive call to her last

night and spent two hours with her earlier in the day trying to convince her to withdraw from the competition. She kept asking him why, never really considering it as an option, but curious. The best answer he had for her, offered again and again: "I know what losing will do to you."

Now Lainie understood.

It was Thom Newberry who feared *he* had something to lose.

That she might say something about them to Lance Clifford and cost Thom his meal ticket.

The "favor" business had shown her what kind of premium Thom put on love.

This turn of events showed her how he felt about her loyalty toward him.

The show over, all the winners gathered on stage with the presenters for a group photo. She found herself in the front row between Walter Matthau, who kept telling her how good she had been as Blanche DuBois, and Lance Clifford, who leaned over after the final setup to request, "Spare me a moment or two, if you will, young lady? We have someone in common to discuss, and there's no time like the present."

Thom had observed them. He rushed out of the wings looking as terrified as he sounded, telling Clifford the limo was out front and ready to speed them to some mumbled destination.

Clifford ordered, "Keep the motor running," and dismissed Thom with a cold look.

He gave Lainie a gracious second-balcony smile and led her by the elbow down into the auditorium to front row seats. Checked for privacy before wondering, "Pray, what are we going to do about you and my boy Thomas?"

"You are guessing I hired private detectives to spy on Thomas and you," Clifford said, looking amused. "I have not done anything like that since *Bulldog Drummond Meets His Match,* a clinker-stinker I did early in my career for Columbia Pictures, one of those seven-day wonders Sam Katzman turned out for that horrid Harry Cohen. Private detectives not necessary, my dear. I have known about Thomas and you from the beginning without the need to snoop. Thomas told me. There are no secrets or lies between us."

"As long as he never brought me around to meet you," Lainie said, struggling to retain her composure, no idea where the conversation was leading.

"Meet you? I have had no interest in meeting you, for reasons you know without having to hear them from me."

"No. I want to hear them."

Clifford waved her off. "Plus the fact you have no permanent residence in Thomas's life—or mine."

"Then why now? What's this all about?"

"Opportunity. Poor Jack's flu. Otherwise, I would have insisted Thomas bring you over to the house for this little chat . . . Thomas has told you his future is in politics, yes?"

"Yes."

"I am determined that absolutely nothing will interfere with that future, which I already have gathering a full head of steam for him. When he completes his work here, he will head for Washington and an important spot with one of our most prestigious Congressmen. You being in the picture could ruin this for us at any time. A risk we definitely would not want to take. Thus, the reason I need your cooperation. Why it is something we must do together, you see? The end credits have rolled on your relationship. Please accept that fact, Miss Davies. It is completely and finally over between you and Thomas."

"And Thom agrees? It's what he wants?"

"Yes."

"He didn't look too happy just now."

"Not. Thomas has had no problem with my plans for him, of

84

course, more proof of his political adroitness, but he did not want me to handle this. He wanted to do it himself with you. Thomas said you would take the news with more grace if it came from him." Clifford paused to send her a look probably meant to make her appreciate Thom's thoughtfulness. "I told him better from me. Less emotion. Less room for argument."

Past being anybody's patsy, she drew on some inner strength and said, "Not good enough, Mr. Clifford."

Clifford tossed away a hand.

Gave her a scornful look.

Retracted it almost immediately, like he had not meant for it to slip out.

"I am prepared to pay you whatever the price to secure your word you will not see or ever again bother Thomas. Name it. I guarantee you it will be more than your share of the profits from the business you and Thomas have been conducting, no matter how much that might be. So, say it, Miss Davies. How much is good enough?"

Profits from the business?

Lainie had no idea what Clifford meant.

Trying not to look obvious, she said, "If Thom tells you everything, you already know how much our business takes in."

"Knowledge offered that I did not need at the time, Miss Davies. I found Thomas's desire to run a sideline business while completing his studies at UCLA commendable, an aggressive and forward-looking pursuit that also augurs extremely well for his future in politics. From what Thomas tells me, you have what it takes to make the business continue working for you without his continued participation. Tonight I saw so with my own eyes, although you are far, far above the likes and looks of any hooker or whore I have ever encountered. Courtesan, if you prefer a politer designation. So, then—how much, Miss Davies? What are we looking at?"

CHAPTER 9

The morning following her meeting with Leonard Volkman, Lainie was in the middle of what had become her ritual daily battle with Sara when the phone rang. She grabbed for it like a boxer on the ropes who's grateful for the bell ending the round.

Petra, Lenny's secretary, was calling to say her suite of offices at Volkman International was available, in a husky, Russian-accented voice as warm as a Siberian winter, tinged with the kind of suspicion Lainie was familiar with—

Petra figured her a rival for Lenny's affection.

She was right about that, but not in any way she could guess.

Nothing Lainie could deal with now.

Nothing had priority in her life ahead of Sara.

She replaced the wall phone and dropped back into her chair at the kitchen table across from Sara, who was still spooning for answers to the mysteries of life deep inside her bowl of oatmeal, like it was the safest place to avoid looking into her mother's eyes.

Lainie knew what that meant. She glanced down at Sara's knapsack, wondering if that's where she was hiding her stash nowadays. Knowing it was a waste of time to make a search, or later, after Sara left for school, to prowl the house like a burglar. Knowing Sara would only hate her more, find a new supply, paying for it—

How?

Lainie winced.

She feared the answer.

Denial was easier.

She took a jolt of coffee and counted the lines of red, yellow, green and blue on top of Sara's midnight black hair. "Where were we?" she said.

"*You* were telling me I look like shit," Sara said after a year of silence, emphasizing the *you*. She had on a t-shirt and torn hip-huggers, low riders exposing a silver ring attached at her belly button, scuffed black lumberjack boots, eye shadow that made her look like a raccoon and a thick coat of base that was meant to hide her zits but only accentuated them.

Sara knew she hadn't meant her outfit. Why else would she hide her eyes, and the other telltale signs that lately were showing up more and more? Lainie played along. "I dressed like that when I was your age, but I was on my own, living on the streets with hardly more than the clothes on my back, shoving newspaper inside my sneakers to cover the holes."

Sara looked up and began playing an invisible violin. "You think I don't know your song by heart by now?"

"It's going to be better again, sweetheart. That phone call—I'm going back to work today. I'm going back into the record business."

Sara didn't return her smile. She checked the time on the moon-faced wall clock and, rising, said, "If you're finished with me, Lainie—"

"Mommy."

"If you're finished with me . . . Mother . . . I don't want to be late for homeroom."

"Glad to hear you plan on going," Lainie said, unable to hold her temper any longer, still too angry over Sara's refusal to tell her what she and the D.A., Harrison Roman, had been talking about when she caught them together yesterday.

"See ya," Sara called, heading off.

"Sara!"

Sara stopped and without turning around said, "What?"

"When will you be home?"

"When I get back."

Lainie sucked in air. "Please be careful, all right, sweetheart? It happens one more time, and they'll take you away from me. You heard them say that. You know I'm not inventing."

"Yeah. Okay."

She went out the door, leaving Lainie to fight back her tears, say a quiet little prayer that Sara would make it through one more day; wonder if she was asking for too much; wonder if the two of them could ever be mother and daughter again.

Volkman International occupied floors seventeen through twenty-two of its headquarters building at the Volkman Plaza. The elevators opened onto a modest reception area on all but the twentieth, twenty-first and twenty-second floors.

It took a special key to get onto twenty and twenty-one. Nobody knew who had the key, what the basis was for permission or what activities occurred on those floors.

Nobody seemed to know anyone who worked on twenty or twenty-one, or were inclined to admit they did.

Twenty-two, Leonard Volkman's private floor, required a call to Petra or, in her absence, one of his other personal secretaries. No one made the ride up unless accompanied by an armed security guard.

The tenants on the other floors were the standard variety of businesses found in any commercial high-rise. Most dealt on a national or international basis, the key reason for their selecting a Marina location—proximity to LAX.

Lainie learned all this from Petra on a whirlwind tour, during which Lenny's secretary sustained her jealous indifference.

She judged Petra, whose last name was Barish, shortened

from Baryshnikov, like the ballet dancer, to be in her thirties, about the right age differential to attract Lenny's attention, along with her "P" name. And her looks. Dark. Exotic. High cheekbones. A swan's neck, long and lean enough for her to carry off the elaborately-patterned Oriental silk scarf draped around her neck and falling past her trim waist, like a border between bosoms too large for the rest of her body and—judging by the way they seemed cemented in place underneath her tight brown cashmere sweater—as authentic as any promises Lenny was feeding her. Wide hips designed for child-bearing, but no match for the bosoms.

Petra routed her down from the nineteenth floor, where the prominent sign on the wall behind the reception counter heralded:

PERPETUAL HEALTH PRODUCTS, INC.
Where 'Living Forever' is a Fact, Not a Destination

The fabric-covered walls were decorated in mural-sized photos of aging, but still-recognizable movie and TV stars glowing with retouched health and displaying products with exotic names like *Power Punch, VitaGlow* and *Super Fix-It 7.*

Lainie knew the company from somewhere, but couldn't place it. Petra grunted away her inquiry and her other questions, sticking to the kind of fat-free, low-cal patter you'd always get from the Animal Farm tour guides.

A familiar-looking man stepped off the elevator as they got back on. He glanced at her like he expected to be recognized. A smile flashed democratically. A purposeful step to the right made it possible for his shoulder to brush against hers as he passed.

He was somewhere in his late forties, a long uninspiring face full of chiseled features on a six-foot frame decked in California casual; curly gray chest hair billowing out from under a silk shirt; both a cross and a Star of David on the gold chain decorating his neck. His aviator glasses worn like a crown on top of his bush of curly Tootsie Roll-brown hair.

"Who was that?" Lainie asked as the doors shut and the elevator glided down to eighteen.

Petra shrugged. "Somebody, I suppose."

"I think I know him from someplace."

"That surprises me not," Petra said, like she'd just heard the punch line to a dirty joke.

Lainie let it pass. Petra Barish wasn't important in her life, only somebody else who qualified for that oldie-but-goodie she had mastered the hard way while growing up fast on L.A.'s nasty streets: *Keep your friends close, but your enemies closer.*

The signs on the eighteenth floor represented a dozen other companies operating under the Volkman International banner. They included Rainbows Unlimited, the company that was fronting Lenny's efforts to acquire Paradise Sands from the city.

As on the nineteenth floor, people rushed through a central area and in and out of doors like manic characters in a French farce, always in a hurry, like Petra seemed to be now, checking her diamond-studded Patek Philippe increasingly as she trotted them around the floor to the beat of rattled-off information as superficial as her occasional grim-lipped smile.

A surprise awaited Lainie on seventeen.

The sign behind the vacant reception desk read:

PERFECT RECORDS

Lainie shot a questioning look at Petra.

"Lenny—Mr. Volkman had a crew work overnight once his partners officially approved the deal," Petra said. She dipped her head a few times, like she wanted Lainie to recognize how much she knew about Volkman operations. "Through there," she said, pointing to double doors on the right. "Everything on that side of seventeen, now it belongs to the record company. Fully furnished, so you can begin to work immediately. Anything you do not like, you let me know. Something you need, you let me know. A budget or a payment? You let me know, and I will take care of it right away, immediately."

"Audio gear?"

"You call to me upstairs, if there are things you find missing afterwards, when you have taken what time you need to look around."

"Staff?"

"Mr. Volkman says hire them. Music people. All but any lawyers and accountants. We already have them for you, here already taking care of all our enterprises. Tomorrow you'll also have a receptionist and some secretarial from our general office pool. You find somebody you like and want to keep, you let me know."

"Mr. Volkman has certainly put a lot of responsibility and trust into you," Lainie said, smiling inwardly at what else she knew Lenny had to be putting into Petra. The poor woman. Petra couldn't know her days with Leonard Volkman were numbered even before he met her. Lenny had the attention span of a gnat, but it never stopped him from dishing up responsibility and trust like giant, mouth-watering slices of chocolate cream pie. Flowers and candy, trinkets, were the commerce of the *hoi polloi*. Smart operators like Lenny, who bothered to really learn about women, knew that giving them value and a sense of self-worth was usually all that it took to turn a loaner into a long-term lease.

She used to wonder why even a smart woman, the smartest of the smart—and Lainie put herself in that category—often didn't recognize the ploy. Or was it a case of refusing to recognize the ploy, self-worth usually being in such short supply?

At least, when Petra was finally sent packing, it would be with some lie that might let her keep a piece of dignity as well as the Patek Philippe. Lenny was good about that, unlike some of the louses she'd crossed swords with in the old days, but not even Lenny's soft soap would wash away the mental scar that came with the territory.

Her scar was bigger, uglier than the one Petra would suffer.

It not only helped destroy her self-confidence but her life.

Now, thanks to another SOB who had made her life a misery and was back haunting her, she hoped to return the favor.

Before Lainie could inquire what companies occupied the other half of the seventeenth floor, a cell phone tinkled its merry melody. Petra pulled the cell from a pocket and identified herself, listened briefly, and said, "Mr. Volkman needs me. Someone will be down to take over from me. You see something, think of something you want, you make notes and get them to me in the morning."

"I thought I'd come upstairs later, before I leave; see Mr. Volkman to thank him and—"

"You're welcome. I'll tell him," Petra said. She turned around to face the elevator, as if Lainie no longer existed.

Petra's replacement stepped off the penthouse elevator making a bugle toot noise. He followed with a stagy bow in Lainie's direction and a raspberry for Petra, who answered with a nasty growl. As the elevator door closed behind her, he launched a middle finger and declared, "Godspeed, you Russky pain in the bloody friggin' arse," before granting Lainie a sidewinding smile.

"If Volkman's hobby horse had gone and displayed any humanity toward you just now, you and me would definitely be starting off on the wrong foot, Missus Lainie Davies Gardner. Name here is Flynn, Rodney. Rodney Flynn. Rod to some, but I answer best to Flynn and to no other man short of God

Almighty Himself."

Lainie said, "Not even Leonard Volkman?"

"This minute the god I had in mind. What say we have ourselves a little drink, you and me, Missus Lainie Davies Gardner?" Flynn raised his unruly eyebrows to the moon.

He looked like he'd just arrived from the Australian Outback and brought the Outback with him. A scruffy khaki shirt over loose-fitting khaki britches. Blond hair pulled into a tight pony tail. Fiery blue eyes full of independence. Average height and weight, a body muscular and full of tension; arms hanging taut at his sides, like he was ready to defend himself at the slightest provocation. Late forties or early fifties.

Lainie said, "What say to you showing me around the offices like you're supposed to be doing, Mr. Flynn?"

" *'Mister.'* A good one, that. Palming me off as my dear departed father to show me who's the boss, are you? Fine, I'm impressed. Is it that you don't drink; that it?"

"Not when I'm working." Said politely, with a smile. Flynn liked to talk. She'd be able to learn from him if she played him right.

Flynn said, "Ah. Hope for us yet. And I confess that I had no intention of luring you away from your appointed task for a wee mid-afternoon libation to help rekindle the spirit and refresh the mind."

A hip flask magically appeared.

"Been in a twelve-step program for years," he said. "I make it a policy never to be more'n twelve steps removed from my local or some reasonable substitute."

Flynn snapped open the flask, smacked his lips and took a gi-ant swallow. He wiped his mouth with the back of his thick hand and proffered the flask to Lainie with a *Just in case* tilt of the head and a soggy twinkle in his eyes. Repeated the process when Lainie declined, adding a toasted declaration: "Here's to them and here's to we, and if by chance we disagree—Fuck them! Here's to we."

This time, sensing she could have an ally in Flynn, Lainie accepted the flask. She said, "To we, Flynn," and made a production of matching his two swallows in a single gulp. Ran a finger towel across her lips and handed back the flask.

He was tanking vodka, which explained why she hadn't caught the smell on his breath. Lainie hadn't drunk like that since her days in record promotion, when sometimes a bar and the booze was enough to get a program director's promise he'd add her single to the playlist.

"I see you're definitely no stranger to one of life's greatest gifts," he said.

"What are some of the others?" she said, expecting him to start rapping gloriously on the current vices of choice, but he surprised her. Without hesitation, he said, "To touch. To taste. To see. To hear. To feel. To laugh. And, of course, to love."

Lainie looked at him with a smile as genuine as her amazement. "Flynn, this could be the beginning of a beautiful friendship."

"One of my favorites, too," he said, as the corners of his mouth tucked into an impish grin and his eyes took on a mischievous sparkle.

The vodka had charged through Lainie's system like the bulls of Pamplona. She had to work to keep her legs from giving out as Flynn guided her around the Perfect Records space, a lot more than she had expected from Lenny and, as Petra Barish suggested, rigged with most of the gear necessary to get her off to a quick start; state-of-the-art in most cases.

When they reached the corner office meant for her, she settled behind the desk and wrote out a list of other items she would need. Flynn parked himself on a visitors' chair, a leg dangling comfortably over one of its arms, the other leg propped on her desk. He bore the sign of a sloppy pisser. She hand-signaled he was on his own for the next swipe from the flask. He accepted the rejection with a wink and drank for the two of them. She was hoping the vodka would loosen his tongue more than it already had.

"What was here before, Flynn?"

"A lot of different businesses, Lainie my lady. Volkman makes a habit of jumping in and out of them the way I fancy he sees himself some Casanova, always jumping to and from a lady's boudoir. Up until five, six months ago it was the friggin' yacht business. A scheme really. Man's smart and shameless, comes to schemes built to make the rich richer and a shitload of insurance companies sadder but hardly any wiser."

"I don't understand."

"Then my pleasure explaining," Flynn said. He looked at the flask but thought better and stashed it. "On another afternoon sometime," he said, "when my tongue's less likely to run ahead of my good sense, as it's on the edge of doing again right now with you."

He unwrapped himself from the chair and reached for a pencil and sheet of memo paper from Lainie's desk. Hastily scribbled a message. Briefly held it up for her to read before ripping the sheet into quarters, then once more and locking the pieces away in a flap pocket of his jacket.

He had written: *Walls could have ears. Sometimes eyes.*

Lainie showed him she understood, pushed her want list across the desk as he rose and adjusted his outfit, as if preparing to leave. "Take this back with you upstairs, please. It's for Mr. Volkman."

He shook his head and waved off the request. "You'll have to call Missus Stalin for that. No messenger boy here, me only playing at one now as a requested favor by my god and yours, the guv'nor himself."

"What *do* you do around here?" Lainie said, figuring him for a Volkman gofer, a clerk or handyman she would ask to have reassigned to Perfect Records, positive whatever Flynn knew was a shortcut to what she needed to learn.

Flynn threw a thumb out the door. "I'm situated direct across the hall corridor from you, in the space you didn't get. The home of Pioneer Productions. Motion pictures and television for the masses."

"Let me guess, Flynn: You manage inventory and shipping or something important like that." Playing to his vanity.

"Nowheres near that important, mate," he said, good-naturedly. "I'm chief cook and bottle washer. The president of Pioneer Productions."

He scribbled another note.

This one had the name and address of a bar and a time for them to meet.

CHAPTER 10

Flynn's note called for six o'clock at Pat Madden's Saloon on Fairfax, a few blocks above Wilshire and the County Art Museum annex. Lainie got there early. He was already at the bar, hands rubbing the backs of two unspectacular secretarial types who were joined at the hip on stools near the entrance.

He ordered up a round for them and made enough racket to prevent any of the dozen or so patrons from missing his presence. It was evident he was a regular here by the way he traded barbs. The worst stings drew the greatest laughter, no anger, suggesting to Lainie they were well-worn comebacks among well-established comrades.

Flynn waved them off with a few final insults the moment he saw her. He repeated her drink order to the bartender, vodka martini straight up, no olive, and a refill for himself without bothering to ID it before steering her to the rear, explaining. "We'll have us more privacy closer to the dinner hour."

En route he paused to show off the shamrock green paper cutout with his name on it, FLYNN, printed in large capital letters, among the hundreds of shamrocks pasted to the wall.

"They're all over, you noticed, but this wall is special," he said.

"What makes it special?"

"More'n because mine's on this particular wall," Flynn said. "You notice it's right by the ladies and gents. People gotta piss and, when they do, there I am for all to remember long after

I'm gone. Them what don't? Piss on 'em." A slur played modest havoc with his diction.

Flynn made more small talk in the minutes before their drinks were delivered by a server in a sweater tighter than Flynn and a mini-skirt loose enough for him to slide a hand up and pat his appreciation. The server laughed like this was an old game, louder when he said, "Still as firm there as my dear departed Great Aunt Minnie ever was, Gracie."

Gracie gave him a giggle and rolled her eyes at Lainie before disappearing. He watched her leave, dah-dah-dahing the theme from *Bridge on the River Kwai;* turned back to Lainie and, raising his glass, recited the same toast he'd offered earlier in the day: "Here's to them and here's to we and if by chance we disagree—Fuck them! Here's to we."

Lainie used it as an excuse to move the conversation.

She teased the martini with her finger and said, "Flynn, what is it you want to tell me that you couldn't say earlier?" No urgency to her question. The same way she might have asked him to name his favorite color.

He checked the room for terrorists and said, "Not what it appears, know what I mean?"

"I don't."

Flynn nodded agreement. "I do." He checked the room again. "My drink? Grand old Irish whisky. Only their imported best. I'm Aussie through and through, the way night is to day, but by way of Ireland. Have I told you that yet?"

"Not yet. You were telling me Volkman International is not what it seems. Exactly how's that, Flynn?"

"Right on. It's not. You are the smart one to notice. I salute you." He touched his glass to his forehead and got it down to his mouth without spilling a drop. "So happens I was brought crying and kicking into this world on an Australian warship parked square the middle of Dublin Harbor, my mum to be and my dad were on board then, on a visit to the Ambassador to Ireland, my grandfather, but that's another story for when I tell it. How my family's fortune disappeared? All due, or so it's been claimed, to the men's liking for slow horses and fast women. I understand you're pretty fast yourself. Yes?"

"I brake for pedestrians. Who told you that?"

"Volkman himself, like it's more than gossip overheard on his part." He shot her an appreciative look. "How's your drink?"

"Fine. When'd he say it?"

"Just before I was sent back down to replace the Russky at your side, himself needing her for backup there for this thing the two of them do on their side every day around this time, and I don't mean dictation. More like dick-tation." He made a circle with the thumb and forefinger of one hand and poked through it several times with his other forefinger, to be sure she understood. "Never a postage stamp Volkman has the Russky licking," Flynn said, doing his eyebrows thing again, like Groucho Marx was also his grandfather.

"I'm surprised Volkman would ask you. Surely there was another secretary, an office boy, somebody not as important, not as busy as you must be running his production company?"

"Right, busy. Good one that. Anytime today you see all my minions minioning about, did you?"

Lainie realized she had neither seen anyone nor felt any sign of activity on the Pioneer Productions side of the floor, except for Flynn poking into her office one last time with a wave and a wink before he left for the day. She had been busy on the phone, calling some of her old key staffers at Blue Pacific Records, hoping they'd be keen for the challenge of joining her start-up label to break Miranda Morgan *Billboard* and *MusicBox* big-time on short turnaround.

She said, "Between shoots, are you, Flynn? The usual staff layoffs?"

Flynn reared back, a wet twinkle in his eyes. "You got that right straight, mate. Between the shoot that never happened and the one that never will. Truth is, it's a bleeding front for Mr. Leonard Volkman and his bleeding company; me, a moving target, you wouldn't want to know how."

"How?"

"I wasn't schooled in the military, I'd be gone faster than chops on the barbee. On my own again. No more dancing to Mr. Leonard Volkman's piper. No fear about the law coming to march me off to bars not like here at Pat Madden's. Cold steel, where I'll eat up what's left of my good years making strokes on the wall to mark my days."

Flynn seemed to be appealing for sympathy before he drifted off again, into a meltdown of words Lainie had to listen to closely in order to understand.

"Off my grandfather's standing as a general, retired, I was taken by the Prince of Wales Light Horse regiment at the ripe age of seventeen, but it was all ceremonial dung, dull as dust for a tumbler like me, so I fixed my way into SAS, the Special Air Services Regiment, and got to Borneo with Three Squadron, going up against the Indonesians. Got myself a souvenir of that engagement from local tribesmen, so come tell me you ever want to see where else you can ring a body part that's not the ear, the nose, the lip, the nipples, but where it's not usually meant for public display." Flynn sent her a lecherous face across the table. "I survived, only to be shipped to the funny place, Nam, with Three Squadron. In country. Part of a four-man team on advance reconnaissance. Was damn bleeding lucky going on near three years before my luck washed out and—" He simulated a series of rifle shots. "Spent the next six months in hospital, in a bleeding coma." He picked up his glass, mumbling, "After Nam, got myself transferred into SAS counter-terrorism, showing I was older but not any wiser."

"You're quite the hero," Lainie said, her cunning tampering with her respect for what she was hearing.

Flynn bolted upright. Squared his shoulders. Gave Lainie a hard, somber stare. Shouted, "All the heroes are dead."

Lainie didn't know how to answer him.

It didn't matter.

Another moment, Flynn drifted off again, trying to make words while his hands fell to his lap and his face floated down onto the table.

His shouting had brought their server, Gracie, running on the double.

She stood knowingly at the table, legs astride, arms folded below her prominent breasts.

"So much for the evening we had planned for later," she said. "Why aren't I the least bit surprised?" Gracie treated the situation with sarcastic indifference, but Lainie had the impression she genuinely cared for Flynn beyond whatever now-disrupted plans they'd made for later.

"How'll Mr. Flynn get home from here?" Lainie said, over a furniture-rattling snore that Flynn probably had used in Nam to frighten the enemy to death.

"He's not far. We dump him in a cab and add the fare to his tab. He's good for it, always saying to be sure and give the cabbie a proper tip, same as he always gives us."

"Let me help."

"That's all right. You go on your way. Some regulars up front, they know the routine by heart. I give him a half hour like this, before the dinner crowd starts. Any sign of life, I get him home myself, on my break. That so, Flynn?"

Her question caught his ear.

He broke into his snore long enough to respond with a grunt.

Gracie bent over Flynn with her breasts parked on the table

and lightly stroked his face, her fingers pushing loose strands of his blond hair back into place.

Leaving the dining room, Lainie almost stumbled cruising past the long bar, thrown off stride by the sight of someone familiar across the bar, his tongue playing with the thick mound of foam topping his beer mug, his attention on the magazine he had propped on the counter, but only after they locked stares, causing him to turn away first.

It was the man she had noticed getting off the elevator on the nineteenth floor at Volkman International, looking as familiar to her now as he had then, but—

—no sudden burst of memory to give him a name.

Lainie quickened her steps out the door and to her Toyota, convinced by the time she had slid behind the wheel that the man, whoever he was, had trailed her to Pat Madden's Saloon from the Marina.

If he had followed Flynn, he would have been inside by the time she arrived and no way would she have missed seeing him. Unless, of course, he had staked himself out on the street to first see who it was Flynn had come to meet. But why would he even think or care about Flynn meeting someone and not on an early run to his usual haunt? Was he a reason Flynn had called himself a "moving target"?

The questions kept coming after she cleared the curb and navigated a left turn at Wilshire.

She was unwilling to settle for the rationale that it was simply coincidence and she had allowed herself to lapse back into the paranoia that first gripped her when the business with the indictments began.

Then, Roy's murder.

Now—

No.

Hardly past the main museum complex, Lainie sensed she was being followed; a white Seville holding to her pace in the outside lane, three cars back.

The Seville was still there when she crossed La Brea, adjusting its lane to the flow of the traffic, usually three cars behind; at times two, but then it would pull back again, even when the lane was ripe for a surge past her.

Dripping sweat, anxious for confirmation, Lainie made an illegal maneuver south onto a side street, whipping around and back up to Wilshire at Highland. The Seville was waiting for her, parked with the motor running, headlights off, a mile farther east, like the driver knew she would come this way. The driver gave her two car lengths, let an RTD bus pass before snapping on the lights and pulling out after her. No way her clunker could outrun the Seville.

Her bag was on the passenger seat. Too frightened to try more games, Lainie dug out her cell phone, intending to punch the nine-one-one button.

Dead battery.

She flung the cell onto the back seat and eased down on the brake approaching Crenshaw.

Reached the cross street as the overhead signal started blinking yellow.

Said a silent prayer.

On the signal's switch to red, Lainie shuffled lanes. She made a wide u-turn in front of oncoming traffic; fishtailed and almost lost control of the wheel battling to straighten out; pulled ahead barely in time to avoid being broadsided by a pickup truck with sick brakes; got the car steady as she rocketed past the Seville, now stuck in traffic behind a blue Pontiac and the RTD bus; shouted her relief and pumped some victory toots from the horn; turned north on the first street; began psyching out the fastest route home.

If the driver of the Seville knew Lainie, the driver could also know where she lived.

No way could she let the driver beat her home.

Sara would be home by now.

Lainie pushed harder on the gas pedal, as if she meant to whack it through the floor, and ignored the posted stop signs.

She arrived at the apartment fifteen minutes later.

The nearest parking spot was a block away.

She covered the distance at the speed of light, was dry-heaving by the time she switched on the porch light, unable to remember if she had done that as usual before she left. With barely a frantic check to see if the Seville was around, she found her keys and got the door open, gave her own safety no further thought shouting "Sara! Sara!" into the darkness before she hit the light switch.

Everything was as she'd left it on her way out to Volkman International, except—

Sara's knapsack.

Where it didn't belong, in the middle of the floor.

Some of her schoolbooks alongside and a couple others half out of the open flap top.

"Sara!" Lainie trying to restrain the rising panic in her voice. Failed miserably. Jarred around by the sound of—

What?

Only the crackle of dry weeds and discarded cans being pushed around by a breeze that also was sneaking inside past the open door.

She hurried over and slammed the door shut, turned the bolt lock and threw the latch into place. "Sara, baby?" More inquiring than desperate, her eyes scouting the room as she took one hurried step after another to the kitchen. Lainie kept her .22 Smithie there, in the cabinet below the sink, inside an empty box of scouring pads, a place she was sure Sara would never think to look. Washing dishes, any form of cleaning around the place, as Sara frequently, loudly, made clear, was outside her lifestyle.

The gun had become one of Lainie's standard accessories long before the avalanche of legal troubles and Roy's murder. The record business came with its own catalog of dangers long before rap conquered the scene and rappers started dropping like bowling pins, especially for a young, good-looking promotion woman working the road. She had never been forced to use the weapon, but she knew how.

Moving through the front room to the bedroom, Lainie held the .22 like a divining rod. The door was slightly ajar. A splinter of light from the naked overhead bulb inside spilled onto her shoes. She nudged the door open more with a foot, at the same time feeling a rush of dread; sensing something wrong in there.

"Sara, baby?"

Nothing back.

She elbowed the door open the rest of the way and fell into a shooter's stance.

Sara was stretched out awkwardly on the floor, dressed as she'd been when she fled the house this morning. Her eyes were shuttered tight, as if warding off whatever nightmare images had contorted her face into an almost grotesque mask.

Lainie was at her side instantly, on her knees, her fingers pressing against Sara's neck, praying aloud for the feel of a pulse, anything to indicate her baby was alive.

A pulse, yes.

Her breathing: normal.

Lainie rolled Sara onto her back, landing a hand on the pool of caramel-colored spew by Sara's mouth. Vomit to the touch and the smell. She wiped her hand as clean as possible on her dress, dried it on the dilapidated carpeting. Gently opened

Sara's eyes. Her pupils were too small to qualify as pinpoints. She was on something, toot or worse.

Sara trembled and just as quickly was still again.

Still no life inside her eyes.

Lainie sat by her side for what could have been a half hour, holding her hands—something Sara had resisted lately—assigning blame solely to herself for whatever it was, anything and everything, that had gone wrong between them.

Knowing better, but at the same time denying it.

She was Sara's mother.

Mothers are not supposed to let something like this happen.

Ever.

She pushed up and crossed to the dresser, found a fresh pair of jammies buried in the dirty underwear Sara was collecting in one of the drawers. Got her undressed and into them. Debated with herself about inspecting her daughter's body for signs of abuse.

That would be committing invasion of privacy.

So what?

The insides of Sara's elbows were clean. There were no signs of a needle behind her knees, between her toes, or any of the secret places junkies learned to use in pursuit of an early death.

Lainie made the sign of the cross. Relief covered her thicker than the sweat seeping out of every pore as she struggled to get her uncooperative sleeping beauty under the covers.

Sara twisted mechanically into a fetal position.

Lainie moved her .22 from the floor to the top of the dresser, undressed and crawled into bed alongside her, positioning an arm around Sara's body in a way that allowed her to keep track of Sara's breathing.

She surrendered to her emotions, crying silently, out of control, against the truths of their relationship; vowing once again to heal it, make it better, get it right this time; save her daughter even as she saved herself; Sara first, if it came to that, as it might.

Her daughter first.

Sara first.

Her daughter first.

Sara first.

Sara.

CHAPTER 11

The new day began as unsettled as the previous day had ended.

Lainie awoke to find Sara gone from the apartment.

No note or signal telling her where.

Panic time again.

She recognized she'd have to suffer it alone.

No calling nine-one-one or Sara's school.

Nothing that would bring someone from Social Services snooping around, deciding there was cause to brand her an unfit parent and take Sara.

She had almost fallen into that pit after Roy's murder, when her whole world was sinking underground. Social Services investigators full of superiority and moral indignation had shown up on her doorstep unannounced, already convinced that placement in a foster home would be in Sara's best interest.

Lainie pulled in support from two dozen of the top music people she'd helped when she was riding high with Blue Pacific Records. They all testified to her exceptional moral character, even those who knew better; to her strengths as a loving, caring and devoted mother, that part all true.

The judge ruled in her favor, on condition she continue the program of psychological counseling she already had Sara enrolled in with a Beverly Hills hotshot shrink, who cut them off cold the day the money well ran dry.

Benny Sugar was one of the people who'd stepped up for Lainie at the hearing.

He was a studio engineer who got his first crack at producing from her, working with a few of Blue Pacific's younger acts. When they scored high on the charts, she moved him as both the engineer and the producer to retreads she was giving a second chance.

At once Benny was minting gold and platinum sides for her, giving a fresh "today" sound to artists no one else wanted anymore, adding gloss to Lainie's reputation as the hottest executive in the business, alongside living legends like Clive Davis, Ahmet Ertegun and Berry Gordy, all of whom tried more than once to steal her from Blue Pacific, the way other execs were panting after Benny Sugar.

Benny, young and idealistic, was aware he owed his success to Lainie and stayed loyal to her. For her part, as she prospered, Lainie wisely saw to it that he also did. In less than two years Benny's royalties were outrageously high enough to let him pay cash for a home in Beverly Hills and a weekend retreat in Laguna.

It wasn't until Lainie quit the business full time that he marched away from Blue Pacific to open his own indie production company, Starshine, in Studio City, where Miranda Morgan was now working and had cut her demos.

Lainie eased the Toyota into one of the few empty slots in the Starshine lot, tracked by surveillance cameras and a pair of beefy lot attendants who made sure she matched her license photo and phoned ahead before opening the gates for her.

The reinforced entrance door to the main building swung open to reveal Benny holding a bouquet of exquisite red roses, his smile as fresh and invigorating as their fragrance. She hadn't recognized him at once.

Benny looked like he had aged forty years in the two-something years since he'd shown up in court for her: A sallow complexion under random wisps of bottle brown hair, the flesh so taut she wouldn't have been surprised to see it crack. A spine unable to support the full weight of his torso, obliging the single crutch parked underneath his left shoulder. A voice that didn't come anywhere close to the passion burning in his brown eyes, grossly magnified inside black frames holding lenses thick as pancakes.

"Welcome, Miss Davies."

Miss Davies.

She'd never been able to break Benny of the habit.

She accepted the flowers and thanked him, averted her gaze so he wouldn't see the sadness blurring her vision.

"Whatever lie you're going to say—don't," he said. "I would rather look like hell than already be on my way there, although it's fair to say I'm pretty close to boarding the boat."

"What happened, Benny?"

"I got sick is what happened. I wanted to get better, but sick had another idea, and I had no choice but to go along. I can still work a sound board, though, so don't worry about Miranda Morgan. Whatever you need, whatever it takes, I'll get it in the grooves for you, like always." He struggled to make a laugh. "Grooves. It's all computers and lasers now, but we still talk grooves. Come on."

He led her up the hallway one slow step at a time, past walls weighted down with framed gold and platinum records, blowups of Benny in the studio with almost every superstar of the past twenty years, all inscribed with words of unstinting praise for Benny and his contributions.

"All thanks to you, Miss Davies," he said.

"Your genius had a little to do with it, Benny."

"A lot," he said, and struggled to make a laugh. "But it needed your generosity, when nobody else was willing to take a chance on me. So, when the office called me at my place in

Santa Barbara, told me what was going on with you and that cutie Miranda, I told them I'm on my way, coming down. My first time here in a long time, since the chemo began, and doctor's orders be damned, seeing as how this was a job for Superman."

"You shouldn't, Benny. Not if your doctors say you're not up to it. I know from Miranda that a lot of top producers and engineers are working here for you now. I'll go with the one you recommend."

"Up to it? Of course I'm up to it. And it's my treat, on the house, so don't give any thought to however long it takes us to get Miranda's demos absolutely primo; mastered and ready for you to go on out there and do your thing."

"I can afford to pay, Benny. I have backing in place that—"

"I can afford to *not* have you pay," he said. "Ah, here we are." He pushed open the door to the studio. "I've been working on her demos since already. You still have a great pair of ears, Miss Davies. The girl's better than fine, and I'm embarrassed to say none of my people picked up on it before you came along."

Benny settled at a computerized board surrounded by banks of screens, slots and drives exceeding anything Lainie had seen before she quit the business full time. She told him so.

"I invented half this stuff, the other half I'll get to improving one of these days," he said. "See that? And that? I own the patents. You think publishing is the pot of gold? Not one of my most important copyrights comes close to what I'm raking in on my patents, and it's just starting. Comes the revolution . . ." Benny made circles with his boulder-sized eyes, bringing on a modest wheeze.

He began fiddling with the sound levers as if he were adjusting them to music only he was hearing, taping a few into new positions. "I'm thinking about adding strings to the first cut, Miss Davies. Maybe a whole symphony orchestra. I have all of the instruments at the tip of my fingers. You'll give a listen and tell me what you think."

He gestured for her silence, but before he could bring in sound, he began coughing, a jag that took a minute to bring under control.

The palm he had used to cover his mouth was full of phlegm. He wiped it clean with a handful of tissue from the giant box on the board utility shelf.

"If you want a cough instead of the orchestra, I can substitute that," he told her, straining to create a fresh smile.

"What I want is a hit, Benny. It's what I need."

"How big?"

"A Number One wouldn't be bad."

"A Number One would be good," he said. He blew onto his hands and rubbed them for circulation. "If we're going to do it for the single, we might as well go and do it for the whole album, don't you think so?"

The Happy Face mask Lainie had been wearing turned real about three hours later, after Benny cranked up the amps and played what he decreed was the final mix on "Scarlet Woman," the cut on Miranda Morgan's demo they'd agreed was the strongest piece of original material.

Shoveling CDs in and out of his computers, sampling from what seemed like a million sources, he'd moved what began as a slow ballad of lament into an up-tempo torch song that came across as an anthem of delivery, never once tampering with Miranda's distinctive voice, the music and lyrics working at counterpoint, never once feeling out of time or place.

The symphony orchestra Benny had injected earlier was now reduced to a phantom refrain at the opening and close, seven notes by a piccolo trumpet the last sound heard; to be used again as the opening on the album's second song, Benny said, to give continuity to the album as well as the artist.

"Miranda's going to be around for a long time," he said, "so why keep it a secret? She's your ticket back into the business, absolutely, Miss Davies."

"From your lips, Benny."

"Why not? I'll add it to the conversations He and I have on a daily basis."

While Benny set up the board for the next cut, Lainie excused herself and headed to the lounge. She was using it as her office, checking the home number every half hour hoping to hear Sara's voice and to finish arranging a meeting for later in the day at Starshine with some old key working buddies from her Blue Pacific years.

The lounge was full of artists and musicians taking a studio break over the loaded snack bar and computer games that had replaced the pinball machines in vogue when she was a major player in the business. The pool and snooker tables were still around, being used by young men and women decked out in body rings and branding, their hair styles from another planet; other status insignias that meant nothing to Lainie. Not one familiar face or tattoo in the bunch. Only the familiar aroma of grass grazing the air, two or three stupids using a corner of the buffet table to dollar bill fat lines of Vitamin C, the typical parade of provocatively dressed groupies tittering around as proof Lainie wasn't an entirely displaced person on the music scene.

Running her messages, she thought, *Some things never change, unfortunately, including a lot of things that should,* but the world became secondary when she heard Sara's voice telling her: "I'm fine, okay, Mother? Fine, fine, fine, so stop calling me. Okay? I'm with my friend Joy. A party at her place tonight, just some of the girls, nothing crazy, okay? I took a change with me, and I'm staying overnight, okay? That's it. So—" Click. End of call, where maybe something like an easy *I love you, Mommy,* would have been nice.

No, not fine, fine, fine, daughter of mine. I've had my cell on all day. You didn't have to answer on the home machine. You've never mentioned a friend named Joy. You didn't leave me a number where I could reach you. Your cell phone has been off all day, whenever I've tried.

Lainie punched in Sara's cell number, got the recorded voice telling her the subscriber wasn't available. She felt small and helpless, but refused to lose her real smile and go back to wearing the Happy Face mask.

Sara had called.

That spoke to something.

It wasn't so long ago Sara wouldn't have bothered.

An hour later, Lainie rapped her nails on the black marble table in Benny's private conference room—the walls full of awards and framed citations, several Grammys among them—and announced, "Enough of our tripping down memory lane, friends. Time to get this show on the road."

She sat at the head of the table. To her right was Stan Currier. To her immediate left was Cubie Wallace, Ira Dent next to him. In the years that Blue Pacific ruled the industry, they were her Three Musketeers.

Her D'Artagnan was Eddie Pope.

"The Man."

Eddie Pope, who made her record industry career possible.

Eddie was the only one who had neither called back nor bothered to materialize.

Not surprising.

Eddie was still working big time, running the show at Chorale, making more in a month than she had ever paid him in a year, plus stock options, performance bonuses and his rake-off from what the business kidded about as the most creative expense accounts in record industry history.

Finding a replacement for Eddie could come later. Right now Lainie needed the likes of Stan, Cubie and Ira if she was going to pull off what Thom Newberry was demanding inside his four-week deadline. It wasn't enough to have Benny Sugar turning out a sure chart-topper with "Scarlet Woman."

Stan was "Mr. Slow and Steady," her sales and marketing maven, who always had his finger on the pulse of the industry, could spot a trend coming a year in front of anybody and never failed to make it pay off.

Cubie inherited the Blue Pacific national promotion job from Lainie after she moved up another notch on the corporate ladder and promptly turned it into an art form.

Ira was the publicity relations genius who routinely confirmed over and over the truth in his catchphrase: *The impossible my specialty. Miracles take longer.*

The only mistake all three ever made, or so it seemed to Lainie, was getting older in a business that thrived on youth. The people running the labels today were at least a decade-and-a-half younger than these guys and looking upon them as dinosaurs properly put out to pasture, or wherever it was dinosaurs lumbered off to die.

The once-stylish Cubie was in his fifties and flabby, his suit with its outdated lapels showing as much wear and tear as him, but still pumped full of the energy he had playing pro ball for the Jersey Barons before they bounced him out of football for sending one opposing lineman too many to the hospital with broken bones.

Ira, a couple years older than Cubie, had a body built on angles and always garbed in basic black, in stark contrast to a bush of white hair and skin coloring that looked like it was never kissed by the sun; an imposing voice that asserted knowledge and authority, still strong, but not so his hands. Ira's hands were full of mild quaking that had Lainie thinking it might be the onset of Parkinson's.

Stan, the oldest of the Three Musketeers, was the perfect picture of an enlistment poster Marine, who always seemed to sit at attention; seams stitched into his khaki pants, part of his regulation work uniform that also consisted of a cashmere sweater and a baseball cap touting an act he was merchandising to the trade. Today the cap advertised Touché, an act her musketeers were breaking about the time Lainie left Blue Pacific.

It hurt her to see the defeat reflected on their faces.

She said, "I understand you all could use a paying gig."

No one gave her an argument. Cubie, always the joker in the bunch, said, "My landlady would appreciate it almost as much as me. Maybe more."

Lainie said, "When we talked, I told you I want to put the old team together again."

"For a one-shot?" Ira said.

"Better, Ira. For the duration. A new label. Perfect Records. Show the business we still know how to pull it off, as good as or better than before."

"That 'we' include thee, Lainie?"

"Positively, Cubie."

"Perfect," Cubie said, making a circle with his thumb and middle finger.

Stan said, "You've been gone a long time, Lainie. Maybe you don't know some things you should."

Reaching into the scruffy leather satchel by his chair, Stan retrieved a blue three-ring binder thick with copies of news clippings and articles inside protective sheets. Each one had sentences, paragraphs, charts and graphs highlighted in various Magic Marker colors. He began quoting from this one and that one and finally closed the cover and made his point: "As much as I hate to admit it, it is a different world out there, not like the old days. I don't know that we'd be in step."

"I don't want that," Lainie said. "I want us marching like always to the beat of a different drummer."

"Who's paying for the uniforms? The way I've heard it, life lately hasn't been too fuzzy wonderful for you, either."

Lainie couldn't remember Stan ever so depressed or negative. His almost sixty years played on his face like a death mask. She fought off the notion of finding somebody else to handle sales and marketing.

"A little bit of both," she said, hiding her concern. "You come aboard, by the end of tomorrow, you'll have your first two weeks in front. All of you will."

Stan seemed to perk up. She realized why. He had mentioned something on the phone about his wife's gargantuan medical bills and no HMO coverage, her condition too serious and far along for her to qualify anywhere. And he had tried everywhere.

"That work for you, Stan?"

"Big time, but I won't shuck and jive you, Lainie. I don't believe any of us would feel comfortable raising your hopes or taking your money if what we have to peddle isn't going to fly."

Cubie nodded agreement.

Ira leaned forward in his chair. He latched his fingers. "I see it on your glamour puss, Lainie. You already have an airplane, don't you."

"A missile, Ira. A rocket to the moon."

All this time she'd been cruising the surface of the table with a CD of "Scarlet Woman" Benny ran off for her. She tossed it at Ira, who nearly fumbled the catch. "Listen and learn," she said, indicating the wall of playback gear behind her.

Ira said, "I have serious problems just turning on the radio, remember?" He passed the CD to Cubie. Cubie eased out of his chair and moved purposefully on the equipment, slotted the

CD and made a few sound adjustments. In another moment, Miranda Morgan was bringing her "Scarlet Woman" alive in a tidal wave of brilliant sound. Ira, Stan and Cubie went into a state of suspended animation. When the song played out, their silence continued, each of her musketeers locked into some conversation with himself until Cubie popped out the CD and held it up like the Statue of Liberty's torch.

"Lady and gentlemen of the listening audience," he said, solemnly, more like Walter Cronkite than the frenzied morning drive disk jock he'd been as a teenager learning the craft in rural Kettle City, Michigan, "Lainie Davies scores again."

CHAPTER 12

Kenyon Military Academy, established a year or two after World War One by General William Tecumseh "Wild Willy" Kenyon, the hero of a long-forgotten skirmish in the Argonne Forrest in 1918, stretched over fourteen acres a mile-and-a-half above Mulholland Drive, almost immediately after the turn off Sternwood Canyon. Wild Willy spent several millions in adjusting the natural landscape to create his vision of a miniature West Point for boys who would benefit from the rigors and disciplines of a uniformed military life on a full-time boarding school basis.

The Academy's motto translated from the Latin as "Win with Honor."

Thom Newberry always translated the motto as "Win or Be Damned."

Newberry reached the guard post and identified himself. The iron gate slid back on the two-lane asphalt road leading to the main quadrangle.

He parked his silver Mercedes—one of the few perks he allowed himself—on Pershing Road and hoofed across Stilwell Square to the Eisenhower Building, marveling at the smell of the freshly cut lawns and surrounding hedges, every line as neat and firm as the bedding on a military bunk.

Jerry was at their usual table in the Patton Library, grim-faced but looking smart in his dress grays, sporting all the trappings of the rank he had achieved since he was enrolled there almost eight years ago at the urging of Lance Clifford, "Grandpa

Lance" telling Thom:

"We both adore the little mouse, my pet, but taking care of the lad under my roof is a problem for your career and mine. No nanny exists who is trustworthy enough to keep from phoning the tabloids and collecting her thirty pieces of silver. It would spell disaster, even in these enlightened times. I propose we pack off the little mouse to Kenyon Military Academy, where I spent some of my own formative years and graduated the better for it. Inflated prices nowadays, but my treat, my pet. Nothing too good for you and your son."

Jerry eased from the chair as Newberry approached his secluded corner of the oak-lined, double-decker library. He stood at perfect attention and saluted. Held the pose until the salute was returned. Sank back down before he could be trapped inside Newberry's extending arms.

Newberry took the seat next to Jerry and did a quick survey of the room. Several other family meetings in progress, full of invented smiles and forced laughter, had caused an overhead conduit of undecipherable chit-chat. He said, "How goes, my man?"

"Fine, sir."

"Those lieutenant's bars look spiffy on you."

"Yes, sir. Thank you for the compliment, sir." Eyes fixed straight ahead, like Jerry was responding to a question from the bookshelves across the room, in a voice fresh out of puberty and not quite adjusted to the new sound, rich and resonant like his father's.

He looked like his father, too, especially in profile. Full-faced, he shared many qualities with his mother, Carla, who was awarded uncontested custody as part of their divorce settlement. At the time it was for the best, Carla threatening to battle Thom for custody in the press, sharing all the "dirty little secrets" she claimed to know.

They weren't dirty and they weren't little, but they were secrets and—she did know them.

And Lance was determined to keep them in their custody, just as later he pushed to send Jerry to Kenyon.

Jerry would still be with Carla, except for her death. Carla's murder was still open on the books of the LAPD, one of those random street killings that in the past decade became as routine in L.A. as traffic lights blinking from green to red.

"Looks to me like you've grown another inch since the last time I was here," Newberry said, grinning.

"Half an inch, sir," Jerry said, and seemed to work at trying to rise up more than his taxed spine already allowed. "Still a ways to go to reach your height, sir."

"I'm not surprised. I was slow out of the chute. Think it wasn't until I was verging on my eighteenth birthday that I seemed to spurt up, almost overnight, like magic. A reason I became a battler when I was a kid, even before I got to your age; the other kids picking on me something fierce. I started giving as good as I got, but then I realized I had something else going for me—"

"Your mind, sir."

"I've mentioned this before?"

"Yes, sir. Several times, sir."

"My mind, yes. My brains. I applied my mind to whatever it seemed this one wanted or needed; that one. Homework most of the time. First I got them trained to come to me, then I got them eating out of my hand. Beats a bloody nose every time."

"Why then, sir?"

"Why what, Jerry?" Inching away for a better look at his son. Uncertain and trying to gauge where the question was going, given it came from a kid who never asked him anything.

"Why then, sir, do you keep me trapped here like a prisoner, in a place that revels in the concept of war and killing?"

Looking squarely at his father now. Indifferent to the surprise Newberry felt charging through his eyes. Answering his father's puzzled expression with a look of harsh challenge.

Newberry so momentarily nonplussed, the best he could do was stare back while he struggled for an answer satisfactory to both of them.

Rod Flynn was waiting for him when he returned home.

They shared a hug and a kiss and adjourned to the bedroom.

Newberry mentioned Jerry's question soon after they fell exhausted into each other's arms.

"What did you answer?" Flynn said.

"I told Jerry it was an especially intelligent question and illustrated how he clearly had inherited his father's mind. I said, 'Jerry Mouse, that's very adult thinking on your part. Keep it up.' "

"Did he notice you still hadn't answered his question?"

"Of course he noticed. I came away very, very impressed."

"But what did you leave him with? I still don't hear an answer."

"I told him I would think about it."

"Still no bleeding answer, mate. Can't even give your own flesh and blood the straight what-for is nothing to be proud over, that's what I think."

"I didn't ask for your opinion, Flynn, so let's get to the subject at hand. What do you have to tell me about Lainie Davies?"

Flynn answered by pulling back his elbow and rocketing his fist forward. The punch caught Newberry on the upper arm. Newberry made a painful sound. "Jesus, Flynn, that one came close to my face. How many times I have to tell you to steer clear of any place visible."

"Not the same thing, getting me to hear and getting me to

pay attention," Flynn said, threatening Newberry with his left hand before surprising him with a hard right to the chest.

The punch made Newberry howl as he fell backward on the mattress.

Flynn was on top of him at once, his lips rough against Newberry's, his fat and feisty tongue pushing hard after Newberry's tonsils. Newberry let Flynn feel him surrender to the intensity of the moment. It was too early for the next go. Hopefully, Flynn would punish him with a solid blow somewhere, but nowhere it would show.

Like he was a mind reader, Flynn let loose another good one, Newberry certain his thigh would be an evil black and blue for a week. He rolled off the bed, announcing, "Off to locate me a refreshment, mate? You?" Swaggered back like a sailor a few minutes later clutching a bottle of Jameson. Plopped down in the leather lounger, legs spread like he was auditioning his pecker.

Newberry pushed himself into a sitting position and let Flynn see his irritation. "Lainie Davies, Flynn. Let's hear it."

"For openers, she's crazy for me. The great old Flynn charm working right as ever. That's what you were after, and that's what you got, mate. I'll be into her confidence full bore before you can say Jack Flash, and after that there'll be friggin' nothing she does or says you won't know."

"Yesterday, what did you talk about?"

"Not much so far to date."

"Dammit all to hell. Let me hear and decide for myself."

The air in Newberry's bedroom thickened.

Flynn looked like he was counting to ten, with a stop at five for another mouthful of Jameson. Turned it into a tic at the corners of his mouth before belching loudly and running a finger across his lips. Said like he was reciting poetry with a bad memory, "Got imported to take her on a tour of seventeen, so didn't have to worm that. She figures me for a bleeding office boy before I set that right and let her know how I'm the one running her next-door neighbor, Pioneer Productions."

Flynn shrugged and tossed over a palm. "What then?"

"No 'what then' for then, mindful of Leonard Volkman's bugs all over the building, I give her more of the old Flynn charm and induce the good lady to meet me later for more chat over a friendly libation at—"

"Pat Madden's Saloon."

"A habit hard as steel. Back where we have the privacy of a confessional."

"You told her about the production company. About the Perpetual Health Food scams. About the two floors under lock and key. About—"

"No friggin' chance, mate. I was cranked and ready to go after some polite words when the good lady up and left me to my own devices, without so much as an explanation, as if the world was coming to an end and she wanted to be there to see it. That's all still on the menu for our next tête-à-tête."

Newberry was convinced Flynn was jacking him around. More likely he got drunk and never got around to passing off the information on Lainie, like he was supposed to. No sense calling him on it. Newberry needed him. Flynn was the perfect prop to help him get the job done. After that, he would be as disposable as yesterday's razor blade.

"Fine, just don't let me down, Flynn. Remember you have a deadline on this."

"As sure as there's a deadline on living. The work with her will get done to your exacting specifications, as promised. Remember how I have an end to my own miseries riding on this, all thanks to you."

"I put you there, I'll take you away."

"When we're finished with her and it's over and done."

"Precisely."

"She locates whatever the frig you're after from wherever Volkman has it," Flynn said, like he was showing off for the teacher. "You're thinking it's stored somewhere on the twentieth or twenty-first floors."

"Yes, along with whatever else Volkman and his band of criminals have going for them on those secured floors."

"Scams, like the one he went and turned my Pioneer Productions into."

"With no little help from you."

"And rue the day that news fell to you. So, honey boy, I still don't know what it is, this golden goose we're after. It being what?"

"Still none of your business."

"She knows, though, Lainie does?"

Newberry let the question hang.

Flynn raised his eyebrows and made a *What do you know about that?* face. "It's the blind leading the blind," he said, and seemed to enjoy the concept. He gave it due process over another swipe of Jameson. "Her record company's a scam like the yachts before her, that part of it?"

Newberry showed Flynn it was another question he had no intention of answering.

"But our Lainie knows something, doesn't she?" Flynn said. "Why else would you want me to be sure after that—" He raced a finger across his throat.

Newberry's pulse exploded at the image painted by the gesture. "I'm ready again," he said, only to shut Flynn up.

Flynn checked the cap on the bottle and set it by the side of the lounger. He unwound and limbered up like a boxer, stretching his legs, adding knee bends, before he aimed for the bed. "In order to understand peace, you have to understand war, mate."

"What's that supposed to mean?"

"How I would-a answered your Jerry Mouse's question, him wondering at you why you'd let him be like a prisoner where they celebrate the idea of war and killing. Same as I'd-a told him you can't ever appreciate living until you experience the dying."

Newberry moaned with anticipation and held his breath against the encroaching stench of sweat and whisky mouth as Flynn got onto the bed one knee at a time and maneuvered him onto his stomach.

Flynn, his own breath suddenly labored, said, "I'd-a told him, Jerry Mouse, it's like you don't ever truly know from pleasure without pain." And rained his fists on Newberry without a care for where they landed.

By the time he reached City Hall, the painkiller had kicked in just enough to erase all but a tingle to go with the delight Newberry had taken in catching the punishment meted out by Rod Flynn, a slight purplish puff on his left cheek just under the eye the only visible sign.

He slowed at the garage entrance on Temple to let the security cop verify it was him and barreled down the steep circular drive to his reserved parking spot next to the mayor's in the VIP compound ten steps from the private elevator reserved for them and City Council members.

He exited on three and flew past the media gang hanging at the main entrance to the mayor's suite, trading bad jokes and worse rumors before being let in to set up for another of Mayor Lawton Welles's interminable press conferences.

Thom recognized he had no one but himself to blame for them.

Keeping Lawton Welles in the public eye was a key part of the election strategy he was confident would take Welles and him to the governor's mansion:

Always find something positive to say that will appeal to at least one voter.

When there's a shortage of issues with a built-in comfort zone, use the cameras and microphones in the conference room to honor somebody or some critic-proof cause with an appropriate proclamation; a day; a week; a key to the city.

Propaganda that isn't shared isn't propaganda.

It's wishful thinking.

Where'd he learn that?

Self-taught in the College of Trial and Error.

The same place he had learned *All good things come to him who hates.*

Disinformation?

Spin?

They were child's play compared to most of the chapters in Thom Newberry's playbook: confirmed techniques and wisdom that would have Machiavelli beggaring at his feet if the wily son of a bitch were still around.

This current problem, as example, was not the problem for Thom Newberry it would be for anybody else. Before Thom Newberry was finished, the mayor would be supporting the bid of Volkman's Rainbows Unlimited for the Paradise Sands property and none the wiser about the blackmail threats that, gone unanswered, would have destroyed his political future.

Sure, easier to have briefed Welles when Volkman first came forward with his threat of exposure, except there was absolutely nothing in the mayor's character to suggest he would bend to the common sense smarts of making a pact with the devil.

Welles was bright, but not the sun.

He lacked the magnetism of a Reagan or a Kennedy, a Clinton, but had the look; honest features down to his Dick Tracy jaw and gray-streaked temples, to project the impression of knowledge and wisdom.

The picture played well on TV, especially with words that were always fine-tuned and sufficiently rehearsed to keep Welles from ever stumbling his way into trouble. The Q&A was always monitored closely, someone, usually Newberry, ready to jump in and push Welles out of the firing line with a quitter comment anytime a reporter's question came out of left field and had the potential for damage, however mild.

Newberry paused. Something he thought he heard one of the reporters say made him turn around—Bob Nakamura of the *City News Syndicate* mentioning Roy Gardner and Harry Roman in conversation with Phil Brown of the *Daily.*

Thom offered them a thumbs-up and said, "Did I catch something you were saying about Hurricane Harry Roman and the old Gardner indictment? What's that all about?"

The newsmen stonewalled him with their expressions and gestures, making it obvious to him he'd heard correctly, and tried changing the subject to the Dodgers.

Newberry took Nakamura by the arm and said, "Bobby, need you but for a minute. You won't miss anything the mayor's planning to gush over today, I promise." His grip was too tight for Nakamura to escape. He had picked Nakamura, not Brown, because he had more chits out on Nakamura. He led him to a private corner behind an arch, catching some curious stares from the media. "What do you hear about Roman and Gardner that maybe I haven't heard, Bobby?"

Nakamura wasn't tricked by Newberry's meaningless smile, but he also remembered the outstanding chits. "Just Roman being his usual Hurricane Harry self. Working the corridor hot and heavy. You doing anything for that swelling? Should, before it turns nasty on you."

"Aspirin and a compress. Roy Gardner. How'd his name surface?"

"Ralph Alexander was hanging with us. Harry says to him something about is he still dogging Cold Cases over at LAPD for his cable series *Crime Old as Time,* unsolved headline makers where the file is opened and worked again? Ralphie says he is, so Harry begins rattling off names, going for a rise from Ralphie. One of the names is Roy Gardner."

"Good show, bad time slot. Did Ralph have anything to say about Gardner's murder?"

"Only that he hasn't heard anything fresh and how come Harry is sounding so curious about it all of a sudden. Harry shrugs the question and away he goes, leaving us to fish for his reasons."

"Come up with any?"

"Didn't give it a second thought." Nakamura's face signaled he had nothing else to tell.

Newberry said, "Let me know, you hear about it happening again with Roman, will you, Bobby?" He let it go at that, aware pressing any harder might send up curiosity dust, maybe get Nakamura checking into a story that wasn't a story yet.

Newberry's secretary, Winnie, leaped from her desk when she spotted him, a mild dread blooming on her face. She wigwagged her arms and pointed at the mayor's door. "Thom, they're waiting on you," she said, clutching a breast like it was about to fall off.

"They?"

"The mayor, the Council president, two others," she said, lowering her flighty voice like she was about to commit treason. "I heard them talking when I brought in some files the mayor wanted. All about Paradise Sands. Sounds like they got him convinced to go on the record today supporting the Council and against the Rainbows Unlimited proposal."

Newberry felt his world collapsing.

Took a deep breath.

Checked his watch.

Barely a half hour to the press conference.

If, in fact, Winnie had heard correctly, enough time to turn Welles around.

He gave himself a minute to collect his thoughts and passed into the mayor's office with all the bravado of a general who has already won the war, mentally damning Welles for stepping out in front of him.

"Sorry about being late getting here, sir," he said, smiling contritely. "Delayed because of my weekly with my Jerry Mouse. You know how that can go with a teenager."

"And from the looks, you forgot to duck," Mayor Welles said. He made a broad face and turned to his visitors to be sure they got the joke. "Park yourself down, Thomas. You should hear what I've been getting an earful of in the past hour."

Newberry didn't need his imagination to guess what he would hear. His mind was already spinning with ideas for short-circuiting the meeting; contemplating the new lies he would have to spend afterward on Harry Roman.

CHAPTER 13

In his office in the Hall of Justice, Harry Roman was having a lousy day.

First it was his boss the D.A. advising Roman by email he was moving Lainie Davies Gardner from the grand jury agenda to the back burner. No reason given, and Roman knew there would be none forthcoming until the runt was ready to share.

Schermerdine set his own agenda.

Period.

The end.

The runt's office was down the corridor, but he didn't have the courtesy—the class—to stick his nose through the door and tell Harry why, or even to burn him on the phone. Hiding behind the computer screen was Schermerdine's style. How many staff meetings had he been through where any issue that called for a hard answer got a fast retreat from the D.A.? All of them since Schermerdine scored his surprise win over Bill Pollard, who always had been a lot better prosecutor than he was a politician.

"I'll mull it over and let you know."

That was the runt's stock answer.

What made the latest e-mail a shocker was how elated Schermerdine had been yesterday, stopping Roman in the hall to say how strong the new evidence was; how much he was looking forward to personally making the pitch; how, once he was done, there would be no question about the grand jury pushing the go button on Lainie Gardner Davies.

Pushing the go button.

How Schermerdine loved saying that, same as he would only go front and center with the grand jury when it was a case sure to grab media attention, like this one, alive and kicking again thanks to the mayor's man, Thom Newberry.

Only no longer alive and kicking thanks to Newberry.

The other reason Roman was having a lousy day.

Unlike Schermerdine, Newberry loved the telephone.

He picked up at once when Roman called and launched his usual *Whazhappening?, Whatc'nIdoferyoutoday?* Soft-shoe massage. Roman cut Newberry short, demanding to know what the D.A.'s change of mind was all about. "I plead guilty as suspected," Newberry said. "Your runt acted after I asked him to jettison the plan. Only for the time being, Harry. Only a temporary delay with the grand jury."

"Why, Newberry? I don't have to tell you what we have against Lainie Davies Gardner is stronger than anything we had going for us against her husband. You keep telling that to me."

"Correct, Harry, you don't. If you'll calm down for a minute I'll be happy to explain."

Roman clamped a hand over the mic of his headset, closed his eyes and silently counted to zero from ten, willing his heart to quit racing. It took a second ten count to get rid of the anger playing havoc with his breathing. "Let me hear it," he said.

"What's been happening here is a little politics."

"I figured that part out for myself."

"A little politics. Not my doing, Harry, and it doesn't thrill me, either. You know how much I want this indictment to happen. So does the mayor. Only, some City Council members are now trying to strong-arm him into taking an affirmative position on the Rainbows Unlimited proposal for Paradise Sands. For the mayor to make out like Rainbows Unlimited is a legitimate company would undermine the entire case against Lainie and could come back to bite Welles on the ass with voters. I did some high-wire sweet-talking and convinced him to hold off making his decision. Meanwhile, I temporarily shut down Schermerdine going to the grand jury on a direct order from Welles. Your boss, he understands politics as well as anyone."

"A lot better than he understands the law. How long is 'temporarily'?"

"Only until I show Welles all over again that it'd be in his worst interests to come out for Leonard Volkman and his gang of criminals."

"The councilmen?"

"First the mayor, then I'll go to work on them."

"Which councilmen?"

"No can say, Harry. Sorry. At their request, and the mayor instructed me to honor it. You know how those things go."

"Politics."

"Politics."

"You think they've been bought off by Volkman?"

"I couldn't say."

"Couldn't or can't?"

Newberry's laugh blasted into Harry's earphones. "A little of both," he said. "Let us keep it at that for now, my friend."

He clicked off, leaving Roman with the unclean feeling he had every time he had to deal with Newberry, certain all over again the only "friend" Thom Newberry ever had or thought he needed was Thom Newberry.

Harry was calling around to people in City Hall who owed him, quietly trying to get a line on who the councilmen were, when his computer screen beeped e-mail. The message was from Jimmy Steiger at the LAPD:

Ruby Crandall's doing her laundry at the Brackens fed lockup for naughty girls, hard time for transporting minors across state lines. Consecutives, with an add-on for knifing a guard that earned "Chips" a lifetime ticket a year-and-a-half ago. You're welcome. Next lunch on you.

Steiger had tagged his e-mail with a clearance code and ID number that would take Roman direct to Crandall's jacket after clicking onto the national law enforcement support services confidential database of the FBI's Web site.

Roman downloaded the Crandall files. Marveled at how, with hardly any effort, Crandall had turned herself into a career criminal, starting at age eleven when she graduated from killing jackrabbits on the family farm in Visalia to using Mommy and Daddy for target practice.

Fortunately for them, she was a lousy shot.

They survived.

A year later, the Crandalls weren't so lucky.

"I begged, but they wouldn't never stop poking fun at me anymore," little Ruby explained to the media, on her way to the bus that would transport her to the Waverly House for Youthful Offenders in Northern California.

Nothing in Ruby's jacket tied her to Lainie Davies Gardner, except for their time at the "Animal Farm," the Federal Women's Detention Center in San Diego. Nothing there to explain what Lainie meant when she accused him of buying Ruby's lies about her from Thom Newberry.

Good old Thom. More tricks than arm up his sleeve. Putting the question to him now was likely to get the same *No can say* answer he had used to shield the identities of the councilmen. Trying to get some straight answers from Ruby Crandall one-on-one was the more logical move.

★ ★ ★ ★ ★

Brackens is one of those off-the-highway California cities built around four corner gas stations, a 7-Eleven and half a dozen fast food franchises located in the central part of the state, paralleling the Interstate the length of a blink and a sneeze without the *gesundheit*. It's home to Montana Brackens Federal Penitentiary for repeat and hardcore women offenders and a major contributor to the community's economy.

Roman made the three-and-a-half hour-drive there the next day. He guided his classic Mustang into a visitors' parking slot about a hundred yards from the prison's main gate, was processed inside, and ten minutes later Ruby Crandall joined him in one of the private rooms allowed for inmates and their legal counsel.

The room was hardly larger than a standard cell, empty except for the heavy metal table and four metal chairs bolted to the concrete floor. The thick concrete walls added an extra layer to the cold atmosphere, chillier after Ruby passed through the remote-operated steel door, trailed by a woman guard the size of a tank.

Ruby settled in the chair opposite Harry.

The guard adjusted Ruby's ankle cuffs binding her to the table before undoing the cuffs on her wrists. The guard pointed to a doorbell-style button rooted to the desk and instructed Roman to use it when their meeting was over or, adding an ominous overtone to her abrasive voice, "If Chips acts up any, the way she's so inclined."

Chips snarled and muttered "Bitch" under her breath, rubbing her wrists briskly as the guard backed out of the room.

She waited to hear the clicks and clanks of the door bolts and checked past her shoulder to verify they were alone before giving Harry an eye colder than a Russian winter.

She said, "Who the fuck are you, and what the fuck's this all about, shit for brains?" Her eyes, tiny black marbles of distrust, skinned him alive.

Harry gave her an impassive stare and didn't answer at once.

There wasn't much to Ruby. She was one of those small creatures who wore their danger like an invisible cloak, intimidating by their presence alone; a mouse of a person, her dark and brooding eyelids constantly blinking a Morse code of menace. Her oval mid-to-late-forties face melted down to a petite chin. A ripe, wormlike scar rising from below the neckline of her orange prison smock. Wearing her black-on-gray hair trimmed almost to the scalp, leaving a layer of five o'clock shadow that looked more like nine o'clock.

Roman was certain he could lift her by his pinky and toss her across the room; as certain she would carry him with her, fingers digging into his neck or trying to bite off his nose with the jagged dragon's teeth that flashed an inkwell black and canary yellow stain whenever she bared her thin, almost invisible lips.

He said, finally, "Ms. Crandall, my name is Harry Roman. I'm your only hope in hell for ever getting sprung from this place."

Ruby finished picking at a nail and moved on to the next. "That arrogant prick Newberry send you?"

At least she was a good judge of character. "Yes," Roman lied.

"He got the deal I want from the D.A.?"

Roman let her stew in silence through another fingernail before he tilted the corners of his mouth to make a brief smile and said, "I am the D.A. I'm here today because I don't believe in middlemen. I need to hear what it is you'll deliver before I deliver."

Crandall folded her arms over her chest and inclined her head, measuring him for either truth or a coffin, maybe both. She shook her head. "Newberry would've told me. He knows how I hate surprises."

"No time. I laid it on him this morning."

"Not buying your bullshit, whoever you said you were. In the time it takes to get here, Newberry could have let me know." She pointed at the button: "You press that damn thing now. Room service will come and get me . . . I said *now,* mister." She leaned forward to give Roman a closer look at the murderous intent flashing in her eyes.

Roman also saw something else: Ruby Crandall was trying to pull a bluff.

It wouldn't be the first time he was in this situation: somebody marked for life or longer, nothing to lose by chipping after some gravy benefits beyond what was on the table. Figuring if it failed to work on him she could fall back on Thom Newberry and the original offer, whatever that might be.

Roman had nothing to lose either. "What else, Ms. Crandall?"

"What else what?"

"There's something Mr. Newberry didn't or couldn't promise you for your testimony that you think I can, that it?"

Ruby cracked a new smile and leaned back in the chair, hands locked behind her neck, and emitted a short series of happy sounds from her throat. "You catch on fast."

"Like a hobo hopping a freight."

"Done that a lot in my time. Newberry promised me you'd slash my time in here."

"Of course. That stands, and"—guessing—"make life a little more comfortable for you. But it's a pass if you're dumb enough to think there's an easy parole in your future. You tried to do a guard, Ms. Crandall. You're lucky the guards didn't try a payback."

"Those bushwhackers did," she cut in, her eyes glowing wild with rage. "I'll always hurt where the sun don't shine, but none of your damn business. And don't call me dumb. I was dumb, I'd be dead now." Banging a fist on the table for emphasis. Eyes circling the room for a landing and finally choosing a spot on the floor. "I heard you loud and clear, you said something about getting me sprung. Only just now you nixed a parole. Let's shit-can the doubletalk first, then we can see where we're heading with this." A command, not a question.

"I said 'sprung' from here, not 'parole.' It's what I meant. I'm talking about working a deal with the feds to have you transferred someplace that's easier on the living."

"Like them white collars get anymore?"

"Like them."

"Newberry didn't say nothing about that."

"Mr. Newberry couldn't. I can."

"Even though I'd be talking about me and Murder One on the stand?"

"Because you're talking Murder One. It's not you I'm after, Ms. Crandall. It's Lainie Davies Gardner. You give her up to me, to a jury, I frankly don't give a damn about what happens to you afterward."

Crandall wilted again on the chair. "What do you want to hear from me?"

"The same as Newberry told me he heard from you. What you'll tell the jury."

Her eyes blinked a thousand times before she closed them for a private appraisal of her thoughts, then opened them and began addressing a corner across the room, where the walls met the ceiling.

Roman found himself listening to the same story he'd heard from Newberry:

How she and Lainie met and became friends at the Animal Farm.

How, years later, Lainie came to her and contracted for Ruby to kill her husband.

Ruby offered details on the killing that either matched everything on record or fit in neatly between the cracks, in a manner that could land like the truth on a jury, even with a defense attorney hammering her on her past, getting an easy admission that her testimony so many years later had been bargained for with the D.A.'s office.

No surprise there.

A textbook tactic always good for a few easy points.

Always easily surmounted by Roman.

Not the problem on his mind right now.

Roman had found nothing in the feds' file on Ruby Crandall tying her to Roy Gardner's murder, to be expected, or what she was offering him now would be worthless, but there was no mistaking this sparrow of a psycho for the shooter who was described in the statements given investigating officers by Lainie Davies Gardner, her daughter, Sara, other eyewitnesses to Roy Gardner's murder.

The shooter was male.

Six-six or six-seven.

Ruby Crandall could lie about a lot of things to get a pass on hard time, but definitely not that.

At once Roman wondered if it was what Lainie meant to tell him when she sprung Ruby Crandall's name and invited him into her place for coffee.

Newberry let me in on it, the lies you're buying from Ruby for the case you think you have going against me.

Roman put the thought aside while he threw the curve at Crandall.

She didn't hesitate before swinging. "Me, a man? Six-six or six-seven? You need to get your eyes examined? Where you going with that kind of bullshit?" Acting somewhere between puzzled and amused, looking to Harry like she already knew.

He told her anyway. "That's the shooter everyone saw, Ms. Crandall. How do you answer me on that?"

She turned over a red and callused palm, giving him a better glimpse at the gang symbol crudely carved out with something not sharp enough, in black dye, between her thumb and index finger: an X in a circle. She shrugged, ran a finger around the tattoo circle several times and said, "Eubie Grass."

"What?"

"Not 'what.' *Who*. Eubie Grass, that's who. As in, Eubie on your case, your ass is grass for certain. I never said I was the shooter. What I said was my gal pal, Lainie, she needed a shooter and came to me. For old times' sake, I gave the girl a price. I took the contract. I tracked down Eubie. More his line of work than mine. Besides, I owed Eubie one. I offered up half my price, knowing it was more than half what Eubie usually quoted. You know the rest. So, how come you didn't know that part already?"

Roman masked his surprise. "Of course I knew. What I don't know is where I can find Eubie Grass, Ms. Crandall? Where can I find him?"

"Like I told Newberry, I haven't seen or heard about him since he took the money and went after the husband. Eubie, if he's out of town, try Vegas. Where he always goes to celebrate between jobs, blowing his payday when he isn't using it to bomb his brains out. Find Eubie, you got your shooter."

CHAPTER 14

Leonard Volkman turned back to Lainie from his penthouse view of the Pacific and told her, "You spend my money like it's going out of style, Lainesky."

Lainie wasn't about to back down. "I'm spending it to give you a hit, Lenny. You gave me an open checkbook, remember?"

"Open, but not open to the kickbacks you're getting."

"What's that supposed to mean, Lenny?"

"What it sounds like—a little grease sliding off the reqs and invoices I've checked is sticking to your fingers," he said, rubbing against his thumb with two fingers. His voice and smile know-it-all pleasant, but contradicted by the fact Lenny had never tolerated being taken advantage of or played for a fool.

Lainie was doing both, of course, but he didn't know that, so it had to be another one of his tests. Lenny was always big on tests, like the last ones he had played on Roy, only that time the tests were tricky enough to score a direct hit on the games Roy was playing on Lenny.

She said, "I told you I'd deliver a Top Five record first time out. That's what I'm doing, Lenny. Miranda Morgan's single, 'Scarlet Woman,' will hit the *Billboard* and *MusicBox* charts at Number One if you stay out of my way. That's where your money's going and will keep going."

"You sound like Number One is a given."

"All I can be is wrong."

Volkman tick-tocked his head. "Worse than that, you'd be

141

disappointing my investors, Lainesky. They're the ones doing the bellyaching, not me, *kapeesh*?" Backing off his hard line, laying the blame like a cautious bookie on his no-names-please investors. Another favorite trick.

"They want to pull the plug on our deal? Fine. Sign off on our deal and I'll take the single down the street. You'll get your money back before anybody else recoups, chump change when you consider how much Perfect Records will rake in on the single. The publishing. The album. Everything that follows."

She had Lenny on the defensive. His head was on the go again, his smile showing he was wise to what he perceived, wrongly, as *her* game: "You know you're locked here for the duration, Lainesky. Just watch how you butter the bread."

"What are you suggesting, Lenny? Maybe dump my team?"

"You're overpaying them."

"Wait until you see the tabs for Miranda's video. Trade ads. Buying windows, listening posts and endcaps from the chains across the board, all their locations, whether or not we want them or need them. Feeding the habits of radio people we'll need to go on the record early. That and more, still the cost of doing business."

Like he hadn't heard her, not letting go, Volkman said, "The recording studio and those payouts? Enough being spent there to build another Taj Mahal. I told Petra she was to order you whatever equipment you needed and we could put on the books, amortize it; the tax benefit. So, what's that all about, that studio in the valley?"

"Starshine is state-of-the-art, and Benny Sugar is a legend. You want to amortize and do your usual tax dodges? I'm sure I can talk Benny into duplicating the studio up here. How's that appeal to you, Your Thriftiness?"

He tossed her a look that told her *Stow the sarcasm* and asked, "How much?"

Lainie threw back the number she'd already discussed with Benny, plus twenty-five percent, the same boost she'd been having Benny add to his invoices and set aside for her. "You go for that, it raises a new question," she said.

"Meaning?"

"Where here? My space on seventeen doesn't lend itself, especially once I finish staffing up. Switch the movie company somewhere else? Is that workable?"

He played with the notion and shook it off. "I got two floors where the space might work out for you. Twenty and twenty-one."

Lainie couldn't believe her luck. She'd figured she would have to stumble her way into making the suggestion herself. "Wherever you say, but we should get Benny Sugar up here for his input."

"I'll think on it," Lenny said, his manner dismissing Lainie while he dug into the desk humidor and began inspecting cigars.

Barely five minutes later, settled behind her desk on seventeen, her temp secretary's voice piped through the overhead, announcing Volkman on the flashing line. She picked up at once. "I thought on it," Volkman said. "Pass-ola on those two floors."

He clicked off, leaving Lainie clueless about his speedy change of mind, making her all the more anxious to explore twenty and twenty-one and get Thom Newberry what he wanted in trade for freedom from worries about—how had he put it? *Anything that'll threaten you or take you away from Sara. Not a grand jury. Not Ruby Crandall.*

Two hours later, she was pretty sure how to go about it—

Easy enough if she could get Rod Flynn to cooperate.

Arriving at Pat Madden's Saloon, Lainie paused at the bar to briefly speak with the barman and Gracie the server, whose scowl said she knew who Lainie was here to meet and made no attempt to hide her jealousy. It was as easy to read as the body inside her tight, turtle-green sweater.

Lainie asked them to slow the service to Flynn and maybe even water his whisky a little, slipping both of them twenties to go with the request. The barman gave her a thank-you wink and quickly folded and pocketed his bill. Gracie looked at hers like it was coated in anthrax and tried shoving it back, insisting, "I don't want your money."

"And I don't want your man," Lainie said. Just as quickly, she turned and went into the ladies' room for one more task before joining Flynn: another check on Sara. In the privacy of a stall, Lainie pressed redial on her cell. She let the home number ring a dozen times before she disconnected, waited a few seconds, pressed redial again. *Damn kid,* she thought. *Should have known better than to take her at her word about staying home.*

Sara's voice blasted her eardrum after the eighth or ninth ring: "I told you I'd stay home, and I'm home. Home, home, home! Stop calling me every five seconds, okay? I am home. I am here." Out of control. But there. Home, home, home. Clicking off before Lainie could tell Sara she planned to join her in about an hour and maybe, if Sara could wait, they could go out for a pleasant, peaceful mother-and-daughter dinner together.

Flynn was at the same table they'd occupied last time, her vodka martini straight up, no olive, waiting in front of the seat across from him. He hoisted his shot glass, a mate to the shot glass he had already emptied, and decreed, "A toast, good lady."

She grabbed for her glass and beat him to the words:

"Here's to them and here's to we and if by chance we disagree—Fuck them! Here's to we."

Flynn downed the whisky with a roar and slapped the table appreciatively. "It's one fine memory you have, among all else fine about you. As fine as the sentiment of that glorious toast, which I'm taking now for bloody certain you share with me."

"For bloody certain," she said, agreeably, giving him the turn-on smile that never failed her, especially in her promotion girl days on the road, the foreplay that got her coveted airplay on even the worst singles ever made in the history of mankind.

Those successes had helped build the Lainie Davies mystique and ultimately got her to the top of the pecking order at Blue Pacific Records. The other promo pros could do it, of course, but never as often or as well. She intended doing it again tonight with Flynn, scoring before too much of the Irish sauce put him under the table. From the looks of him, she might already be too late.

Flynn aimed his chin at her, investigating her over his nose. "Besides my charm, how was it you were so inclined to invite me to my own local?"

"You're an interesting man, Flynn, and I was anxious to hear the rest of it."

"The rest of . . . ?"

"The rest of your story. Last time we only got as far as—"

"My thrilling and unparalleled wartime exploits and heroic derring-do," Flynn said.

His memory was precision sharp for a man who minutes later had turned sloppy out-to-the-world drunk, Lainie thought, her suspicions about him rousing again. "How did you wind up in the movie business?" she said.

"No trick that," Flynn said. "Back in civilian life and working the odd job as a bouncer in nasty London nightclubs, I met up with movie types who benefited from my knuckles and repaid me with bit parts, usually as a 'crim,' a criminal. I found a natural attachment, me seeing me up on the big screen.

"I hooked up with a film school to learn the craft and anything else that went into making movies. Sat down and wrote a screenplay based on my adventures, and it came to the attention of a fine gentleman, Sir Lew Grade, who bought it for production and me along for the ride. I'm a fast study and saw how it was easier to make movies than war, although neither as much fun as making love . . ." He gave Lainie an eye. "Also, how much money there was to be made, a thought that brought on another kind of orgasm in myself. I also saw that the really big money was over here in America, so *Goodbye, London,* and *Hello, America.*"

Flynn made a musical sound. "I formed my own production company to write, produce, direct and maybe even bloody star in some of the pictures. I did the old bouncer routine at some of the trendier clubs until I caught it lucky with some big spender types, who bought the idea of their names on the screen as bloody executive producers—to impress the wife and mistress, you know?—and quick as a wink invested enough for me to make some low-budget, straight-to-the-video-store pictures . . . What's holding up my refill? You see any evidence of Gracie anywhere? Gracie!"

Flynn looked like he planned to get up and search for her.

Lainie reached over and put a tight lock on his hands, flashed him her best ga-ga face.

"Fantastic what you pulled off, Flynn."

"Almost as good as a whack on the old banana."

"Not too old, I hope," she said, provocatively. "That how you landed Leonard Volkman?" Steering the conversation toward learning if there was an upside to his relationship with Lenny that would force her to rule Flynn out of her plan for getting inside the twentieth and twenty-first floors.

"Friggin' Leonard Volkman, he bloody found me, you mean. Not the other way round, no matter what stories you might hear." Twisting his neck like he was trying to unscrew his head, at the same time finding her leg with a shoe and running it up and down.

Lainie let him. "How so?"

"Phone call from the blue one day and I'm being invited to visit with the great man. He's seen my movies and wonders if I'm interested in forming a joint venture of some sort, says his secretary. The one right before Petra. Polly, her name. Looked like one. Learned soon enough how Volkman put that beak of hers to use. That parrot, definitely no stranger to a cockatoo." A wink to underline the joke.

Gracie arrived with Flynn's refill and a look for Lainie that said she didn't enjoy seeing Lainie holding hands with her man. Lainie let go, moved her leg away from Flynn's reach.

Flynn attacked the whisky glass in one swallow, gave the empty a curious study.

He looked up at Gracie, demanding, "When did they begin watering the whisky here?"

"No such thing," Gracie said.

She turned on her heels and sped away, Flynn calling after her, "I expect better the next time, and that time's right now, you bloody hearing me?" He looked at Lainie with a hound dog expression that begged for sympathy.

Lainie showed Flynn she understood and accelerated the conversation before he got too smashed to be of any use. "You were about to explain how Volkman played you for a fool."

Flynn looked at her like he knew better. Lainie was certain she'd blown it until his head began bouncing. "He fucked me over good," Flynn said. "Worse'n was just now done to me with my whisky."

He explained how Volkman proposed funding a Pioneer Productions slate of four films annually, leaving Flynn free to run the creative end. Write, produce, direct, act if he chose to, in films turned out on a budget of anywhere up to a hundred twenty million dollars.

Pioneer would headquarter in the Volkman International

building as part of the deal, to run seven years, with an option to renew for an additional seven subject to the mutual approval of Flynn and Volkman's parent organization.

It read like no risk, all reward to Flynn.

Who could ask for more?

Not Flynn.

A dream come true.

A dream?

"Sheer bloody friggin' heaven," he said, musing over the fresh whisky finally delivered by Gracie, letting her see on first sip that he knew this one also was watered. "Only it turned out to be a private hell like you would not imagine."

Lainie didn't have to imagine. Years ago, she'd heard the Volkman playbook from Roy so often she could recite it from memory. How Lenny and his man-eating sharks would zero in on an industry that came with some glamour attached. Find some startup or struggling company, an entrepreneurial visionary, a desperate schnook. Offer the deal of a lifetime.

Once the paperwork was out of the way, Lenny began taking control. The structure of every contract allowed the ultimate power transferred to Lenny and his board of directors if certain terms, conditions and deadlines were not met.

The fine print was a tossed salad of contradictions that guaranteed failure and a quick takeover.

At that point, a new company was formed, usually with a foreign base, and taken public through channels operated by the gang of underground investors whose identities Lenny never revealed. Not long after, following quiet manipulations to boost the value of the stock, the new company bailed out, taking a substantial profit as it dumped its shares and declared bankruptcy.

The dreamers like Rod Flynn were left with a carcass and worse: the blame—because the original paperwork always divested Volkman and his umbrella companies of any liability in the event of failure. The dreamers wound up mired in a court battle they had no chance of winning, in a prison cell or dead by their own hand, but not always.

A number managed to hang on to their relationship with Volkman International, Lenny having found something in them that appealed to his dishonest nature, usually fruition of their own dishonesty. He kept them around, paying them well enough to make them a part of newer, bigger, better scams that came around almost as regularly as the mailman.

When Flynn got to that part of his tale, his anger boiled over.

Lainie signaled she had a question. "That why Pioneer Productions still exists and you're still up there?"

The question angered him further.

"All I ever wanted to do was make some bleeding great movies, not become the prisoner I am to his whims," Flynn said. "Volkman liked the idea of being in the picture show business, even though we never have, and I'm bleeding certain never will, get one made. Gets him places full of glamour. Gets him those young skirts ready to drop their knickers, trade a piece of ass for a part in a movie. Volkman holds over my head the most damaging paperwork, what can mark the friggin' bloody end of me if it ever got out and fell into the wrong hands. So I do the nine-to-five in a bunch of empty offices, pretending, on a wage I could earn back home digging ditches. I dream now of the day I'm out from under Leonard Volkman's greasy thumb instead of being the whipping boy to never-know-what."

Flynn, suddenly more embarrassed than angry, swallowed what was left in his glass and turned away from her.

Comfortable with what she'd heard, Lainie said, "Flynn, how would you like to get even with Volkman?"

"For you or for me?"

"Maybe for both of us?"

He turned back, and they locked eyes for a long minute before Flynn quit finger-wiping his empty glass and said, "There's a motto been inscribed on my family crest for hundreds of years that goes: *It's not over until you win.*"

"Is that a yes or a no?"

"Means how and when do we go about whatever this devilish idea of yours might be?"

Driving home, Lainie played Flynn's story over again in her mind, searching for any inconsistencies that might help her define an eerie sensation she couldn't shake, that he was somehow jacking her around for his own private reasons. The hail-fellow, don't-give-a-damn, live-for-today-and-leave-a-beautiful-corpse attitude he cultivated with her and everyone came across so real, so without letup, that it came to seem as big an act as she was playing with him.

She didn't trust Flynn entirely, but she had to trust someone.

Hopefully, she'd done nothing to set off any bells and whistles with him. She had Flynn in her pocket now. She needed to keep him there at whatever the price.

He had jumped at the opportunity—

Too quickly?

Was that what bothered her?

That he had jumped too quickly?

It was one of the reasons she had held off telling him everything she had in mind for their private invasion of the two secured floors at Volkman International. She needed to think about it more. If she had figured wrong about Flynn, she wanted the latitude to make adjustments without giving away anything that would offset the overall plan she was still giving a final tune-up in her mind.

Exercise caution in the time of crisis was something Roy had always preached at her, especially in the early record business years when her temper ran at mach speed in her need to get everything done now.

N-O-W.

Right and fast and damn the cost.

Roy's guidance matched his goodness right to the end, when the assassin's bullet put him out of his miseries and for a time seemed to close the book on hers.

Another of Lainie's reasons:

Flynn had come on to her more and more aggressively with every slug of whisky, as if the watered drinks were whetting his appetite for her.

Too drunk too fast to be that drunk at all?

She toyed with him, letting him sniff the perfume of possibility, but had no intention of carrying it as far as the bedroom. She'd be playing the game only as long as it took to check out twenty and twenty-one. He would be expendable after that, like any independent promotion man after a record he was working slipped off the charts.

Sara became Lainie's excuse to Flynn for shortcutting the conversation and ducking out before he could stretch his shoe any further up the inside of her thigh.

Sara.

Lainie reached for her cell on the passenger seat and called for the fourth time.

For the fourth time no answer.

Sara had told her she would stay home, so why wasn't she picking up? Where was she?

Lainie floored the gas pedal, indifferent to the speed limit, stop signs and signals, as if she had the white Seville tracking after her again, her worst fears for Sara's safety fueled by her imagination.

★ ★ ★ ★ ★

Home.

Instant relief.

Sara was in bed, asleep, the TV crackling to some grotesque-looking trash band making ghoulish noises on MTV.

Lainie adjusted the bedcovers and settled a light kiss on her forehead, causing Sara to stir and swat at the air as if she were attacking a fly.

Lainie backed away softly and into the bathroom, where a few minutes later she was in the tub sponging off the sweat, strain and fears of the day.

She stopped thinking about Flynn, about cracking the twentieth and twenty-first floors, and relaxed over memories of earlier times, settling on the UCLA Stage Arts Awards and the Blanche DuBois-*Streetcar* scene that won her the acting scholarship with Tracy Roberts; her showcases at Tracy's that got her an agent, who scored her a few small television roles, some lines in a Sly Stallone movie, before she decided acting put her life in the hands of others on a daily basis, and that wasn't the kind of life she was after.

She was never one to take "no" for an answer or wait tables waiting for the next audition and the "big break," though that's how she had been day-jobbing lately, minimum plus her share of the tips at Jocko's Joynt, this year's trendy hot spot for industry movers and shakers.

The "big break."

Not for her.

Lainie wanted to be the one who dished out "no" for an answer.

She was determined to become that person.

Music had always been her true passion. She had a nice if not spectacular singing voice. Tracy's classes in music calisthenics helped make it good enough for her to audition and land the occasional second or third lead in budget-deprived stage productions outside L.A., "Ado Annie" in *Oklahoma!*, the grown-up "Baby June" in *Gypsy*, that sort of thing. But it wasn't what caused her shift from acting into the record business.

Lainie owed that to Glenn Stanley, a friend from UCLA who was now lead singer with a grunge band called Snuff Dreams. The band was drifting from one local hole to another, buying its way onto multiple bills and living off the sale of CDs—pressed at their own expense, on their own label, Dead End—after every gig.

They had bumped into each other a few times, and she'd taken him up on his invitation to see the band. She made it to their Hole in the Wall date, decided they were at least as good as the leading hard-rockers, like Guns 'N Roses, and other grunge bands out to revolutionize the sound of music, like No Tall Giants.

Glenn wrote all Snuff Dreams' songs, building them around dark and depressing themes and explosive contemporary social issues. Rants about hypocrisy, child abuse, betrayal and self-destruction. They were controversial, but she felt they were important enough to get heard.

She had asked Glenn why Snuff Dreams seemed to be the best-kept secret on the L.A. club scene. He'd shrugged and said, "No label, no distribution, no promotion, no airplay. You want a hit off this, Slim? It's quite the exceptional weed. Imported all the way in from the San Fernando Valley outback."

"What comes first?" Lainie asked, taking a hit off the proffered joint.

"My guess would be the chicken."

After Glenn came down from his cloud, he told her airplay would make the difference, get them the golden goose, but that would take some minor miracle, like a major rant coming from

MusicBox or *Billboard.*

Lainie did her homework.

The next Monday, the day promotion men pitched their best to *MusicBox*'s review guru, she was there with a copy of Snuff Dreams' album. The reception room was wall-to-wall bodies. They spilled out into the hallway.

The scene was worse than take-a-number, which everyone had to do, but numbers didn't matter. Appointments didn't matter. First calls went to the veteran promo men who had special pull based on something none of the other lesser lights cooling their heels chose to put any other name to.

Pull Lainie didn't have.

Or patience, either.

She hung in for about fifteen minutes, squeezed between two neophytes from loser labels discoursing about the rising price of stepped-on Colombian, before she crossed over and tossed her crumpled number through the reception window.

Three minutes later, Lainie had located a back door into *MusicBox*'s editorial offices.

She wandered a maze of corridors until she found a door with the nameplate she was searching for:

MATT HORNER

THE REVIEW GURU

Without knocking, Lainie turned the knob and stepped inside.

The Review Guru sat facing his wall of sound gear, thumping his palms on his thighs to something that sounded good, but not great.

Metallic.

Riding a music curve already slanted downward.

He wasn't aware of Lainie until she leaned over the desk and knocked on the back of his bald head.

The Review Guru sputtered something unacceptable in any

church of any denomination and spun around, at the same time using the desk to push himself onto his feet. His expression turned from rage into a question mark when he saw who'd come knocking.

"Who the hell are you?"

Lainie smiled pleasantly. "The lady who's come bearing a gift. Your next big hit."

"My next big hit will be in your face if you don't scram," the Review Guru said, already assaulting her with garlic breath.

"You'd hit a lady?"

"My grandmother, she pulled your kind of stunt. Besides, you don't look like no lady to me, so scram, I said."

"I don't have to be a lady, if that's what it takes to get you to listen. If I get on my knees, it won't be to beg you."

"You don't have to tell me."

"The third cut. The band disagrees, but I think it's the revolution."

"I'm counting to one, and then I'm calling security."

"Jesus, Matty, cut the girl some slack and give it a listen. The third cut. Prove her wrong."

Until then Lainie hadn't realized anyone else was in the Review Guru's office.

Over her shoulder, she saw the man half-sitting, half-reclining in a visitors' chair against the back wall, his hands clasped on his stomach, outstretched legs crossed at the ankles. A look of bemusement dancing on his face.

Lainie said, "Listen to the man, Matty. Good advice."

That was her introduction to Eddie Pope.

What Eddie did exactly nobody ever spelled out, only that Eddie was "The Man."

Eddie was "The Man" to see if something needed doing or fixing or made to happen in the record business. The Man, although half a glance told anyone Eddie Pope was still hardly more than a boy. He was Lainie's age, maybe a few years older. An angel's face under a bushel of surfer blond; blue eyes that shone like kliegs but gave away nothing Eddie didn't want you to observe. An athletic body that might work on a soccer field, but was too short for basketball. A commanding voice to go with his commanding presence, except for those times he chose not to be any more obvious than the wallpaper.

Getting Eddie Pope to do your tricks was nowhere near a cheap proposition.

He was expensive. His price, once he quoted it to you, was non-negotiable, a take-it-or-leave-it proposition that the smart people took even when it meant leaving a blank check behind, which it often did.

Better to have Eddie on your side than not at all was frequently heard in radio and record circles, never so loud as to hint at the unspoken codicil, *The Man's connected to the mob.*

The way he dressed, his abundant smooth-as-silk charm when he chose to turn it on, how he dropped a lot of words East Coast-style, it all added credence to the concept.

Make no mistake. Eddie knew what was said about him. It amused Eddie, and he used it. He made it work for him. But he never owned up to any mob connection, not even with Lainie after they got to be as close as they became. That was years down the line, after she found herself in desperate need of somebody to help her save her skin at Blue Pacific Records. It had to be somebody who could pull vital strings she was in no position to pull for herself; a somebody like The Man.

To her surprise, Eddie volunteered for the job.

He showed up unannounced at her office, much as she had invaded the Review Guru's domain years before, and announced himself available. "Let's just say I'm an old dog trying to check out some new tricks and leave it at that?" he answered her question.

"I can't afford you, Eddie."

"What I hear, you can't afford not to. Besides, I say you can. Which office you have in mind for me? The one next to Ira Dent looks about right. I'll need my own private line out. Don't bother with a nameplate on the door. I know who I am."

To this day Lainie remembered calling after him as he headed out, "Who are you, then?"

He leveled her with his cool blue eyes and said, "I'm your D'Artagnan, of course."

It had been a stupid question for her to ask.

She'd known the answer since Day One, when he egged on Matty Horner to play the third cut on Glenn Stanley's Snuff Dreams album.

Matty went for it and threw on the CD; at once swung into the groove, like he was first in line for the second coming; raised his right hand like he was enlisting and declared the album his prime pick for next week.

Lainie raced around the desk and surprised Matty with a hot kiss.

Eddie dodged his as she whooped her way out of the office.

That night she celebrated with Glenn and the band, went on a high that took her past heaven for the first time since she'd gone cold turkey clean and sworn off. She woke up with a head the size of Texas.

The following Saturday, she had a headache to match.

She hit the newsstand early and picked off a *MusicBox* from the stack, rifled the pages until she found The Review Guru's column across from the Hot 100 chart and—

That lying son of a bitch!

His prime pick was some scuzz bucket single from some scuzz bucket album by some scuzz bucket band that couldn't ever begin to match what Glenn and Snuff Dreams delivered.

She knew it in her heart; her soul.

Knew it was true without having to hear the scuzz bucket single. She tossed *MusicBox* into the gutter. Spent the rest of the day holed up in her apartment and got drunk on cheap red. Scrambled between tears and moans over how she would ever be able to face Glenn at Tracy Roberts's next class. Or ever again.

D'Artagnan rode to the rescue.

Somehow Eddie tracked her to Tracy's studio. He was waiting for her outside, blending in with other students who were hunkered down against the wall and blowing whispers of blue cigarette smoke into the evening breeze. He sprang up and grabbed onto Lainie's shoulder as she passed, laid an angelic smile on her.

"I got good news for you," he said. He pointed to a pale green Ferrari parked across the boulevard. "Over there."

Two minutes later he was behind the wheel, studying her as she shifted in the passenger bucket into a comfortable, defensive position. He anchored her with an amused expression and seemed to be trying to burrow beyond her eyes into her mind.

"You're blaming Matty for what didn't happen," he said. "Don't."

"He lied to me when—"

"Everybody lies. That's the truth."

Lainie started to tell him how lousy the scuzz band had to be compared to Snuff Dreams. He cut her off with a gesture. "First commandment of the record business: Don't knock what you don't know. It always comes back to haunt you."

"You heard Snuff Dreams. You saw his reaction. You—"

Eddie Pope reached over and pressed his fingers against her mouth, transforming her complaint into a mumble. "Matty's pick was the single I was up there to see him about. I won, you lost. Like everyone else hoping to score with him last week. Any week I'm up there."

"You bought him, bought the pick, that it?"

"Matty Horner is not for sale. Let's say I already own him and leave it at that."

"You let me leave his office knowing he was putting on a show for me? You could have followed me out. Told me. Saved me the aggravation."

Eddie shook his head. "Wasn't the time or place. I wanted to hit you with good news, not bad news. That needed time. A few days. It's done. Signed, sealed and delivered. Why I'm here tonight."

"I suppose you think I know what you're talking about?"

A new look absorbed Eddie's stare. "The second commandment of the record business: Don't presume what you don't know. Give your mouth a rest, and I'll be happy to share the good news."

She stopped herself from telling him to shove it and sucked up the Ferrari's sweet leather smell. The car was probably two or three years old, but the leather smelled first-day fresh. So did the discreet cologne Eddie was wearing, not so weak it was lost against her Number Five. Chanel was one of the few luxuries Lainie allowed herself.

Eddie turned from her and started talking to the air outside the windshield. "The cut's a winner, so's the band," he said. "I took the album home with me and ran it all. I decided early on, *The girl has got ears, as well as all her other fine attributes.* What it was I couldn't understand, *Why is she looking to give away what anyone in the business knows could be worth a million? You could see she also had brains among all her fine attributes. So, was out of her mind?*"

"Because I'm not in the business. Because I was trying to do a favor for a friend."

As if he hadn't heard her, Eddie said, "Her mouth, maybe a little too big, but even that's a fine attribute for someone selling to people who don't usually want to buy. No, I decided. Not out of her mind. She's not in the business or I would have known her. She was probably trying to do a friend a favor."

"I just told you that."

"I decided then and there she was worthy of me exercising a favor."

"I learned a long time ago where favors come from and where they lead." Her words leaped at him like an unchained tiger. "I don't need a favor from you or from anybody."

"Yes, you do, Lainie Davies, but I wasn't thinking about doing a favor for you. I was thinking about doing a favor for people who don't ever mind owning a favor from me. You get out of my car now and you'll be going back to your past. What I'm here for is to offer you your future."

The phone rang, snapping Lainie out of the past.

Back into the bathtub.

She reached for her cell phone on the drying stool and answered with her name.

Harry Roman responded with his. "Please don't hang up on me," he said. "You need to hear what I have to tell you."

"Haven't you already said all there is to say, none of which I wanted to hear in the first place?"

"I might be wrong about you, Ms. Gardner. Have I ever said that? You actually might be innocent of the—"

Whatever he was saying was lost in the blur of movement as Lainie pulled the cell from her ear and snapped it shut.

CHAPTER 15

The day hardly begun, Thom Newberry was wishing Friday over.

He was desperate to escape from City Hall and a mayor fixated on the damned Lindbergh Beacon, the signal light originally mounted on top of the imposing twenty-eight story building in 1928, in the days before radio and radar communications, as a guide for pilots approaching L.A. Airport.

The Beacon was currently more important to Lawton Welles than anything Thom was doing to bring damage control to a Paradise Sands situation that could totally derail plans the mayor had to run for governor.

The mayor's plans?

Hell.

His plans for converting a Lawton Welles victory into Thom Newberry's own greatest triumph. He was determined not to let anything or anyone stand in the way, not even the mayor, no matter what.

He had waltzed into the mayor's office first thing this morning to give Welles an update on Volkman International. Not the entire story, of course. Only enough to let him appreciate how well the mayor's man was looking after his best interests.

Before Newberry could get a word past *Good morning, Chief,* Welles had popped from his chair waving the phone he'd been cooing into and called across the room, "A fire to put out,

161

Thom. Roaring blaze. It needs your immediate and total attention."

Newberry guessed aloud it had to do with the latest San Fernando Valley campaign to secede from L.A. He and by default the mayor had hedged on taking a strong position on the insurrection, recognizing it might reflect badly on the Welles candidacy and cost him several hundred thousand gubernatorial votes, possibly the election.

"Not that," the mayor said, showing more teeth than intelligence. "I know you have that issue well under control by now." Welles aimed his eyes and chin at the ceiling. "The Lindbergh Beacon, Thom. Some time middle of the night it stopped beaconing, or however you say it. Lots of phone calls already, all telling me how we need to get the Lindbergh Beacon back in working order. Y'know? The symbol of our magnificent city. Y'know? I don't want to alienate any of our fat cats, like this latest call. Gellman. Telling me how he's gotten used to the light guiding him home nights in his Cessna something or other."

"I'll handle it."

"Yes. You're still the best, Thom. They don't make 'em any better than you." He saluted Newberry and, forgetting he was wielding the telephone, bashed himself on the temple.

Back in his office, Newberry instructed Winnie to get the Maintenance and Electrical boys climbing up to the roof of City Hall. That took care of the Lindbergh Beacon in time to make time for a crisis that really might be a crisis—

A collect call out of the blue from Ruby Crandall, on a payphone at Brackens Federal Penitentiary.

Ruby said, "Something's been playing on my mind since the other day, Newberry, so I decided to hear it straight from the horse before I step up on any witness stand and do my thing."

He cut in quickly. "Watch your words, Ruby."

"Why? We being tapped? Taped?"

"Just be cautious," Newberry said. She didn't have to know he automatically taped all his conversations, in case someone said something he could use. In a case like this, however, where the spoken word might come back to haunt him, he was too smart to do a Nixon. He clicked off the recorder.

"What we fucking talked about before?" she said.

"Nothing's changed. Our understanding still stands."

"The D.A. came on up here to see me, who sweetened the honey pot to make sure we're all digging the same ditch? You said it was okay for him to be here, right?"

"Right," Newberry said after a moment, hoping Crandall hadn't heard his grab for air an instant ago or the slight quiver infecting his voice as he guessed, "Harrison Roman, the assistant district attorney."

"Roman. Tight-assed, but a cute one, I was into men."

Jesus K!

How had Roman stumbled onto Ruby Crandall? He'd never mentioned Crandall by name to Roman, never talked in more than general terms and then only about "evidence."

His voice back under control, Newberry said, "A good man, Harrison Roman. First-rate. He'll be working the trial, yes."

Lainie.

He had dropped Crandall's name on Lainie to reinforce the importance of her doing what he told her needed to be done, and—

Lainie and Harry Roman were talking.

That had to be it.

About Ruby Crandall and what else?

Not good, not good at all, but first things first.

"You went over your testimony with Mr. Roman?"

"He said you said so. What I needed to hear first. Why I called in the first place."

"How you were approached to do a special favor for a friend?"

"Yeah. Some fucking favor. And the rest. But nothing before he said he would sponsor me to one of the feds' country clubs, the way you couldn't ever."

Newberry stopped breathing, as if that could keep him from hearing what he knew Ruby Crandall would be telling him next.

She said, "So, Newberry, 'splain to me how come this D.A. Harrison Roman didn't know nothing from nowhere about Eubie Grass?"

He gave himself a moment before answering.

The lies flowed easily.

Crandall hung up sounding satisfied, but the question of how to handle the Eubie Grass situation stayed with Newberry the rest of the day. He hadn't expected Roman to do the kind of digging that would lead him to Crandall or, for that matter, any kind of digging. He should have known better.

He flashed on earlier in the week, catching Bob Nakamura of the *City News Syndicate* and Phil Brown of the *Daily* outside the mayor's suite, whispering about Roy Gardner and Harry Roman. He should have foreseen Roman zeroing in on Lainie. Roman had the kind of aggressive nature that would not allow him to take somebody's word for anything. It was the quality that made him such a good prosecutor and could eventually get him elected district attorney.

The surprise was Lainie volunteering Ruby Crandall's name to the guy who would be trying for a second time to send her to prison. If he'd thought that might happen, he'd have held back mentioning her while engineering Lainie into the Volkman situation.

A lesson learned.

Early evening, Lance was waiting for him, as usual, outside the front entrance to the Friars Club, where he spent four afternoons a week playing hearts in the members-only card room. Lance was laughing at something Jack Carter was saying as Thom glided up to the curb and gave the Mercedes horn a triple-toot.

Lance signaled for another minute and a fraction of a second later broke out a bigger laugh, gave Carter a hug and headed over. He eased cautiously into the passenger seat, leaned over and kissed Thom on the cheek. "Sweetheart, it always does my heart so very, very good to see you," he said.

"No more than mine," Thom said, meaning it.

They no longer lived together, hadn't for years, but their closeness remained.

Lance gave him a certain comfort and feeling of security even greater than the inheritance he knew was coming to him one day, the Holmbly Hills mansion on Sunset, the cars, the stocks and bonds, whatever cash was in however many bank accounts Lance had. Whatever Lance got from their relationship, he'd never expressed. It was one of those secrets locked away wherever actors hide truths they can't bring themselves to share with anyone, the same way they hide their real selves behind costumes and makeup, funny wigs and fake mustaches.

Lance said, "Jack was telling me about this big movie producer talking to a writer and telling him, 'I have been on this job for fifteen years, and in that time I have read thousands of scripts. Maybe six or seven were good. Yours is the best I have ever read so far! The action is nonstop. Every gag works. The characters are beautifully delineated from beginning to end. Their motivations are honest and real. Every act break is organic and does not feel like a false ending for another commercial break on TV. The humor, as good as anything you hope to get from Doc Simon or Larry Gelbart. The story arc is flawless. Flawless! Unfortunately, all we're buying this year is crap.' "

Lance broke into a sustained laugh. He repeated the punch line, *Unfortunately, all we're buying this year is crap,* and reprised the laughter, frowned when Thom didn't laugh hard enough to suit him. He allowed himself a rumbling chuckle before permitting the smile to leave his face and checked out the window as they crawled along Wilshire Boulevard in the stop-and-go traffic.

"Your cheek, boy, you usually do a better job of hiding the bruise," he said. "Rough trade will be the death of you one day, but not too soon, please. The one good funeral oration I ever delivered was in *Bugle Call* for that irascible Johnny Ford. Halfway through it had me shedding more tears than even dear Olive Carey."

Lance's spirits lifted as he launched recollections of the shoot, dropping names like Duke Wayne, Henry Fonda, Ward Bond and Harry Carey, Anna Lee and Maureen O'Hara, and moved on to stories about movies he'd done with Hitchcock and Wyler.

More and more, Thom caught Lance retreating into his past, real and imagined. It often made him wonder if that was the reason he was still around. He had been a significant part of Lance Clifford's past and had come out much the better for it. If not for Lance, he would have crashed and burned—along with hopes for a meaningful career—in the wake of his disastrous affair with Carla.

A great lay, Carla, insatiable in the sack, but Carla lacked the brains and looks to ever be more than what she was, the secretary to the dimwit congressman Lance had set him up to work for following his graduation from UCLA.

Thom had humpety-humped Carla for a couple reasons:

He could close his eyes and believe it was Lainie he was riding the merry-go-round with. Strange as it might appear, he missed Lainie, although he recognized that dumping her at Lance's insistence was the right decision.

More than that, by gaining Carla's trust, he also was able to screw out of her the kind of insider information useful in ac-

cumulating favors that down the line would help seed his political future, by covertly passing it along to other congressmen
and to key members of the press corps.

Exercising his usual charm, Thom quickly had her believing
he was in love with her. He fed her the belief until the backfire,
the night she took him to dinner at the Rotunda; announced
she was carrying his child; and cooed about marriage, a
honeymoon in Paris or on some exotic island, the dream home
with the white picket fence.

Panic-stricken, Thom phoned Lance.

Lance accepted the news with an eternity of silence, then:
"Well, Thomas, we'll have to do something about that, won't
we?" As if the crisis were no more than discovering rats nesting
in the basement. "Leave it to me, dear boy."

When Carla refused the idea of abortion—against her
religion, she'd said, sloughing off Thom's reminder that what
got her knocked up in the first place also was against her
religion—Lance stepped in and made all the wedding arrangements.

He paid for the honeymoon in Paris and threw in London
and Rome stays as his gift.

He brought them back to Los Angeles and bought them the
house Thom still occupied.

He welcomed little Jerry Mouse as if he were the one who'd
given birth.

When it became time to dump Carla, Lance financed the
settlement that kept her close-mouthed on the "dirty little
secrets" she knew. He seemed more reluctant than Thom to let
her take custody of the boy but said, "Nothing is forever,
sweetie," calmly, with none of his usual dramatic flair, eyes
tracking something in the distance that only he could see.

When Carla was murdered, Lance paid for her funeral.

The expensive casket.

The lavish floral tribute from a grieving husband.

After the service, Thom suggested he move with Jerry into the Holmbly Hills mansion. Lance answered with a broad, mock crazy expression, declaring, "Sweetie, it is no place to raise a son or a career."

Thom felt it was an offer he had to make, but he was relieved.

Crawling under the covers with Lance was not enough for him anymore.

Never had been.

He needed privacy, the freedom to explore his darker side without having to sneak off or account for his time. He thought he was doing a good job of it until the night they were returning from a visit to some of Lance's old closet buddies at the Motion Picture Retirement Estates, and Lance commented apropos of nothing:

"Thomas, I won't ever mind what's going on in your life so long as you don't get caught by anyone else."

"Meaning?"

"Come, come. I'm the real actor in this family. Meaning exactly that. Don't do anything to disgrace or embarrass me or Jerry Mouse, and I will be satisfied. Do we understand one another, my dear boy?"

And Lance continued to finance Thom's life, never demanding any form of ownership—no lease, no license, no mortgage.

Their date tonight was for a screening at the Academy, the new one by Scorsese.

Fifteen minutes before the movie ended, Thom's cell phone began massaging his thigh. He waited until they were in the lobby and Lance got caught up in conversation with a gushing anchor from *The Insider* before checking the message screen.

Somebody calling from Kenyon Military Academy.

At this time of night?

His pulse quickened.

Fearing something had happened to Jerry, Thom pressed re-dial and counted the seconds before someone answered and connected him with Commandant Bisenius. Bisenius tried put-ting a smile in his voice, explaining, "We completed our nightly room checks shortly before I thought to call you, sir. Your son, Allen Clifford Newberry—"

"I know his name. What's going on?"

"Cadet Newberry went unaccounted for. We scoured the compound and could not find him. I called you to inquire if, perhaps, you might have taken him home for the weekend and inadvertently neglected to sign him out in the Academy register, sir . . . Mr. Newberry, you there, sir? . . . Mr. Newberry?"

"I'm on my way over."

"Unnecessary, sir. In the time since I phoned, we located Cadet Newberry halfway down the canyon, attempting to hitch a ride. We'll be dealing with him in our usual manner, restrict-ing him to the grounds twenty-four seven and on disciplinary detail; all visiting privileges cancelled for the next two weeks."

"What didn't work the first time he ran away. Or the second. Or the third."

"Boys will be boys, sir, but be assured we'll have whipped them into men before they graduate KMA."

Newberry clicked off. Lance had finished his interview and scribbling a few autographs, and joined him. "You look like death warmed over. Why?"

"Jerry Mouse. He'll be the death of me yet."

CHAPTER 16

Harry Roman was striking out on Eubie Grass.

The search Jimmy Steiger at LAPD had run on the man Ruby Crandall said pulled the trigger on Roy Gardner produced zilch. The name hadn't come up anywhere, Jimmy said, not even on the runs he'd requested from the FBI and Interpol. A big fat zero all around.

Was Grass a figment of Crandall's imagination?

That would also explain why Thom Newberry hadn't mentioned Grass to him, but—

Newberry hadn't mentioned Ruby Crandall to him, either.

He could drop over to City Hall and face Newberry with the question, but his old cop intuition told him to make that a last resort. If Newberry was playing games with him, wiser to play his own game with Newberry, see if they crossed the same finish line together.

Or if not, why not?

Roman wanted Lainie Davies Gardner convicted strictly on truth and enough evidence to support the truth. If it wasn't there on accessory to Murder One, he would still have all those other charges to get her ticketed away to hard time by a jury.

That was the logic that brought Roman to Las Vegas for the weekend, to check out the name with some old well-connected connections who, even after all these years, didn't trust him enough to settle for a phone call. They liked the ex-cop live and in person, with a careful pat-down for a recording device, usually with apologies and a *You know how it goes, old pal.*

The two-bits slots between meetings had been as lousy to him as his contacts and he was down to his last hope: Phil Crenshaw.

Crenshaw was one of those shadow figures with links to all the hotels that still had reputed ties to the old mobs that used to run the desert town. Nobody knew what he did for a living, only that he was never short of a bankroll, a high-end car or a super-sized showgirl falling out of her low-cut gown and too beautiful for Phil, who would never be among the top five-million finalists in *People Magazine*'s annual "Sexiest Man in the World" issue.

Roman had put out the word around town that he was look-ing for him, but Crenshaw was a no-show until late Sunday afternoon at McCarran Airport, about an hour before his return flight to Burbank. Crenshaw slipped onto the stained waiting-area seat alongside Roman and buried his meat-wagon nose in a *USA Today.* "I understand you're looking for somebody?" he said.

Roman said, "Someone you might know, Phil," struggling not to stare at the elegant six-foot-something Egyptian goddess buffing her nails across the waiting area. He bet himself she was Crenshaw's current fling; she had all the trimmings.

"I know lots of people. Yours have a name?" Crenshaw said, like he was talking to the pictures in the sports section.

"One that doesn't work: Eubie Grass."

"Or with me. Anything else?" He looked up from the *USA Today* and aimed his oversized rose-tinted shades at the Egyptian goddess. She gave him a royal nod and went back to her nails.

Roman repeated the physical description Ruby Crandall gave him, coupling it with what was known about Roy Gardner's shooter.

Crenshaw thought about it. Played his palms over his bushy

sideburns. Put a fist to his mouth and filled it with a smoker's hacking cough. His raspy voice carried the same clue.

"Sounds like the fickle finger's on Berry Berryman. What's the story?"

Roman told him, leaving out any reference to Lainie.

"Yeah. Sounds like Berryman," Crenshaw said, his head bobbing agreement.

"You know where I can find him?"

"Yeah."

"Care to share?"

Crenshaw ate some time, making it appear like a tough call and gave the question a *What the hell* noise. "For free, Harry, because I know you won't forget."

"I won't forget, Phil. I never have."

"Last I heard, Berry Berryman was back in L.A., using the name Rudy Schindler."

"Somebody in L.A. who can lead me to Rudy Schindler?"

Crenshaw rose and stretched, dropped the *USA Today* on the seat and chuckled to himself. "Try the information desk at Forest Lawn," he said.

Roman watched Crenshaw fade into the airport crowd before he whipped out his cell and called the cemetery.

A sweet-voiced woman told him that Mr. Schindler had become maggot food in the Mt. Sinai section on Forest Lawn Drive eight months ago, although she didn't put it in quite those terms. It was a shaded plot with an excellent view of the 134 she was explaining as he clicked off wondering, *Now what?*

Roman's pets let him know they weren't happy about him having abandoned them. May Whitty and Joe were slow to greet him at the door and wandered away after sniffing at his pants for clues to where he'd been and with whom, satisfied the time wasn't spent with another dog. The rest of his brood didn't even bother.

Searching out the others, he thought, *So much like humans, my pooches. Possessive and jealous, no matter how true or deep the underlying love. Protective and loyal to a fault. They'll always let you know what they're thinking—no lies in the way they look at you; no deception in the way they wag their tails. Is it any wonder I prefer them to humans?*

The pooches were in their usual parking places in the house or in the back yard, asleep and indifferent to his approach. They knew his scent and that was enough. He gave them all a chunk of friendly stroking and assurance that Daddy loved and had missed them, winning some friendly stirs and purrs before heading for the kitchen.

The bowls of food had barely been touched. He freshened them along with their water bowls. Rescued a Dos Equis from the fridge. Popped the lid and was taking a hearty swallow as he settled at the kitchen table when he heard nails clicking on the linoleum. The newest member of the family, his fox terrier, Michael J., had trailed after him.

Michael J. attacked his food bowl before heading over to Harry. Harry lifted Michael J. onto his lap and stroked and talked to him, as if the terrier were a person, bringing Michael J. up to date. He held nothing back, thrilled to have a friendly ear to share the major frustration that set in after he learned Rudy Schindler was dead.

Roman said, "I'm back in the hands of Newberry on that one, pooch, unless you have a better idea?" Michael J. eased onto his back in full surrender to Harry's coddling. "And if that's not bad enough, he stonewalled on the indictments. No chance with the grand jury until he says so, the way it's playing out . . . Why would Newberry get me back onto the Lainie Davies Gardner case, get me all hot and bothered, but hold back on information that'd let me move forward with her prosecution?" Michael J.'s eyes half opened, sending Harry a message of doggie satisfaction, not an answer to the question. "So I'm on my own with that one, am I, pooch?"

Harry worked over the puzzle and the Dos Equis for ten or fifteen minutes. The look on his face gradually regrouped around a smile. "Michael J., let you in on a secret? Your old man is a little slow and dense sometimes, but—he ain't stupid. Newberry's been playing me. This isn't about Lainie Davies Gardner or the old indictments or Roy Gardner's murder. It's to cover up something else that's going down. Me around to make it look legit. Misdirection by the mayor's man. The mayor's magician. Hocus-pocus stuff."

Roman eased Michael J. off his lap and back onto the floor. He rose and padded across to the fridge for a fresh beer, gently rubbing at the arthritic pain torturing his sloping right shoulder.

The fox terrier sniffed out an acceptable spot on the linoleum and rounded his tail a few times before settling down.

"Where it's at, Michael J., where it's at?" Harry said. He toasted the fox terrier with the Dos Equis. "Somewhere else is where it's at. Your daddy intends to find out where." He took a swallow. "I think, first off, Daddy tests the theory with another run at the lady in question, Mrs. Lainie Davies Gardner herself."

Karma came into play during the week.

Newberry got him on the phone, all good cheer, small-talking the weather and the state of Harry's health, making it sound like he really cared. Harry went along, answering in kind before neither had anywhere left to go but the reason for the call.

Newberry jumped out of the pregnant pause first. "I owe you certain information to make your case against Lainie Davies Gardner. I want you to know I'm close to delivering."

Harry muzzled his surprise. "The fraud issues or the murder?"

"Both. How's your Saturday night week after next?"

"You tell me."

"Lainie Gardner's tossing a party at the Marina for some new record company of hers. I think you'll find it worth your while to be there."

"Why's that?"

"I took the liberty of putting your name on the guest list," Newberry said. "I'll see you there, and you can learn for yourself. Here's my secretary to fill you in on the details."

Afterward, Harry debated whether he should have pressed Newberry about Ruby Crandall and the late Rudy Schindler, but the timing had felt wrong. He moved on to wondering what this Perfect Records business was about, how this singer Miranda Morgan fit in the picture. *Patience,* he ordered himself. *Patience, Harry.* He added the party date to his calendar.

CHAPTER 17

Lainie had no time to spare against the four-week deadline imposed by Thom Newberry. She was already two days into the third week when she met Flynn for breakfast at a coffee shop east of the Third Street Promenade on Olympic Boulevard, far enough removed from Marina del Rey to reduce the risk of being spotted by anyone from Volkman International.

She arrived a half hour early, pulled into the parking lot behind the shop and guided her Toyota to a vertical slot at the far end. The lot was large enough to hold a hundred or more cars. In spite of the hour, it was already three-quarters full. Excellent. A crowd was the best place to be when it came to hiding in plain sight.

Passing inside the shop, she was embraced by the overpowering smells of breakfast. Lots of fried eggs and toast. Bacon, sausage and hash browns on the griddle. The invigorating aroma of freshly brewed coffee mingling with the murmur of undecipherable conversations.

She did a quick survey. No one she recognized at any of the tired green and red plastic-covered booths in the forward section. The signpost on the floor said: *Please Seat Yourself.* She headed to the rear, checking faces left and right.

An elderly couple was moving out of a corner booth. The woman, using the table for leverage, made it to the aisle first and unfolded her walker. Her less-agile husband struggled to spring himself from the bench seat but couldn't navigate the space. His body began trembling.

Lainie hurried over to help him up. Assisted a waitress with the old man's wheelchair. Watched the three of them head up front while a busboy cleaned the table and set it for two. Sat down facing the entrance.

After several minutes, the busboy returned to pour her a cup of coffee.

Flynn said, "Make that two. Mine straight black will do just fine, my good man."

He slid into the booth across from Lainie.

The busboy filled their cups and retreated.

Lainie said, "I didn't see you come in, Flynn."

"You were busy being an angel of mercy, good lady. The good Lord will certainly bless and keep you comes that time." He reached for the menu.

When the waitress arrived, Lainie ordered half a grapefruit, two eggs easy over, hash browns, a toasted bagel.

The waitress said, "The number six, honey. You only had to say you wanted the number six to make my life easier."

Flynn smiled and said, "The number zero for me." The waitress threw him a questioning look. He said, "In other words, I'm up for nothing just now, you darling creature. Coffee'll do me just fine."

The waitress frowned and left.

Flynn sent her a wave before he drew a small brown bag from a coat pocket.

He unscrewed the protruding cap and in a moment was pouring a thick brown liquid into his coffee cup.

"A little hair of the dog to help me past last night's revelries," he said. He toasted Lainie. Blew on the cup before taking a cautious sip. Smacked his lips, smiled approvingly and repeated the process. "So, good lady, who goes first with our devil of a scheme?"

Lainie started, cautiously adding a layer to what Flynn already knew, pausing only when the waitress returned with her order. "My part's handled," she said. "My Three Musketeers have been working overtime on the Miranda Morgan launch. Three hundred RSVPs so far. The key trades and consumer press accounted for. Indie distributors and rack jobbers. Honchos from the major chains. Every retailer, every radio station that reports to *Billboard, MusicBox* and *Radio & Records.* Almost a hundred names on the want list are from out-of-state. They're coming as our guests, all bought and paid for. First-class air. Suites at the Peninsula. The whole *schmear.*

"Stan, Cubie and Ira, this is their thing. There's been nothing like it in years. Ira got Jay Leno to introduce Miranda. She'll be doing his show the next night, backed again by a band only a Benny Sugar could assemble on short notice—Hal Blaine, the Rock Hall of Fame drummer, and other players from the old Gold Star Wrecking Crew. More TV appearances are already in place for her. Miranda will break out as a star before she sings her first note."

She paused for a bite of her bagel while she gauged Flynn's reaction.

"If you're happy, I'm happy," he said, sipping from his coffee cup. "I have my crew lined up, too, mate. We're shooting in digital, like Lucas did for the last *Star Wars.* Stanley Dorfman is my director, and he'll also do post on your Miranda's first single or any full concert you peddle to VH-1 or somewhere. He's top of the heap, our Stanley, going all the way back to John Lennon and before." He took another sip.

"History I'm aware of, Flynn, but it's not what I want to hear from you this morning. If you couldn't make it happen, what I need from you, tell me now, Flynn. You don't have to break it gently."

"Couldn't make it happen?" Irritation flashed over Flynn's

face. He reared back, cocked his head, spoke slowly and deliberately. "My history with Three Squadron, with SAS, should've been enough to inform you otherwise, Missus High and Mighty. Not to mention my saying for a fact how I'd get the job done for you. For a bloody fact." His coffee cup was empty. He took his next swallow straight from the brown bag. Swiped at his lips. "All I'm down for, it's either done or will be before your high-falootin' muckey-muck guests are arriving at Volkman International. You have to hear more than that?"

"Humor me," Lainie said.

Flynn made her wait a minute or two, like it was some form of punishment.

"I got a copy of the original plans and blueprints from the Building and Safety Department downtown," he said. "Nothing special about twenty and twenty-one was called for. No variances asked for before the building went up, none or any improvements since the building inspector's original sign-off, except on the twenty-second, for Volkman's private gymnasium and sauna. So, all we know going in, there was raw space."

"The elevators?"

"What we already knew without the plans. I talked to the company what installed them, passing myself off as the new maintenance super. We can bypass the security locks easy enough, not so easy the security cameras. The picture feed goes straight to the monitors twenty-four hours a day. We'd be seen and as cooked as a Christmas goose before we set a foot on either floor."

"Back doors?"

"No surprises there. Like all the other floors, part of the same path up and down from the basement. The fire department would never have it any other way."

"And we can use them to crack the two floors?"

"I'm not so sure as you're sounding. I came across nothing

to tell me one way or the other if the back sides of the doors aren't rigged to keep out trespassers. Nothing saying those doors aren't extra strength or fixed with special alarms or under security cameras. They could prove a more tricky risk than the elevators."

"What I hear you telling me is—"

"We can't get there from here," Flynn said.

He seemed to enjoy watching her face drop. He took another swallow from the brown bag and cracked a gleeful smile. "It may be what you hear, good lady, but not by any stretch what I'm telling you. I'll be giving you your heart's desire comes the night of your party. Tell me what floor you want to begin with, twenty or twenty-one, I'll have us there quick as a wink."

"How, then?"

He told her.

"Flynn, I can't afford for this to go wrong."

"Understood loud and clear, and something else: You're yet to fess up about what it is Newberry wants you searching for up there."

"I have. I told you. I don't know."

"And I'm supposed to believe that?"

"Yes."

"We're risking arrest or worse in order for you to go on a treasure hunt not even knowing the treasure you're hunting for? Not even a needle in a haystack?"

"Not even the haystack."

"Tell me, then: Why go and take the risk, mate? What do you have to gain?"

"My life back, Flynn. That's all. Only my life."

Her answer set off a curious mix of confusion and compassion in Flynn's eyes. He raised his brown bag saying, "Here's to we." With that, he slid from the booth, dug a roll of bills from a pocket, peeled off five singles and set them on the table, using the coffee cup as a paperweight. "Should cover my share and the tip, mate. I'll have me a fast pee and be on my way."

Lainie watched Flynn head up the aisle and follow the sign to the restrooms. She got the waitress's attention, motioned for the check. Waiting, her mind played with her mixed feelings about Flynn, wanting to trust him more than she did, but—

But *what,* she wondered.

Maybe the drinking?

She'd known enough alcoholics in her life to know they were capable of creating more problems than only behind the wheel of a car, like the bastard drunk driver who had killed her mommy and daddy, rest their souls, and almost killed her.

Yes. Maybe the drinking.

That concept crashed and burned several minutes later.

Waiting for the slow-as-evolution overweight man behind the cash register to run her credit card, staring out the window onto Olympic, she was surprised to see Flynn on the street corner across the boulevard, engaged in animated conversation with a woman.

The woman's back was to her, but there was something familiar about her.

Lainie's first thought was Gracie, Flynn's waitress-girlfriend from Pat Madden's.

She was wrong.

When the woman turned and hurried away after taking a hug and a kiss from Flynn, she saw it was Petra Barish, Lenny Volkman's secretary.

Lainie phoned Thom Newberry from the car.

His secretary said, "Mr. Newberry has been wanting to speak with you, Mrs. Gardner, but it's a personal matter presently has his complete undivided attention."

Newberry's callback came after she'd been at the office for

an hour. By then she'd brought Lenny Volkman up to speed on the status of the Miranda Morgan launch and half-listened while he growled through his now-routine complaint about her spending habits.

Flynn materialized in the doorway and threw her a wave, as if he were seeing her for the first time this morning.

She skimmed some memos from her Three Musketeers.

She got Cubie Wallace on the line to tell him it was cool to bring in six more station managers and program directors.

"Big-timers under thirty, saying it's no to me until our buzz started buzzing," Cubie said. "Twelve bodies total counting their spouses or playmates."

"Just do it, Cubie. Any others who fit the profile we need. Tell Stan same thing goes for him."

Her tone darkened the minute she heard Newberry's voice eschewing any greeting and demanding in her ear, like thunder racing down the mountain, "Where do we stand?"

"I can have whatever you want after the weekend. What am I looking for?"

"Saturday. I'll tell you Saturday, when I see you."

"See me?"

"The party you're putting on down there for this singer of yours. What's it? You sound surprised that I know about the party? That when it's happening, Lainie? Saturday, during the party?"

"You know about the party?" Wondering who'd told him. The hype. So strong, it had carried downtown to City Hall?

"I'm bringing the mayor's proclamation with me—'Miranda Morgan Day' in the City of Los Angeles. The mayor has a prior engagement or he'd be coming himself, pressing the flesh, flashing the smile and doing the presentation for the cameras, not me."

Ira Dent. Of course. That's how Newberry found out about

the party. Ira was always one for inviting a government biggie to proclaim a day or a week for one of the acts. Even got a day from the President of the United States once for the Statues of Liberty.

"You haven't answered my question yet," Newberry said. "Saturday during the party, is that it, Lainie? Is that what you're planning, my little girl?"

When she arrived at Benny Sugar's Starshine Studios, Benny himself was playing the sound board as Miranda Morgan and her backup band of all-star players rehearsed in Benny's largest and best space, working out every aspect of their make-or-break showcase Saturday at Volkman International. The plan called for her set to run twenty minutes, Miranda doing only original songs from her debut album, closing with the breakout single, "Scarlet Woman."

Lainie, watching the rehearsal from a back corner, had been firm about "originals only" when she and the musketeers first sat down with Miranda to plot the show. History had taught her that using cover material from an album, however great in the grooves, leads an audience to make comparisons with the original artists. "Miranda Morgan must defy comparisons; we're not going to do anything to feed it," she told them. "She's one of a kind, and that's the only way we're going to treat her."

Heads had nodded around the table.

Ira Dent quickly aimed an index finger at Miranda and quipped out of *Forty-Second Street,* "We're sending you out a youngster, Miranda, but you have to come back a star." Tap-danced his nails on the conference table to the wave of laughter.

Miranda applauded Lainie and gave everyone a look that said Miranda Morgan already owned the world.

Lainie had loved her show of confidence, but now, sitting in the rehearsal hall, she was uncomfortable with what she observed on the makeshift stage. Unquestionably, Miranda's voice was in gear, but she was something of a dancing klutz.

Not *something*.

A klutz of the first magnitude.

Everybody else there looked to be suppressing the same thought. The band members. Stage and film production crew members. Stanley Dorfman, trying to mask his apprehension while jotting down notes in a slim pad on the camera angles he had in mind. Billy Carlton, the Tony-winning choreographer Lainie had brought in from New York to work with Miranda, at a flat twenty-five grand for two weeks.

Billy was tracking Miranda from the foot of the stage like a Texas twister, gunning her directions while at the same time keeping a cigarette parked in the corner of his mouth. "Take five, everyone," he called and sped over to Lainie. He parked in front of her with his hands on her shoulders, his deeply ridged forehead pressed against hers. He said, "The look on your face says you're seeing disaster in the making. Me, too, but that's today. When we get to Saturday, all will be well with the world."

"Why am I having a hard time believing you, Billy?"

"Probably because you're here," he said, and soft-shoed away from her squealing with laughter. Back at the stage, he made a megaphone of his hands and called, "All's well that ends well, Lainie." He gave her two thumbs up and spun around to Miranda, who was reworking her hair into braids on top of her head. "All right, my darling. This time we're going to concentrate on your two *right* feet." He leaped onto the stage and pirouetted to Miranda. Began pushing her around like a puppet master trying to give life to Pinocchio.

Lainie caught herself wishing she cared as much as Billy did about how well Miranda performed on Saturday night. She cared. She didn't wish failure on Miranda any more than she wanted to deceive her musketeers more than she already had.

But that was not what Saturday night was about.

Saturday night was about the twentieth and twenty-first floors of Volkman International.

Lainie became aware somebody had moved a folding chair next to hers and was settling into it. Her heart began palpitating out of control. Without turning to confirm a cologne smell she knew as well as she knew her own skin, she said, "I would have thought by now you could afford something better."

Eddie Pope laughed and said, "I was in the neighborhood and didn't think you'd mind me dropping in, Slim."

"All for one and one for all, my D'Artagnan."

"Tell me something I don't already know," he said.

Chapter 18

Saturday night at the main entrance to Volkman Plaza, giant kliegs roamed the star-filled sky and stretch limos pulled up one after the other, dropping off passengers at a golden archway. It was the starting point for a fifty-yard stroll on plush crimson carpeting, scrutinized by the two or three hundred people behind red velvet security ropes who had been drawn by curiosity and a warm breeze to the Marina usually a ghost town on weekends. The media vans were double-parked out front, and news crews jockeyed with their mics and cameras whenever a new limo arrived.

Pink- and red-colored banners hung from the arch and all the flagpoles that formed a ring at the core of the plaza. They pictured the unfamiliar face of an attractive young woman exuding sex like some film vamp from the twenties or thirties, a Theda Bara, Clara Bow or Jean Harlow.

Under her photo were the words:

Miranda Morgan. Scarlet Woman. A Legend Is Born.

By eight o'clock, Volkman Plaza lacked breathing room.

It was overcrowded with guests waiting patiently in a series of long, snaking lines that fed into security check points outside the single entrance to the canvas circus tent that had been installed in the middle of the plaza.

A dozen plainclothes officers from the private security firm hired for the night by Perfect Records mingled with the guests.

They were armed for any emergency, as were six other officers posted by the row of trailers immediately behind the tent.

The biggest trailer was Miranda's.

The others were for her band and backstage personnel.

Inside the circus tent, behind the rows of folding chairs set up theater style in front of the visible stage, guests were greedily attacking rows of buffet tables stocked with exotic foods. Bar stations were pouring high-end champagnes and call liquors.

Lainie luxuriated in the sights, sounds and smells of impending success heading away from Miranda's trailer, where she had just delivered a *go-out-and-get-'em-sister* inspirational message to her nervous artist.

Miranda's forehead and underarms had been waterfalls of sweat. Lainie saw this as an excellent sign. It meant the artist cared enough to come out swinging like an Oscar de la Hoya, aiming to score big, a knockout, with the first punch. She only wished she had more confidence in Miranda's abilities on stage. Billy Carlton had wrung a lot of improvement out of her, but she still wasn't a Tina or a Janis, anywhere near.

Lainie also wished she had more confidence in herself, in what she was about to attempt in the Volkman International building, where a second celebration was underway. This one was for guests who had received special engraved invitations to an ultra-exclusive reception hosted by Leonard Volkman in his penthouse suite.

Security procedures were not as rigid at the building.

It would work to her advantage later.

She hoped.

This party was for Volkman's family of investors, many of whom had flown in for the event from Las Vegas, Detroit, New York, Chicago, and as far away as London, Rome, Paris, Tokyo and Hong Kong, as well as potential investors and the heaviest of heavies on the Perfect Records list.

It had been Lainie's idea.

Volkman resisted at first, but she wouldn't quit suggesting it was good for his business, good for his image. He shrugged and said, "What the hell. What's another hundredG, the way you're already pissing away my money anymore?"

Once past the lobby entrance metal detectors, the special guests were escorted to one of four elevators that whisked them direct to the twenty-second floor. A fifth elevator was reserved for guests being given special attention by Volkman's secretary, Petra Barish, who knew most by name and personally escorted them upstairs.

Thom Newberry, the Marina's City Council and Board of Supervisors members, and the Assemblyman and State Senator who had flown in from Sacramento were on the list to be given her deluxe treatment.

The record industry people on the Perfect Records list, including Eddie Pope, were in the former category, as were Lainie's musketeers and Lainie herself.

The moment she stepped from the elevator, Lainie began navigating through the crowd, pausing for brief handshakes and hugs, cranking her head left and right on the lookout for Eddie. She spotted him across the lobby, assailed by industry people who rarely if ever were able to get this close to the head of Chorale Records.

Eddie was making like everyone's oldest and best friend, in the usual Eddie Pope manner.

His expression registered relief when he saw her.

He excused himself and moved in her direction.

They met in the middle of the room and exchanged quiet eye contact before she took his hand and guided him to the floor-to-ceiling double doors to Leonard Volkman's office.

They passed through and into another solid block of bodies.

An animated Volkman was holding court in front of the

picture window, currently little more than a black curtain of glass assailed by slow-moving swipes of klieg light.

Lainie recognized all of the half dozen people in his circle. At one time or another they had fit into the various schemes perpetrated by one of Volkman's dummy corporations. They'd gotten away clean, unlike Roy, when Volkman conveniently forgot to mention *their* names in his deposition to the district attorney. In her mind ever since, they were as guilty as Lenny Volkman for Roy's death. They made room for Lainie and Eddie to join them, spent some insincere smiles and meaningless chitchat before drifting away.

Volkman said, "I was glad when Lainie told me you were coming, Eddie. Been a long time."

"Years."

"The Blue Pacific days, that right, Lainesky?" He bit down on his giant unlit Havana and waited for her acknowledgment. "I remember thinking you were a guy going places, but nowhere near the *macher* you became, grabbing the brass ring with Chorale Records. Brass? Shit. Gold."

"Platinum . . . I'm flattered to hear you keep that kind of track, Mr. Volkman."

"No, you're not. He's not, Lainesky." He made a throw-away gesture. "What I remember the most about you, Eddie, is how Lainesky always credited you with her climb to the top at Blue Pacific Records. It was what? Some stunt she pulled over at *MusicBox* got your attention?"

"I was impressed enough to get her a gig at *Billboard,* yeah, and a deal for the band she was pushing, Snuff Dreams. She did all the rest herself, up until you and your people took over the label and you tried to shit-can her."

Lainie said, "Eddie, please, that's history."

Volkman shot Eddie Pope a *Who me?* look and tick-tocked his head. "Was the money boys did it. We were scaling the company for a fast turnover. They didn't like the idea it would be a girl leading the charge. It was out of my hands until I got that call from friends of yours."

"Just one."

"But the right one . . . With friends like that . . ." Their eyes commingled understanding. "So later, when Lainesky finally split Blue Pacific, she was the one who made the decision. Right, Lainesky?"

"With Roy and for Roy, Lenny. Please. Can we talk about something else?"

"Right. Christ, did Roy fall head over heels for you. So hard he couldn't concentrate on working our numbers half the time you were around. All the time . . . So tell me, Eddie. Your one friend, he helped you catch the gold at Chorale?"

"Lenny, enough," Lainie said. "Please."

She didn't like the grim turn Eddie's face was taking.

Eddie said, "My friend was killed not long after the business with Lainie at Blue Pacific Records, Mr. Volkman. Otherwise, you might have gotten a call from him about the time you were talking to the D.A."

"I suppose," Volkman said, like he wasn't supposing at all. He turned away from them to return the wave of an overdressed, jewelry-dripping couple that had called his name.

Lainie glanced at her wristwatch.

Almost time for Flynn's plan to swing into motion.

Volkman said, "So, you're here tonight for old times' sake, that what, Eddie? That it?"

"Actually, scuttlebutt, Mr. Volkman. From what I heard on the street, Lainie is back in business with an artist who has the same potential for greatness she caught with Snuff Dreams. Everybody still talks about how high and how fast she got that band to the top of the mountain."

"The same as the hype she feeds me about Miranda Morgan

every time she needs to dig deeper into my pockets."

"If Miranda is half what I hear, I might be interested in buying up her contract from you and bringing her over to Chorale. She would have a better shot with us than with the indie you're using, as good as they are. You be up for that?"

Volkman searched Lainie for an answer.

She showed him nothing, busy thinking, *Come on, come on, Flynn. Keep to the schedule.*

Volkman said, "Everything and everybody's got a price, Eddie."

"Maybe think about yours, Mr. Volkman." Eddie flashed him a weak smile and excused himself, telling Lainie, "I'm heading that way to say hello to Nat Walpow, Slim. Catch up with you after the show."

Seconds later, as if Eddie had never existed, Volkman said, "So, Lainesky, where is that little girl of yours and Roy's? You said something about bringing her tonight?"

"Sara's back at the tent, Lenny. My guys Stan and Cubie are goal-tending her. She wanted to meet the band. You know how kids can be?"

"Yeah. Exactly. Married a couple in my time."

While Lenny enjoyed his joke, Lainie checked her watch. *Come on, come on, Flynn.* She said, "In fact, I should get back there. We're closing in on show time."

One of the guards who'd been working lobby security appeared from nowhere, banging into Lainie without bothering to excuse himself while angling for Volkman's attention. His eyes were tiny pinwheels of anxiety. He drew closer, connected his hand to Volkman's ear and began whispering breathlessly.

Volkman's mouth opened in seeming disbelief.

He lost his cigar to the floor.

His face turned ghostly white.

His eyes bulged and recklessly zigzagged the office.

Lainie didn't need to be told to know what Volkman had just heard.

Flynn's plan was in motion.

The guard had reported a bomb scare to Volkman, telling him someone phoned to say a bomb planted in the building would go off in thirty minutes.

Two days ago at the coffee shop, Flynn had set his hand over his heart and said, *"Believe me sincerely on this one, mate. A bomb threat's the finest excuse and the fastest way in the world to empty out a building fast, like a hundred meter dash at the Olympics. In the panic to evacuate, you'll slip away and safely do your search and rescue."*

"How do I get onto the floors, Flynn? You haven't told me that part."

"Or you telling me what you're going after for Newberry, good lady."

"I still don't know. When I told Newberry it would happen on Saturday night, all he said was, 'See what you see and let me know after the stage show you're planning.' "

Her explanation seemed to satisfy Flynn but didn't break their standoff.

"All in good time," he said. *"When the call is made and the panic begins, I want you to go along with whatever happens next."*

Lainie gave Volkman a few more moments of solitary dread before asking with a show of concern, "Is there a problem, Lenny?"

Volkman stared vacantly at her.

Blue veins were throbbing at his temples.

His mind appeared to be spinning in overdrive.

The guard stepped in closer and said quietly, "I just passed him word from over to the tent, Missus Gardner. It seems somebody just got himself shot over there. The gunman might still be running loose, hiding somewhere, so no one's supposed to leave here until further word."

Lainie's face contorted in panic. She opened her mouth. No sound came out until: "Sara. I have to go find—get to Sara. I have to make sure she's all right."

Lainie pivoted and pushed her way through the crowd to the bank of elevators.

She hammered on the *Down* button, bouncing from foot to foot, demanding at the digital floor monitor, "Move, dammit. Move, move, move."

Volkman's voice boomed out behind her, begging for attention.

Lainie looked over her shoulder. Volkman had moved to his desk and was speaking into a cordless mic positioned there earlier, for when it was time for him to thank his guests and send them on their way downstairs to the tent. His voice wasn't entirely composed. His snow-capped smile, even at this distance, was unrealistically wide. It seemed to split his face in half.

He said, "I have been informed our show will be starting late this evening. That old saw about technical difficulties beyond our control. It shouldn't be too long, so please party on while I bring up a hundred or two hundred of my other nearest and dearest friends to tell the rest of you how wonderful I am."

One of Volkman's security people stepped to Lainie and said, apologetically, "Sorry, but the elevators are shut down, Miss Gardner. Orders from the police, in order to keep everybody up here and safe for the duration."

"My daughter's in that tent, Jack. Not you or anyone's going to stop me from going to her. Get the power turned back on. Do it now."

Jack exhaled a heavy sigh and turned up his palms. "The control panel is on the basement level, Miss Davies. To do that I'd need to go down in the elevator." He thought over what he said and blushed.

Petra Barish materialized at the guard's side. Lainie gave her a look of desperation while the guard explained the problem.

Petra made a show of enjoying Lainie's distress and told the guard, "I'll take care of this, Jack." The guard saluted her with two fingers to his forehead and moved off. "This way," Petra said.

Lainie followed her across the reception room to a side door that was marked: *No Exit.*

Petra unclipped a ring of keys from a belt loop, found the one she wanted, and used it to unlock the door. "It takes you to where you want to go," Petra said. "Go now."

She pushed open the door. Lainie slipped through. The door clicked shut behind her and a key turned in the lock. Before she could acclimate to the darkness of the chilly stairwell, a burst of light blinded her. She slapped her hands over her eyes for protection.

Flynn said, "Double-checking it's you, mate. You ready for our glorious adventure?"

"My daughter, Flynn. I've got to get to my daughter. I've got to get to Sara."

"Ease up on the panic," he said, aiming the Mag-Lite at a wall. The beam bounced back to catch them in an eerie illumination. "Sara is fine, and all's right with the world. I had my man make it a shooting down below instead of a bomb scare over here."

Lainie settled against the door and threw him an evil look. She caught her breath. "You could have let me in on the secret instead of scaring me half to death."

"Only half?" A shrug. "I'll do better next time, I promise." An impish grin.

She had an urge to slap his face.

If Flynn noticed, he didn't let on.

He said, "Actually, it came about over a change of mind too

late to tell you. I realized there'd be far too much panic with a bomb scare and the picture of buildings going boom and down and people caught to death. Could shut down everything longer than the time you crave, the twenty or thirty minutes. Do us a whole lot more harm than good."

"You were positive we needed crowd confusion here in the building, not the tent, as a safety net breaking in and out of the twentieth and twenty-first floors."

"That was before I had this."

Flynn fished something from his pocket and offered it to her.

It was an oddly shaped key, the kind watchmen use clocking in at checkpoints.

"Like a magic wand," he said. "Opens a door and shuts down the security system on the floor—sound alarm and spy cameras the same time—everywhere in the building you want to be. You get to the door, you punch it into the red hole just above the handle. Give it a full twist and wait for a click, then inside you go."

Flynn uncorked a winner's smile and flashed her a thumbs-up. "We had something was similar, I was seeing service with SAS, only, like me, a whole lot less sophisticated."

Lainie looked the key over. "Where'd you get this, Flynn?" Certain she knew the answer before she had finished the question. "Petra Barish, right? She gave it to you."

For a moment Flynn looked like he wasn't going to answer. "More like I gave it to her, mate." He pumped his fist. "Let's just say it was my sacrificial indiscretion made on your behalf, after which I borrowed it from the bird's nest."

"How do you know Petra didn't run straight to Volkman when she realized the key was missing and tell him you stole it? You must know they're lovers."

"Know it? I counted on it. That so, about her running, we wouldn't be on this side of the door right now. Volkman, he would've demanded to know how I come to be in any position to snatch the key from her. Petra's far too smart to kick her goose that also lays the golden eggs." He danced his eyebrows. "You plan to stand here chatting the night away?"

Lainie recognized Flynn was right.

Even with the unexpected luxury of more time, there was a limit to how long she'd have to check out the two floors. Once the crank call was exposed, Miranda's performance would be back on track. The people in the building would head for the tent. Volkman would expect to find her there, given how she'd raced off panic-stricken to make sure Sara was safe. Twenty minutes, thirty max. Keep it to that, she decided. "Let's get this show on the road," she said.

Flynn handed over the Mag-Lite. "I'll be waiting here when you get done."

"I thought you wanted inside those rooms with me."

"Better I'm where I can handle the odd emergency. You got your cell phone with you?"

"Of course."

"Keep it on. And me mine. A problem either end, get right to it."

"What kind of odd emergency, Flynn?"

"Mate, I knew that, I'd have it out of the way by now."

Lainie took the stairwell down one cautious step at a time, preceded by the sharp light of the Mag. She used her shoulder against the wall for balance, treading lightly to dim the sound of her heels on the metal to a soft echo. She hit the twenty-first floor landing undecided whether to start there or on the floor below.

Twenty-one kept her nearer to the party crowd, if something went wrong and she had to hurry back and lose herself.

The twentieth put her a floor closer to ground level, giving her a minute or two advantage if she ran late checking for whatever she was checking for.

"Silly, stupid reasoning either way," she mumbled under her breath. "Thom Newberry's game, refusing to say what it is. That's his own stupidity. All it does is prolong the time I'll have to spend on either floor." Lainie ordered herself to cut it out. Now. This second. She was over-thinking the situation. Letting the anxiety and the tension get to her.

She flipped an imaginary coin.

It landed on its edge.

She cursed her imagination and flipped the coin again.

Tails.

That made it the twentieth floor.

When she reached the landing on twenty, she heard what sounded like footsteps bouncing around the stairwell. She couldn't tell if they were above or below her. Flynn, maybe, but Lainie couldn't be certain. She thought better than to whisper after him.

She doused the Mag, removed her shoes and quickly stepped over to the steel door. She found the door handle and the hole Flynn had instructed her about. She went after the round key, which she had placed in the small security pocket of her tuxedo slacks.

She missed the keyhole.

She poked around in the dark as the sound of footsteps grew louder, certain now someone was heading up the stairwell.

Her poking became more anxious.

No, maybe down.

Heading down the stairwell.

Lainie stowed the Mag between her thighs and urgently felt around the door with both hands. She located the hole again, but in her hurry to insert the key lost her hold on it. The key hit the floor with a metallic ding. She moved to retrieve it. The

Mag slipped loose, fell and made a large clanging sound on the landing, then a rolling noise.

The footsteps stopped.

So did Lainie's breathing.

She closed her eyes and counted off a silent ten.

She counted to ten again.

She eased onto her knees and felt around in the dark, blindly patting the cold metal until her palm came down hard on the key. She felt around more and located the Mag. She scrambled onto her feet and over to the door.

Listened for footsteps.

Got silence in return.

She moved the Mag within inches of the door and chanced the light. Found the red-rimmed hole. Got the key inserted. Turned it a full twist. Heard the click Flynn told her to expect.

She pressed the door handle down and pushed hard.

The heavy steel door rolled aside. When the opening was wide enough, she jumped inside, wheeled around and pushed the door shut. At once she heard the click again. This time the door had relocked itself.

The room was silent, cold and pitch black.

While she recaptured her composure, she thought about the Mag.

Safe to turn it on?

Lainie knew she couldn't go stumbling around in the dark. She threw the beam forward, almost ceiling high. It hit a bare wall and bounced back at her. The walls on either side also were bare. She stepped forward, turned around and aimed the Mag at the back wall. Only the door she had entered through; on it, a blinking green light that had no meaning for her. She knew she had offed the video cameras and the sound alarm when she turned the key. Maybe it was an indicator that the door lock was operational again. As good a guess as any.

She scanned the back wall for a light switch, thinking, *In for a penny, in for a pound.* Thinking, *Who ever said that to me first? That lead singer with the first Brit band I ever took on the road, what's his name?* She had slept with him, she remembered. All they wound up doing, sleeping together, whatever his name too far gone on his free-basing to rise to the occasion. She berated herself for letting her mind wander.

Instead of a switch, Lainie saw two numerical keypads, one on either side and about six inches away from the door.

She moved closer to check them out and—stubbed her toes on something.

Her toes!

Mother Mary and Joseph, she thought. *My shoes. They're still outside on the landing, on the other side of the door.*

Her heartbeat became the loudest noise on the twentieth floor.

So be it.

Nothing she could do about her shoes now.

Lainie clicked on the Mag, aimed it downward. Her toes had connected with a medium-sized metal storage box someone had stranded in the middle of the concrete floor. She stepped around the gunmetal gray box and followed the Mag trail to the pad on the left of the door. She moved the light to the pad on the right and inched in for a closer look.

The pads were identical.

Nothing to indicate purpose.

Tapping in a combination of numbers would probably make something happen.

She told herself, *Clever girl, Lainie. Figured that out all by your lonesome, did you?*

She turned from the door with the Mag's beam at waist level, randomly wandered the room. Saw the bank of elevator doors across the room, a similar door to her left, on the wall she'd gauged was facing the ocean. To her right was a half-open, high double doorway, a dark wood in color. Even with their crusted layers of dust, the doors were the only decorator touch in otherwise empty space, a roomful of nothing.

Except for the storage box.

And ten folding chairs.

The chairs were open, arranged in a circle in the middle of the area, as if meetings had been held there. Crushed cigarette butts and discarded carrier bags and boxes from various fast-food places near most of the chairs.

She wigwagged the Mag left and right and up and down across the room. The box, the ten chairs and the discards. Nothing more in space she reckoned was a third again larger than Perfect Records' share of the seventeenth floor. That meant the space on the other side of the doorway was less than the space allocated Flynn's Pioneer Productions.

Lainie scooped up the metal box, parked it between her arm and her chest and headed across to the doorway. The Mag was intruding on the darkness, four or five feet in front of her, when she heard a noise to the left, like the purring of a well-tuned engine. Lainie froze, doused the light and glanced over her shoulder. The floor indicator above a middle elevator was lit and moving.

It stopped.

The elevator door fired out a thickening shaft of light as it started to open.

Lainie leaped through the double doors and did a fast back-pedal against the wall, feeling new gallons of sweat on her forehead and under her arms as footsteps clunked onto the twentieth floor.

A shimmer of yellow light crossed into the room from the other side.

Somebody had turned on the lights and was wandering around.

The shuffle of rubber soles squeaking and groaning under the weight of heavy steps drew closer to the half-open doorway.

Lainie pushed herself tighter between the wall and the door, one arm rigid by her side, the other pressing the box against her chest. She couldn't recall the last time she'd felt so threatened.

The wild teenager, the prototype Sara, on the prowl with Thom Newberry? At the Animal Farm, where she came as close to being killed as she'd ever come? Her years in promotion, fighting off the constant army of DJ sluts who refused to take *Not this trip, baby,* for an answer?

The footsteps stopped, sounding like they'd quit in front of the doorway.

Lainie braced herself for discovery. She sent her mind into high gear and in seconds had managed to dream up an excuse for being here: the fear for her daughter's safety the instant she heard about the shooting at the tent.

She remembered getting to the elevator, banging on the down button and—nothing after that.

How she'd wound up unconscious here?

No idea.

Would the story play?

The lie was certainly big enough, stupid enough and unbelievable enough to be believed.

She stepped away from the door to allow herself enough room to glide noiselessly to the floor. She put aside the Mag and the metal box and angled into a fetal position, arms crossed at the wrists and wedged between her thighs, her head resting on the bare floor.

She closed her eyes and waited for a hand to check her for body warmth, for a pulse, for a clue she was alive.

She would rouse to the touch with a startled suddenness and

201

appropriate sound effects, rattled by the face staring down at her, back away feigning uncertainty and outright fear, but—

The footsteps were retreating.

Whoever had stood by the door was moving away, not into the room.

It made no sense to Lainie.

She let a few minutes pass, then a few more, not daring to move or open her eyes, hearing only a few distant, undecipherable sounds.

She opened an eye.

The light that had spilled over from the other room was gone.

She couldn't stay like this forever.

She would have to chance making a move.

If someone was out there somewhere, so be it.

The lie could still work.

Maybe.

Lainie rolled into a sitting position and crawled like an enfeebled cat to where she could check out the other side of the door, careful not to drop the Mag, which she carried locked under her chin; extremely vulnerable were the darkness to give way to another eruption of light.

She wanted to scream for the sake of screaming, shed anger on her nagging fears. It was as if everything that had ever gone wrong with her life was catching up with her in this moment. She sniffed the air and came up with nothing but more of the dust that began clinging to her skin the moment she stepped inside from the stairwell.

A light popped on from somewhere to her right.

Her head snapped up.

She screamed, a primal scream she could no longer hold back.

The Mag fell to the floor.

She grabbed for it, but not fast enough. It rolled out of her reach.

Lainie gasped in air and released it in tiny sputters.

Waited for something to happen, but—

Nothing, except for the dim light forming a narrow traffic lane in the middle of the dust-infested darkness.

She looked to her right and saw the source.

One of the center elevator doors was open, as if it had been summoned to the twentieth floor. Was someone getting ready to leave, or was it that someone had gotten off, making it two people who were about to come after her?

Lainie did a swift backward crawl through the doorway, shifted around and against the wall with her legs spread apart, like they were when she was a little girl playing lonely games of jacks. She reached for her cell phone in the inside pocket of her plush velvet tux jacket, clicked it on and tapped in Flynn's number. He was holed up on the penthouse stairwell landing waiting for her. He might have a better idea what to do than she had, which right now was no idea at all.

She halted after the first six digits. The rest of Flynn's phone number had fled her mind. She demanded herself to remember. Begged herself. His number returned and retreated in the same flash. She closed her eyes and cleared her mind. His number formed like a movie title on the insides of her lids. She tapped it out before she could forget again. Pressed the cell against her ear and heard—

Nothing.

No ringing.

No dial tone.

No metallic voice advising her the subscriber was unavailable or had traveled outside the coverage area.

The tiny green screen giving her the reason:

No Service.

Lainie cursed under her breath and returned the phone to her tux pocket.

Decision time.

She couldn't spend the rest of her life here.

She burst out laughing at her inadvertent joke. If people were about to come after her, this *could* be where she'd spend the rest of her life. So be it. *In for a penny, in for a pound.* Jay Lowy. That was his name, who'd said it. *Jay Lowy.* The British rock idol. Thought he was another Mick Jagger, in a world where one Mick Jagger already was one too many.

Lainie felt around for the metal box and tried opening the lid. It was locked. She shook the box and heard nothing rattling inside. She decided to leave it behind. She got up and brushed herself off. Straightened her outfit. Ran her hands through her sweat-drenched hair. Drank a gallon of dirty air. Pushed away a short mumbled prayer with her breath and started on a dead run for the open elevator.

As if it were rejecting Lainie's decision, the elevator door began closing.

She dodged around the collection of chairs, increased her speed, reached the door about the same time she felt her legs preparing to buckle under her.

She squeezed her eyes shut and leaped sideways at the narrowing opening.

Too little too late.

Lainie slammed against the door panels. She bounced off into a hard landing that caused her to grimace and cry out in pain. She opened her eyes and was startled to see the light from the elevator grow larger, then smaller again, then larger, as the doors kept opening and closing. She clambered onto her feet, turned around and saw why:

The high heels she had left behind on the other side of the stairwell door.

Someone had positioned her heels to prevent the safety buffers on the elevator doors from connecting and allowing the doors to shut all the way. When the doors opened all the way again, she jumped in and retrieved her shoes. She knew she had failed miserably at what she set out to accomplish. Right now she didn't care. She didn't care about trying to answer the new questions the past fifteen or twenty minutes that felt like fifteen or twenty years had raised. All she cared about was getting the hell away from here.

She slipped her heels on, but before she could decide which made more sense, to go up or down, the elevator made the decision for her.

It took her to the ground floor level.

The doors opened, and she found herself staring at the man she had first seen on her tour of Volkman International, who'd stepped off the elevator on the nineteenth floor; who had been at Pat Madden's when she met Flynn there the first time; who could have been driving the car that followed her home.

The man looked at her wordlessly.

His expression said even less.

He stepped into the elevator.

She averted her eyes and brushed past him, raced out of the building and headed for the party tent.

CHAPTER 19

Thom Newberry spotted Lainie entering the staging compound behind the party tent. He was sitting about ten yards away from the band trailer, observing a dozen or so grubby types in *look at me* outfits, makeup and fright wig hairdos who were hanging around outside the way he remembered freaks parading on a carnival sideshow platform.

An exception was Jerry Mouse. Thom had requested special authorization to bring him tonight. It wasn't so much that he thought Jerry Mouse would enjoy seeing Miranda Morgan. He wanted Jerry Mouse to see his father on stage, observe how important and well-respected he was. God willing, something positive might rub off on the kid and turn him around a little. For certain, no harm giving it a shot.

Lainie, of course, was his main reason for being here. His future was riding on her ability to deliver for him the way she'd always managed to deliver in the past, before he gave her cause to despise him. He cut off reflecting before it wandered into wondering what life together might have been like if fate had dealt them different cards.

She saw him making air circles in her direction and started over.

A second or two later changed course.

She continued past him to the band trailer, up to one of the goony girls wearing a lot more makeup than clothing, her miniskirt the size of a pocket handkerchief. It was the same goony girl Jerry Mouse had made a few moves on, none successful, and was trying with now. Lainie yanked a joint from the girl's lips, crushing it under her heel. Their heated exchange of words got louder and drew attention from the other band groupies. Jerry Mouse not quite sure what to do, angled his head up, searching for an answer from the beams of light dancing in the tranquil night sky.

Thom gave the girl a harder look. He smiled and grunted out some chuckles, his head swinging left and right with the realization she was Lainie's kid, Sara.

Like Lainie, Sara was a string bean, tall for her age, maybe an inch taller than her mother had been around that age, but the real tip-off, now that he was seeing her past her discordantly colored ribbons of hair that extended down past her waist, were her eyes. They were possibly larger and rounder than Lainie's. He was certain, were he closer, he'd find them the same vivid shade of emerald green.

Thom started over.

Lainie signaled him to stay where he was.

She turned back to Sara and Jerry Mouse and, her voice only a murmur, said something.

Jerry Mouse seemed okay with it, Sara less so. They headed to the stage entrance to the tent, where rent-a-guards checked the laminated passes hanging around their necks and checked out Sara's bag before signaling them through the metal detectors.

Lainie joined Newberry. "So that was your Jerry. Nothing like you."

"Your daughter, everything like you."

"She pissed me off big time. I leave her and the first thing she does is change into that outfit, like she's going from here to a working girl's corner on Santa Monica. That and the grass. Usually behind my back, especially since she swore she'd stay off the stuff."

"Like mother, like daughter." His grin stretched to his ear-lobes.

"You always were a fast one with the compliments."

"I meant, a close look, and you immediately see she's the spitting image of you."

Not at all what he meant.

"Your son. You poured him into a uniform, no less. You tell him tonight was Halloween and he was going trick-or-treating?"

"He's a cadet at Kenyon. Top of the class. Straight A's; a four-point-zero grade average. Jerry'll be a cadet colonel and running the academy cadet corps by next year."

Spoken with enough fatherly pride to cover his lies.

She didn't have to know better.

Lainie said, "I would never have guessed in a million years it was him, if he hadn't said something; name-dropped trying to make an impression on Sara; on me. Wasn't that one of your tricks, Newberry?"

"What I dropped was acid. Never a hallucination that compared favorably to the real-life you, though."

"Save the bullshit for somebody who cares," she said. "I told them to go inside and grab some good seats in the VIP section before the place filled up. I hope to hell it won't be a case of lightning striking twice."

"For them or for us?"

"Over my dead body."

She murdered him with her look, and that was all it took to snap Thom out of his game and the thought that maybe she would be good for one more bang, for old times' sake; to see if Lainie could still turn him on, keep him going, like nobody else ever had, man or woman.

He made certain she saw his eyes grow cold before he spoke. "How's it coming, my little girl? You remember you have something to tell me after the show?" Her expression leapfrogged from scorn to contempt. The lock he put on her eyes was inviting her to fire away, he didn't care. He said, "Maybe now? You ready to tell me now?"

Lainie looked away.

It seemed to him she was using the time to construct her answer.

He couldn't tell if it was going to be good news or bad news until she ran a hand through her hair, from the back of her neck up and around to her forehead, then slicked the strands to one side. It was a Lainie tic that always signaled bad news. He thought he had trained her out of it.

Lainie's features grew taut. "It didn't work out the way I planned."

"How so?"

"I got onto twenty, but somehow they found out I was there and came after me before I had a chance to check out the floor."

"Who came after you?"

A shrug. "I never saw, only heard. I managed to hide and get to an elevator before anyone could get to me."

"Twenty-one?"

She shook her head. "It would have been next."

"You see anything on twenty?"

Lainie worked her fingers through her hair again. "Nothing to see. Some chairs. A metal box, like a safe deposit box. Nothing special. I heard someone, and I hid until the elevator came and I made a run for it."

"How'd you get in there in the first place? I thought the elevators didn't stop there."

"This one did. A special key for the back door. I stole it off the desk of Volkman's secretary."

"The Russky with the big tits."

"Yes. Petra."

"Petra Barish. You still have it?"

"Why?"

"You still have the key?"

Her hand moved to a pocket of her slacks. "Yes. Why?"

"I want you to go back now and try again."

"Now? That's craziness, Thom. They knew somebody was prowling around up there. There's bound to be more security, probably on the floor itself. Both floors. Maybe during the week, but it can't happen tonight."

"I'll say it again. Tonight."

"I have another week before the deadline you gave me."

"You have a new deadline. Tonight."

He said it so Lainie understood he was giving her an ultimatum, not a choice. He allowed her a silent minute to hate him. She took two. "I'm going," she said. "Until I get back, you make sure your Colonel Jerry Mouse behaves himself around my daughter; doesn't turn into a rat like his old man."

Thom watched her wheel around and march off.

She got as far as the corner of the tent and halted, then made a sharp turn and marched back. She stood closer than before. He felt her breath on his face, hot as the fury in her voice, matched by the resoluteness burning in her eyes as she gripped him by the shoulder and said, quietly, "Do us both a favor, Newberry. Tell me what I'm supposed to be looking for."

CHAPTER 20

Lainie found Sara and Jerry Mouse in the VIP section of the circus tent and knelt in the aisle alongside them. "I have an emergency, something that needs taking care of," she said. "If I'm not back before the show's over, I'll meet you backstage in Miranda's trailer."

Sara said, "Whenever," and gave Jerry Mouse a look.

Jerry Mouse returned the look. "She's in good hands, Mrs. Gardner, ma'am, so go ahead and take care of your emergency and don't worry about a thing." He proffered an edgy smile.

Lainie didn't have time to speculate about its meaning. She rose and moved toward the rear of the tent, hand-slaps for a few friends and false smiles here and there on the way out. No time for anything else. Definitely no time for small talk.

Her thoughts were consumed by gut-wrenching fright over the concept of going back up to the twentieth floor and—if she didn't find there what Newberry was demanding—moving to twenty-one. She had no idea where Flynn was. This time she'd be strictly on her own.

She was halfway there when she realized the building was emptying.

The VIP partygoers were on their way to the circus tent.

She'd need a reasonable excuse for heading back upstairs. And if she did manage to get back onto twenty—

No, she decided. *It's not going to work. Not tonight. Whatever lies I have to go back and tell Newberry in order to buy more time,*

211

that's what I'm going to do.

Lainie made an abrupt turnaround and, lost inside the flow of guests, headed for the tent.

She peeled off a short distance from the entrance, speed-walked to the backstage area and ducked inside Miranda's trailer, planning to hide out there until the show ended. Afterward, she'd feed Newberry the best lie she could come up with.

"Thank God you're here," Billy Carlton said, racing over. "Your star is refusing to go on." He jerked a thumb over his shoulder at Miranda. She was at the dressing table, staring at herself in the mirror like she was studying a stranger.

Lainie's mind automatically shifted gears. She padded over to Miranda and, addressing the mirror image, said, "It's show time. Let's go."

Miranda said, "Not. I can't do it, Lainie. A bummer, I know, but I can't. I won't. I won't go out and make a fool of myself for you or anyone."

Lainie closed her eyes to a moment she'd played out a hundred times before with baby acts getting ready to vomit their confidence in the dressing room. Hunkering down, she said quietly, "Here's the deal, Miranda. Until you're a Streisand, you better save your prima donna crap. Dig? Now, get up off your ass and get out there."

"And if I don't?"

"You don't wanna know, Miranda. Trust me about that. You really don't want to know."

CHAPTER 21

Harry Roman checked his watch. The show was a half-hour late getting started. No sense it would begin any time soon, not that anyone in the jam-packed tent gave signs of caring. There was too much free food and booze, too much glamour on the hoof, too much excitement stirred by news crews patrolling the room.

He caught himself wondering how many actually cared about Miranda Morgan. Little of the gossipy chatter he overheard from the command post he had assigned himself at a corner of the bar at the back of the tent had anything to do with her.

"Miranda as in Marvelous" tote bags were in evidence, and some guests had pulled their "Scarlet Woman" t-shirts over their outfits. Some tote bags were being used as seat-holders, but more seemed to have been abandoned with the press kits, promotional paraphernalia and hand-signed copies of Miranda Morgan's first album still intact.

He was guilty, too, having dumped the tote on a pile next to a trash bin after stuffing the CD and the t-shirt into a jacket pocket, where the bulge balanced the modest bump created by the Glock parked under his belt. Party security had given him a hard time about the gun, calling over a couple uniformed for-real cops for backup, but the moment turned all-smiles and a wave-through once he flashed his D.A. ident card and badge.

Harry's gaze roamed the tent from the party area to the stage area. He figured there were enough temporary rows of uncomfortable-looking white folding chairs for about three hundred. For anything over that, plenty of standing room here at the back. Some people had already taken their seats; many fidgeting, checking the time, showing other signs of impatience at the late start.

He suspected the delay had to do with the private party in progress in Leonard Volkman's penthouse suite. That's where he supposed Lainie Davies Gardner and her A-list of recognizable faces were hanging, Lainie working the crowd, charming anyone who could do her or her record company any good. He'd not seen her around here at all.

He checked his watch again.

Caught a sense of people starting to drift in.

The only face he knew belonged to Sara, Lainie's daughter. She had slipped under the rope six or seven minutes ago with a boy about her age, who may have thought he was heading for an ROTC drill. They'd taken front row seats off the center aisle. Sara looked to be ignoring the boy the first few minutes, before he leaned over and said something that caught her attention. Their conversation immediately had become lips-to-ears close, with frequent checkouts to see if anyone had overheard them.

Somebody in a tux with out-of-date lapels stepped onstage and up to the microphone.

He said, "Ladies, gentlemen and assorted others, if I may have your attention." Thump-thump-thump. Tapping the mic. "What's it? This mic dead or am I?" Thump-thump-thump. Removing the mic from the stand and wandering the stage. "On my way up here, somebody stopped me to ask if I knew why Hell's Angels wear leather. I told him, just a guess—" Beat. Beat. "It's probably because chiffon wrinkles too easily." He waited out the laugh. "Someone else, the gentleman there in the low-cut evening gown"—pointing with his chin—"he wants to know how high you should be if you're going to make a parachute jump." Beat. "Three days of steady drinking should do it, sir."

A ripple of laughter turned into applause when people recognized it was Chick Rainbow, the old-time comic who'd recently won an Emmy for his co-starring role on the *Daffy, Dizzy and Moi* series.

Chick acknowledged them with his famous chipmunk smile.

He said, "The people behind this magnificent extravaganza have asked *moi*"—pausing and mugging to be sure everyone understood the reference—"have asked *moi* to apologize for their tardiness in presenting the talented, beautiful and marvelous Miranda Morgan. I'd say that even if I knew who the hell Miranda Morgan was . . . Some guests were delayed and are only now gracing us with their M&Ms, I mean with their eminence." Aiming his index finger at the back of the tent. "So, Miranda Morgan, our own 'Scarlet Woman,' should be coming out to excite you like I always do—in another year or so." He did a slow bow-off, throwing kisses and milking the applause every inch of the way.

Miranda Morgan's band members ambled onto the stage and settled in.

Plugged in the electrics.

Fiddled for sound and tune, vamping chords, tramping into a common riff that became a time-filling melody Harry knew but couldn't name.

Harry's eyes drifted back to Sara and the boy in the uniform.

A woman in an expensive tux outfit was kneeling in the aisle telling them something. As she rose, turning her profile full-face, and moved hurriedly up the center aisle like she was late in catching a bus, he confirmed it was Lainie.

She slapped a few hands being held out in greeting, like a basketball player heading for the locker room, but didn't stop for conversation. Her smile seemed forced. She looked troubled beyond anything he'd noticed on her face before tonight.

Harry decided to follow her. Call it old cop instinct, his sense that something definitely sour was going down. Why else would Lainie Davies Gardner be racing off like that, instead of sticking around for her new star's grand entrance and a show that had to be costing her, actually Leonard Volkman, a small fortune?

He gave her a twenty-second head start past the tent's rear exit, abandoned his barely-touched Dos Equis on the bar counter and sprang after her.

Roman hung back as Lainie maneuvered her way through the human tidal wave spilling out of the Volkman International building and heading for the tent. She arrived at the entrance, charged her way inside past rent-a-cops too busy with the departing guests to give her more than a glance and a nod, sped through the metal detector, and onto an elevator.

Roman picked up the pace, but his Glock set off the metal detector.

Four linebackers, all of whom looked ready to kick ass if his explanation didn't satisfy them, blocked his entry. He stretched his arms parallel to the ground and told them where his D.A. ident and badge were. One of the beef trust moved in a way that obscured his view of the elevator floor indicators.

By the time Roman received his *Thank you for your cooperation and have a nice night,* the elevator Lainie had used was heading down again.

The doors slid open and eight revelers staggered out.

Roman recognized the pretty-faced aging brunette who looked like she wouldn't be able to pass a crooked line test as an actress famous for being famous. She hesitated in passing him, then took a step back and turned to face him. She took his hand and jammed it onto her breast. He felt her nipple puncturing her multicolored silk chemise. Her tongue went after his tonsils and growled at him when he gently pushed her away with his free hand. "You know what any other man would give for that?" she said, angrily, slurring her words.

"Two dollars?" The words just slipped out.

She looked at Roman with pity, slapped his face—connecting so hard he thought she might have dislocated his jaw—and stumbled off after her friends.

Roman rubbed his jaw and pretended not to notice the beef trust looking at him with a combination of awe and amusement. He said, "Do you know who Mrs. Gardner is?"

The beef trust checked among themselves. The one with biceps the size of watermelons said, "Lainie, who owns the record company that's throwing the show over there?"

"Her. You see her just now, when she came in and got on an elevator?"

Heads shook. Shoulders shrugged. Palms turned to the dome ceiling.

Trying to be helpful, the one without a neck said, "She could've been on her way up to Mr. Volkman's party, but it's ended, so maybe up to seventeen, where her record company is?"

Roman thanked him and headed back to the tent.

No sense in trying to track after Lainie now.

No reason to stake out the lobby waiting for her to come down.

For sure she'd wind up back at the tent for whatever might be left of Miranda Morgan's debut performance or, at the very least, to retrieve her daughter.

He'd wait there for her.

The lights were dimming as Roman eased inside the circus tent.

The audience was quieting down, people scrambling to find seats as a single spotlight created an empty circle at center stage. A drum roll danced softly under Chick Rainbow's voice booming overhead like a god: "Ladies and germs, with no further adieu-dieu from me, here she is. Please say hello, welcome, greet, send money and whatever else, the marvelous Miss—" A beat. "What's her name?" Ripples of polite laughter as he patted himself searching for a slip of paper he found in a pocket. "Here it is . . . Miss. Miranda. Morgan."

Roman likened the modest applause to payback for the free party as Miranda la-la-la'd her way into the circle of light. Her revealing crimson-colored chemise floated provocatively with the breeze caused by every little move she made. Her hair, worn equally free, spilled over her shoulders like the mother of all waterfalls.

He remembered her buzz cut, navel orange the day he tracked Lainie to the recording studio in the valley. That had to be a wig Miranda was wearing. No matter. She was creating her own look to go with her sound—a new version of Sex Personified—and he thought, "So long, Cher. Goodbye, Madonna. Hello, Miss Miranda Morgan."

She wasn't much of a dancer, but she was game. Every misstep was offset by a flash of attention-getting flesh. By the time she settled onto the piano lid and launched into a mournful "Scarlet Woman" as her closing number a half hour later, she owned the crowd.

They'd been on their feet hooting and stomping from the first number, Miranda scoring with both the uptown belts and the sultry ballads. They were demanding more, shouting for an encore, but that was the show. Chick Rainbow raced out to share the last bow with her. He took Miranda in his arms and locked her in a body-bend to suggest the sex act, mugging a *How about that?* before leading her off the stage, carrying on outrageously, like he was the one who'd won the night.

The house lights came up, and Roman looked down front to

see if Lainie had joined Sara and the ROTC commando. It took a minute. Other people were on their feet and moving to the aisle. Lainie wasn't there, nor her daughter or the boy.

Roman's head spun everywhere checking faces on the move, exiting the tent or aiming for a bar station and one more for the road. No sign of anyone. He cursed himself for not being more careful. He elbowed his way out of the tent and around to the staging area.

He saw Lainie. She had emerged from Miranda Morgan's trailer and gone into the band trailer. Moments later, she re-appeared with a disturbed look on her face. She charged at the man approaching her and began shaking him by the lapels. He reacted with surprise and struggled to free himself from her grip.

Roman recognized the man: Thom Newberry.

He'd become as disturbed as Lainie. He roared up the stairs into the band trailer. He was out in less than two minutes. His desperation visibly more intense now, maybe even more so than Lainie's. He crashed inside the gang of groupies hanging outside the band trailer, bounding from one cluster to another.

Lainie joined him, keeping a strangler's grip on Newberry's arm while he weaved about, seemingly asking questions and not getting the answers he wanted. Somebody said something that made Newberry pause. Their conversation lasted another minute before he turned to Lainie and turned his palms to the sky.

Her shoulders caved and her whole body seemed to shrink. She stood as motionless as well water.

Newberry wheeled around, dug his hands into his pockets and walked off.

Her head bowed, her hands finger-laced behind her back, Lainie began a slow walk to Miranda Morgan's trailer.

Roman yanked over a chair, scrubbed it clean and dry with a

discarded cocktail napkin, and plopped down. His curiosity over what he'd just seen was running too high to let him quit tracking her now.

He had a second thought:

Maybe he should be tracking after Newberry.

It was Newberry who'd put him on the invitation list, got him down here tonight, broadly hinting he would have new information to deliver about Lainie.

Yes. Newberry.

There was still time to catch him.

Roman got up and started off in the direction Newberry had taken.

He had barely covered twenty feet and was about to break into a sprint when somebody stepping away from the show tent bumped into him hard and threw him off stride.

Roman moved to his right.

The man again moved in front of him.

Either the guy was soused to the gills or he didn't want him going anywhere.

Roman moved a third time.

So did the man.

It was like they were practicing a clumsy fox trot.

"Excuse me," Roman said, as if it were his fault.

He was adding an apologetic smile when the man said, "Looks to me like you're carrying, Harry."

"What? What's that supposed—How do you know my name?"

"That bulge down there under your jacket, too high to think it's just you're happy to see me," the man said, ignoring the question.

"It's a t-shirt," Roman said, working a half-truth while studying the man's face. It was familiar and not familiar at the same time.

"Me, too," the man said. He used his head to indicate his left hand, which was jostling a bulge inside the pocket of his windbreaker. "My t-shirt is a Smith & Wesson .357 Magnum. Model 19, short barrel. A little longer now 'cause I got it silenced, same as it'll do to you if you try making fun and games with me."

Roman moved his arms out eight or ten inches, palms parallel to the concrete. "If it's about money, my billfold's in my hip pocket, on the right side." He moved to fetch it.

"Quit it," the man said. Harry stopped and swung his arm back.

The man stepped aside. "Now I want you and me to take a little stroll. You start. I'll tell you where to go, Harry. I'll be right behind you all the way, me and Mr. Smith and Mr. Wesson."

Roman realized why the man looked familiar to him.

He'd never seen him, but he'd heard him described more than once.

By Ruby Crandall.

In Vegas by Phil Crenshaw.

Roman said, "You're Rudy Schindler." The man took the news without expression. "I'm right, aren't I? That's exactly who you are. Rudy Schindler."

"You did your homework; you'd know how Rudy Schindler's dead and buried, pushing up daisies," the man said. "So just get a move on, Harry. We haven't got all night." He giggled. "You especially."

CHAPTER 22

All Lainie cared about was getting home and finding Sara.

That's where the sassy girl with the body like a walking tattoo parlor had told Newberry she'd be. Sara had said she was going home with her friend, Jerry, and to tell that to anyone who came around asking.

Her friend Jerry.

Suddenly Jerry was her friend?

Sara was too guarded to ever make friends so fast, on a first meeting, no less. Sara never did. What Sara did do was disobey her mother. That was the art Sara had mastered. *Tell that to anyone who came around asking.* As opposed to what? The truth?

Lainie blamed herself for what was happening.

She should have known better than to think Sara would listen when she'd told her to head to Miranda's trailer if the show ended before she returned. Was that what triggered her taking off, as in *Whatever mama wants, mama doesn't get?*

The boy, Thom's son. Jerry had said, as polite as an airport porter wangling for a bigger tip, "She's in good hands. Don't worry about a thing." Thom's son. "Don't worry about a thing," he'd said. She rebuked herself for not at once knowing better than to accept Jerry Mouse's word for anything. The acorn doesn't fall far from the oak tree. She should have seen past his smile, a junior version of his daddy's lying smile.

★ ★ ★ ★ ★

Lainie found Flynn sprawled out on the hood of her Toyota when she reached level four of the parking structure across from the Volkman International building. On his back, one arm draped over his chest, the other dangling. His face branded with wounds that looked like they'd been made by an insignia ring. Nasty swelling around both eyes. Blood crusted under his nose after running onto his lips. His nose possibly fractured.

She feared Flynn was dead until a snore erupted from him, sounding like a biker jump-starting his monster hog, his breath stinking from alcohol. She scooped up his open hip flask from the oil-stained concrete below his dangling arm and confirmed it was empty. The smell matched his breath. She slapped his face, again, once more, only producing more snoring and a creepy kind of smile.

In desperation, she balled her fists and began beating on him.

That got Flynn's attention.

His eyes burst open, and he shifted upright into a sitting position, as if he were waking from a nightmare. His hands slipped. He lost his balance and rolled over onto the fender. Onto the ground on the driver's side.

He leaped to his feet and into a boxing stance. Recognized who he was aiming at. "Why the hell you go and do that for?" he said. He checked his surroundings. "What the bleeding name of bloody hell am I doing here?"

"Get out of my way, Flynn. Get away from the door. I'm in a hurry, damn you."

"Not without me." He wheeled around the back of the Toyota, yanked open the door and ducked into the passenger seat before she could move the car into gear.

Lainie gambled that the freeways would take her home faster than her usual route using surface streets. Except for a minor slowdown as she approached the wraparound to the 101 north from the 10 east, the gamble paid off. She used the 101 until the Vermont exit, covered the rest of the drive in less than five minutes.

She and Flynn rode in silence the first fifteen minutes, sharing the golden oldies cranked out over KOLD, the station that touted itself as "*The* Hearing Aid for the Young at Heart."

He'd tried breaking through to her several times, but she was too intent on getting home to Sara. He leaned over, snapped off the radio and began rapping to himself.

How he'd heard sounds that said they weren't alone in the stairwell.

Steps coming up.

Him worrying for her.

Taking it carefully down the stairs to be certain Lainie was safe.

No sign of her on twenty-one, so on down to twenty.

"And what do I find there, outside the door, but the good lady's high heel shoes," he said to the cars whizzing past, faster than the twenty she was hitting over the speed limit. "Like she's retired for the night and expects them back from the porter, shining like the sun come morning, or—"

"I get the idea, Flynn. Enough."

"So what was that about, the high heels?"

"I heard the sound you heard. I got through the door and shut so fast I forgot and left my heels behind."

"You have them now. How's that come to be? Last I saw of them I was picking them up from the floor and wondering the same way I'm wondering now."

Lainie was not into giving him the answer or getting into the puzzle of it.

"I tried calling. The cell couldn't crack the walls," she said.

"Or mine when I tried after you, like the only one who could is Superman . . . I had your shoes, and I was dialing you, and from nowhere I'm suddenly being punched around like Mike Tyson's punching bag. Wham, like that. Wham-wham-wham. Too gone to fight back before I even know I'm in a fight. I wake up wondering if somebody got the license number of the train before it left the station, scared to death for what's the case with you. The heels are gone, and I'm thinking, *All someone had to do was ask and I'd give up the bloody friggin' heels.* I help myself to my painkiller and know I can't get onto the floor to find you. I don't want to chance anybody seeing me and asking a piss pot full of questions, so I ease the pain some more and start working my way downstairs, all bloody hell twenty floors, hanging onto the handrail. I don't know where you are, but I do know where to find your car. That's where I head. If it's there, a good chance so will you be sooner or later. I can only guess what happened after, about how my medication sent me off on a nice peaceful slumber. Exactly how you found me . . . Now, good lady, your turn?" Lainie shook her head. "So, mate, then maybe—What's the big hurry-up?"

Lainie wanted to say it was none of his business but lost to an inexplicable need to share her concern with him.

Anyone.

She told Flynn about Sara, blurting and stammering out more than about tonight, maybe because it might show him, show herself, she was not the one who had caused the problems, but the one who wanted to make it all better.

Flynn reached up to the tissue dispenser hooked to the visor and passed one to her. "All we ever can do is the best we can. After that, we cross our fingers and pray for the best."

"You wouldn't talk that way if you were a father and it was your child," she said, dabbing at her eyes.

"I am and there was a time not so far back it was so." He grew muted by memory. Several moments passed before he confessed, "I did the best I could, mate, until I drank more and trained myself to quit caring so much. Either that or take the easy road to not waking up in the morning."

Lainie glanced over and saw him inflicting the pain of memory on himself. Maybe she and Flynn had more in common than she'd ever have suspected. Her personal fears subsided. She reached over and patted Flynn's shoulder.

He added a grin and a snort of air, a brief mutter of acknowledgment to his vague stare out the window. Nodded and raised a hand so she could see that he had his fingers crossed for her. "We'll find your Sara's just fine," Flynn said, as if it were for his benefit as well as hers. He held onto the thought briefly. "The Newberry boy, if he comes out of anywhere near the military, I know from my own life he'll be well up for taking care of her. It's what the military does. More than stick you in a uniform and teach you how to march. Wait and see. It's probably just Sara and Jerry Mouse running off to have a go at some innocent kid fun."

"What I'm afraid of, Flynn. I've seen what kids today consider innocent fun. Have you?"

He had no ready answer for her.

Lainie's apartment was empty.

Exactly as she and Sara had left it eight hours ago.

No messages.

Only empty rooms to worry in.

Flynn draped his jacket over a chair, found his own way around and returned from the kitchen muttering, "I wanted to drink milk, I'd buy me a cow." Lainie gave him a blank stare. "My portable Pat Madden's. Fear I went and lost it in the rumpus." He put fingers to his face, pulled them off like he'd touched fire. "Jesus Almighty. I look as bad as I just felt?"

She almost said he looked like a Big Mac, super-sized, but let it pass. She sank onto the couch, pushed herself into a corner and wrapped herself in worry, tapping at her mouth with a handful of knuckles.

"If you think I'll leave you now to your own devices, I don't think so," Flynn said. "Fear can always use a friend. I'm going to check myself in your loo and take comfort from a shower, that sits with you?"

"Fresh towels in the drawer next to the bathroom door," she said, absently. "The second drawer down."

After five minutes, she heard water running, Flynn shout-singing in a cracked voice to a Beatles song, barely on melody and screwing up the lyrics. She corrected the words in her mind, anything to give herself relief from dread, until the chiming of her cell phone startled her.

She leaped for it calling Sara's name and was telling the cell *Hello* in a voice somewhere between desperation and hope before she recognized it was not her phone. She'd yanked Flynn's from his jacket on the chair; a pat confirming hers was in a pocket of her tuxedo jacket. She was about to click off when she heard, "Who is this? Hello? Hello, is this—" A number recited. "I'm calling Rod Flynn. Is this his number? Is he there? Hello?"

The last pause became a dial tone.

Lainie dropped the cell phone back in Flynn's jacket and retreated to the couch.

She hunched forward with her arms hand-locked between her legs, thinking at mach speed. Trying to make sense of the call. Trying to remember if Flynn had ever said he knew Thom Newberry past anything she had ever told him when she drew Flynn into her scheming confidence.

No.

Never.

Nothing to explain why Newberry had just called him on his cell phone.

Lainie began a mindless tour of the room, her conversations with Flynn during the drive home on playback. In telling him about Sara and Jerry Mouse, not once had she mentioned the boy by name. Not "Jerry." Certainly not "Jerry Mouse." At no time had she said Thom's son was attending a military academy or anything to suggest even remotely how that was the case or that the boy was wearing a uniform tonight.

What she smelled now was more than his alcoholic's breath.

Flynn was suckering her.

He was playing a game.

He was part of Thom Newberry's game.

Part of this damned business Newberry had blackmailed her into.

Maybe that's what she'd sensed originally about Flynn, why she'd injected a margin of caution into their relationship.

She was trying to fit Petra Barish into the equation when he materialized, clutching a towel around his tight midsection. His blond hair was out of its ponytail and hanging over his muscular shoulders, sending beads of water down his arms and into his thick mat of graying chest hairs. She had the impression he was posing for her benefit.

"Anything yet?" he said.

She shook her head.

Flynn held the pose another few seconds. "Just keep your cool, mate. There's a don't-worry happy ending to all this. I feel it in my bones." He flashed a thumbs-up and headed back for the bathroom, made an *Oops* noise after he seemed to accidentally drop the towel low enough for her to survey his plumber's crack.

When she heard the bathroom door creak closed, Lainie raced back to his jacket. She checked over her shoulder before retrieving the cell phone.

She did a swift check of the names on his autodial.

Thom Newberry was there.

So was Petra Barish.

Theirs were not the only names she recognized.

Flynn returned from the bathroom dressed, his face buried under cotton swabs held in place by Band-Aids, his eyes barely more than slits fighting to work inside a pair of purple hills. He settled on the secondhand stuffed armchair at the wall to her left and announced his intention to stick around, insisting it was important for her to have somebody there in case something were to happen that she couldn't handle by herself.

"I'm not suggesting or wishing bad things," Flynn said. "It might only be for company you have to drive off at some bloody ungodly hour to fetch Sara. Tomorrow comes, I can call a cab to get me back to the Marina for my junk heap of a car."

Lainie was too fatigued to argue. Besides, Flynn was enough of a big mouth, she might hear something to go with her suspicions. She knew, meanwhile, she'd have to be careful about keeping up her own guard. What Roy had quoted to her more than once returned to mind: *Keep your friends close, but your enemies closer.*

Flynn wondered about the TV.

She was in no mood to be entertained but turned it on and tossed him the remote.

He toured the channels until he found a movie to his liking, a western with John Wayne and James Stewart. He turned up the volume a notch, looked to make sure she had no objection.

She let him see it was okay, stretched out on the couch with one of the pillows propped under her head, the cordless house phone as well as the cell within reach on the coffee table. She ignored the movie and studied the fractures in the cottage cheese ceiling while her mind replayed the evening. There was something she was forgetting that might provide a clue to the truth about Flynn, about his relationship with Thom Newberry, with Petra Barish, with—

Lainie's cell phone sang out.

Hers for sure this time.

Flynn glanced over. He lowered the sound as she twisted around, swept the cell off the table and poured an urgent "Hello, yes, hello?" into the mouthpiece.

Lainie listened.

And listened.

And listened.

Until the horror of what she was hearing turned into a ferocious scream.

Lainie's legs failed her as she struggled to her feet. She lost her grip on the cell phone. Saw the blur that Flynn had become leap over to grab her before she hit the floor. Felt the blur easing her back onto the couch. Saw the blur scoop up the phone. Heard the blur challenging, "Who is this? What in the bloody friggin' hell is going on?" Heard the blur demand, "Tell it to me again, Newberry. Slow the bloody frig down and tell it to me again, damn you." Felt herself giving in to the dark.

CHAPTER 23

Newberry was speeding north on the 405, almost at Sunset, when he received the frantic call from Jerry Mouse, otherwise the drive from Marina del Rey to El Segundo would have taken ten or fifteen minutes. The turnaround south added a half hour of drive time, complicated by an eight-car fender bender that tied up two lanes of the freeway.

"Sir, I have a problem, and I need help," Jerry Mouse had said, trying unsuccessfully to mask a terror in his voice Thom had never heard from him.

"A problem? Me, too. You're my problem. Your problem can't be anything next to what I've been experiencing since you disappeared on me tonight, mister. What the hell do you think you're up to, anyway? Where are you?"

"El Segundo, sir. I really need your help this time."

"El Segundo? What are you on, the grand deluxe tour of bedroom communities? Try not to miss the Chevron refinery or the Hyperion Water Treatment Plant."

"Sir, I really think you—Please, Daddy, this could be really ugly after the cops get here."

"The cops? What do you mean the cops?"

"Daddy, I have to get off the phone now. I have to get back. Can I give you the address where I am?"

Newberry scribbled the address on the think pad mounted on top of the Mercedes's dash and read it back to Jerry Mouse to be certain he had it right.

"What's that ruckus I hear in the background, Jerry?"

"You'll see when you get here," Jerry said, hurrying his words. "I need to get back to her now, okay? I need to see if she's okay, sir."

"She? Sara, right?"

Jerry Mouse had already clicked off.

Newberry floored the gas pedal. He swerved to avoid kissing a Pontiac Grand Am that picked that moment to cut in front of him. The woman behind the wheel stuck her arm out the window and flipped him the bird.

The city of El Segundo was what Newberry always referred to as a "blink" community.

You're driving. You blink. You miss it.

It was located south of the commercial charter and freight terminals behind LAX, a tight squeeze between Hawthorne on the east and Manhattan Beach and the ocean on the west. It had a Main Street that ran north and south for three or four blocks, studded on both sides of the narrow asphalt road by rows of mom-and-pop stores that looked like they had been doing business there since Teddy Roosevelt was calling the White House home.

Most of the homes looked as old. There was no consistency to their style, nothing that suggested the post–World War Two-tract developments that mushroomed in the San Fernando Valley. A high school campus right out of *Grease* or one of those Annette and Frankie movies always popping up on cable. A library off Main, on West Mariposa, new enough to look out of place. No fast-food franchises, except for a lonely Subway off Imperial Highway.

The address Jerry Mouse gave him was several blocks past the Fantastic Café and Scoops Ice Cream Parlor, on Serendipity Street, off Main and then a few left and right turns. It belonged to a small, undistinguished Craftsman out of the twenties set back about ten yards from the street, the well-groomed front lawn enclosed by a used-brick and black wrought-iron fence.

All the house lights were blazing behind drawn shades. Driving by slowly in search of parking, Thom observed shadow figures in constant motion. The front door was wide open, night flyers swarming around the porch. Lots of kids Jerry's age, give or take, were racing in and out, hooking up with other kids who'd gathered on the lawn.

The curb in front of the bungalow was full of cars on both sides of the street.

Thom wedged into a spot about a half block away.

He checked for signs of police on the way back and up the brick entrance path guarded by neatly trimmed mid-thigh-high hedges.

No cops.

No sign of Jerry Mouse in the clutter of kids in the compact living room. Those who weren't on cell phones were hanging from the wall or sitting like statues. See-nothing stares. Some with painted faces and fresh tear stains. Isolated sobbing, especially the younger girls. Some faces Thom thought he remembered from the staging area behind the tent.

He guessed Jerry Mouse had run off with them to party, induced by Lainie's kid. Jerry Mouse wasn't social enough on his own to get that kind of invitation. He was an unruly loner, who so far showed no signs of turning into a social charmer like his old man, with his old man's powers of persuasion that one day would escalate Thom Newberry to the top of the mountain.

Thank God for nepotism, Thom thought, as he often did. *I can ever get Jerry Mouse in line, he'll wind up on easy street. If not . . .*
He quit there, as he always did. Junked that possibility as an impossibility. Jerry Mouse was absolutely going to get in line,

sooner or later, one way or the other.

Thom pushed forward, cutting through the living room to the dining room, also crowded with somber faces. He was on the verge of going through the door to the kitchen when he heard Jerry Mouse calling. He turned and saw him dodging heads and bodies, waving at him from the hallway arch, urging, "This way, sir."

Thom worked his way over and followed Jerry Mouse about five feet and through a door to his right.

The bathroom.

Jerry Mouse threw the bolt lock on the door.

He turned and gave Thom an imploring look.

He opened his mouth and tried to say something, but no words would come out.

Thom stared at the girl's body slumped over on the toilet seat, her head buried in her lap.

Stared at the girl sitting lifeless in the empty tub, her blood making an eccentric pattern from what looked like a series of stabbing wounds on her naked chest above the scoop neck of her bloody tank top.

He demanded, "Jesus Christ! What happened here?"

"I killed her," Jerry Mouse said, a river of tears flooding his cheeks. "I killed her, Daddy."

Thom saw bloodstains on Jerry Mouse's uniform. The gunk on the uniform appeared to be vomit, explaining the smell stinging his nostrils. He grabbed Jerry Mouse's shoulders, shook him to silence while flyspecking the bathroom. His eyes fell on the door bolt as someone began hammering from outside, yelling, "Hey, dudes, you ever coming out? I got a giant pee needs my immediate attention."

Thom screamed at the door: "Shut the fuck up!" Stepped over and gave the bolt a comfort push. He didn't know how much time he had before any police arrived, or even if they had been called. He needed to hurry through this with Jerry Mouse, who had bent forward with his palms pressed against the wall to keep it from caving in. "Tell me what happened," Thom said, coolly.

"I already told you, Daddy. I told you and told you and told you. I killed her." He wiped at his eyes.

Thom gave him an angry look. "Lower your voice and stop your cry-babying, you little prick," he said and froze. He'd not meant to call Jerry Mouse that. It had slipped out as his mind switched to possible ramifications beyond the boy. No good, this situation. No good for him. For Thom Newberry. For the bigger picture. The last thing in the world he needed now or ever was a killer for a son, Goddamn it.

It may have been the shock of hearing his father call him a "little prick." Jerry Mouse turned mute, but couldn't turn off the tears quite as fast. His breathing sounded like a marathon runner struggling to cover the last hundred yards. Thom made a wide semicircle with his hand. Jerry Mouse saw the slap coming, turned his head. Thom's palm landed swat-hard on Jerry Mouse's ear, not the cheek he was aiming for. Jerry Mouse didn't flinch. His wet eyes stared blindly at his father. He hand-toweled them off. Wiped his fingers over the blood and puke on his uniform. Looked at his hands and reasoned what had happened. Wiped his hands on his trousers. Stood looking up at his father helplessly.

Thom gathered his emotions, stepped forward to lay a comforting hand on the shoulder of Jerry Mouse, who quickly stepped back rather than accept his father's touch. Thom didn't pursue it. Injecting what he hoped Jerry Mouse would recognize as his true concern, he said, "I see what happened here. What I'm asking you is why? What was this all about?" He pointed at the body in the tub. "Why did you kill her?"

"Am I going to go to prison, Daddy?"

"Answer my questions first, please, Jerry Mouse."

"Just Jerry."

They locked eyes for a moment.

Thom recognized that the boy was on something and thought, *Jesus, first murder and now drugs on top of that.* "Please, Jerry. Do this for me? Answer my questions?" He watched the question tumble in his son's mind for several seconds.

"From when, sir?"

Thom glanced at the door. "Did you call the police?"

"Not me."

"Someone else?"

"I think."

"You're not sure."

"Negative, sir. People saying to call the police when I went out from here and told them what happened."

"Nobody else was in here when it happened?"

"They were, sir," Jerry Mouse said. He pointed out the girl in the tub; the girl who was slumped over on the toilet seat.

Thom turned his head briefly, rolled his eyes. The kid definitely was on something. All the signs were there. He'd broken his promise to stay clean after—how long now?—three years since his year of rehab?

"What were the three of you doing in here?"

"Her," Jerry Mouse said, indicating the dead girl in the tub. "She said she had something for me, and she brought me. Roofies. I didn't want one. She was flying already, but she took it instead. Then a Wagging Willie, and I don't know the other." He dropped his chin onto his chest and thought for a moment. "I really don't know . . . That's when *she* came busting in." Indicating the girl on the toilet. "She's all screams, saying and yelling, *Are you trying to steal my man, you bitch? You trying to steal my man, you goddamn bitch? You find some other cock to suck, you cunt bitch whore.*" A hint of a smile flashed across Jerry Mouse's face.

"I think she likes, liked me, her talking to me that way, don't you think so, sir?"

"Who wouldn't like you, Jerry? Please go on."

"Thank you, sir . . . She starts screaming back—her—and I just want it to end. I say that and she—her—she takes hold of me and says, *I'm leaving you bitch, and I'm taking my man with me.* We don't get as far as two steps before she—her—jumps at her, and she's waving this switchblade knife she's got from I don't know where. Like she's going to use it on her. It's then I jump in. All I wanted to do was stop her, sir. Take the knife and go. Next thing, we're fighting over the knife. And she's—her there—she's cheering me on, saying things like *Do her, sweetmeat. Do the bitch. Come on and do her good. Teach her a lesson.* I mean, I was her man and all . . . Next thing, she—her—she's pulling away from me, holding onto herself, and there's this look on her face I can't begin to tell you, and she's holding onto herself and I see all this blood coming from her, and I grab onto her, and I try to keep her from falling back, but she falls anyway, not too hard though, into the tub there and—"

Jerry Mouse sputtered to a stop, like a car running out of gas. He stared blankly at his father.

His hands seemed to gesture an appeal for help.

"What happened next, Jerry?"

"She sits down there and grabs onto my belt and pulls me over. She says, *I owe you a reward for being such a good honey, honey.* She unzips me, and she reaches in and, well, I don't. I didn't. I couldn't. I . . . I look over at the tub, and all I know is she may still be alive and need help. I move away, and I zip up, and I say to her, *I'll be right back.* She gives me this look, and then she falls over the way you see she is now. All I can think of is how she's just died. I go out and tell the first people I see to hurry and get nine-one-one or the police or something because of what's happened. Some of the guys go on over to see what I mean. They go crazy and shouting what's happened and I—"

"Did you tell any of them you killed the girl?"

"Only for them to call the police is what I said. Right away, I came back here and called you on my cell and told you what happened, because you always know what to do. I locked the door again, the way you said, to not let nobody in until you got here."

"The girls? That one?"

"Everything was the same. Nothing changed. Exactly like you see them now. That's all, until I got scared you maybe changed your mind about coming, and I went out looking for you." He hung his head, nervously slapped his thighs. "What now, sir? What now, Daddy? I'm having to go to prison over this, aren't I?"

Thom held off Jerry Mouse's question with a gesture. He moved over to the girl on the toilet and checked her for a pulse. Found it. Eased her back into a sitting position and took a long, hard look at her, cursing the girl to himself for creating a problem that could bring down his world.

He stepped away and searched the floor; saw what he was looking for. The switchblade. Jerry Mouse had dropped it onto the yellow shag rug at the base of the sink cabinet. He snatched it up and carefully wiped it clean inside a hand towel. With equal care, he hunkered down and laid it in the girl's right hand, folded her fingers over the lean black handle. The right hand, not the left, because her Darth Vader watch was on her left wrist. That meant she was right-handed, as was Jerry Mouse, so he'd have the direction of the knife wounds working for him.

"What are you doing, sir?"

Thom rose and stepped over to Jerry Mouse.

He wrapped him in his arms. "You were in here, and you forgot to lock the door," he said. "They came in yelling and screaming at each other. She pulled out the knife and had stabbed her friend to death before you could do anything about it. You told people to call for help. That's it. That is what happened. That is what you tell the police when they get here. Do you understand, Jerry? Do you? Do you understand what you have to tell the police?"

"You're asking me to lie, sir?"

"I'm asking, do you want to go to prison, Jerry?"

CHAPTER 24

Lainie sat on the bungalow couch with Sara bundled in her arms, frozen asleep, feeling sadness for the mothers of the girl who'd been killed and the girl who'd be standing trial for her murder, at the same time thankful she'd be taking her daughter home alive. Sara may have been one of the last of the partying kids to learn about the killing, the police explained after she and Flynn arrived at the crime scene. She had been identified to them by Mr. Thom Newberry when she and Mr. Newberry's son, Jerry, returned to the bungalow looking like disheveled fugitives from a crude backseat quickie, higher than the quarter moon now disappearing inside the crisp blanket of fog drifting in from the ocean.

"Why would he bother to point Sara out?" she'd asked the officer who seemed to be in charge, hardly more than a teenager himself, hiding his inexperience behind a silly wisp of a mustache.

"To corroborate the boy's story, Mrs. Gardner."

"If she wasn't here when it happened, what was there to corroborate?"

"The part that had to do with what happened before what happened happened, ma'am."

"That's so, Mom," Sara said. She was standing between Lainie and Flynn, her tired eyes and careful speech showing she had been scoring more than a few hits and snorts, but otherwise sobered by the situation. Flynn as a precaution against her falling had a tight grip

around Sara's waist.

Mom.

Lainie couldn't remember the last time Sara called her "Mom."

Actually, she could.

Forgetting those circumstances was easier.

Sara said, "They wanted to know what we were doing here since we're not locals, Mom. I told them how we were at the Marina for your show?" Lainie nodded agreement. "This girl, the one who OD'd, she came up to us when we were back there with the band. She said she'd been eyeing Jerry because she always gets hot over any guy in a uniform, her father being regular Army and all—a colonel—like it was some big heavy deal, and did he want to lam with her and some friends to a really torrid house rave here in Segundo.

"Jerry liked the way she was doing finger rolls on his chest and said, Sure, why not, but only if I could also go. I told her it'd be cool and not to worry after she gives me a look that says she doesn't want a turf war over him. We arrange to sneak off and hook up once the show began and, so, that's what we did."

The officer said, "How did you expect to get home?"

"I always do, don't I, Mom?" Sara turned her head and looked toward Jerry. "I'd bring Jerry it came to that, seeing as how his father and my mom go back way a long way together."

"You weren't around when Jerry headed for the bathroom with this other girl?"

"You already asked me that. He already asked me that, Mom."

"I just wanted to be sure what I heard, Sara."

"I saw her sniffing around Jerry and the colonel's daughter starting to show her fangs, that's all. Jerry was doing his party by that time, and I was into mine." She gave Lainie a defiant look, as if daring her to make an issue of it now.

Lainie sat as patiently as she could under the circumstances, waiting for the police to dismiss them, enjoying the rare nearness of Sara, who had chosen a deep sleep as her escape route from reality. Having Sara so near was comfort enough for her.

She glanced across the room. Jerry Mouse was still being questioned by one of the cops. His father was close by in deep conversation with Flynn, but caught the fearful look Jerry Mouse flashed him. Newberry stopped aiming daggers at Flynn, answered his son with a curious stare that seemed to substitute for a question. He received a brief nod in reply and appeared to blink back his approval.

It seemed to Lainie that a private Morse code had passed between them. A moment later, something Newberry said to Flynn ignited Flynn's anger. Flynn answered by taking a wild swing at him. The swing missed Newberry and instead hit the cop who'd been questioning Jerry Mouse. The cop had about a hundred pounds on Flynn and shoved him against the wall, warning him to stay put.

Flynn was beyond listening and launched one on the cop. Large though he was, the cop was as agile as a gazelle. He dodged the punch, drew his patrol club and brought it down on Flynn's shoulder. Flynn hung in the air a few seconds. He tried catching a chair for support, missed and hit the ground hard.

The cop's partner was on him like freckles. He wrenched Flynn's hands behind his back and cuffed him. Looked up at Lainie and between chugalugs of breath said, "I'm afraid you and your daughter will have to go home alone tonight, Mrs. Gardner. Your friend here's going to be spending the night as the guest of El Segundo's finest."

Newberry told the other cop, "I'm prepared to file assault charges against the son of a bitch, Officer. Teach the son of a bitch the lesson he deserves."

Most of Sunday passed without incident for Lainie.

She cut herself off from the world.

Ignored the ringing and singing of the phones.

Unplugged the answering machine.

Sat on the couch in her bra and panties like a cramped Buddha, her legs tucked under her, oblivious to the golden oldies trying to take her backward in time over KOLD, "*The* Hearing Aid for the Young at Heart."

What Lainie heard was playing in her mind: the present and the future.

The TV set was off, but she stared on end at the blank screen as if her thoughts were unfolding there. She didn't like what she saw, but it didn't get better any time she tried switching thought channels.

She always returned to Sara, who had feigned sleep on the drive home the instant Lainie tried talking to her and, once home, had buried herself underneath the covers for what became a fitful slumber. With Sara came worries, fears, the sad conclusion she was failing her as a mother. The wall of Sara's making kept them apart no matter what she did or how hard she tried to better their relationship and make it work.

Getting Sara into a rehab program was an answer, but not the solution. Drugs weren't the only problem polluting her daughter's life. It didn't take a shrink for Lainie to know that. An even bigger problem at the moment was Thom Newberry and what she knew from experience he was capable of if he didn't get his way.

She had only a week left to get Newberry his answers about the two floors at Volkman International or he'd make good on his threats to tell the D.A. whatever he had to say that would put her back in a courtroom for fraud or for Roy's murder. Were that to happen, no matter what the outcome, she would be branded an unfit mother and Sara would be taken from her.

No.

The possibility was unacceptable.

It was not going to happen.

She would get Newberry before she let that happen.

Get him before he could get her, whatever it took to make that happen.

"What. Ever," Lainie said, flashing a fist at the TV screen.

She got up and crossed to the bedroom. Eased the door open enough to check on Sara, who was thrashing about, fighting her demons her way. "Don't you worry, baby, no matter what happens, it's you and me," Lainie whispered across the room. "No one's coming between us. You may be a pain in the ass, but you are my pain in the ass."

Acting on other thoughts that had been growing through the day, Lainie padded to the phone. She got no answer trying the numbers for Cubie Wallace or Stan Currier, a busy signal for Ira Dent. She gave it a minute and tried Ira again. He picked up before the first ring, like he had been anticipating the call.

"Oh, ho, Lainie. I thought it was the *Times* calling me back. We got disconnected in the middle of the chick reading me tomorrow's coverage on Miranda. Almost up to the raves we're due from the *New York Times* and the Hollywood trades. We have to wait a week for *Billboard* in print, but it'll be like I wrote it myself. Remember me saying 'Scarlet Woman' would open at Numero Uno? Let's say nothing that I heard from any source makes me believe otherwise. Stan and Cubie also have been getting fantastic feedback since the show last night. You have scored once again, my brilliant leader."

Ira carried on like that for another minute, making it impossible for her to get a word in before he broke a burst of silence to wonder, "And whatever happened to you last night? You were MIA for the backstage photo-ops. When I tried connecting with you earlier today, it was like you no longer existed."

"Something came up, Ira. I can't go into it now. Why I called. I need a favor."

He didn't hesitate. "Your slightest wish, madam."

She explained what it was.

"Give me an hour to get there," Ira said. "What fun. I've never been a babysitter before."

By the time Ira arrived fifty minutes later, she'd showered, thrown herself into a tank top and a scruffy pair of stonewashed farmer's overalls, bundled her mess of hair inside a Dodgers cap, and rummaged the pockets of her tuxedo slacks for the key that unlocked the back doors to the twentieth and twenty-first floors at Volkman International.

Lainie didn't want to park in the plaza garage, in case she had to escape from the building as quickly as possible. She found curbside parking on a side street a block away and, unsure how tight security might be, moved her .22 from her tote bag to the trunk of the Toyota.

She strolled through the plaza enjoying the warmth of the late afternoon sun hanging in a cloudless crystal blue sky. The party tent and the show trailers were history, but the maintenance crews were still sweeping up and making trash bag mountains.

Building security was back to normal. A lone guard behind the lobby desk was working the Sunday *Times* crossword puzzle with a thick pencil stub he kept moving between his tongue and the paper, which he had folded into quarters. He looked up when he heard her footsteps and quickly traded suspicion for a grin. "Some heck of a shindig you threw last night, Lainie."

"Thanks, Scooter. You get a Miranda Morgan t-shirt?"

"Missed out. Was hoping to get my hands on one for the little woman."

It was the answer she'd hoped for. "We kept some emergency extras in Stan's office. I'll bring one down for you. A small or medium do it?"

Scooter cackled. "I guess you've never met the little woman. I don't suppose you have something in an extra-large, would you?"

"I find one, it's yours."

"Mighty kind of you, Lainie, even for you to only have the thought."

She scribbled her name, floor and sign-in time on the register and headed to the bank of elevators. Only the elevator center left operated on weekends. She took it to Perfect Records on the seventeenth floor.

She stopped in Stan Currier's office to sort through the box of surplus t-shirts she knew would be there. Stan habitually over-ordered, to have a ready gift on hand for some rack jobber or retailer he wanted to sell or impress—what she'd be doing shortly with Scooter.

In her office, Lainie wandered the room impatiently. She tested and retested her memory of last night and kept thinking through the scheme she had conceived at home and worked and reworked on the drive over. She recognized it was far from perfect. A gamble. A risk. But one worth taking. After fifteen minutes, she took the elevator back down to the lobby.

Scooter looked up from his crossword puzzle with a hopeful smile.

"Extra-large." She placed it on the counter along with four other t-shirts she'd brought down in her tote bag. "These are mediums and larges, for family or friends."

"Really thoughtful of you, Lainie. I appreciate it."

"Scooter, maybe something you can do for me?"

He gave her a questioning look.

"What brought me back here was to find a diamond earring I lost last night. I thought it might have fallen off somewhere in my office, but it wasn't there. The other place it might be is Mr. Volkman's suite. While I was up there with the VIPs last night.

You think I could go have a look around?"

He weighed the request.

She saw it made him nervous.

"Strictly against the rules, anyone up there without a proper authorization, Lainie. You think it might've been in the circus tent, lost there someplace, backstage area, maybe, when you were there?"

"I first missed it after I left the building, Scooter, before I got there. It's not that it's worth a lot; it's a family heirloom, the earring. Irreplaceable. From my mother to me, her mother before her. I was planning to pass it on to my little girl, Sara."

She screwed up her face like she was about to spring an emotional leak.

"Gee, Lainie, I wish I could, but—"

"You're authorized to check the floor, aren't you? If you spotted something amiss on the surveillance screen or—"

"Not really," he said. "That were to happen, I punch in the silent alarm to headquarters. They do nine-one-one and hurry the dickens over here loaded for bear."

It wasn't the answer she wanted.

Her mind was whizzing after something, anything, to persuade Scooter when he checked the digital clock mounted in the control panel and said, "Tell you what, Lainie, it's about time for me to post the floors. Nothing in the rule book says you can't tag along, head up there with me, but it'll have to be fast-like."

Lainie felt Scooter's eyes burning a hole in her back while she checked around Lenny's suite, on her hands and knees in a few places, explaining how these were areas where she had spent time last night.

A minute or two after his boot began tapping impatiently, she made a jubilant noise and held up the earring she had brought from home and palmed. Cut-glass, but she was counting on the security guard not to know the difference.

"Scooter, you're my hero," she said. "My darling Sara would have been devastated. I can't ever thank you enough."

"Do unto others," he said. He helped her to her feet, escorted her back to the elevator.

"I'm going to one-stop down at my office to call Sara with the news. Maybe do a little work, pick up some files. Unless that breaks another rule?" She knew better.

"Fine and dandy, Lainie. You go ahead. You finish before I'm back downstairs from clocking the floors, remember to log out."

"You got it," she said, and settled a light kiss on Scooter's cheek. He brought his fingers to where her lips had landed and blushed a molten red.

Lainie stepped off the elevator and onto seventeen, drew one deep breath, then another, and sprinted across to the rear exit door. One more deep breath before she dashed up the back stairwell. Taking the steps two at a time. Pulling on the handrail to propel herself faster to the twentieth floor.

On twenty, she wiped off her sweat with a sleeve and dipped into the coin compartment of her tote bag for the key that would disable the sound alarm and the spy cameras.

The key slipped out of her hand.

She caught it mid-air and shoved it into the red hole over the door handle.

Gave the key a hard turn.

Waited for the click that got the steel door moving before she started breathing again.

The room, so ominously dark last night, was alive with recessed lighting.

Everything else was as she remembered.

She crossed through the double doors into the other section

of twenty and almost tripped on the gunmetal gray storage box she had left behind. She pushed the box aside with her foot.

The recessed lighting was also on here.

She saw what Thom Newberry was counting on her to find: Files.

She'd entered a wasteland of raw, unfinished space that was filled with row upon row of legal-sized filing cabinets and what seemed like hundreds of mahogany and glass library cases containing more of the storage boxes.

Lainie hurried to the nearest row of cabinets, sailed it down and back, randomly opening drawers and spot-checking file folders. They all involved companies Leonard Volkman and his gangs of partners had brutalized and then turned out to pasture. She remembered most of them, especially the names she came across that had given Roy his worst days of regret for his role in turning dreams into nightmares for the thousands of investors who'd bought into Volkman's con.

Once she had a sense of how the files were organized, Lainie charged the aisles hunting for the one Newberry had specified and described last night. His words hadn't come easily, but rather as if he were committing a cardinal sin, and he'd started to balk when he reached a major point of explanation.

She cut him off, saying, "Not good enough, Newberry, so make up your mind. What's it going to be, the lady or the tiger?"

"You know all you have to know. Go do it. Just go and do it now, or do I have to remind you all over again that if it's over for me it's also over for you, my little girl?"

Lainie gave him a searing look. "Your little girl will take her chances," she said.

She turned and started to leave.

Her bluff scored.

Newberry was on her tail before she was ten feet away.

★ ★ ★ ★ ★

Lainie grew increasingly frustrated moving from aisle to aisle, section to section, sliding open drawers that should have yielded the file Newberry wanted. She searched for the mayor's name, *Welles, Lawton,* the obvious starting point. Other possibilities on the short list Newberry had rattled off. Even *Newberry, Thom.* She reversed first and last names, contradicting the other files she came across. Nothing worked. She moved onto the library cabinets. They were full of metal boxes in all sizes. They were problematical, identified sequentially only with numbers; no names; no way to effectively sort through them.

The logical move now was to head to the twenty-first floor.

Check it out for a second collection of filing cabinets.

Hopefully find one that would yield the Newberry file.

Lainie leaned over to pick up her tote bag and heard a shuffling noise behind her. She froze and listened hard for it again, hoping not to hear it; hoping it was only her nerves playing tricks; hoping it had been room noises, what her music video editors were always laying down on the audio track as "atmosphere."

A man's voice Lainie didn't recognize dispelled the notion, quietly suggesting, "If you're packing a weapon, do yourself a large favor and don't go for it. I'm behind you with my friends Mr. Smith and Mr. Wesson." She shook her head. "Remove your hand with your fingers spread wide . . . Thank you . . . Now, the way you see it in movies—Rise all the way. No false moves. Then turn around and face me."

It was the man she saw on the nineteenth floor when she toured Volkman International. From Pat Madden's Saloon, the first time she met up with Flynn there, who probably trailed her home. From last night, downstairs by the elevators after she managed to get away from here.

That man.

Gripping the Magnum in one hand, the loose metal storage box in the other.

"Those shoes look more comfortable than the pair you had yesterday," he said. "I don't know how any woman's able to walk in spikes like those."

"That was you in here?" He blinked and Lainie took it as *once for yes*. "You scared me half to death." Trying not to let him see he was doing it again.

"I could have taken it all the way, that was what was in the cards for you, only it wasn't. Not last night, anyway."

"Today?"

"Depends on you, Lainie." Motioning her with the Magnum to move out ahead of him, calling directions that led her to the back door.

He told her where to stand and stepped up to the keypad on the right. He shifted the box to under his arm and punched in a series of numbers one-handed.

The steel door glided open.

He motioned Lainie upstairs, saying how good the Dodgers cap looked on her and how he sometimes went to Dodgers games on the company's box seats behind home plate, especially if he had a taste for some chili dogs and the roasted peanuts, maybe the roasted peanuts more than the chili dogs.

At the landing on twenty-one he said, "Use the key." He kept the Magnum trained on her while she exercised visible care taking the key out of the coin compartment. "Lead the way in," he said. Waited for the door to close behind them and the green light to begin blinking.

The recessed lighting was on, revealing a floor filled almost to the ceiling with packing cases, boxes and cartons of every size and dimension, the contents indicated on each in letters printed large and bold with a thick black marker.

251

"Where's Rosebud hiding?" Lainie said, louder than she thought.

He said, "The sled?" Gave her a sly look that boasted *Bet you thought you could catch me on that one.* "This looks like a junk pile, but not really. Every time we take one of the companies under, we inventory the remains and keep what we think we might have use for again. It's what all of this stuff is. C'mon, you head that way. Not a Yellow Brick Road but it'll have to do. Ray Bolger, remember him? He was also a Dodgers fan, but that was before, in the Ebbets Field days back in Brooklyn. That's what Ray Bolger told me once, the scarecrow. He was sitting right in front of me, with—get this—Cary Grant."

There was hardly room to walk, only unpredictable paths and detours that took them to the other side of the building and—

Harry Roman.

Roman was pacing inside a glass enclosure about the size of a three-car garage, four thick walls topped by a flat corrugated metal roof that created a room within the exposed beams of the infrastructure. The room reminded Lainie of the rows of dioramas she and Sara had spent time surveying on visits to the Natural History Museum, but this native habitat was straight out of a modest suite at a cheap Las Vegas hotel. No privacy except for a paneled area at the rear, which she figured for the bathroom.

Roman stopped at the sound of their echoing footsteps.

Turned up the rage already visible on his gnarled face.

He shot a finger at them, charged forward to the wall and said, "Mrs. Gardner, I should have guessed before now that you're in on this." His hair was as unruly as his clothing. His eyes showed serious fatigue, and he needed a shave. "Kidnapping on top of Murder One spells special circumstances in this state, Mrs. Gardner, and that makes you prime for a lethal needle."

"How melodramatic of you," the man said. "By the size of that claim, I don't suppose it'll make a difference if we substitute 'dead' for 'kidnapping.' " He raised the Magnum to be certain Roman got a good look and understood his meaning.

Roman didn't flinch. He stepped closer to the wall, by the narrow entrance door fronted by a glass holding pen. With his lips almost touching the glass, he said in a mocking tone, "Dead is not a problem for you, Schindler." He wagged his finger at Lainie. "Obviously a killing doesn't mean a gnat's ass to you, either, Mrs. Gardner. Just when I was close to thinking you didn't have a part in your husband's murder. Thank you for showing me the truth, Schindler."

Roman wheeled away. He flung himself on the sofa, locked his hands under his head to make a pillow and closed his eyes to the company.

Lainie looked at Schindler for an explanation.

Schindler said, "The D.A. explained last night how you hired me to kill Roy Gardner. A story he heard from one of your ex-playmates at the Animal Farm."

"Ruby Crandall."

"That was her."

"What did you say?"

"Me, talk to a D.A.?" Schindler gave her a *You've got to be kidding* look.

"Tell me something, then. What's going on? With me. With him."

"Don't forget Newberry."

"Newberry. What's going on, Schindler?"

"Rudy."

"What's going on, Rudy?"

"Wanted you to see who it was on your tail last night, and

not for the first time, before I busted him. You can call it a show of good faith. Like with the shoes. Like watching out for you with Rod Flynn."

He attempted a benign smile, adjusted the gaudy Star of David and cross resting on his hairy chest, as if that would sanctify his answer.

"Rudy, that doesn't answer my question."

"Not mine to say more than that, Lainie."

"Who, then?" she said, although she already knew the answer.

"Our next stop," Schindler said. "Here, hold on to this for a change," he said, and handed over the metal box. He moved the aviator shades from his crown and motioned with the Magnum for Lainie to start back for the other room. "We're off to see the wizard," he said.

CHAPTER 25

Leonard Volkman said, "Nothing goes on in here that can get past our security systems, but I'm giving you an 'A' for effort for the clever way you gave it a shot today, Lainesky. Last night, a 'B' or 'B-plus,' because of all the help you got going in. What do you think, Rudy?"

"Like 'eye in the sky' in Las Vegas, only lots better. On the ground. Underground. In the walls. Dust gets tripped up, that's how good the systems are."

"Better than anything law enforcement has. If the feds ever cracked through I'd be taking daily dumps behind bars, my fat *toochis* freezing on a toilet bowl without a seat."

Volkman walked around his desk to join Lainie and Schindler in the conversation area, pausing to adjust a small Cubist oil by Picabia. "A Cuban Spaniard from Paris who hit his stride later on with Dadaism; Duchamp and that crew," he said. He pronounced it *Due-champ*.

Lainie fought the urge to correct him and his Harvard education.

Volkman settled into an armchair across from them and stretched his hairy legs, crossing them at the ankles. He was dressed for tennis, all in white, except for the blue Gucci loafers; no socks. A monogram and a silly Volkman family crest of someone's invention over his heart.

Lainie said, "That the case, why'd you let me get as far inside twenty and twenty-one as you did, Lenny?" Volkman leaned

255

forward and grabbed a handful of mixed nuts from the large Tiffany cut-crystal bowl on the coffee table. Picked some flecks off his teeth. Gave her his best paternal smile. She examined his eyes for give and caught the answer for herself. "You wanted me breaking in. You expected it."

Volkman applauded her and quickly plucked a Havana from the humidor on the coffee table. He tossed it to her, calling, "Give the little lady a great big one . . . The way I wanted it from the get-go or it never would have happened, Lainesky. See, Rudy? I always told you she had the brains to go with the guts." Returning his smile to her: "You figure out why yet?"

Lainie didn't have to give the question thought.

She said, "Malibu. Rainbows Unlimited. Paradise Sands."

He threw her another Havana.

She said, "Thom Newberry."

"*Gevult.* Rudy, Lainesky keeps this up, I'll be out of cigars before you know it."

"Don't bother," she said, dropping the two Havanas into her tote bag. "You've both been playing me—you and Newberry."

Volkman finger-tapped his temple for Schindler to see. "Brains up the wazoo. I always figured her to be smarter than her husband."

Lainie ignored the remark. "Who played me first, Lenny?"

"Who do you think?"

"I think you set me up for Newberry to come after me, to make your scam work."

"*Exactamenté.* The scuzzball kept putting himself in front of the mayor and gumming up the works, parking the decision in neutral for Rainbows Unlimited, my partners and me. I put up with it until I knew his game for sure, then put my own game into play."

"Newberry's game. What is it?"

"What the game always is with shadow players who start

confusing themselves with the main event. Power and money. Money and power. They let ambition take over their lives. He thought, because we let him beat us on other deals over the years, he had the edge on us. Could outsmart us. A cancer of the ego is what all these supercharged angles players develop. It grows and grows and grows and grows until"—he snapped his fingers—"it destroys them. Newberry, this poor schnook, he made Paradise Sands a carrot dangling in front of us. Expecting us to cave in and help him step up to mayor. Governor. Congress. The White House. The White House, for Christ's sake. How's that for getting out of line? Trying to work a shakedown. Guy's brain dead and doesn't know it."

"Why not just kill him?" Lainie said, only half in jest. "Over and out. The end of your problem."

Volkman went for the nuts again. "Too much government looking over our shoulder right now to do it the old-fashioned way. Besides, we have some other Newberry types in other parts of the country who are valuable to the partners and could benefit from seeing what happens when anyone tries to outplay me. I let this arrogant SOB Newberry know what was what if he refused to fall back in line and gave him a deadline. Six weeks to unleash the mayor and deliver Paradise Sands."

"Holding the file over his head."

"*Exactamenté.* Leading him to think he can find it down on my mysterious twentieth or twenty-first floor."

"Leading him how?"

"Slowly but surely, starting with your boy Flynn."

Lainie gasped.

Volkman laughed. He said, "Catch that, Rudy? Smart as she, there's nobody ever catches all the angles, not even me . . ." He got up and rotated some cracks out of his neck and shoulders, did a series of leg stretches and knee bends. "He got nailed somehow by Newberry and went over without a fuss. No surprise. Flynn's always smarted over how I yanked his movie company out from under him. Newberry's snitch, so we made it easy for Flynn to learn what we wanted him to learn."

"Petra Barish."

"See, Rudy? She's back on track . . . He thought he'd won Petra with his transparent Aussie Irish charm. Ha! You think you're an actress? That one's really some performer and not only in the sack. Petra spoonfed him what it took to see he didn't stand a rat's *toochis* of cracking those floors for Newberry by himself. Newberry needed someone like—"

"Me."

"You. Someone who had a skintight history with me."

"When Newberry got me to meet him, it was clear he knew I thought—next to him—you were the biggest bastard who ever came into my life."

"I made certain word got back. Also word on how there was more I could have told about you when I gave my depo on that lousy fraud business, like tying the whole bunch of bananas to you in spades."

"How I was behind Roy's murder," Lainie said, throwing a look at Schindler. "Also that word? That where he came up with it, Lenny?"

Volkman shrugged. He said, "Newberry went from salivating to out-and-out rabies. How that would give him a lot more ammo to hold over your head and keep you on track until he was satisfied. You must have hurt him deep, Lainesky. More than once he told Flynn how he was out for revenge over something from the past. How he'd lived for the day that would be coming."

"I told him *No* once. It wasn't the answer the great Newberry wanted. That also explains why I was suddenly finding Harrison Roman anywhere I looked."

Volkman turned his palms to the ceiling to tell her *Of course.*

"Also why I made it easy for you to come up and make the record deal with me, but not so easy that you would feel the fix or give Newberry something to suspect."

"What if I hadn't shown up on your doorstep?"

"Never entered my mind. I even bet Rudy it would have something to do with the music business. You always were one to play to your strength."

"Figure a way to get onto twenty and twenty-one."

"Sure. And see enough to figure out what Newberry wanted was a file of some sort."

"Like the file inside the box on the floor?" Lainie had settled the box next to her on the sofa. She picked it up for him to see.

Volkman shook his head. "If you tried twenty-one first, you would have found a box all by its lonesome, just like that one. And, just like that box—empty."

"Empty?" Lainie switched her eyes away from Volkman rather than let him gloat over her momentary bewilderment. She settled on one of the Picassos, a still life, the mismatched pieces presenting a single view from dozens of angles. It took her mind off a straight line, and somehow cleared her confusion.

She turned back and let him see her smile, which he answered in kind.

He reached in for another cigar, sent it twirling to her with an overhand toss.

She made a one-handed catch.

Volkman said, "Tell me what you think." He leaned back with his hands behind his head and draped his feet over the coffee table.

"You were conning Newberry when you made your threat. You figured the scare would be enough to have him get the mayor in line on Paradise Sands and you'd take him out down the road. You were surprised when you learned from Petra Barish how Newberry was reacting. The bottom line: You didn't have a clue what file he was after, but you knew it had to be pretty damn hot. That's when you contrived to get me involved. You figured he'd have to identify it to me, so I could lift and deliver it . . . How's that, Lenny?"

She returned to the sofa and dropped the cigar into her tote bag.

"You coming back today tells me you know which file it is, if you didn't already know last night, before Rudy called me to say you were on the prowl again and I had to cut short my regular Sunday game."

She tapped the tip of her nose. "A file name straight from the horse's mouth."

"But you still wouldn't be able to find it, because of the way the catalog works. Tell me which file Newberry said, and you are officially out of the loop. You get to keep our record deal, and I do what has to be done with Newberry—for both of us."

"First, I want the story on Harrison Roman and that glass house on twenty-one."

Volkman thought about it.

He signaled Rudy Schindler to answer her.

Schindler said, "It's where we entertain the people who need entertaining. When they've been entertained enough, we send them off on a nice long vacation." He kissed his fingertips and threw them away.

Volkman said, "My special gift to you, Lainesky, to make up for how I had to ignore you and your kid the years since Roy got killed. You'll never-never be bothered by Roman again, and when I'm through with Newberry the D.A. won't ever have cause to remember your name."

"Let Roman go, Lenny."

Volkman reared back. "You're putting me on."

"You want the name of the file, let Roman go. Let him go or stick me in there with him, those are your options."

"Rudy, I ever tell you she wasn't just smart but also crazy in the head?" His expression lost any sign of humor. "Lainesky, you better have a good answer for talking to me that way, or I'll have to seriously consider punching your ticket."

"He's a bastard like you and Thom Newberry, but I owe him one, Lenny."

"Do better."

"Payback for something Roman did for Sara."

"Do better."

"A gangbanger turned a gun on her and might have killed my kid, except Roman turned it around. Roman turned it around, or my baby girl might have been lying dead in the street."

Volkman parked his face on his clasped hands and thought about it. "The son of a bitch goes ahead and hauls your tight little tush into court down the line, you're on your own. No help from me. We go back to square one, like the last time. We clear on that?"

"Thank you, Lenny."

"Rudy, after we know she's delivered the file to Newberry, go explain the facts of life to Roman and send him on his way." He turned back to Lainie. "By then, I'll have made some calls. Applied juice where it counts. Made sure nobody who matters gives Roman the time of day if he decides to get noisy."

"I have your word on that?" Lainie said, exploring his face.

"The whole sentence," Leonard Volkman said.

Lainie got home to find Ira Dent gone.

Flynn was parked in front of the television watching a "Thin Man" movie over cartons of Chinese take-out. "Sara is fine," he said, misreading the look on her face. "A sound sleeper, that one. The sound is snoring sometimes, but don't we all?"

He was causing her apprehension, but nothing she could do about it now.

She had to play Flynn like she didn't know his real connection to Thom Newberry.

"Where's Ira?" she said, dropping her tote on the table by the door.

"No need for two to babysit your little princess, so I sent the good man packing. Come, sit. There's a spare pair of chopsticks. You look famished."

"Maybe later. The last time I saw you, the cops were hauling you off to jail, Flynn, and Newberry was screaming for your scalp."

"He's why El Segundo's finest held me as long as they did, until a few hours ago, in one of the worst cells where I've ever had the honor of adding my initials on the wall. The bleeding arse never showed, and, when they called him, Newberry said to forget it—How are you doing? I needed to come over and be certain you and Sara were none the worse for last night's ordeal."

Lainie responded with a gesture, was about to ask him to go, lie that she needed to crawl into bed and grab some sleep, when he said, "So, how'd it go?"

"How did what go?"

"Your return trip to Volkman International? Ira said that's where you'd flown."

"He must have misunderstood."

Handling the chopsticks with ease, Flynn fed himself a large glob of steamed white rice and began exploring the other cartons. "The little dump smelled like the grease pits I remember from Nam and after, when I was shuttling between Tokyo and South Korea, but this sweet and sour pork is some of the best I've had anywhere." He helped himself to another chunk. "You had best try some before it's all gone." He locked onto her eyes. "Ira didn't misunderstand, good lady, so—what is it you don't want me to know?"

It wasn't a question Lainie intended to deal with.

She had too much to sort out first, including how to handle Newberry when she called him tomorrow. She was positive it wouldn't be the way Volkman wanted, all she was positive about, except for not wanting to accidentally drop any information Flynn could carry back to Newberry. "I had to pick up some paperwork," she said. "That's all. And what makes you think I have to answer to you?"

"What kind of paperwork?"

"What is this, Flynn, the Inquisition *redux*?"

"Making conversation, mate. You recall I do have something of a vested interest in this business." He used a finger to draw an invisible circle around his face. "This is not from yours truly walking into a meat grinder, you know?"

"Thank you, but please go now. I'm tired. I need to be alone. I have things to do."

Flynn shook his head vigorously. "Something went down earlier that's come between us. Say it. Tell me the answer and then I'll go, fair enough?"

He rose from the table in a way that made Lainie feel threatened. She eyed her tote bag. Her .22 was still there, not yet returned to its usual place in the box of scouring pads under the sink. Reluctantly, she was going to have to prove to Flynn just how serious she was about him leaving.

Flynn spotted her move. He covered the space between them in seconds and cuffed her wrist with a tight grip while he reached inside the tote with his free hand. He pulled out the .22 and pushed the gun barrel against her heart.

"Sexy that," he said, washing his lips with his tongue. He let the gun linger briefly before lowering his arm. "Why would you want to go and do a thing like that to me?"

Lainie reached into the tote bag again and came up with one of the Havanas Volkman had tossed her. "This, not that," she said, hoping Flynn would buy her commingling of sincerity with indignation.

"Ho! One of Volkman's special illegal imports," he said. "Tell me you wrestled it away from him at gunpoint for this terribly nasty habit you've acquired in the hours since we parted."

"I carry the .22 for protection. The cigar I picked up at the party last night. I brought it back for Ira, but you're welcome to it. A goodnight gift. Good night, Flynn."

He accepted the Havana, sniffed at the cellophane wrapper and slid it into a shirt pocket. "A sad substitute for the truth, Mrs. Gardner. I would much prefer knowing what is truly going on. What did Volkman tell you to cause this change between us? Whatever Volkman told you, he was as wrong as the rain that never knows not to fall in Southern California."

Lainie understood Flynn was not going to leave until she gave him an answer he found acceptable. She gave him one that was mostly the truth. "Lenny said, whatever else you claim to be, you're really a dirty, rotten snitch for my bastard ex, out to do your worst against Lenny and me." She had put herself in the equation to get a reaction. How he answered would let her decide how much else he should know.

Flynn floated a smile at her and said, "My best, good lady. Out to do my best by you."

"You ain't no friend of mine, Flynn. I've felt bad vibes about you from the time we met. Now, thanks to Leonard Volkman, I understand them."

"Not at all what I've been feeling about you," he said, showing her a face that held back nothing. "Not where it's at between Newberry and me, either."

"You're saying you're not a snitch for Newberry?"

"I'm saying I'm more than that."

He pulled out his billfold and flashed a gold shield, like a proud fisherman posing with the record-breaking marlin he just caught. Gave her a moment to find her breath. "It's not from no cereal box," he said. "A federal agent putting your taxpayer dollars to work for you."

Lainie stared voiceless at the shield.

"I've been out a long while getting the goods on Leonard Volkman and all of his partners in crime," Flynn said. "Thanks to you, I'm farther along now, feeling closer than I've ever been to another feather in my distinguished cap."

"You've been using me."

"I use everybody, mate."

"Thom Newberry."

"You don't know the miserable worst of it between that filthy bugger and me." He made a clucking noise. "The sacrifices people do sometimes for God and country."

"Petra Barish?"

"We brought the Russky into play when the timing seemed right. Pet's the prime cut of top sirloin Volkman prefers on his barbee. Not bad either, the tastes I've had."

"Two-timing your waitress friend, Gracie, or is she one of yours, too?"

"Gracie's like my grog. Something to help relieve the stress of the day. I've never been one who's satisfied with a handshake."

He did the Groucho eyebrows thing, but Lainie saw more than humor igniting his eyes. Flynn was coming on to her. She couldn't deny her own electrical charges. She couldn't explain them either.

Flynn held Lainie's look, eating her alive. He cleared his throat and said, "Besides the obvious, I needed Gracie for cover, to make my act look more the better after I learned from Pet that Rudy Schindler had been put on my tail by Volkman."

"And what do you need me for, Flynn?"

"You cooperate now, help me get the goods, your life goes on unattended after I finish up with Volkman."

"And that's all you need me for?"

"All, but I want you for myself."

"If I forget and call you 'Roy'?"

"After a while you won't need to be reminded."

Some moments and emotions defy a rational explanation.

This was one of them for Lainie.

She felt her nerve-endings ignite as they hadn't since Roy's death.

She and Flynn were at each other at once, finding places to put their hands and lips and dissatisfied with everywhere they found, growling under their breath like they had had enough even before they'd had any, until—she remembered Sara in the next room and forced herself to stop.

"No good, no good, not here," Lainie said, unsure of her words as they spluttered out and collided.

Flynn understood. He said something to her with his mouth on her ear, and all she heard was the thunder that comes before the lightning.

A few minutes later, they were in the back seat of his car, doors locked, windows tight against intrusion, at it like two kids discovering sex, like sex was of their own invention; half-dressed, half-undressed; oblivious to the cramped space making a jigsaw puzzle of their body parts. Later, spent, piecing themselves together, Lainie said nothing. Flynn said less. No words would make a difference now except *again*, and hearing it was unnecessary.

CHAPTER 26

Thom Newberry stood to greet Lainie as the maitre d' led her to his table. It was nearing one o'clock, and the elegant dining room at Hillcrest was already filled with regulars, the ultra-wealthy West Side businessmen he had courted so successfully over the years and several old-time comedians. The comics were living out the legacy of the show business legends who had helped found the exclusive country club on Pico Boulevard, across from the 20th Century Fox studios, when it was built in the forties: Jack Benny, George Burns, Groucho Marx, that ilk.

Newberry was not a member. It was a luxury he couldn't afford—yet—but not the club he'd choose even if he could. Created in an era when Jews weren't admitted to any of the posh country clubs around L.A., it was still too Jewish for his taste. He was into martinis, not matzo balls. His status as a welcome guest came through his political ties, of course, currently Mayor Welles and the *quid pro quo* he hinted about over a few belts and the sumptuous Hillcrest buffet with potential campaign fat cats.

The maitre d' pulled out the chair next to him for Lainie and pampered them with a stage smile before leaving them to a review of the day's menu.

When she made a move to hand Newberry the gray metal box she was carrying, he shook his head and pointed at the floor. "You're not permitted to talk business in the dining room—against the bylaws—and putting something like that or an attaché on the table is definitely a no-no," he said. "It's in there?"

"I didn't drive across town to deliver an empty box or for a free meal."

A waiter came to take their drink order.

Newberry encouraged her with a look.

"Coffee," she said.

"We have to do better than that," Newberry said. "After all, we are celebrating." He ordered a split of champagne and after the waiter retreated said, "Did you look at the file?"

"You said not to. Don't I always do what you tell me?"

"That's my little girl."

Lainie repudiated the statement with a look. She turned her head away and spent a few moments checking out the private dining area behind them. Thom recognized several at the long table, heavy contributors used to City Hall access. Table-hopping was also a no-no at Hillcrest, but he'd find a way to lobby them after he was through with Lainie; sharing the little surprise he had in store for her.

The waiter returned with the split and her coffee.

He filled Newberry's glass.

Lainie shook her head and turned her glass face down. "Just the coffee," she said.

So Lainie, Thom thought, *always taking the simplest things and blowing them out of proportion.* He reached for the glass and turned it face up. "Pour, Abie. I'm sure my guest will feel differently once she hears what I have to tell her."

Abie did as instructed and disappeared. Newberry raised his glass. Lainie raised her coffee cup with both hands, moved it up by her mouth and blew on it. Newberry decided it wasn't a contest he had to win. "Cheers," he said, and took a hefty swallow that left his glass half-empty. She took a sip and settled the cup on its saucer. She clasped her hands on the table and waited for him to say something.

"How'd you pull it off yesterday?" he said. She told him. "You're smart as ever, Lainie. No. Smarter. This smart back when, they never would have caught you at the border and your life, mine, they might have worked out a whole lot different."

"The border was your idea."

"A lot different," he said, as if he hadn't heard her. "What would you have done if that security guard hadn't allowed you upstairs?"

"Tried something else."

"Or if you'd been caught on twenty or twenty-one?"

"But I wasn't, was I? There's the box. The file's inside it. You said you had something to tell me. Tell me I'm off the hook with you."

"Locked."

"Locked. Tell me I'm off the hook, Thom."

"And you didn't look at the file?"

"I couldn't look, Newberry. Even if I wanted to, it was in that damn locked box. Crack it open and see for yourself."

"Then how did you know it was the file, Lainie?"

"The file name you gave me was on a master list on the floor clerk's desk. The master list also specified the location. The number assigned the file corresponded to the number on the box, right below the combination lock."

She leaned over to pick up the box.

Newberry stopped her. "No business at the table, remember?" He emptied his champagne glass and patted his lips dry with his napkin. So far everything she was saying matched the report he got last night from Flynn. He needed to be certain before he sent her on her way again. "The combination?"

Lainie shook her head. "You're strictly on your own in that department."

"The key that got you onto the floors?"

"Rod Flynn has it. He came by for it last night. He needed to get it back to Volkman's secretary first thing this morning, before it was missed and the wrong people started asking the wrong questions."

"He could get it again from her if he had to?"

"I don't know, and I don't give a damn. Tell me I'm off the hook. I have a daughter I need to get back to." Her fingers began a nervous dance on the table.

"How is Sara?"

"Lousy, but she'll live . . . Jerry Mouse?"

"He's close to being a basket case, but he'll get over it. Kids have a great resilience, more than most adults . . . No, I'm not quite ready to let you off the hook yet, my little girl."

Newberry enjoyed watching her eyes burn into him while she digested the advisory he'd just delivered so casually, a bee sting as a preview of the greater pain coming. He hoped Lainie was sensing that. Was there a greater joy in life than getting even?

"I'm sure you're about to explain what that means," she said, gathering the reins on her composure.

"Minor, minor," he said, fluffing his hand in the air. "You're too smart to think I'm going to give you your Get Out of Jail card until I open the box and check the file. I do that, get inside the box, check the file and see it's the right one, you pass Go."

Lainie sat motionless, burying him with her eyes.

Newberry was in no hurry. If Lainie was holding out on him, if she'd held out on Flynn, this was her break point. He looked down and began removing imaginary pieces of lint from his sports jacket. She mumbled something. He gave it a few beats before looking up. "I couldn't hear you. What?"

She rattled off a series of numbers.

"What's that? Your picks in this week's lottery? The jackpot is up to how much? Twenty-one or twenty-two million? Oops. Sorry. I confused the jackpot with the two floors at Volkman

270

International."

"The combination, damn you. Go open the damn box, Thom. Do it now. Pick up the box and take it to the men's room. There's a golf course here. Take it to the locker room. I don't care where. Take it someplace, and open it now."

"You love giving orders, don't you, my little girl?"

She repeated the combination. "You want me to write it down for you?"

"It's tucked up here," he said, tapping his head. "I'll get to it later, maybe back at City Hall, and I'll let you know. I may have more questions."

"Like what?"

"Like, you lied about having the combination. You also lie when you told me you didn't look at the file? Maybe you even ran a copy to keep for yourself, thinking it might do you some good somewhere down the line?"

"Maybe I switched files on you. How did you forget to come up with that one?"

Newberry shook his head and stood up. "I'll be back shortly." He picked up the box and crossed through the main dining area to the men's room. He locked himself in a stall, settled the box on his lap and worked the combination lock.

The number on the tab of the file folder corresponded to the number on the box. He put the box on the tile floor away from a wet spot and checked the folder's contents. At once he was seized by panic. Nothing that should have been in the folder was there. Not one document. Not one photograph. Not one negative. Not one—

Newberry grabbed for the box. He dumped in the file and spun the lock.

He managed to keep his paste-on smile in place back to the table. Lainie was drinking champagne now, her body less tense than it had been ten or twelve minutes ago. He set the box on the table and angling over it, arms at his sides with his fists pumping air, struggling to keep his voice down, said, "You miserable bitch."

Lainie pointed to the box. "Shouldn't it go back on the floor, Thom? It's a no-no on the table, I understand." She toasted him with her glass. Took a sip. Cracked a smile. Said, "Nice choice."

"Funny. You're a funny miserable bitch." He felt his face burning sunburn red, his veins stretching at his temples and on his neck. "You did run a switch. You switched files. You got the box open. You saw what was there, and you made the switch."

Lainie's eyes grew huge. She pressed her fingers against her lips. "Oops." Made the smile again. "I mentioned switching files first, remember?"

"Where is it? Where's my file?"

"Right next to my Get Out of Jail card."

A fat cat heading out of the private area patted Newberry's shoulder in passing. Newberry acknowledged him with a bright greeting he barely got out. He turned back to Lainie and took a rich swallow of air. "You win. You're passing Go."

"Not yet, Thom. This time I want it in writing. When I get it in writing from you, from the D.A.'s office, from the feds, then and only then do you get your file."

"No, I can't. I don't—"

"Sure you can. You don't get me what I just asked for, the file and the copies I made this morning will be on their way to the D.A., the feds and the media before you and your mayor can say, 'Not guilty, your honor.' "

"What about Volkman?"

"You'll still have a week to get your boss the mayor to ramrod the Paradise Sands deal for Lenny. You do that, Lenny will have no reason to go after the file—or your scalp."

She checked her watch. "I'm due at the Marina for a meeting

with Miranda Morgan and my staff, Thom. Anything you want to tell me before I leave?"

Newberry connected with Flynn on the drive to City Hall. "We have a problem," he said, and explained what had occurred with Lainie.

"You can't trust anybody nowadays, can you, mate?"

"Save it for the classroom, Flynn." He was in no mood for philosophical rhetoric. "You still have the key to those two floors?"

"I got it back bright and early to Volkman's main squeeze, or there would've been hell to pay."

"Can you get your hands on it again?"

"Can I get my hands on Petra again, you mean."

"I want you to get the key. I want you to go into those rooms and find the damn master list she described. I want—"

"Hold on, mate. I get the friggin' key and somehow manage to get to those rooms, nobody noticing, you just told me Lainie has your bleeding file."

"I said she claimed to have the file."

"So, what then?"

"Whatever file she stole out of there, it's not the one I want. It never was."

He heard Flynn suck in his breath, like he was trying to swallow the mouthpiece because it led to a bucket of the lush's favorite booze. "Never? What kind of game were you—"

"Not in my lifetime would I trust getting that file from that cunning bitch. I wanted to see if someone could get onto those floors. If she got caught, so what? She made it twice, got the lay, got the file. Harmless shit. Nothing I can't wheel and deal around. The bitch will be on her way to jail, stripped bare, when I get through with her. It's your turn now, Flynn."

"Meaning? You testing me next in line, that so?"

"Call it opportunity, Flynn. It's your opportunity to keep enjoying the finer things in life. Whether you do it or you have Volkman's Russky whore do it for you or with you, I want you to get onto those floors and get me the real file."

"And if I get found?"

"That's your problem, damn it. You solve mine."

"After which you fuck me like you're fucking Lainie?"

"Not if you deliver."

"I'm FedEx, UPS and the U.S. post office rolled into one, but why should I believe you?"

"What are your options? You have three days."

"Generous bastard that you are." Flynn drank the phone again. "I suppose this real file of yours has a name?"

Newberry told him and a minute after he'd clicked off on Flynn, was leaving a message on Lainie's home machine. "It's me. I have it all in the works for you already. Your specifications."

CHAPTER 27

"We're shipping 'Scarlet Woman' gold," Stan Currier said. "The orders blossomed after Miranda's gig Saturday night. We're already into reorders, and I have to get us a second pressing plant or we won't make the first shipping dates, that's how good-to-go we are."

Lainie looked at him appreciatively. "Whatever it takes, Stan. Do it."

She turned to Cubie Wallace, who was sitting across from Stan at the conference table, and indicated it was his turn. The promotion man's smile absorbed his face. "You can safely bet we're staying Numero Uno on the charts for a second and third week. That's the bottom line until sales kick in. Figure the sky's the limit."

"Cubie, you're too much," Ira Dent said.

"Cheap at half. And how's the God of Publicity scoring?"

"You saw the action Saturday night and the coverage? The magazines and the talk shows that were dragging their feet, now they're standing in line begging me for a shot at Miranda, and, of course, I've started greasing the wheels on getting her a performing spot on the next Grammy Awards." He turned to Miranda, who was sitting quietly at the far end of the table absorbing the conversation. "Did you remember to twinkle this morning, little star?"

Cubie corrected Ira: "Big star."

"Gigantic," Stan said.

Miranda spent a few moments watching herself polish the table surface with her fingers. She looked up, pushed her oversized shades onto her forehead and said, "I've been grooving on the test pressing since Sunday. There are some cuts, three in all, where the mix isn't right. I want to go on back into Starshine and get Benny Sugar working on the remix, maybe some overdubs in some spots he didn't think of."

Lainie found a neutral place for her eyes to land and pursed her lips, doing a mental count of how many times over how many years she had heard this from newly inflated egos.

Cubie eased over to Lainie. He cupped his mouth and muttered only loud enough for her ears, "A biiiiig star."

Stan said, "We can't afford the delay, Lainie. We don't want to lose the momentum of—"

"Piss on the momentum," Miranda said, cutting him off. "I need mo' verb and mo' reverb is what I need now. That's my picture that'll be going out on the album, Stan, not yours. I am the one who lives or dies with 'Scarlet Woman.' " Her face a portrait in defiance.

Stan started to answer.

Lainie stopped him like a crossing guard. "What you're saying, Miranda, is that you know better than Benny Sugar?" Miranda, briefly pensive, nodded. "Also, better than me and everyone around the table who loves what's already planted in the grooves and has been kicking ass to get you a hit?"

"I wasn't comfortable saying anything before this, Lainie."

"You're comfortable now, though."

"Yes."

"Grand, because I want you to be comfortable. Do you know what stillbirth is, Miranda?" Miranda's brow knitted, like she wasn't entirely sure where Lainie was taking the conversation. Lainie planted an elbow on the table and her chin on her fist, trapped Miranda with her eyes. She said, "You owe everyone in this room an apology, young lady. I don't hear it in the next thirty seconds, 'Scarlet Woman' is dead in the water." She ran a finger across her throat. "Zap time. Your album will never see the light of day. It'll be over, gone, pfffft!, goodbye."

Miranda pushed herself onto her feet. "You can't. You wouldn't."

"I can. I will. You think I can't, read the fine print in your contract." A show of looking at her watch. "Fifteen seconds and counting."

Miranda grabbed her shoulder bag and stomped out of the conference room.

Ira, Cubie and Stan watched her go.

One, then all of them, began laughing.

"Déjà vu all over again," Cubie said.

Ira said, "They always come back looking different when they're reincarnated. Business as usual, boss?"

"Of course," Lainie said, and to Stan: "What are we doing about the internet, Stan?"

"Covered, Lainie." He shuffled through his files until he found the color-coded sheets he wanted and pushed them to her. "Our 'Scarlet Woman' Web site's getting its last tweaks, and we're still road testing the single. Free downloads on a hundred and fifty sites around the world. Great response."

"At that price, what else?" Ira said.

Lainie tuned out as Stan recited his statistics, her mind back on Harry Roman, wondering if he had been cut loose from the glass room. She told Stan to continue and headed for her office, where she called upstairs to Leonard Volkman. Petra put her through.

"Didn't we have this conversation about two hours ago?" Volkman said, letting her hear he resented her checking up on him. "You let me know you had made your delivery at Hillcrest. I delivered. Over and out." He hung up.

Lainie studied the dead phone. She tapped out the number of the district attorney's office through automated information. A bored secretary with a surreal Valley Girl accent told her Mr. Roman was in a meeting. Lainie opted against leaving word.

She dawdled through routine business and made calls of the nice-nice variety that Cubie insisted were necessary to lock into the indie radio promotion cliques that wanted her personal guarantee on their fees—two or three times their standard weekly five-figures—and radio station managers and program directors who needed their own kind of guarantees.

Lainie got home earlier than usual, fearing Sara might not be there.

She was, in her jammies, staked out in front of the television and deep into a carton of chocolate chip ice cream. She looked up from the "Addams Family" rerun long enough to say, "Surprised, huh? I told you not to worry; I wasn't planning to split anytime soon."

"Not surprised in the least, baby," Lainie said, hoping she'd carried off the lie.

"The least, that must mean the most then because seeing me here, you look like I'd have figured you to look if I told you I'm preggers."

Lainie felt the color on her face dive onto the floor. "Tell me that's a joke."

"A joke."

Lainie caught her breath. She settled alongside Sara, who offered her the spoon. She took a large glob for herself, then spoon-fed as much to Sara. "How you doing, baby?"

"I'll live, I suppose." She rescued the spoon and dug out a glob of ice cream for Lainie, then for herself. Using the spoon as a pointer at the TV, she said, "We have bigger monsters in our family than any one of them."

Lainie shook her head. "Meaning?"

"Nothing," Sara said, blankly. "Forget it."

"It must mean something or you wouldn't have said it."

"It means the phone is ringing?"

"What?"

Using the spoon as a pointer again: "The phone there. It's ringing."

Lainie answered with a subdued, "Hello." Jerry Newberry was calling for Sara. She passed over the receiver.

"What's up, soldier-boy?" Sara said, neither sounding nor looking happy about being on the phone with Jerry Mouse. "No. Oh, shit. Oh, God. Oh, God." Whatever he'd said had spun Sara into near-panic. "Where? Yes. I will . . . Yes, soon as possible . . . Jerry, you dumb fuck, don't you go and do something stupid. Promise me. Promise me, Jerr . . . Jerry?"

Sara dropped the phone and grabbed for the remote. She puddle-jumped stations until she connected with a live newscast whose field reporter was pumping a breathless, Hispanic-flavored baritone into a *This Just In* kind of account. The entrance to Bay Cities Emergency Hospital was prominent in the background.

"Doctors now report the young unidentified girl is in extremely critical condition and is not expected to survive," he was saying. *"They have confirmed that she is the thirteen-year-old girl who allegedly stabbed and killed another girl at a wild party that raged out of control last Saturday night in El Segundo."*

The reporter described how the girl, being treated for an overdose of illegal drugs she had consumed at the party, attempted to take her own life a few hours after being moved out of the Intensive Care ward. She'd apparently taken a ceramic vase holding a bouquet of roses into the bathroom. Cracked it in the sink. Used the sharpest piece to slash both wrists before driving it deep into her stomach.

"Unconfirmed reports from sources close to the scene told me exclusively that the child, who was found bleeding on the bathroom floor, wrote a note in her own blood on the mirror," the reporter continued, going pop-eyed to express his emotions. *"The note in her own blood said she was acting from guilt and remorse over killing her friend at the party. My exclusive sources said the suicide attempt happened about an hour after her parents explained what she was being accused of and police had asked her a series of questions relevant to the killing. The girl told the police she had no memory of anything, but"*—putting a choke in his voice—*"it's appearing that perhaps, she did . . . Back to you in the studio."*

A transfixed Sara suddenly lurched over the arm of the couch and vomited. When she'd finished heaving, she wiped the residue from her lips and across her pajama top, pushed to her feet and headed for the bedroom, telling Lainie, "I need to get dressed and go. I need to go meet Jerry, Mom. I told Jerry I'd go meet him."

Lainie started after her. "No," she said. "I understand why Jerry would be troubled by what we just learned, but it has nothing to do with you, baby. He was there when it happened. He saw the murder take place. He's probably feeling he was the cause, so some of the blame for this suicide attempt falls on him. It's Jerry's problem, baby. You weren't there. You don't have to make it your problem."

Sara stopped at the door, her hands gripping the knob. She said, "You don't get it, do you, Mom? It never happened the way Jerry told the police. That girl in the hospital, she didn't do it. I did. I did, Mom. I killed the other girl."

CHAPTER 28

An hour before Jerry Mouse's call to Sara, Harry Roman showed up unexpectedly at Thom Newberry's office in City Hall. Newberry's secretary caught his intercom cue to plead unavailability, put on an insincere smile and offered to schedule a meeting for tomorrow.

Roman answered with a bulldog growl and bolted past her.

Newberry looked up from his computer, unperturbed, like he had anticipated as much. "It's okay, Winnie. Close the door behind you and don't disturb us . . . Harry, old buddy, grab a chair."

"Thanks, old buddy," Roman said, his words dripping sarcasm and anger contorting his misshapen face as he shambled over. Without preamble, he launched the subject that had brought him here from the Hall of Justice and demanded answers.

Newberry listened patiently to Roman's recounting of history. When it was his turn, he said, "I explained it to you once before, Harry. It's all politics. Your boss the D.A. told you to turn down the burner on Lainie Davies Gardner and Leonard Volkman, because of Volkman's Rainbows Unlimited proposal for Paradise Sands. Instead, you ignored a direct order and went your own way. You turned the burner to high." He lifted his palms off the desk with suddenness, as if they had touched fire. "Ouch! All it got you was third-degree burns. Does that answer your questions?"

"Not all of them. Not the parts I don't know, Newberry. I came here hoping to hear those parts from you. What I asked you for and you ducked just now, old buddy."

Newberry shrugged. "Politics, remember?"

"Politics also that the D.A. fired me twenty minutes ago?"

"Fired? Indefinite suspension, the way I heard it, Harry."

Roman adjusted himself in the guest chair and threw one leg over the other, showed him a twitch of a smile. "What did the runt do? Grab the phone and call you the minute the deed was done?"

"The second call, actually. The first was Schermerdine wondering if Mayor Welles would object to your being put on indefinite suspension. That was before he met with you."

"A little professional courtesy between county and city government?"

"Still politics, Harry."

"And you told him?"

"Mayor Welles would have no objection."

"And still politics after the second call and you heard what I had to tell him?"

"Only to let me know your new status was official and to suggest we had some new developments we needed to go over in depth. The D.A. always prefers a face-to-face to the phone."

"New developments." Roman blew a laugh to the ceiling. "That gangster prick Volkman has me kidnapped and locked up in his building in a glass cage you'd expect to see in *Planet of the Apes,* and he's calling them *new developments*?" The laugh again, full of throaty disgust.

"I don't know what that means, Harry." He tried to keep his response nonchalant although Roman had told him more than he'd heard from Schermerdine. Roman had set off warning bells, arousing steep concern as well as curiosity.

"Up on that twenty-first floor of his?"

Newberry shook his head. *A glass cage?* Neither Lainie nor Flynn had ever said anything about a glass cage.

Roman said, "A goddamn glass cage. All the comforts of home to go with the gun-toting ape I think murdered Roy Gardner and expressed his appetite more than once for making me go away for good. You know the name Rudy Schindler, Newberry?"

Not a word about Rudy Schindler.

Newberry shook his head. "But you're still here."

Roman massaged his bad shoulder. "Maybe because that's also politics, me still being around? Maybe you know something about Rudy Schindler you can tell me? He's used names like Eubie Grass and Berry Berryman in the past." Newberry threw up his hands. "You lying to me, old buddy?"

"Hardly."

"Then Ruby Crandall has been lying to me about her little chats with you? The zipper-mouth you bought from that sweet little ol' career crim? Also politics?"

Newberry recognized Roman was through buying into his game. "You don't want to go there, Harry."

Roman pretended to search the office. "It would seem to me I've already been there and back, Newberry. Why do I sense you and your mayor just may be up to your collective asses in alligators?"

"What do you want, Harry?"

"Besides more truth than you've ever given me?"

"Answer the question."

"I want my job back."

"What else?"

"I want off the leash you and Schermerdine put me on."

"What do I receive in return?"

"My faulty memory when I go back in front of the grand jury and get my indictments on Volkman and Lainie Davies Gardner.

I also rope Rudy Schindler. A pretty package that'll grow to include kidnapping, extortion, ADW, attempted murder, false imprisonment, but you and your mayor will remain on the outside looking in. How's that for a return?"

"If I pass on your generous offer?"

"You'll read all about it in tomorrow's newspapers, old buddy."

"Either way, Harry, you know you're talking like a dead man."

"What movie did you steal that line from?"

Newberry propped his chin into his palm and tapped his fingernails on the desk. He spent several moments making out like he was weighing his decision. "It sounds like a bargain to me," he said, turning back to Roman, hoping he'd sounded sincere. All he wanted now was Roman out of his office, so he could call Volkman, tell him they had a serious problem. "You want to shake on it?" He extended his hand.

Roman pushed back in his chair. "Definitely not if it means touching you. You are a toilet bowl that needs flushing, old buddy."

Newberry put on a false smile and let the remark pass without comment, thinking how Volkman could set all the deadlines he wanted, threaten all he wanted about the Paradise Sands deal, but it wasn't going to happen as long as Roman was around and running off at the mouth. Volkman wouldn't need a crystal ball to see he had to purge the plague called *Harry Roman* that was terminally endangering all of them.

Roman rose and toweled his hands over his chest and thighs. The connecting door to the outer office swung open as he turned to leave. Winnie was filling the space almost as well as the door did.

She said, "I know you didn't want to be disturbed, Mr. Newberry, but your son insisted." Her brown eyes blinked nervously behind thick lenses that made them appear as large as bottle caps.

Newberry reached over for the phone, wondering why no light was flashing until Winnie stepped aside to reveal Jerry Mouse in full military uniform.

"Ma'am, please don't forget to send in my friend Sara when she gets here," Jerry said. He stepped forward, did a sharp turn, and shut and locked the door. He removed his cap, stationed it inside his belt and assumed an at-ease position. "I need to speak with you, sir; really bad. Do you know?" He appeared confused and agitated. He realized they were not alone and studied Roman for familiarity.

"Harrison Roman," Newberry said. "This is my son, Jerry Mouse."

"Jerry."

"My son, Jerry. Did the academy sign you out?" Newberry said, rising.

Jerry Mouse swung his head left and right. "Do you know the news, sir?"

Newberry wanted to give the brat what-for, but it could wait until they were alone. He turned on a broad smile. "I'll have someone get you back to Kenyon before the evening roll call, and they won't even know you're missing."

Jerry Mouse dismissed the suggestion with a gesture. "The girl, she tried to kill herself, sir. It's on the news. She tried to commit suicide for killing the other one. The one you made it look like she'd done it. Where you said for me to tell the police—"

Newberry slapped the desk. "That's enough, Jerry Mouse." He turned to Roman, shook his head and put on a sorrowful grimace. "My son has ADD challenges he can't always control, like an extremely vivid imagination that erupts like a volcano."

"Sir, Daddy, did you hear me? If that girl dies, it will be our fault. Yours and mine." He shifted his attention back to Roman. "It'll be our fault, me and my father, that she did that. She got high and OD'd, but she had no idea about anything else. No idea. Not one."

Newberry shrugged. "See what I mean, Harry?"

"Sir, I need you to pay attention," Jerry Mouse said, pleading with him. He withdrew a service revolver from his hip holster and aimed it at his father.

Roman gave Jerry Mouse an incredulous look. "Is that cap pistol loaded, Jerry?"

"Real gun, real bullets," Jerry Mouse said, adding with a certain amount of pride, "It's the Kenyon Academy way."

"How'd you get the gun past security?"

"Here at City Hall they know who I am, sir, so they don't bother anymore." He shifted his eyes back to Newberry.

Newberry mentally assayed the damage Jerry Mouse was causing him and, in those same split seconds, found a solution that, if handled correctly, would be immediate and definitive. He said, "Yes, I knew, Jerry."

"About the girl and all?"

"Yes. From Mr. Roman. That's why he's here."

"Why he's here, sir?"

"Why I'm here?" Roman said, as confused as Jerry Mouse.

Newberry steered around the desk to his son and took a position behind him. He leaned over and spoke softly inside the whisper fence he'd made with the hand cupped alongside Jerry Mouse's ear. "Mr. Roman is a former police officer, and he figured out what really happened on Saturday night. He put it all together, son."

"All of it?" Jerry Mouse said, a notch louder than his father.

The question carried across the way to Roman.

"All of what?" Roman said. "You plan on letting me in on the secret?"

Newberry whispered, "Mr. Roman wanted me to know before he called his cop buddies. First me, then the cops are coming to get you. Mr. Roman said he was going to prosecute us and see to it that we're both sent away to prison for life."

"Daddy, I couldn't. He can't . . . That's not fair." Jerry Mouse was buying into the story. He screamed at Roman: "That is not fair. I never meant for her—" The rest of his words reduced to an undecipherable gush. His blood red eyes turned glossier.

"If she died, Mr. Roman said it would go even worse for us. She did die, son. The girl has died. We saw the news on CNN a few minutes before you got here."

"On the CNN news." Jerry Mouse looked at the TV set on the wall cabinet shelf. Tears streamed down his checks and pockmarked his neatly pressed academy jacket.

Roman said, "Saw what on CNN, Jerry?"

"Her dying, on the CNN news," Jerry Mouse said, unaware he'd answered Roman. By the second, he was turning into an emotional disaster area. The service revolver wavered in his two-handed grip.

"Guess I have to go and find out for myself," Roman said, crossing to the couch in the conversation area. He plopped down and searched for the remote.

Newberry had repositioned himself with his arms around Jerry Mouse. He inched his hand along his son's arm, got his finger inside the trigger guard on top of Jerry Mouse's and gauged a good fix on Roman, confident what had worked for him once could be made to work for him again.

This time it would be Jerry Mouse who had committed murder, not a damn teenaged girl who'd gone and put his son into such a tailspin. The boy was only fifteen. A call or two would guarantee that Jerry Mouse wound up in a juvenile facility doing easy time. Later, once he'd put Lawton Welles in the governor's mansion, he'd get Jerry Mouse an early release, see to it that the sealed court proceedings were expunged. Memories are short. Any possible damage to his career and reputation would be fully repaired by the time the boy got out. Everything would be back on track, and—

Newberry kissed the shaved back of Jerry Mouse's head. He told him gently but firmly, "We can't let Mr. Roman do this to you, son. We can't let him destroy your life."

Roman said, "Oh, there it is," pointing to where he'd spotted the remote on the coffee table.

They were Roman's last words.

The bullet caught him in the chest. It flung him hard against the couch, his arms slapping the cushions, then into a crash dive onto the coffee table. A hand landed on the remote, popping on the TV.

The gunshot had exploded like a sonic boom.

For a few moments it deafened Newberry to the buzz of the intercom, a pounding on the door and the distant voice that belonged to the picture emerging on the flat jumbo screen.

Jerry Mouse had descended into a trance of sorts. He stood as rigid as a steel beam, the revolver still aimed at Roman, his eyes trying to decipher the meaning of Roman's lifeless form.

Newberry steered him to a desk chair and picked up the phone while Jerry Mouse turned away to focus again on Roman. Winnie was on the line, desperate to know what the noise was, if Newberry was all right.

Newberry said, "A horrible accident, Winnie. My boy has shot and killed Mr. Roman."

"What's that you're saying, sir?" Jerry Mouse said, his attention divided between Roman and the TV. The pictures were signaling the start of a fresh newscast, the sound hardly more than a background murmur. "It was you who—"

"Jerry, everything will be fine. Let me handle this."

"Yes, sir," Jerry Mouse said, distracted again by the television.

Newberry moved out of his hearing range and cupped the mouthpiece. He said, "Winnie, I want you to call building security and the police. Get them here on the double. The paramedics for Jerry Mouse."

"Is he hurt, Thom?"

"My boy went crazy all of a sudden, for no reason at all. He still has a gun," Newberry said, not answering the question; thinking: *Set up the concept of temporary insanity. Get Jerry Mouse short-term outpatient time with a county shrink instead of any juvenile time at all. It'll definitely put more top spin on the sympathy I'll be playing the media for.* "And, Winnie, keep the media away until I can frame my statement and a declaration of concern and support from Mayor Welles."

Jerry Mouse had moved from the chair to the table.

He picked up the remote and raised the level of the TV sound.

The Asian woman staring dramatically into the camera outside Bay Cities Emergency Hospital, mic in one hand, the other covering the receiver in her ear, was saying, ". . . Yes, that's correct, Gary. Doctors here are just as amazed as we are. They tell us that the thirteen-year-old, who was so close to death less than an hour ago, has improved dramatically and now looks like she will pull through this terrible ordeal. Being so young is what may have made the difference, they said, and—"

Jerry Mouse clicked off the set and called across the room, "Sir, you lied to me, sir. You lied to me, Daddy."

Newberry aimed a palm at him, cocked his head, said, self-righteously, "For you, Jerry. Not to you. For you."

"Why would you go and do that, Daddy?"

"You didn't hear what I said, Jerry. For you, son. For you."

He started toward Jerry Mouse, halted when Jerry Mouse hurried into a shooter's stance and leveled the revolver at him.

"I heard you, Daddy. I just don't believe you anymore. You

called the police on me just now, and just now I hear the girl never died at all, the way you said."

"Jerry, please. I must have misunderstood what I heard. Don't do anything foolish. You and I, we'll get through this horrible business together." He moved several tentative steps closer. "Put down the gun, son. I want you to give me the gun."

"Yes, sir," Jerry Mouse said, and—

Fired.

The impact spun Newberry and sent him flying toward the desk. He crashed against one of the visitors' chairs. Grabbed it like a pillow. Dragged it along as he sank to the floor. Looked up and forced his eyes to keep open against the descending darkness.

He saw Jerry Mouse standing over him, heard Jerry Mouse wondering, "What are we going to do now, Daddy?" Not sounding like he really needed or wanted an answer.

CHAPTER 29

Thom Newberry's office door opened, and Jerry Mouse stepped into the reception area revolver first, facing a frantic Winnie, who hadn't seen or chose to ignore the gun pointed at her. She pushed past the boy and charged through the door calling her boss's name. Seconds later, she screamed.

Sara, who'd been nervously pacing the room alongside Lainie since the gunshots and the lack of a response to her banging on the door, started for Jerry.

Lainie caught her arm. Ordered her not to move. She understood the desperation on Jerry Mouse's panic-driven face as he called over, "Sara, my daddy, he lied to me about the girl. About the police."

Sara tried undoing her mother's grip. Lainie squeezed harder and ordered Sara to stay put. She said, "What happened in there, Jerry?"

Jerry Mouse shook his head. "He lied to me about the girl, Mrs. Gardner. He lied to me about the police. Lied about Mr. Roman in there."

Hearing Roman's name startled Lainie. She tried hiding her reaction. "Talk to me about the lies, Jerry."

Jerry Mouse rotated his head, fast, like he was trying to unscrew his face from his neck. "Parents aren't supposed to lie to their children."

"Of course not. Mr. Roman, did he also lie?"

Jerry Mouse's face spun out of control. "Sara, my daddy told me he found out, but I don't know. I didn't tell anybody anything. Not Mr. Roman or anybody."

Sara showed she understood. Under her breath said to Lainie, "Let me go to him, Mother. I can get him to put down the gun."

"It's not going to happen, baby. Stay put."

"He'll do it for me, Mother. I told you what he did for me Saturday night."

"That was then. This is now." She fought off Sara's attempt to spring loose.

Jerry Mouse said, "What's that? What are you saying?"

Before Lainie could attempt to pacify him with a response, Newberry's secretary charged through the door like an angry rhino. She shoved Jerry Mouse between the shoulder blades and threw him off balance. He reflexively pulled the trigger. His wild shot whizzed within inches of Lainie's neck before thudding into the paneled wall behind her.

He was like a tightrope walker struggling on the high wire but regained his balance and turned in time to sidestep the brick-sized glass paperweight Winnie intended to bring down on his head. He fired blindly. A puncture hole formed on her chest and spilled blood.

Winnie came at him again. Jerry Mouse fired again. She staggered to a full stop, her face filled with wonder, her globe-round eyes staring back at him in disbelief. She dropped to the floor and rolled onto her side, crying for someone to help her. Jerry Mouse glanced down at her. "He lied to me, Winnie, or not any of this would have happened," he said, then repeated himself to Lainie and Sara.

An explosive boom brought down the corridor door.

An LAPD officer in a flak jacket twisted into view, his assault rifle ready to fire.

At once he was shouting demands at Jerry Mouse.

Sara wrenched free of Lainie, yelling "Don't!" as Jerry Mouse appeared ready to raise his revolver. She stepped into the line of fire between Jerry Mouse and the officer. The cop, young, grim-faced and determined, ordered, "Out of the way, miss."

Instead, Sara backed up to Jerry and said, "Quick, get an arm around me and put your gun to my neck."

"I wouldn't—"

"Chill and do it, Jerry. My turn to try and help you."

The cop shed his initial amazement. "Are you crazy, miss?"

Lainie moved to the cop and pushed his rifle aside. "She's my daughter. Let me have a minute to talk some sense into them."

The cop said, "More of us out there at the ready. Some people still haven't quit for the day. We can't risk them getting harmed. Better we settle it quick, or we take him down in here."

"A minute."

The cop nodded.

Lainie began an approach on Sara and Jerry Mouse.

Jerry Mouse's answer was a fast retreat backward into his father's office.

"Not on your life," Lainie shouted. Leaped after them. Made it through the door before Jerry Mouse could untangle himself from Sara and got it closed.

Jerry Mouse had visited his father often enough to know about City Hall's back alleys. These were the private corridors that allowed city officials to come and go away from prying eyes. Important to him now were the stairwells developed expressly for work crews brought in for "Project Restore" following the Northridge earthquake of ninety-four that caused relocation for more than a thousand workers from the fifth through the twenty-seventh floors. Most of the stairwells had not been used since the project was completed.

The maze of a trail he ordered Sara and her mother on began at a door by the bookcase at the rear of his father's office. He was using it for the third time, he said. The first time was when Daddy moved into City Hall and explored the building with him and his Uncle Lance. The next time it was the two of them, when Daddy took him all the way to the top to check on something that was wrong with the Lindbergh Beacon.

"Charles A. Lindbergh was the first man who flew across the Atlantic by himself, nonstop," he said, blankly, as if he were reciting a book report from memory. "Go through the door there and across." The door he indicated had a sloppy "12" splashed on its rusted brown surface in white paint. "The next walk takes us across the building to the equipment elevator that goes from twelve up to twenty-seven. There's no thirteen. Someone was superstitious. We go straight to fourteen."

Lainie took a deep breath and coughed out dust she had been swallowing during the race Jerry Mouse had them on. The boy was too fragile to deal with logically. There was no sense in trying to talk him back downstairs. If it were just the two of them, no Sara, she could attempt something, but otherwise—

No.

Definitely not.

The boy had shot three people.

He obviously had developed some inexplicable bond with Sara, but say something wrong or the wrong way, and there was no guarantee he wouldn't squeeze the trigger a fourth time.

Or a fifth.

Sara was uncharacteristically quiet, perhaps because she also recognized the danger or correctly read the look Lainie kept flashing her.

Lainie should have figured it was too good to last.

Jerry Mouse was wondering if they knew how tall City Hall was when Sara turned and said with the know-everything wisdom that comes from being fifteen, "Dude, I don't know what exactly you're looking for, but whatever, you're not going to find it here."

"Sara—"

"Chill, Mom," Sara said, running her palm at Lainie's face. "We have to go back down, Jerry."

"Over four hundred and fifty feet," Jerry Mouse said. "Four hundred and fifty-two to be exact . . . The cop, he was going to shoot me, Sara. Down there in Daddy's office. You saved my life downstairs."

"Dude, the way I saw it, you were going to shoot him. I was out to save the cop."

"No, not so. I've had it up to here with lies already, so you shouldn't."

"Cross my boobs," Sara said, puffing out her chest.

"You don't have any, and I don't want to hear anymore, so turn and go that way," Jerry Mouse said, wagging the revolver up and down. "Do it, and you, too, ma'am. Please. Just do it."

They stepped from the elevator on the twenty-seventh floor which, with twenty-eight, formed the Tower area. Jerry Mouse flipped the lock switch, called a direction that took them through open space that served as a repository for workmen's gear— some areas more orderly than others—and carried the lingering sweat of vintage day labor.

"Not the original terra cotta tile on the walls," Jerry Mouse said. "The original tiles fell off when the ninety-four quake hit. Getting City Hall back in shape? It ran up a cost of a cool two hundred and ninety-nine million dollars. Cheap at half the price, my dad always says."

He continued his rambling, piling on historical details about City Hall and the Lindbergh Beacon, sometimes repeating himself, but always speaking with authority, until they reached the door he wanted.

"It's for the stairwell that goes to the beacon," he said. "No other way up and only one other way to get down." When they reached the landing, he said, "Go ahead inside and make yourselves comfortable. Have a look around."

The turret-shaped area was small and confining. Its cement walls alternated with tall windowless openings that created a cross breeze pregnant with the hum of early evening street and freeway traffic and the undecipherable noise patterns of a Civic Center that was emptying. A circular stepladder base dominated the center of the room. It rose almost to the break in the roof. The Lindbergh Beacon topped it like a crown jewel.

The computerized timing system controlling the beacon had switched on the powerful light and was shooting it into the star-dimpled melancholy gray sky as if it were reaching for the moon. The tower was otherwise dark, barely enough brightness creeping in from outside to let them monitor their movement.

Jerry Mouse said, "We'll be in here for a while. Make yourselves comfortable."

Lainie said, "How long is a while, Jerry?"

Jerry Mouse opened his mouth to answer; at once must have realized he didn't have an answer. He gave the door a few shakes. "We'll be here a while, so make yourselves comfortable."

"They'll come looking and find us up here sooner or later, Jerry."

"Yes, ma'am. It's a tactical imperative." He threw a smile at Lainie the way somebody might throw a dog a bone.

Lainie eased down onto the cold cement floor. It was damp from teasing drizzles that recently had broken a long-term drought, sending an instant shiver-inducing chill up her spine. Sara, who had settled into the same cross-legged position alongside her, didn't react or seem to mind. Lainie reached over and took Sara's hands in hers. Sara let her.

Jerry Mouse moved around behind them to a spot that gave him a clear view of the door and the base of the Lindbergh Beacon as a protection wall.

Nobody spoke for several minutes; the boy's breathing at times the loudest sound in the room, except for a laser-like whine from the beacon.

He broke the silence, wondering, "Does your mother know the truth about what happened Saturday night, Sara?"

Lainie answered the question for her. "If you mean how it was my daughter who stabbed that poor girl to death, yes, I do, Jerry."

"It's what I mean, ma'am, but I don't know where you got that idea from. That's not the truth at all about what happened Saturday night. Why would your mother say something like that, Sara?" Lainie swung around to confront Sara, who averted her stare and tried to pull her hands free. "I said, why would your mother say something like that, Sara?"

Lainie said, "Why would I say something like that, Sara?" tugging at Sara for emphasis.

"She was giving me a hard time about coming to see you, like you asked me, Jerry. I had to tell her like something that would make her spring the wheels—like it was my fault what you were being put through."

Relief covered Lainie like a shroud. "Then the girl in the hospital, she did do it. She did kill the other girl."

"Oh, no, ma'am," Jerry Mouse said. "I was the one who did it. It was me. They got in a fight in the bathroom, the two of them. I tried to stop it. Next I knew I was stabbing and stabbing and stabbing away. When he got there, my father made it look like the girl did it. Daddy told me what I had to say to the police to keep from going to prison and all."

"And Sara, she wasn't involved?"

"Not exactly, ma'am." Lainie gave him a puzzled look over her shoulder. "Sara, she was there when it happened—in the bathroom with us, the three of us, all three. Like four of us there when it happened. Sara, too."

Lainie recoiled from his explanation, not sure what to make of it. Fearful she'd next be hearing that Sara had been party to the murder, however accidental it was beginning to sound. She released Sara's hands. She held her daughter's face with both hands, making it impossible for Sara to turn away from her. Sara's eyes said Jerry Mouse was telling the truth.

"Tell me the rest," Lainie said, with as much authority as she could muster.

Jerry Mouse came around the beacon's base and stood directly in front of them. "You don't have to, Sara, you don't have to be in trouble like I am. I told you that when it happened and said for you to go away fast."

"Dude, stop waving the damn gun in my face." He eased it over so that the barrel stared down at Lainie. "Her, too, dude, for Christ's sake."

Jerry Mouse frowned. "You shouldn't be taking the name of our dear Lord in vain, Sara." He raised the revolver so that it aimed at the opening in the roof. "I got to keep the safety on for now, for you, though not later, when they come after me."

"I'm waiting for my answer," Lainie said.

Jerry Mouse and Sara traded glances.

He said, "It's always important to obey your parents," and threw her an encouraging smile.

Sara said, "I was doing party-hearty with a primo dude when I saw Jerry being leashed into the bathroom by this chick who had been woofing after him from when we hit the rave. I figured he'd get his nuts toasted and nothing wrong with that, but then in went the prom queen who heated up to Jerry backstage at your Miranda Morgan blast. She has this mean as shit look and barges right in, and one of her tats didn't have to say 'trouble' for me to know it. So, I spring loose and head on over, figuring Jerry might need a helping hand out, knowing from our rap that this is a new kind of action for him? They're into it, and then the prom queen pulls out her blade and—"

"I got between them," Jerry Mouse said, interrupting. "The rest was the way I already told you, except for Sara being there, who I told to get away quick, because she didn't have to get into trouble like me."

"I shouldn't have listened to him, Mother. I'm as guilty as him. Jerry's nice and all, but a nerd who didn't belong at the rave. I shouldn't have encouraged him to go when the prom queen did her number on him. If I hadn't and he didn't, none of this would have happened. Both those girls would still be alive instead of dead, and Jerry would never have shot his father or the others and—"

Jerry Mouse said, "A nerd? That's what you think?"

"In the nicest way I could mean, Jerry, and I think we have to go downstairs now."

Jerry Mouse sprang the safety and got off a shot that cracked into the roof.

"You think a nerd would do that?" His anger building.

"I said, 'in the nicest way.' I could have called you a wuss, y'know, dude?"

Lainie said, "Jerry, it will only get worse the longer we stay up here and the police have to come after you."

"I'm not going to prison, ma'am."

"No, you're not. Everything I hear and everything Sara says means it might even be self-defense. Probably is. Even if it were more, you're too young to be sent to prison." She didn't add the obvious, that he would wind up someplace a juvenile offender could receive the psychiatric care he desperately needed.

Jerry Mouse responded with a puzzled look.

He fired again without aiming.

The shot clanged against the Lindbergh Beacon, throwing the light off course.

He said, "How many wusses you know who can handle a firearm as good as me? Or nerds? Or—?" His eyes shifted to the left, almost spilled off his face as he moved a few steps away. Some new confusion was crowding his mind. "Sara, why are you trying to trick me like my father?"

"Say what, dude?"

"You said both of them were dead, but I watched it on the TV news that the girl in the hospital was getting better all of a sudden and not dead like my father lied. Now you lie to me. She's lying to me, ma'am. Is it because she thinks I'm a nerd and a wuss and—?"

He moved the revolver and sighted onto Sara.

Lainie rolled herself in front of her daughter. If anyone was going to get shot up here, it was going to be her.

She said, "It's not a lie, Jerry. Whatever your father told you, Sara has told you the truth. We heard the news on the radio when we were parking. The poor girl seemed to be improving, but almost as quickly she did another turnaround and died. Sara is telling the truth, Jerry. So am I. Put down the gun, all right?"

"So my father, he didn't lie to me?"

"Not the way it turned out, Jerry."

"Wow." He eased up on the gun. Looked up at the light and sputtered a laugh, like he was seeing something amusing. "You ever see the movie where this dude is way up on top of an oil tank or something and he's saying *Top of the world, Mom,* or something? He shoots down at the cops who are trying to capture him, and the oil tank explodes and him with it?"

"I think so, Jerry. Why?"

He shrugged.

"Just wondering, ma'am. You think up there where the Lindbergh Beacon is, outside at the very top, it would feel like it felt for King Kong when he was up on top of the Empire State Building? Swatting back at all the planes that were shooting at him before he went falling to the ground?"

"I don't know, Jerry. Let's go downstairs now, okay?"

"I think I want to check it out first, ma'am."

He gave a little salute, holstered the revolver and double-timed the stepladder base. He reached the top and squeezed between the beacon and the aperture before disappearing entirely.

After a minute or two, Jerry Mouse poked his head back inside.

"More like the top of the world," he said.

He moved out of sight again.

After another moment, having given the Lindbergh Beacon a slight adjustment, so that the beam caught him as well as the night sky, he screamed, "Top of the world, Daddy! Top of the world!"

CHAPTER 30

Leonard Volkman was patrolling the walls, aligning frames that had gone out of kilter, when Petra ushered Lainie and Flynn into his office. Rudy Schindler, lounging over a can of soda in the conversation area, grunted confirmation. Volkman adjusted the frame of a small Rouault and, expressing satisfaction, wandered to his desk, inviting them with a gesture to occupy the visitors' chairs.

He helped himself to a cigar and said, "The business at City Hall two days ago, it solved a shit-load of problems for us, but did it answer the big one? Did Newberry have a chance to set the mayor straight on the Paradise Sands deal before that sick-o kid of his punched his ticket and took a bungee jump the hard way?"

He sat down and toyed with the giant Havana waiting for an answer.

Lainie winced but otherwise ignored his coarse attitude. "We met at Hillcrest, and I gave Newberry the box with the file. He checked it out and said it wasn't the right one. He accused me of running a switch on him. I didn't know what to make of it, so I played him. I said, yes, I made a switch, and he would get the right file after he guaranteed the mayor was in line for you."

"That lying son of a bitch. I absolutely got him the file you said he was after. It wasn't one that could come back to haunt us as much as him, so no skin off my nose." Volkman leaned forward pointing at Flynn. "You know any better?"

Flynn gave him a look. "Why should I, mate?"

"Don't 'mate' me, Flynn. You tell Flynn why he should or should I, Lainesky?" He didn't wait for an answer. "Because you've been Newberry's snitch around here. Why else do you think I okayed your being here with her, because I'm lonely for your company?"

"Who went and handed you that piss water?"

"I got snitches of my own. You think Petra's big mouth to go with her big boobies is only good for one thing?"

Flynn flashed a grin. "What did Petra say?"

"Only that you told her about the file when you got the key to twenty and twenty-one back to her, but not which one. You said you planned to make your own pass at cracking the floors and scoring the right file, because that's what Newberry ordered you to do."

"A *very* big mouth," Flynn said.

"Here's the deal. You tell me the right file, and I'll make other arrangements with the mayor before the vote next week on Paradise Sands. I'll call us square, and you can pack your bags and lose yourself for good."

"I don't think so, mate."

The sound of metal on glass drew Lainie's attention. Schindler had settled his soda can on the coffee table, pushed up from the couch and moved to a position almost directly behind Flynn.

Flynn looked over at Schindler and acknowledged his presence. "Why do I suddenly feel threatened?"

Schindler said, "Maybe because you answer Mr. Volkman's question and tell him what he wants, or you're worse off than just feeling threatened."

"I get to visit your little glass playroom?"

"What do you think?"

"I think I'd be safer smoking six packs of fags a day."

Volkman said, "You're damn cocky for an asshole who—" and stopped mid-sentence. He pulled his brow tight. Filled his eyes with suspicion. Gave Flynn a hard look. "Who was it told you about the glass house?"

"A verrry big mouth," Flynn said, smiling lasciviously.

Volkman shook his head. "I never told Petra or let her go on either twenty or twenty-one, so she had no way of knowing the glass house even existed." He began tapping one-handed on the desk while exploring his Havana; looked up after several moments and trained his eyes on Lainie. "You, though, Lainesky. You're another story."

Flynn said, "A story that'll have a happier ending than the one you're up for, mate."

"Try me while you have the chance."

Flynn reached inside his sports jacket. Schindler made it his cue to pull out the Magnum holstered under his arm. He stepped forward and settled the weapon at the nape of Flynn's neck.

Flynn said, "Nothing rash now. I'm after my billfold and something you should see."

Lainie said, "His badge, Lenny. Flynn's a federal agent."

"And long on your case, mate." He placed the billfold on the desk and pushed it toward Volkman using the palm of his hand. Volkman opened the billfold wide enough to confirm the presence of a gold shield; let the lid fall back.

Flynn said, "More shields where that one came from, only an elevator ride away from us, you or Schindler still thinking about doing anything foolish."

Volkman pumped out a clump of noisy breath. He said, "Go finish your soda pop, Rudy." Schindler holstered the Magnum and retreated to the couch. "You been at this a long time, Flynn?"

"On your arse since before we set you up to buy the movie

company. Doing the nasty with Thom Newberry to get a line on his dealings with your other companies after I picked up that clue from Petra."

"I should have seen you're a switch-hitter, one of the boys who go both ways."

"Any way it takes to land sharks like you."

"I'm not landed yet, Flynn."

"You just don't know it." Flynn pulled a search warrant from his jacket and waved it at Volkman. "What we learned from Mrs. Gardner and that one file you gave her was enough for us to get this. My people are about to give the twentieth and twenty-first floors a spring cleaning that should do you in once and for all in a court of law."

Volkman shook his head. "It's a big ocean . . . Lainesky, you know about this all along?"

"Short term, Lenny. Not until I got home Sunday. Flynn was waiting for me. He said it was either cooperate and catch a break or—" She turned her palms to the ceiling.

Flynn said, "Mrs. Gardner does right by us in court, she earns a pass from her grateful government and can live happily ever after, provided it's the whole truth and nothing but we get from her."

"The truth, when did that ever count for anything?" Volkman said. He studied Lainie. "It ain't over till it's over, kid, so no hard feelings," he said, and tossed her the Havana.

CHAPTER 31

Two weeks later, Flynn drove Lainie to Lance Clifford's mansion in Holmbly Hills. It hadn't changed in the years since she'd cracked the grounds looking for Thom Newberry after her release from the Animal Farm, except, this time, shrouds covered the statues she had once identified as Thom and black silk mourning bands adhered to the arms of other bronze and plaster-cast male torsos in the garden surrounds.

Lainie had ignored the memorial service at City Hall honoring Newberry's memory, but wanted to be at Clifford's from the moment Flynn told her about the intimate gathering the aging movie star was planning for his longtime lover—fifty or sixty of the friends and lovers they had in common—and for Jerry Mouse, his "nephew."

By pulling the strings always available to celebrities, Clifford had arranged for both bodies to be released early by the coroner's office and had them cremated. Their co-mingled ashes were reposing in a decorative antique urn on display in the lavish shrine Clifford had commissioned from an art director buddy at one of the movie studios.

The shrine was a marvel of curlicue gold, glitz and glitter, the towering centerpiece of the precisely-manicured walking gardens behind the mansion. It stood about twelve feet high, with an "eternal flame" burning on the top.

Lainie's reaction had jumped from amazement to amusement when Flynn described the shrine to her. "It fits perfectly into

Clifford's world of make-believe," she said. "He's put Thom and Jerry closer in death than they ever were in life."

Clifford was at the shrine when they arrived, the center of attention, surrounded by seven or eight men and women of varying age and attire clinking champagne glasses raised on high in some sort of toast. She recognized several from the movies and TV, the tallest one from the NBA playoffs.

He saw Flynn, excused himself and headed over, covering the short distance at a cane-assisted pace that disputed the vigor in his voice. He greeted Flynn by name, gave him a warm embrace and turned to stare at Lainie. She read more than sadness on his face and in his dark-circled, red-rimmed eyes swollen with grief. His wrinkles were as deep as irrigation ditches. The hollows under his cheeks dispelled any memory of the matinee idol Clifford once had been. He was a sick old man now, unable to rise to full height, his glorious prime long spent. His body fit badly inside a custom-tailored suit, the patterned silk handkerchief falling from the jacket pocket the only colorful thing about him.

His face and his jaw dropped when he recognized her. He moved a hand to his forehead as a shade against the sun and squinted to be certain. "What, pray tell, is she doing here?" he said, like spit, no attempt at charm or civility.

"I've brought you something," Lainie said. "Is there someplace private we can go?"

"You can go to hell for all I care, Miss Davies."

"Mrs. Gardner."

"By any name," he said, contemptuously. "Flynn, what's this about? Why do you insult me by bringing here this tramp relic from our Thom's past?"

"You'll be interested in the why of it, mate."

Flynn's easy smile disarmed Clifford.

"My study. I'll join you in ten minutes," he said. Turned and headed back to the shrine, one difficult step after the next.

Lance Clifford's inner sanctum was a study in traditional show business ego, the red silk-lined walls lost under elegantly framed autographed candid and posed photographs of the movie star with other stars and prominent celebrities, and posters from his film and stage triumphs. A key light captured the golden glow of the "Best Actor" Oscar protecting the mantle, putting to shame the Golden Globe, Emmy and Grammy awards scattered about like so much ho-hum.

Lainie was testing the Oscar for weight, guessing it at about eight or nine pounds, when the double doors slid into the walls. Clifford powered in on a motorized wheelchair. He slowed to a stop in the middle of the room, settled a frown on his face, bundled his hands in his lap.

"Yes? What? I have guests I must get back to," Clifford said, his unrelenting slit-eyed stare shifting from Flynn to Lainie, challenging her to say something that would validate her presence.

She put the Oscar back and padded over to her tote bag, propped against the head of the grizzly bear rug by the armchair in which Flynn was lounging. She took out the file folder that had been so coveted by Thom Newberry and settled in the armchair next to Flynn.

Clifford's expression turned curious. He shook his head, like he had no idea where this was leading.

Lainie said, "I asked Flynn to bring me here because I thought you might like to see what killed Thom, Mr. Clifford." She leaned forward and held up the file folder. "This is what killed Thom."

Flynn appealed to her quietly, from the side of his mouth, "A bit louder, mate. He's deaf in one ear and maybe seventy-five percent keen in the other."

Lainie repeated herself.

Clifford said, "You do not have to shout, Miss Davies. I am not deaf. What does that have to do with my young man?"

"With you, also, Mr. Clifford." She told him about Newberry's commanding her to his office at City Hall, threatening her with a new trial, with prison and, worst of all, with losing Sara, unless she got into Volkman International, got him what turned out to be—

"This file, Mr. Clifford."

"Flynn, this is so much phony baloney. You believe it, the phony baloney she must have handed you before she took her phony baloney to me?" His voice had gone as loud as Lainie's, the way it is with people too vain to drop an aid in their ear. "I was made to think by Thom that you were smarter than that, Flynn."

"Smarter'n by half, Lance, but why she's here with me, Mrs. Gardner. She's telling it all true, mate."

"What are the two of you up to? What's the game? Thom called you a good friend, Flynn, but this? I am having my doubts."

"His punching bag and battering ram is all what I ever was about with him, Lance." He signaled for Lainie to continue.

She said, "Thom led me to believe this file was—like everything else I ever knew about him—still about him. It was about keeping the mayor's skirts clean and Thom's with him, so the mayor could get elected governor and Thom could keep climbing onward and upward. That wasn't the case at all. Ultimately, I learned the file he coveted was all about you, Mr. Clifford. Letters, documents, photographs that would reveal you as the pus in a pimple if any of it ever were to be made public. Even in these enlightened times, when the truth comes out of closets regularly and your reputation wouldn't be tarnished anywhere but in your ego, and even though your career is into the twilight zone—"

"Only today my agent called with a major offer!"

"Of course," she said, and looked away, not interested in measuring the toll this brush with reality and truth was taking on Clifford. "I was amazed, sir, Thom doing maybe the only decent thing he'd ever done in his life for someone who was not Thom Newberry. For perhaps the one person in the world he had affection for beside himself and his son, Jerry. Ironically, it got Thom murdered by his son and caused the death of a poor, sad, confused, lonely, miserable boy who deserved better out of life and never had a chance."

"Damn it, woman. Why tell me this? To taunt me before you run off and expose me to the world, exacting some delayed revenge for my coming between you and Thom and taking him away from you those many years ago?"

Lainie laughed. "On the contrary. I came to thank you." She turned to face him. Clifford cranked his head away and settled his gaze on the Oscar. "If it were not for you taking him away from me for yourself, running me roughshod out of Thom's life, I might have been crazy enough, blinded enough by love, to stay with Thom. Marry Thom. Wind up destroying my life before it had a chance to start. There'd be no me. No career. No Roy Gardner. No Sara. So I owe you for all that, Mr. Clifford."

She rose and crossed to the wheelchair.

Dropped the file on his lap.

Clifford made a harsh noise in his throat and looked up at her. "I have absolutely nothing to apologize for."

"Certainly not to me," Lainie said. "Let's go, Flynn. We have better places to be."

They passed around the wheelchair heading for the door.

Clifford called after her, "Are these the originals? Is this everything? Are there copies? Were any copies made?"

She ignored him and kept walking, flushed with an over-whelming satisfaction.

The next stop for Lainie and Flynn was the Beverly Oaks Hotel and what she considered "their" bungalow, where they had been meeting three and four times a week since the night she returned home from Volkman International and found Ira Dent gone and Flynn babysitting Sara.

Verging on two in the morning, they were lounging naked on the exotic pink carpeting in front of the bedroom fireplace, draining a second bottle of Cristal while Sinatra serenaded them on the radio with "My Funny Valentine," when Flynn surprised Lainie with a question that hit her like a sharp jab in the ribs.

He said, "You planning to ever tell me about the meeting I hear Volkman had with you and your old mate Eddie Pope?"

The question was so out of place.

So left field.

An unwarranted reminder of the circumstances that brought them together.

A fresh warning not to let her heart rule her head.

She said, "Why? What difference?"

"Why not? An innocent inquiry, you delicious creature."

"Nothing's ever innocent with you, Flynn."

"So, keeping secrets, are you?" Flynn pulled her back to him and planted a wet kiss on her neck. His champagne breath had undertones of brandy. He'd been sneaking at the hip flask again—those *Excuse me* trips to the john—despite his promise to cut down now that he had her for his Energizer Bunny. How he had put it: *My Energizer Bunny.*

Like every man she had ever known, he came with as many faults as he had virtues, but a greater voltage power than she'd known since Roy; that, and he posed as great a threat to her as Thom had. As Harry Roman had. She could admit now she had suspected after that first night in the back seat of the car that there was not going to be any true love here for either of them, only heat, passion, the need to know, only the lesson she had learned the hard way as a kid surviving on the pitted streets and dark alleys of L.A. and codified later by Roy: *Keep your friends close, but your enemies closer.*

She said, "Saving the news for the right time."

"Of course, and no time like the present?" Flynn moved his kisses to her ear, then down to her left breast, then to the right breast, where he let his lips linger, making it difficult for her to tell him only what she thought he should know.

"Eddie called and invited me to join him at the meeting. It was yesterday."

"Ah, yesterday, when all your troubles fade away?" He hummed a few bars of the Beatles song. "Some of them, anyway."

"Eddie put a deal to Lenny in terms Lenny understood."

"Like one thief to another?"

Eddie was the one standup guy in her life who had never been anything but. Lainie let the put down pass. "Eddie's bought me out from under Volkman."

"A deal the way you wanted?"

"The way Eddie offered to make it happen. He's acquired Perfect Records and its assets, including Miranda Morgan. We'll be moving to his company, Chorale, as a boutique label. I'll continue running Perfect, with my Three Musketeers on board as part of the deal. Effective immediately."

"How generous of Volkman. Not his nature to walk away from any of his investments before working some swindle on thousands of people." Flynn was beginning to slur his words. "You wonder why?"

"Nothing to wonder. Eddie is cashing him out a hundred percent for two-and-a-half times Volkman's investment to date. There's a pro rata on Miranda Morgan's record sales and publishing, but that's cash down the line."

"Payable to one of his shell companies located where the IRS can't reach?"

"Nothing Eddie or Lenny talked about."

"You and Lenny. What else you and Lenny talk about?"

"He asked about Sara. How she was getting along."

"How human of him . . . No mention of the Paradise Sands proposal, now it's finally up for City Council vote day after next? Or how the vote might go?"

"No."

Neither feeling nor sounding as sloshed as he had only seconds ago: "The mayor, if he was planning to veto the deal it went Volkman's way?"

"No."

"How my agency might be doing with the grand tour through his files from twenty and twenty-one?" A question so damn obvious as to be insulting.

"What do you do for an encore, Flynn? Spring a lie detector test on me?"

"Just asking, mate."

"Playtime's over," Lainie said.

She drove home on main streets full of calm in the ghost hours before sunrise. There were few cars on the road and fewer people, except for the homeless who were as common as cracks in the sidewalk. They were in crude shelters in inlaid doorways and roofed bus benches, their shopping carts piled high with the refuse of past lives parked nearby.

Her windows were rolled tight against lingering exhaust fumes, burned tobacco and the fetid sweat of people always in a hurry, as if speed were the panacea for whatever about their daily lives needed fixing.

She hated these streets this time of morning. They took her back too far. To days she never wanted to experience again, even in memory, although she knew they would never leave her any more than she could entirely leave them behind. However well Lainie managed to flee her past, it always caught up to her again, like some shadow of truth that never lets go, but only becomes temporarily invisible as part of a gigantic hoax life loves to play.

Arriving home, she showered to scrub Flynn off her, scrubbing herself hard enough with a wire soap brush to raise exquisite pain and narrow avenues of blood.

Failed to achieve any of the relief she craved.

Fell into bed hoping for a few hours' sleep before her daily visit to Sara.

Sara had seemed in control of herself and her emotions after the police got them down from the tower. She got through their gentle interrogation dry-eyed; smiled when they offered her a department psychologist to help her past any post-traumatic stress; turned and, clenching her eyebrows and stretching her mouth into silliness, delivered a *They've got to be kidding* look to her mother.

Lainie should have recognized then that it was an act, before Sara woke up screaming, blaming herself for the deaths of Jerry Mouse and the two girls; plummeted into a downward spiral that landed her beyond hysteria before the paramedics arrived, sedated her and whisked her off to emergency at County General.

Thinking about Sara, sleep became impossible.

CHAPTER 32

Sara was at Safety Net, an expensive rehab clinic hidden about forty minutes from L.A. in a gated community of million-dollar homes in Northridge. Eddie Pope had reminded Lainie about the place and insisted on paying for it after making the phone call that cut through what he referred to as "the usual check-out-the-bank balance red tape crap."

She'd told him, "You don't have to do this, Eddie."

He blew her off with a gesture. "If I did, I wouldn't, Slim. Besides, you'd never get Sara in Safety Net otherwise. Not on your bank balance."

Sara's doctor was an intense, pleasant man in his late twenties with a thin lemon-colored mustache and a voice like body lotion. He greeted Lainie with his usual deference and inquired after Mr. Pope while guiding her to Sara's private room, one of twelve in the home's two-story west wing.

"You should be able to notice some modest improvement over yesterday and a world of difference since a week ago," Dr. Starnes said, ushering her in. He announced "Sara, it's your mommy here to visit with you again," and left them alone.

A world of difference?

Lainie noticed nothing of the sort.

Sara was sitting in a straight-back chair staring out the window, exactly as she'd left her yesterday, a cardboard cutout that breathed.

Lainie called, "Hi, baby."

No acknowledgement.

She headed over with a chair, gave Sara a kiss before settling down alongside her. She reached for her hand. It was cold. She warmed it between hers, asking, "How are you, baby?"

Nothing back.

"Time for me to go, baby," she said after twenty minutes of small talk that failed to pull so much as a flinch. She gave Sara another kiss, returned her chair to its place by the wall and called from the doorway, "Goodbye, baby. See you tomorrow."

Driving back to her new office at Chorale, she cried most of the way.

Rudy Schindler was waiting for her in reception, his face buried in today's *Daily Variety*.

He looked up at the sound of her approaching. "We need to talk," he said.

There was a retro-fifties diner a few blocks away, the waitresses in cutesy canary-colored costumes, nickel juke boxes and make-your-own toasters at every counter station and booth, the smell of grease everywhere. It was between meal hours. The place was relatively empty, mostly company gophers waiting for coffee and Danish orders at the pick-up spot by the cash register.

Lainie and Schindler settled across from one another at a small back booth, Schindler on the side facing the front entrance, trading silence until the waitress took their orders and roller-skated away. He looked up from pouring a pound of sugar into his coffee. "Mr. Volkman wants you to know you're about to be busted," he said.

It was not what she expected to hear. She'd been guessing Lenny had sent Schindler to see her after receiving reassurance she'd be keeping her word to him. As part of the deal that gave Perfect Records to Eddie Pope, she swore not to do the kind of show-and-tell for Flynn and the feds that gave up anything damaging about Lenny beyond what they agreed would keep her guarantee of immunity in place.

She said, "For some reason déjà vu all over again, Rudy? Lenny decide to drop the dime on me like the last time, in order to save his miserable wrinkled ass?"

Schindler gave his coffee a few more stirs. He lifted the cup two-handed and took a sip. Nodded approval. Settled the cup and used an index finger to trace some of the scars carved on the table's lime-colored linoleum surface, mostly awkwardly rendered hearts, punctuated kid-style with initials and arrows.

"Not the story, Lainie. As long as you stay straight, Mr. Volkman, he has that piece of the pie under control. Nothing they're gonna find in the files or anywhere that can throw him or his partners into the pit. The files he keeps around are strictly for show. The files that really matter? No place anybody can get to before we get there first. You don't believe it, ask your cockhound friend Flynn the next time you go see him at your cozy little Beverly Oaks Hotel hideaway."

"Lenny's been spying on us?"

"No cameras or bugs in the bungalow, that what you mean. Your coffee's getting cold."

Lainie pushed the cup aside. "If it isn't Lenny, who's busting me, Rudy?"

"Who do you think? It's Flynn, unless you do something about it and fast."

She went silent, unsure where the truth was.

Motioned him to tell her more.

Before Schindler could continue, the waitress skated back balancing a cafeteria tray on the palm she held above her Dutch Girl cap. She repeated Schindler's order in detail, the Big Bonanza Breakfast Special, but didn't bother to identify Lainie's fresh-squeezed orange juice, regular-size. Schindler watched her wheel away in reverse on one foot. "A cutie, but too young and not enough meat on her bones," he said.

"How is Flynn busting me, Rudy?"

Schindler spent a minute watching the rotary blades on the ceiling fans turn while he finished a jaw full of fried eggs and a shriveled slice of bacon, washing it down with coffee. "The way Newberry had it in mind. Same way Roman had it in mind. They're both dead, but your old buddy Chips Crandall is still alive and kicking."

Lainie didn't want to believe him.

Schindler's face left no margin for doubt.

She said, "How would Chips know to get to Flynn or Flynn to her?"

"Wasn't necessary. Lance Clifford, the fairy actor? You and Flynn at the wake yesterday for Clifford's co-pilot on cruises up the muddy brown river and Newberry's wreck of a kid? You upset the fairy something fierce, right into a humungous flitting frenzy to beat the band."

"I was there to do Clifford a favor. Present him with a file full of crap that would have broken his ego into bite-sized pieces if its contents ever got out. You know that. Lenny knows that."

"Not the what, the how. How you did it. Clifford took offense, leaving the old bitch out for a taste of your blood. He was on to Flynn first thing in the a.m."

"On to Flynn how, Rudy?"

"Newberry didn't keep all his papers at City Hall. The ones he wanted ultra-safe he kept at home or at Clifford's place. Clifford went through them and found some affidavits, one from Chips Crandall, explaining how you went to her for help getting your husband's ticket punched. He let Flynn know, and Flynn one-stopped to pick up the affidavit between girlfriends."

"Between—?"

Lainie couldn't get the question past the word.

"You and Gracie," Schindler said. He paused to pad his

mouth with a mound of home-fried potatoes and onions drenched in ketchup. "Flynn has this thing for double-dipping. He usually heads to Gracie's pad after you've been serviced, satisfied and are steering for home."

Lainie had never asked Flynn for fidelity.

Flynn had never offered fidelity to her.

That was that, but the affidavit—?

Was the past ever going to stop haunting her?

Schindler said, "We own Gracie. We bought her goodwill the first night Mr. Volkman had me check out Flynn. I tracked him to Pat Madden's Saloon and saw him taking a shine to her. Gracie knows how to get Flynn bragging on her as much as he bangs, even when he's not spinning on too much grape. First thing afterward she passes the word to me."

Lainie looked up at Schindler from her orange juice, her mind working like a mongoose. "The affidavit also names you, doesn't it, Rudy?"

"No." A blue-ribbon smile. "It names Eubie Grass."

"Who's dead."

"Same as Berry Berryman is dead."

"And even Rudy Schindler, any strangers go checking the way Harry Roman did."

"They get to me, same name, but only a coincidence. You know how many Rudy Schindlers there are in the world? Me and some famous architect. Maybe a thousand other Schindlers floating around."

"Except I know you're the Rudy Schindler who killed my husband for Chips."

"Not for Chips. For you, Lainie. Chips bought my services for you."

"Her word against mine, it ever came down to that."

"Which is the reason Mr. Volkman had me come tell you," Schindler said.

Lainie had that figured. "If Flynn busted me, Lenny knows I'd turn for keeps—on him, on you—rather than lose immunity. Is it time for me to start looking over my shoulder, Rudy?"

"No problem with that, but it's not what Mr. Volkman wants. He figures you're a better bet than Flynn is. He wants Flynn going on the long voyage, not you, but needs you to make it happen. Fast-like."

"How fast is fast?"

Schindler snapped his fingers.

"That fast . . . When do you see Flynn again at the love nest?"

"Tomorrow straight from the office, or isn't that"—snapping her fingers—"fast enough to suit you?"

"You go and do your thing, but get it done before three in the a.m. At ten minutes before three give Flynn his goodnight kiss and split. Go into the lobby. Ask the front desk to call you a cab. Stir things up so they remember you. Anything that establishes where you are at three in the morning, only not in the bungalow with Flynn."

"You are the thorough one, aren't you?"

"Why Mr. Volkman hunted me down, put me on his personal payroll after I did your husband."

"What if my watch is running slow, Rudy?"

"Then you better know how to run fast, Lainie." Schindler let her wrestle with the idea a few minutes longer. "So, what's it going to be, Lainie? What do you want me to go back and tell Mr. Volkman? Yes or no?"

CHAPTER 33

Lainie spent the next day with guilt as her constant companion, condemning herself for again accepting sin as her mortal friend, marveling at how the best of intentions so often come wrapped in bad deeds, how the worst lies too often serve a greater good than the truth, while the best lies have a way of becoming the truth.

It should have been a wonderful day for her. Sara had squeezed back at the touch of her hand and said words that sounded like *Love you, too,* when Lainie said her goodbyes. *Luhyt.* The first utterance in weeks from Sara, and Lainie heard it as she willed it to be.

I love you, too, baby. More than life itself.

News about Eddie Pope's acquisition of Perfect Records had spread like summer pollen, and there was a pile of phone messages waiting for her when she reached the office; more e-mails than she could answer in a year, a lot from people who had shunned her when she was sitting out the trial date with Roy. Stan, Cubie and Ira repeatedly burst into her office with updated reports confirming it was a home run for Miranda Morgan. Even Miranda came in, contrite, like a Born Again Humble, expressing her thanks and appreciation, almost like she meant it. The classes she had taken with Lainie at Star Bright had helped her, but Miranda was still a semester shy of total conviction.

Lenny Volkman was having a wonderful day, of that she was certain.

Driving to the office, the radio had blasted out the news between the traffic and weather reports that the City Council had voted unanimously to accept a proposal for the Paradise Sands property submitted by Rainbows Unlimited. The business consortium headed by prominent civic leader Leonard Volkman of Volkman International was chosen over two proposals that appeared superior after Mayor Lawton Welles hailed it as "one that will bring a new dimension of growth, progress and prosperity to our great metropolis of a city, and a magnificent doorway to the future of all of California, not just Los Angeles."

However Lenny had made it happen, he'd shown her once again that he not only owned the hat, but all the rabbits.

Flynn, meanwhile—

Did Flynn think he could bust Lainie Davies Gardner on a murder charge if she didn't help him bring down the Volkman empire? Was that it?

Probably.

Certainly.

Definitely.

Flynn had no reason to think otherwise.

Flynn thought he had a rabbit.

She heard it in his voice when he phoned her to confirm the time tonight and said, "I have something I need to show you."

"Fantastic, can't wait to see," she said, making it sound like she believed it was something hiding behind the zipper on his fly.

He laughed with her, but his laugh sounded unconvincing.

She was barely through their bungalow door at the Beverly Oaks before Flynn carried her into the bedroom for a tangle on top of the covers.

He shed any semblance of his usual romanticism as speedily as he rid her of her clothing, added an overload of aggression to his passion. She performed with a mounting concern that he was turning into some beast she'd recognized from her past but had never seen in him.

Afterward, Flynn apologized and volunteered an explanation, the slur to his words more pronounced than usual. His breath could become a blowtorch if she put a flame to it. "Volkman taking his toll," he said. "It came clear today that files that produced nothing of value so far won't produce anything valuable in future. They're another of Volkman's clever deceptions. For every scam company of his that comes and goes, he creates scam files for people like me come looking his way."

Flynn laid a kiss on her shoulder, making nice to a small bruise he'd created, and ran a finger-brush through her hair. She smiled back and traced his body with her hand, wishing she didn't have to play the game with him until three in the morning.

He said, "First I hear today how he's won over the city on his Malibu scam, then this about the files. The man lives a charmed life. He's slippery as a cobra and twice as deadly."

"Flynn, do we have to talk about Volkman?"

He left the question unanswered. "I don't suppose your Roy Gardner kept duplicate sets of his questionable services to His High and Mighty Lordship and you could lead me to them?" He was trying to sound playful.

She wasn't going to be fooled by him again. "Sweetheart, there's something else on your mind. Can we cut to the chase?"

"Just you on my mind," he said, with a melancholy twist that rang true. "I've stumbled into something bad to show you."

"Then why show it?"

"For all the bad it does you, it might do myself some good and then you in the bargain."

"Show me, then."

"First things first," he said.

Flynn's lovemaking was gentler this time. She followed him into a nap, her mind as thankful for the rest as her body. Not yet nine o'clock. Another six hours of this—

Sleeping and screwing with a dead man who didn't know that yet, no matter what else Flynn thought he knew.

Lainie woke up certain something was wrong about tonight— not sure what—eyes goggling out of a dreamless sleep.

She checked the digital on the side table:

Closing in on midnight.

Flynn was asleep on his stomach, his face turned away from her, one arm dangling over the side of the bed.

Her stomach was growling. She'd had nothing to eat since late afternoon, and then only a vending machine sandwich, a paper-thin slice of baked ham and a hard slice of American cheese, a lettuce leaf, held together by an inch of mayonnaise between two slices of day-old white bread; a package of Oreo cookies; an Eskimo Pie for energy.

Lainie inched apart from Flynn, taking care not to wake him as she shifted onto her feet. The pale glow from the outdoor path lights trying to crack the sleep curtain guided her out of the bedroom. In the parlor, modest flames from the low-burning gas fireplace were harvesting what remained of the pressed wood logs. She used the light to reach the serving cart and champagne Flynn always had waiting for them. The ice bucket had their usual starter bottle of Cristal. The ice had turned to water. She popped the cork anyway and drew straight from the bottle.

She raised the rounded swivel lid of the copper cart to see what dining surprise Flynn had ordered this time. Last time it was pressed duck. She had never liked pressed duck. She found it too fatty and the taste too flat for her, no matter what condiments she applied.

Flynn's surprise tonight was far less to her taste than the pressed duck ever was:

A legal-size brown manila envelope.

No markings.

She didn't need them to guess what was inside.

Lainie settled at a corner of the couch, clicked on the reading lamp, took another swallow of Cristal and put the bottle aside before she began a careful reading of the blue-backed notarized affidavit Thom Newberry had pulled out of Ruby Crandall.

The sworn document, however inaccurate and incomplete, brought back memories Lainie didn't need but had never been able to fully discard. Chips had gotten enough of her facts right to make it a painful resurrection. In words and sentence structure that spoke to help from Newberry or someone, Chips described how surprised she'd been when Lainie showed up at Brackens full of smiles and cartons of cigarettes; plastic sacks loaded with candy bars.

They had never been on friendly terms at the U.S. Federal Women's Detention Center in San Diego, so it made obvious Lainie needed something from her. She needed somebody to kill her husband. She wanted Roy Gardner dead, as early as possible, and the price was no object.

"I said I might be able to oblige her," Chips recounted in the affidavit. "There were some personal commitments Lainie would have to make, for friends of mine on the outside who could use help. Lainie said that was easily done. I had her take care of that first. When I heard back that Lainie had delivered on her word, I put her together with a friend of a friend who was known to be good at dealing with this kind of business matter, a real professional."

There was more.

It sounded like Chips was responding to questions that

weren't on the affidavit:

"Not long after, I heard that her request had been satisfied, and that's all I know, except there's no doubt in my mind Lainie Davies Gardner was behind the murder of the individual she identified to me as her husband, Roy Gardner, or that the murder of Roy Gardner was carried out by an individual known to me as Eubie Grass. I have not heard again from the person I know as Lainie Davies Gardner about the murder of her husband she bought and paid for or anything else, not even so much as a thank you."

Lainie settled the document on her lap and reluctantly reminded herself, *Yes, yes, yes, you bitch, I needed someone to kill Roy, and you were the only one I knew who might help me. What you learn from negotiating, the right deal always wipes out the bad blood between people, even when it runs as deep as it once did between us. Only I never in my life, then or ever, said to you or anyone that I wanted Roy Gardner dead, you lying bitch. I never said I wanted Roy dead.*

That could not be farther from the truth.

I loved Roy with all my heart and soul.

I wanted Roy alive.

Roy wanted Roy dead.

For his sake and mine.

For the sake of Sara, our precious daughter.

But I never shared that with you, Chips. It was none of your business. You wouldn't have cared anyway. If anything, you would have gloated. You're one of those people who find great joy and satisfaction in the misery of others, who will use any opportunity to inflict suffering. Their pain is your pleasure.

My pain you would have judged a victory, probably the way you've been doing since you squealed through your affidavit. I can only guess at your reward for giving it to Thom Newberry, someone else who always rooted for the wicked witch and cheered when Snow

White bit into the poisoned apple.

My pain was Roy's pain.

I would have continued to suffer gladly with him, but he wouldn't hear of it.

That was Roy.

Our upcoming trial was weighing heavily on him. It stunned him when I also was indicted on charges, especially since he'd been promised protection for me from Leonard Volkman, right from the beginning, when he first used me as a signatory on some of the sour deals, or my name and my prominence in the music industry, where it would help to impress the more deep-pocket investors.

Roy trusted Lenny, so I trusted Lenny for Roy, although I knew from the day I met him he was a person who would screw you out of a smile and complain afterward how you'd neglected to thank him for the privilege.

At first, did I know what I was getting into?

Yes. Roy explained it to me. And that was that.

The evil deeds we do are often the things we do for love.

Have you ever felt true love, Chips?

As the situation grew darker for us, Roy sank deeper into depression. Sleepless nights and severe headaches got to be oppressive beyond comprehension. So did the physical pains he passed off as temporary symptoms of stress, even whenever it got bad enough to cry about. The drastic weight loss he attributed to a lack of appetite, joking, "Honey, I'm full up eating my heart out over what all this is doing to you and Sara."

His doctor revealed the ugly truth.

Two kinds of cancer chewing at his body, the kinds that get worse and never go away before they get you.

One night, unable to unbend, the agony on his face too grotesque to describe, Roy begged my help. "I am too much the coward to take care of the problem for myself, dear one, so please? Find someone to pull the plug on me? Please? The sooner the better."

Begged me.

And that also was that; the evil deeds we do; the things we do for love.

Where you came into the picture, Chips, and soon I was talking to Eubie Grass on the telephone, only he was Berry Berryman then.

He was everything you said he would be, only greedier.

Cash up front.

Tell him who was on the menu and leave the cooking to him was how he put it.

I told him who, but I also reminded him who was paying and told him exactly what I wanted.

I gave him a day, a place and a time when I would take Sara and some of her friends to the movies. Said how long we'd be away from the house. How Roy would be home in bed alone, doped out on pills that took him to a planet where nothing ever hurt. I told him to do it in a way that made it look like Roy had fallen asleep and drifted away peacefully on one final voyage, to an even better place.

I told him, most of all, don't let Roy suffer.

I told him, most of all, don't let Roy suffer.

I told him, most of all, don't let Roy suffer.

I had myself convinced I could handle it, Chips, that I could explain it and let it work for Sara, too, once she was over the initial shock of losing her beloved daddy.

Berryman said he understood. He didn't say he intended to ignore my instructions, until afterward—the one time I heard from him afterward—after he had blown off Roy's head in front of my Sara, with Sara in her daddy's arms.

He was calling, he said, to brag how his recipe was better than mine.

Roy hadn't suffered—it was too quick and certain for that—and about Sara being there, about it being Sara's birthday? Sorry, but doing it his way no one would ever think to suspect the wife was behind the murder. What wife would be evil enough to let something like that happen in front of her child?

"I did it your way, the cops come looking at you, next thing I know they could be looking for me," Berryman said. "My way, you're in the clear, no chance of suspicion rolling over onto me unless you let it happen. I know you won't, though, because of the kid. If I thought otherwise, I'd have dished up that entrée to include you."

I remember screaming at him, words I never used, Chips, including all of your favorites.

I remember him laughing into the phone and saying, "I don't ever like to leave anything to chance, especially not someone who's—"

"In any position to do me dirt," Lainie said, looking up from the affidavit.

That's what Berryman had told her.

"*—in any position to do me dirt.*"

Lainie stared at the front door of the bungalow, recognizing what it was she had sensed was wrong about tonight. Berry Berryman-Rudy Schindler intended to cook two geese tonight, not only Flynn's. Hers was the other one. She should have seen it when he laid out the plan for her. Schindler, who pictured himself a master chef, had taken her into the kitchen with him on the deadly menu he was cooking up for Flynn tonight.

That was out of character.

Schindler had given her the recipe to avoid becoming a suspect: "At ten minutes before three give Flynn his goodnight kiss and split. Go into the lobby. Ask the front desk to call you a cab. Stir things up so they remember you. Anything that establishes where you are at three in the morning, only not in the bungalow with Flynn."

Thoughtful.

Considerate.

Too thoughtful and considerate for a contract killer practiced in self-preservation, who'd once advised, "I don't ever like to leave anything to chance, especially not someone who's in any position to do me dirt."

Lainie was in that position now, unlike when he defied her instructions about killing Roy.

That time she'd made herself an accomplice to murder.

This time it was Schindler's own doing.

Springing her from suspicion was not doing himself any favor.

He'd want her dead and buried.

He probably had Lenny's blessing for that, Lenny figuring she'd be more dangerous than Flynn ever had been if he let her walk around with knowledge of Flynn's murder to hang over his miserable, double-dealing head.

That's how Lenny's trick-book mind worked.

Chance was for suckers in Lenny Volkman's world as well as Rudy Schindler's kitchen.

Tawdry headlines blaring:

TWO VOLKMAN INTERNATIONAL BUSINESS ASSOCIATES MURDERED DURING SECRET BEVERLY HILLS LOVE TRYST

Probably as close as Lenny figured an investigation would get to him.

Forget three a.m., she decided. Schindler was going to show up sometime between now and three a.m. He might already be outside, a system in place to get inside the bungalow and kill both of them.

Lainie threw the affidavit back onto the service cart grill and made a guarded trip to the front door to double-check the locks. She worked her way by the fire's glow to the bedroom. Rifled through her tote bag for her .22.

It wasn't there.

She flashed on the last time she saw it—this morning, when she pulled it out from its hiding place under the sink and parked it in the Toyota's glove.

Flynn, he must be carrying.

Lainie crossed to the bed. He didn't appear to have moved since she left him. She shook his sweaty, hairy shoulders. That got her irritable grunts and his dangling arm swatting away at invisible insects. She pounded on him. "Flynn, wake up, you stupid damn drunk." Got senseless mumbles in response. "You carrying a gun, Flynn? Tell me. I'm trying to save your goddamn life." More mumbles. Swats, one that caught her hard on her thigh and made her yelp.

She flipped the light switch and checked the clothing he had neatly hung in the walk-in closet. Nothing. Of course not. He would be more likely to keep any weapon closer than that on a night he planned to bust her.

Lainie returned to the bed. She dug under Flynn's head and the pillow, came up empty-handed. Between the mattress and the box spring. No. Underneath the bed. Nothing. The side table drawer. Empty. All the dresser drawers. All empty.

Lainie rushed back to the parlor. She hit the lights and hurriedly checked everywhere, first under the creamy velvet cuddling rug in front of the fireplace, another one of his favorite places for them to make love; the couch cushions; even around the pair of butane tanks in the heating cabinet of the copper serving cart.

Flynn was as good at hiding his weapon as he'd been in disguising his identity.

Back in the bedroom, Lainie rushed through picking up the clothing he had pulled off her and strewn around the room. She was jamming her blouse into her slacks when she thought she heard crackling noises outside the window. Footsteps crunching the blanket of dead leaves that even a light breeze would regularly steal from the tall oaks decorating the bungalow grounds.

Rudy Schindler or her imagination playing tricks?

CHAPTER 34

The footsteps weren't Lainie's imagination. They appeared to be trudging north toward the service door off the kitchenette. She raced over, uncertain if the door was locked. It wasn't. She depressed the door lock and slapped the chain into place, stood bent over, her hands on her knees and fought for breath against a rising pulse, against a whirlwind of wooziness pummeling her head.

She heard somebody testing the doorknob and dropped to all fours. A few harder twists on the knob before the click-click-clicking stopped, superseded by the sounds of leaf-crunching footsteps receding into the silence of the night.

Lainie sprang up and grabbed the wall phone.

Got as far as nine-one before she broke the connection.

There would be too much for her to explain later.

The cops might get Schindler, but they would have her, too.

After ten minutes that lasted for an eternity, Lainie pushed aside the lace curtains on the kitchen door and connected her face to the windowpane with her hands. She didn't see, hear or sense anything. She opened the door a crack. Only the breeze causing a discordant symphony of noises as it swept over the carpet of leaves and through the bushes and the trees; the monotonous drone of electricity coursing through the overhead power lines.

She reached for the phone again and punched the key for the hotel operator.

She had to do something about Flynn.

She didn't want to die with him, but knew she would never be able to live with herself if she didn't try helping him. Uninterrupted rings before a computer voice clicked on to report all service stations were temporarily unavailable and please leave a message; someone will return your call as soon as possible.

Similar messages when she pressed the specified keys for the concierge, a bellman, valet service, housekeeping. Each time she ordered something and requested immediate delivery in a no-nonsense tone of absolute authority. Tourist pamphlets. The newspaper. A laundry and dry cleaning pickup. Extra blankets and pillows.

Call out enough foot traffic to the bungalow, and Schindler would have to be a total fool to do anything but quit and get the hell away from here.

Seconds later Lainie left the bungalow.

She fled down the path leading to her Toyota, parked on Canyon Oaks Drive, the street that provided direct access to the hotel grounds and made it unnecessary for bungalow guests to bother with valet parking at the main entrance. She stopped when she reached the last stretch of chest-high hedge before the sidewalk and checked behind her. No sign of Schindler. She peered over the hedge, down the block about ten or fifteen yards to her car.

All clear.

She took off for the Toyota.

Halfway there realized she'd left her tote bag at the bungalow.

All her keys were in the tote.

She told herself, *Hotwire the damn Toyota.* When was the last time she had hotwired a car? Not since she and Thom and their gang of runaways took the occasional joyride or needed wheels for some quickie hit on a 7-Eleven. Did she even remember how? *Like roller skates or riding a bicycle,* Lainie reminded herself.

She peeled off her jacket and approached the window on the driver side, pausing to pick up one of the weather-beaten, cantaloupe-sized decorative rocks lining the hotel's exterior bush wall. She hefted it a few times and smiled at the familiar feel.

Lainie folded the jacket into quarters and settled it against the driver's window. It would dull the noise of the breaking glass when she pounded it with the rock.

Four solid hits and the job was done. She pushed the stray pieces of glass out of the way to get to the door lock. Used her jacket to clear the seat of glass residue before she settled behind the wheel and felt for the wires she'd need.

Seconds later, Lainie had the Toyota humming and ready to roll.

Like roller skates or riding a bicycle.

She threw the gearshift into reverse and eased the car away from the curb, said relieved goodbyes under her breath to Schindler and to Flynn. At once realized her mistake. She should have stayed focused on her need to escape instead of conjuring up the image of Flynn asleep on the bed in his drunken stupor—helpless.

Leaving Flynn for Schindler to kill was too big a price for her to pay.

There was need and a reason behind what she had done for Roy, but running away now would make her a true accessory to murder.

She weighed this truth against what it might mean for Sara.

"Sorry, baby," she said, and cut the motor.

Found her .22 in the glove.

Hurrying back to the bungalow, she avoided the lighted walkways, making her own path on a hunkered-down run behind the hedges, pausing briefly once or twice to check for any sight or sound of Schindler.

A bellman passed her heading in the opposite direction, complaining to himself about how cheap some people could be, twenty-two-five a night for a bungalow and the best they do for a working stiff is a stinkin' Abe Lincoln.

She reached the hedge across from the bungalow and got her nerves under control before chancing a stare.

Flynn was standing barefoot in the doorway, half in and half out of his clothing; his shirt sloppily buttoned, his belt hanging loose. His long blond hair disheveled, hanging like a curtain over his shoulders. His eyes looking like they were fighting to stay alert. His smile hardly better while the young woman in the pink and white housekeeping uniform handed over two pillows and blankets. She hesitated long enough to recognize no tip was forthcoming and scooted off the porch wearing an expression almost as sour as the bellman's had been.

Flynn, clutching the pillows and blankets to his chest, stepped forward and watched her disappear before starting back into the bungalow.

Lainie dashed through a break in the hedge calling his name in a desperate whisper and reached him before he could close the door. "Flynn, we need to get out of here." She gave him a strong nudge that caused him to drop the pillows and the blankets as he stumbled forward.

She spun around and locked the bungalow door. Stooped to pick up the pillows and the blankets saying, "Grab everything and get your ass in gear, Flynn. I'll explain later."

Before Flynn could respond, Schindler said, "Thank you for making it so easy for me, Lainie. I followed the bellboy in." He was inside the bungalow, to her right, his Glock aimed where he'd blow a tunnel through her when he squeezed the trigger. "So thoughtful of you to come back," he said, like kids sound Christmas morning, when they look under the tree and discover their letter to Santa reached the North Pole.

Lainie said, "Thank me by dying."

The muscles in Schindler's face constricted and did a little dance.

He said, "Not exactly my plan for tonight."

"Change of plans," she said, and squeezed the trigger of the .22 she'd concealed behind the pillows.

The shot caught Schindler in the chest and threw him against the wall, his head cracking the frame on a picture of love-smitten angels as he dropped the Glock.

Her second shot burrowed into his stomach.

Lainie told him while he could still hear, "Consider it a payback for what you did to my daughter, Schindler." She became aware of the .22 being eased away from her and asked, "What now, Flynn? Am I under arrest?"

Flynn packaged the gun between his belt and his belly. "Hold your ground a minute," he said, and headed for the bedroom on unsteady legs, returning at a more confident gait with the hip flask. "Better," he said, hand-wiping his lips.

"Am I, Flynn? Under arrest?"

"Do you see me holding you here at gunpoint? What you did was self-defense, on top of which you went and saved my bloody friggin' life. But there is something we need to clear up." He crossed to the service cart grill, brought out Ruby Crandall's affidavit, raised an eyebrow at the open lid and Lainie. "I see where you already took a peek at Exhibit A?"

"I've read better fiction, Flynn."

"You're saying it's not true what Chips Crandall had to say?"

"There's more to the story than what's there."

" 'More' that would make me think better of you?" Lainie shrugged. "An honest response," Flynn said. "I admire honesty in a person. A rare quality this day and age."

"Where do you want me to begin?"

"I don't."

Flynn strolled over to the fireplace, stoked what was left of the pressed logs and tossed in the affidavit. The blue flame from the gas jets took it like sharks on blood. Ashes floated upward.

"The shame," he said. "The original and so far as I know never a copy in existence that anyone would know to go searching after. You should leave now." He gave Lainie a pretty smile and saw the question rising on her face. "It's not every day I have my life saved," Flynn said. "Besides, I'll probably get a raise and a promotion after I tell my story to the press; how he came stalking me to shut off an investigation permanently, and how I got him before he could get off a crack. You here would be bloody awkward for me to explain, so go already, Mrs. Gardner. Get your memorable arse away from here."

"Thanks, Flynn."

He saluted her, tipping the flask to his forehead. "Comes another time I have the urge to hold you, good lady, it still won't be for questioning."

Lainie kissed her fingers and blew it to Flynn.

Flynn caught the kiss mid-air, pressed it to his heart and said, "Here's to we."

"Here's to we," Lainie said, smiling at him as if all their yesterdays were wrapped inside a million tomorrows.

CHAPTER 35

The next afternoon, Eddie Pope was waiting outside for Lainie when she pulled up to the Safety Net in Northridge. He answered her honk with a wave, snapped his smoke into the gutter and stepped over to the Toyota. "You going to get that window taken care of?"

"Soon, Eddie."

He blew out a sigh. "You know I don't like what you're doing. Neither do the doctors. Sara is a long way from a full recovery, Slim."

"I asked for your help, Eddie. Not an opinion."

A gesture of resignation. "I have them running Sara's papers. She's waiting for you in reception. At least she's no longer some candidate for a vegetable garden."

"Thanks, Eddie. Take it out of what I have coming from the record company."

"I told you, my treat. No arguments." He passed her a thick white envelope, which she leaned over and put in the glove without checking. "When you need more, you know where to find me . . . You're sure this is what you want, Slim?"

"It's what I want for Sara. A fresh town means a fresh start for both of us."

"If things don't work out, you don't find what you're looking for, come back. I'm holding down the fort for you, that's all."

"You're the whole rainbow, Eddie."

★　★　★　★　★

Lainie and Sara spent the night at a motel outside San Jose, after a quiet ride up Pacific Coast Highway on a day that threatened rain but never delivered on the ominous black clouds that had trailed them north. Lainie carried most of the conversation, what there was of it. Sara made a few comments, even initiated a topic or asked a question of no consequence based on some news item or a song that got her lip-synching the lyrics.

She strained to smile whenever she caught Lainie studying her, like a smile was a fair barometer on her condition. She called her "Mommy" when she addressed her, but the way she said it was another indicator something about Lainie played hard on Sara's mind. Several times, Lainie started to ask her what but stopped, fearing what she might hear.

The one time Lainie almost finished the question, Sara caught on in that mother-daughter way of non-verbal communication. She hurriedly turned up the music and joined Richard Harris in a loud chorus of the Jimmy Webb song about a cake left melting in the rain.

Worn out by the hard drive and the tension between them, Lainie fell into a trancelike sleep. When she woke the next day, it was almost noon. Sara was gone. So was the Toyota.

Sara had left behind a note on the pillow of her twin, on a sheet of motel memo paper.

In her cramped, tiny block-printing, she'd written:

MOMMY DEAREST, WHEN I CALLED OUR HOUSE YESTERDAY TO SEE IF YOU WERE ON YOUR WAY, I GOT THE MACHINE. I PLAYED THE MESSAGES TO SEE IF ANYBODY MISSED ME. NOBODY DID. I

DON'T THINK I'LL MISS YOU. GOODBYE. YOUR DAUGHTER, SARA SUZANNE MARIE GARDNER.

Lainie grabbed after her cell phone and speed-dialed the apartment. She punched over the salutation and skipped past more than two dozen messages and hang-ups before one stopped her and sent her heart into deadfall.

"Hey, sweetmeat. Longtime . . . It's—"

Ruby Crandall.

The voice familiar and ugly:

"—Chips Crandall, sweetmeat. Still doing my thing at Brackens. I've been seeing on the news how you still have your own thing going, so I thought to call. Excuse to say hello . . . First you go and pay me to help you get your husband murdered. Then that damn D.A. who made promises he didn't get around to keeping, and you just happen to be there? Now it's Rudolph Schindler, he was calling himself, who I get to do the big number on your hubby, getting him free room and board on a coroner's slab. I don't know how you worked that magic, sweetmeat, but I know it's you, bitch. You let it get to be a habit; you and me will be together again before you know it. Won't that be fun? Well, gotta go. As usual, the pussy parade here at the phone's already longer than John Holmes's dick."

Lainie put down the cell phone. She hugged Sara's note to her breast and told the empty room, "No, baby, no. That's not it at all. That's not the way it was."

ABOUT THE AUTHOR

Robert S. Levinson is the best-selling author of eleven prior crime-thriller novels, *Phony Tinsel, A Rhumba in Waltz Time, The Traitor in Us All, In the Key of Death, Where the Lies Begin, Ask a Dead Man, Hot Paint, The James Dean Affair, The John Lennon Affair, The Elvis and Marilyn Affair,* and *Finders, Keepers, Losers, Weepers.* His short stories appear frequently in the *Ellery Queen* and *Alfred Hitchcock* mystery magazines. He is a Derringer Award winner, won *Ellery Queen* Readers Award recognition three times and is regularly included in "year's best" anthologies. His nonfiction has appeared in *Rolling Stone, Los Angeles Times* Magazine, *Written By* Magazine of the Writers Guild of America West, *Westways,* and *Los Angeles* Magazine. His plays *Transcript* and *Murder Times Two* had their world premieres at the annual International Mystery Writers Festival. Bob served four years on Mystery Writers of America's (MWA) national board of directors. He wrote and produced two MWA annual "Edgar Awards" shows and two International Thriller Writers "Thriller Awards" shows. His work has been praised by Nelson DeMille, Clive Cussler, Joseph Wambaugh, T. Jefferson Parker, David Morrell, Margaret Maron, William Link, Heather Graham, John Lescroart, Gayle Lynds, Michael Palmer, James Rollins, Thomas Perry, Joseph Finder, William Kent Krueger, Christopher Reich and others. He resides in Los Angeles with his wife, Sandra, and Rosie, a loving Basenji mix, who thinks she rescued them. Visit him at *www.rslevinson.com* and on Facebook.